THE EMPEROR'S ENEMY

Also by Jasmine Mas

Villains of Lore

Blood of Hercules

Bonds of Hercules

Visit jasminemasbooks.com
to learn more about Jasmine Mas.

THE EMPEROR'S ENEMY

JASMINE MAS

HARPER
Voyager

Harper*Voyager*
An imprint of
HarperCollins*Publishers* Ltd
1 London Bridge Street
London SE1 9GF

www.harpercollins.co.uk

HarperCollins*Publishers*
Macken House,
39/40 Mayor Street Upper,
Dublin 1, D01 C9W8
Ireland

First published by HarperCollins*Publishers* Ltd 2026
1

Interior illustrations: Siana Park
Chapter heading images: Maria at Steamy Designs
Stock images: © Nasira's studio/stock.adobe.com (Rose);
© sorrapongs/stock.adobe.com
(Paper texture)

A catalogue record for this book is available from the British Library.

ISBN: 978-0-00-883471-5 (HB)
ISBN: 978-0-00-883472-2 (TPB)

Printed and bound in the UK using 100% renewable electricity by CPI Group (UK) Ltd

FSC
www.fsc.org
MIX
Paper | Supporting
responsible forestry
FSC® C013604

The practice of naming storms after women is rooted in bigotry. This book is dedicated to taking the power back.

CONTENT WARNING

This is a dark fantasy romance and contains graphic death, electrocution, and excessive violence. For example, a man is stabbed multiple times . . . but beware, he might secretly enjoy it.

A NOTE ON LANGUAGE

Please note that a few of the characters in this book speak using these simple archaic words and phrases. The rest of their words are modern for ease of reading.

thou = you (subject)
thee = you (object)
thou art = you are
'tis = it is
'twas = it was
shan't = shall not

CONVOCATION

"She is violent and uneducated. I vote no. Her soul is far too brash . . . She smells of righteous chaos. Her moral code is as extreme as her temperament. Look at her—she's only ten years old and she's gotten herself addicted to adrenaline in a pitiful attempt to distract herself from hunger."

"I agree with Babilon's assessment. The child does not have what it takes to represent us. I advise we find a person of—"

"She is exactly what we need."

"Barren, be *practical*. We've all weighed her soul. She's a menace—"

"Barren's right. She's a virtuous menace. I like the girl. She reminds me of myself when I was younger. I also vote yes."

"Moor, this is *not* what we need. If I recall, when you were young, you nearly flooded Antichthon with your—"

"Calm down, Scorpio. You always try to hold my past against me. Is it not high time we fight for a better future?"

"No. The status quo must be maintained, or the entire system will crumble—"

"A broken system must be burned to the ground. I agree with Moor and Barren. I vote yes. It's time we choose a virtuous antagonizer. Let us see what the girl can do."

"Glacia, please. This is a *grave* mistake. She's going to ruin everything and sow chaos—"

"I hope so. It is decided. Her test begins today."

THE DEMOCRATIC PAPERS: DAILY NEWS

The Birth of a New Hope: The Bear of the North Captures Royal Mage

STORIES OF HOPE **BY: NORA JAMESON**

A once-in-a-lifetime miracle has occurred. Zora Ravenal, the great Bear of the North, has taken the most powerful Royal Mage and the Emperor's right-hand man—Tarantula—as her personal hostage. Shortly after the capture, Zora survived the Iron Ritual. She joins the twins, Axel and Ella, as a Knight Mage who can nullify the destructive storm magic Royal Mages wield.

Zora reminds us that we aren't just two warring continents separated by the Moor Ocean—our Commonwealth on Westmere, and the Empire on Azote. We're Antichthon, a beautiful world that deserves peace.

Zora is confident we're stronger than the Empire. "I've seen it with my own eyes. Our target-seeking missiles terrify the Emperor," she told us with a grim nod. "Despite the Mist, we still have our technology. If our ancestors could break free from their shackles in the platinum mines, discover the Iron Ritual, and fight the Empire back to Azote, we can defeat them in this age once and for all."

At her knighting ceremony, with fearsome dire bear scars stark across her face, Zora promised the Crimson Army, "Tarantula is trapped in my private quarters, and rest assured, he suffers nightly by my hand."

Blessed be the bone daggers of Zora, the fearsome Bear of the North.

Tarantula has met his match.

See below for the portrait of Zora's capture of Tarantula by master painter Marge.

THE EXCELSIOR GAZETTE: DRACONIS NEWS

A NEW ERA OF STRENGTH: EMPEROR ALEKSANDER AND EXPANSIONISM

CROWN COVERAGE — BY: VELIXIA XARON

Our illustrious High Emperor, Aleksander the Sadistic, continues to show his cunning with the expansion of Draconis politics to Westmere. The *Democratic Papers* are spreading their propaganda lies, claiming our most ferocious Royal Mage, Tarantula, has been captured by a pathetic human woman.

With a smirk on his divinely handsome lips, the Emperor assured us there was no cause for any concern. "There is no universe in which these ridiculous falsehoods are true. Everything is not as it seems. Games are afoot, and the Commonwealth has *never*, in all its sordid history, matched our cunning."

A man of great conviction, the High Emperor today mirrored what he told us in an interview a decade ago, when he was just a boy. Back then, when asked about how the winner of the Storm Wars would impact the future of Antichthon, he said:

"The victor will own the world, and I *never* lose."

1

A Story of Survival

Fresh blisters burned, blood-soaked toes slipping inside my combat boots, as I followed behind the rest of the red-clad recruits.

The Draconis Empire will fall in my lifetime.

To build up endurance, we ran single file across the rolling desert dunes of Scorpion Valley. My long braid rhythmically bounced against the scabbard of my standard-issue sword, and my sweaty balaclava pulled tight, sticking to my salt-covered cheeks.

A serendipitous turn of events—we were *finally* outside the military hangar and doing something other than boring formation drills. I'd take running over standing still any day of the week.

Rule of survival: Enjoy the adrenaline rush.

Long silvery streaks of storm magic danced above in the violet sky. Within the world of Antichthon, the continent of Westmere was renowned for its three unique ecosystems. We were in the Middlelands' desert, infamous for its unforgiving heat and rust-orange dunes.

All Westmere was as beautiful as it was deadly, a world full of treacherous storms, dangerous dire beasts, and strange magics.

I was still grateful to be here, despite all the trauma.

Lucky, blessed girl.

Blinding sunlight burned my eyes as I looked back at the ornate spire-covered facade of the Scorpion Hole. Stones wavered through the heat haze. Even from this distance, the gray brick gothic exterior of the military base contrasted sharply with the white interior of the hangar.

"Tighten up formation, recruits!" the Admiral shouted from the front of the line as he led us farther away from the base.

Two months ago, I joined the Crimson Army, leaving behind the snowy forests of the Northern Commune. *I miss you, Mom.* Her gentle voice whispered in my ear, *"If you do something for those you love, it's not a sacrifice. It's a gift."*

I was going to take down the Draconis Empire. No matter what it took.

I will win.

Perspiration dripped from my lashes, burning my eyes as I lost myself in the high of running-induced delusions of grandeur.

"Patchy Beard Man is mean," Squire, my tiny pygmy owl, hooted from where he balanced on my shoulder, silver storm magic wafting from his yellow beak.

"No, darling," I whispered quickly. "Remember, we're playing the *quiet* game." Recruits looked back, shooting me and Squire glares.

The Admiral, whose beard was scraggly at best, turned with a fierce scowl. "Who said that?"

"Me!" Squire squawked happily.

I grimaced.

Squire weighed barely two ounces and stood as tall as my pointer finger, but what he lacked in size, he made up for in being vocally problematic. *He inspires me.* We'd been best friends since I found him years ago in the North, crying on an icy branch because magic had gifted him speech but no one to talk to.

"I've *told you* to be quiet, simpleton bird," the Admiral said as he ran backward.

"No speak to me," Squire gasped with outrage, fluffing his tawny feathers. "Rude man."

I covered Squire's head, and he nibbled playfully on my finger. "Please accept his sincerest apology," I said, not for the first time. "He doesn't mean it."

"Yes, I do!" Squire hooted from behind my hand (not helpful).

The Admiral's face reddened, but he shook his head and turned back around. Pygmy owls were a highly endangered protected species, and Squire had said he would kill himself if they separated us, so there was nothing the Admiral could do; it was one of Squire's more intelligent moments.

Recruits grumbled as we picked up the pace.

"Uneducated Northern peasant," Kane, aka recruit number Five, said under his breath as he ran in front of me.

His tone made it clear he was disgusted by my heritage, specifically that Northerners prioritized trade apprenticeships over traditional education. Unlike him, I never attended Steelden, the Middlelands' most prestigious military university.

Instead, I started my apprenticeship with Tracker Gareth on my tenth birthday. He taught me everything I needed to know. The forest was my happy place, and even though I didn't have the stomach for killing like Gareth did, I was good at it. Therefore, I became a hunter.

With talent comes duty.

The North was isolated from the rest of Westmere's Communes by mountains, so we survived using a cooperative land-based economy. Nostalgia was bittersweet, softening the hunger pains that had plagued my childhood. Because of the escalating Storm Wars, our food supply was dwindling.

Guilt gnawed at me for leaving, but before I left, I'd drawn a map of all the active traps and given it to the council with extensive instructions.

Sure, the North wasn't perfect.

When I was only thirteen, Gareth was mauled to death by a

dire bear while snowboarding, but at least he'd died doing what he loved. In his memory, I hiked up mountains for hours just so I could race back down, throwing death-defying flips.

Gareth didn't just teach me how to snowboard; he showed me that when you loved something, you gave *everything* to it. No exceptions.

Kane turned, his face hidden beneath his balaclava. "You don't belong here," he said pointedly as I held his gaze. He waited for me to react, but mentally I was far away, playing chess against myself—an old distraction technique I used to use on my longest hunts.

Kane looked away first.

He always did.

Squire hooted as he pecked kisses onto the side of my cloth-covered sweaty face while I leaned forward into another steep hill. My worries drifted far away as I lost myself in the peaceful rhythm of jogging; sand whistled in a low hum across the sloping mounds.

It was a glorious day to be alive. I could run like this forever.

Vibrations shook my boots.

I paused on the top of the dune.

Hiss.

A strange crinkling, scraping sound shuddered below.

"Number Six!" the Admiral shouted. "Get back into—"

BOOM.

Sand displaced with a hissing screech as a monstrous creature breached out of the dune in a blue-green blur. It was larger than a dire horse.

Mammoth serrated pincers clacked as it soared through the air with unfathomable speed; blood splattered in a gruesome arc; recruit number Two let out a high-pitched wail, then fell abruptly silent. Her torso dropped to the sand. She had been cleaved in two by the pincers; her legs dangled from its maw as it turned away.

It was the desert's namesake: a deadly dire scorpion.

Silver wafted from the magically mutated beast. Dire scorpions formed colonies in the caves along the river canyon to the west, but they rarely ventured this far into the dunes.

The Admiral pointed at the beast. "Fall into formation. Draw your swords—" He was cut off as he rolled to the ground, hit by recruit numbers One and Three, who fell into each other as they scrambled to get away. Recruit number Four retched violently, cursing the old god for abandoning us.

Meanwhile, the dire scorpion finished swallowing and swung back around with its pincers raised.

Two middle eyes stared at us, and its stinger was raised high—it was longer than my forearm. On the side of its exoskeleton, five pairs of additional eyes swiveled in different directions. Somehow it was looking at all of us simultaneously.

Squire trembled on my shoulder. "Me scared."

"Look away, dear," I whispered, and he turned his head obediently like he always did on a hunt, staring behind me.

The dire scorpion opened its jaw wide.

On instinct, I went to grab my bone daggers, but I wasn't wearing my hunting leathers. Swearing, I drew the sword we'd barely touched so far in training.

The wood handle and steel blade were unfamiliar in my sweaty grip. The weight was off-balance and too elongated. *This monster is going to be impossible to beat— Stop it, Zora.*

I took a deep breath and cleared my head.

Rule of survival: Don't you dare panic.

"We all need to approach it at the same time from opposite sides," Kane whispered beside me, drawing his sword with practiced ease. He looked back to the others.

Recruits One and Three were now sprinting away across the dunes, and recruit number Four was holding number Two's head, crying into her auburn hair. The Admiral stood off on a different dune, watching us as he slowly backed away.

Kane scoffed and turned to me. "Fine. The two of us must

approach simultaneously. Their stingers are highly venomous but have a rigid range of motion. They can't attack laterally. Follow my lead." I distantly remembered him bragging about being valedictorian of Steelden.

Kane inched left with his sword held close to his face in a two-handed grip. I followed his direction, heading toward the right, but I raised my weapon forward with one hand like I would my dagger, arm extended to put as much space as possible between myself and the beast.

Its many eyes swiveled, tracking us with beady intelligence. Eight spindly legs shifted, and every single eye focused on Kane.

A weight settled into my gut, instincts screaming at me to change course. It looked *hungry.*

I stopped. "I don't think we should get this close," I whispered as I redirected and stepped slowly toward Kane. "Are you sure it can't attack laterally?" Trepidation mounted with each tense second.

Kane scoffed. "I'm positive, *peasant.* You need to follow my lead—"

The stinger exploded dexterously to the left, heading straight for Kane, laterally; I lunged at the same time.

Thud. My blade sliced the venomous appendage clean off, but the edge of the stinger clipped Kane's forearm. He shrieked as he fell to his knees, the fast-acting toxin working immediately.

"Run!" the Admiral bellowed as he turned and sprinted. Recruit number Four staggered to his feet and ran after him.

The dire scorpion scurried backward, screeching in pain as its blue blood splattered across the sand, gushing from the injured tail. Pincers clacked together loudly, but instead of retreating, it did what every predator did when it sensed injured prey. It focused on Kane, its distended jaw salivating.

"Zora?" Squire hooted.

"Don't look yet," I ordered harshly, legs shaking with the urge to run for safety. I'd take a deadly dire bear over this monster. At least I wouldn't have to stare at twelve creepy eyes as I died.

Kane whimpered in pain, clutching his arm. His flesh was slowly turning black. He'd live if he got it amputated before the venom reached his heart.

Click. Click. Click. Razor-sharp pincers clamped together menacingly, a hair-raising warning, as the dire scorpion kicked back sand like it was preparing to charge.

I took a step backward.

Kane didn't deserve my kindness because I was just a poor, uneducated peasant to him. I was *lesser* because I didn't have gold coins in my bank account or a fancy education.

"*Number Six, get out of there!*" the Admiral shouted from a distance.

A good soldier followed orders. My feet slipped. I stood on the very edge of the dune.

I prepared to flee.

The scorching desert disappeared, and I blinked rapidly in confusion. I lifted my palm up. Thick snowflakes melted with pricks as they drifted onto my warm skin.

What in the damned?

It was real.

I was standing among familiar towering fir trees coated in glistening ice. The Barren Forest of the great North, *home*, stretched all around.

My breath came out in frosty puffs, condensing in the freezing temperature. Snow drifted softly, gathering on my shoulders and hand.

The sharp scent of storm magic burned my sinuses, and a bright emerald light glittered in my peripheral vision, but when I tried to focus on it, nothing was there.

I spun in a circle, snow crunching loudly beneath my boots.

"Help me!" Kane begged with a tortured sob.

The hair on the back of my neck stood on end. Kane kneeled in the forest, crying as he stared off at a looming shadow in the trees.

My heart pounded painfully beneath my ribs, racing with anticipation. Hand steady, I raised my sword toward the shadowy beast.

I charged.

The desert reappeared in a disorienting blink.

What WAS that?

My fingers prickled with pain as biting cold became suffocating heat. Blinding sunlight bleached everything with whiteness. The dire scorpion was a teal outline in the light.

Concentrate, Zora.

I swiped up Kane's discarded weapon as I sprinted past him. Holding my breath, I slid on my knees in the sand, leaning back as far as I could. *Please let this work.* I swung both swords out wide in a timed arc, aiming for its pincers. My spine pressed into the sand as I flattened myself.

The dire scorpion let out a high-pitched whistling wail. Bright blue blood sprayed my face. Its jaw opened, saliva splattering, and it fell to the sand, centimeters in front of my bent legs. The creature gasped as it bled out.

Severed pincers twitched on the sand with final electrical impulses.

Zora: 1.

Dire scorpion: 0.

"Me look now?" Squire chirped.

"I wouldn't—"

He screeched with horror, straight into my ear.

"Told you," I muttered as I got to my feet, wincing as I wiped my eyes with my sleeve. We were alone. The Admiral and other recruits were all gone.

Kane cried out, and I tipped my head back to the sun.

You can do it, Zora.

How difficult can it be?

A few minutes later, I ran with Kane across my shoulders over the *endless* sand, arms and legs burning from strain as I deeply regretted my life choices.

The sterile white hangar wavered in and out of focus. Intense nausea from overexertion made it hard to think. *Pure agony.*

"You're hurting me, peasant," Kane whined as his head bobbed limply. *Good.* We were about the same size, and he was *not* light. Sadly, if I didn't hurry, the venom would get to his heart, which would defeat the point of helping him.

I was in too much pain to speak and wished with each strained breath that I'd left him to die. Another blister on my heel ruptured with a sharp sting, and my left calf seized up with a cramp.

I didn't stop.

"Silence, coward!" Squire hooted as he balanced atop Kane's injured arm (helpful).

Finally I lunged into the shadowy hangar. Leaning forward, I dropped Kane unceremoniously onto the polished floor, right in front of the row of parked dust-covered jet planes. Saliva and sweat ran off my face as I keeled over, heaving, struggling not to pass out. *Everything* hurt.

"Scorpion venom," I whispered to a soldier who shouted for help as I gagged.

Dark spots slowly receded from my vision as my heart rate calmed enough that I could stand up straight. Still tremulous, I feigned indifference as I walked away from Kane's slumped form. *I need to lie down.*

Medic Sara sprinted out, gasping as she stared down at the blubbering man and me walking away from him. "How could you throw down an injured soldier like that?" she asked, her eyes full of condemnation.

Because he's annoying.

She shook her head at me with disgust. "Stupid Northern peasant." She stabbed him in the neck with antivenom.

My stomach dropped, but this time from humiliation.

A group of nurses I recognized but didn't know by name helped her cart Kane away on a stretcher. He'd live.

Raising my tingling arms, I leaned back, trying to get feeling in my overtaxed, numb appendages. Someone pushed water into my hand, and I gulped it greedily.

My elbow banged into a tall figure.

The Admiral stared down at me, his expression inscrutable. "The Marshal wants to speak with you. Follow me."

Why does the elected leader of the Democratic Commonwealth, the highest position in the military and the leader of the Storm Wars, want to talk to me?

The Admiral walked away before I could ask anything. I staggered after him through the busy hangar into the long white halls that led deeper into the base.

He stopped, and I nearly collided with him again. Holding on to the wall for balance, I tried not to whimper as pain radiated down my exhausted legs. Stiff dark uniforms with identifying red trim headed toward us in formation.

Shadow Swords. The most highly trained, competent soldiers on the base, second only to the twin Knight Mages. They flew the helicopters and protected the Marshal.

The Shadow Swords parted, revealing a prisoner in shackles. The temperature in the hall plummeted. The prisoner towered above the Shadow Swords in stature and ferocity, his demeanor unsettling.

What.

The.

Hell?

Time warped as the prisoner approached in slow motion, chains clattering. I officially was suffering from a curse; there was no other explanation for *this* much bad luck.

Pale skin, unique milky irises ringed with the palest blue, and messy blond curls sauntered through the hall. He had the elegant, tightly coiled physique of someone who regularly fought to the death—and won.

A bright blue spider tattoo stretched across the lower left side of his face, rows of platinum hoops jangled in both of his ears, and *DANGER* was embroidered in bright orange across the chest of his gray jumpsuit.

The deadliest of all Draconis Royal Mages, the Emperor's right-hand man, and a recent prisoner of the Storm Wars.

Tarantula.

His platinum mask fit snugly across his disgustingly handsome face—the mark of his creed as a Royal Mage. The narrow metal covered only his brow and half of his nose, while high cheekbones jutted beneath his cold eyes like razor blades.

Named after the arachnid tattooed on his face, he somehow sauntered elegantly *even* with his hands and ankles chained together. The shackles overlaid his personal decorative platinum wrist cuffs; the opulent accessories shone bright, identifying him as Draconis royalty.

A thick metal collar sat tight around his throat.

Light refracted across the walls, making me blink. Priceless fig-sized diamonds studded the collar. They must have been from the Commonwealth's Treasury coffers. Legend had it that large diamonds counteracted storm magic, which meant the Crimson Army had nullified his powers.

He's magically castrated.

I wished he was dead.

The memory of Aurora's sightless green eyes had me standing tall despite the pain. *My sweet best friend.* We had grown up together as close as sisters. I'd helped her dye her hair pink the same day he killed her. As if that wasn't enough, he then threatened my mother's life. Tarantula was part of the reason I'd joined the Crimson Army two months ago. I *yearned* for his demise.

"Scary spider man," Squire chirped on my shoulder.

Tarantula strode past, and the corner of his bloodred lips lifted as he leaned toward me tauntingly. For a second, he faltered.

His eyes narrowed as he took in my disheveled state. "What happened to thee?" he asked, leaning close enough that I could see his pupils expanding and my bared teeth reflected in his platinum mask.

I swung my tired arm.

Crack.

My fist slammed into his cheek before he could react, knuckles splitting against his mask, but I barely registered the new wave of pain. All my senses were focused on the evil.

"Harder," he said coldly.

Rule of survival: Always attack first.

I swung again but missed.

He'd dodged.

"Thou *filthy* serf, I dare thee to do that again." He raised his cuffed hands, fingers touching his blood-streaked mask. "The Emperor will make thee pay for this," he purred tauntingly.

"What game are you two playing?" I asked, overwhelmed by his manic intensity and the mention of the sadistic Emperor. "Why do you care so much about me?" *I'm just a* serf *from Westmere, after all.*

"Thou know the answer." For a bewildering moment, I could have sworn his lips curled up with satisfaction.

Hand throbbing, I backed away from him. "What are you talking about?"

He scoffed but didn't elaborate.

A flush of terror burned hot across my chest. His proximity was *terror inducing.* I'd rather fight a hundred dire scorpions than suffer his presence. *Despicable man.* I had no idea what he was alluding to.

Tarantula leaned toward me.

A dark-haired Shadow Sword grabbed my arm and yanked me back, throwing me behind his body protectively.

Tarantula's eyes flatlined, and he lunged toward us. *SIZZLE.* Electricity exploded from the diamond collar around his neck, and he dropped to the floor.

It's also a shock collar?

The Shadow Sword stood over Tarantula, holding a small square device in one hand. He turned the round dial up with his thumb, and sparks intensified, leaping from the collar as Tarantula writhed.

A fog of blue rolled through the hall at our feet. It tendrilled into long strands and slowly rose, heading for the shock collar.

The Mist.

No one knew where it came from, just that centuries ago the Mist appeared and spread across Antichthon like wildfire, shutting down all working technology. It was why the aircraft in the hangar were mostly unused and only a few helicopters were taken out for short training exercises.

Tarantula crawled toward me, teeth bared savagely as he fought through the electricity.

The Shadow Sword turned down the dial before the Mist could render it inert. Then he expertly brandished his sword, pressing the point to Tarantula's forehead, halting him.

Tarantula leaned into the blade, blood welling as he ignored everyone else and smiled cruelly up at me.

"I'm going to kill you," I mouthed silently, meaning every word.

Tarantula winked mockingly like he had a secret.

"Number Six, come with me," the Admiral said, and I obeyed on instinct, following behind him, desperate to put space between myself and the man on all fours. Between the dire scorpion and now Tarantula, my nerves were shot.

Zaps sizzled as the electrocution resumed in the hushed hall behind us, but Tarantula took it silently. An abnormal gust of icy wind whispered across my neck.

I glanced back.

The white bottoms of Tarantula's eyes were visible, giving him an inhuman appearance. The magic-dampening diamonds glittered on his shock collar as phantom fingers of wind wrapped around my throat.

The sensation whispering across my neck couldn't be his storm magic.

Right. *Right?*

A few minutes later, I wiped dried blood off my face and tried to calm my racing heart as I stood in front of the Marshal in an empty room. The Admiral had bowed low as soon as we entered, then left alongside the Marshal's cadre of Shadow Swords, giving us privacy.

The Marshal—*Kalen Reeves*—wore her signature red suit and black cape, the dark material draped behind her. A horizontal scar bisected her forehead, and on her right breast gleamed the oversized gold pin of a Knight on a horse. She also wore a tight red cap that designated her rank. Her blue eyes were unsettlingly shrewd up close, and it felt like she was staring through me.

Her opinion of me was stark across her face—*Northern peasant.* I regretted voting for her.

She was supposed to defeat the Empire and end the Storm Wars, not keep the most dangerous Royal Mage alive and let him walk around the base.

In the tense silence, her gaze narrowed on the facial scars that I knew were stark against my bronze skin. The ones on my spine were worse, but I always kept them covered. She focused on the longest scar, which bisected my eyebrow and the corner of my lip. Unlike the rest of my white marks, it glittered a metallic silver, the color of storm magic.

In my very first week apprenticing in the North, I got separated from Gareth. A dire bear charged out of nowhere, swiping its claws across my face and back as I twisted away hopelessly.

Strangely I'd woken up the same day, tucked safely in my bed, with the gaping wounds fully healed. Someday I'd find out what my magical scar meant, but for now, I was just grateful to be alive.

Lucky, lucky girl.

"You saved recruit Kane's life," the Marshal finally said, her voice deep and commanding. "His family is extremely prominent in the Middlelands. What do you want as a reward? I can offer you a higher salary, time off, or honorable leave of service—"

"Put me through the Iron Ritual," I blurted.

The Marshal blinked rapidly. "Excuse . . . me?"

The secretive ritual was infamously held on this base. It had a minuscule survival rate—*a one in one hundred thousand chance*—but those rare few who lived developed a unique form of defensive magic that dissipated storms.

They became magical Knight Mages and weapons of the Commonwealth in the Storm Wars. Their sole life's purpose was to battle against Royal Mages, the magical storm-wielding elite of the Draconis Empire.

I needed magic if I was ever going to get revenge on the Emperor and properly ruin Tarantula. The North would starve to death if their reign of terror continued unchecked.

"You'll die," the Marshal scoffed. "Only two people have survived it in *the past century.* It's a—"

"Put me through it," I said, refusing to quail at the impossible odds because I had to try. *For Aurora and Mom.* The North deserved a better future, free from starvation and tyranny.

Don't lie to yourself. I wanted to hurt the Emperor and Tarantula. My heart was in my throat, full of longing for change, but my skin was crawling off my bones, fingers twitching with violent, vengeful desires.

"You don't mean—"

"Put me through it," I repeated with force. I might not have control over what I wanted, but that didn't mean I wasn't going to get it.

Rule of survival: Practice existential audacity.

"Fine. Your funeral." She gestured for me to leave the room.

My tired legs turned to stone. "Right now?" I hadn't thought she'd *actually* agree that easily.

"Yes, soldier. Move." She arched her brow like she was calling my bluff, her gaze seeing straight into my dissonant soul.

"Perfect," I whispered, feeling faint.

Before I could second-guess my precarious decision, I was escorted through a door with *IRON RITUAL* written on its surface above the alchemy symbol for blood: an upside-down triangle with a line through the middle and a droplet in the top section.

I paused inside the threshold. A single upright gurney was in the middle of the white room. A narrow empty tank sat beside it, and tubes were connected to the glass, needles hanging from the other side.

Nothing screamed *mystical.* The space was mechanically austere. *Where is the magic?*

Heaviness slammed into the back of my head. Someone shouted something outside the room, and it sounded like . . . *Tarantula's voice*? Everything went dark.

Lashes fluttering, I forced open heavy eyelids. Freezing cold air bit my naked skin. I felt groggy, like a significant amount of time had passed, but I had no way to tell for sure.

I was strapped to the vertical gurney. The empty tank was now full of a bubbling dark scarlet liquid. *Blood.* It was a shade of red so deep it bordered on black, glittering with tendrils of silver magic. I sniffed. It reeked of . . . *evil intentions*?

Teeth chattering, I tried to stay conscious.

Drip.

Drip.

Drip.

A needle dug into a raised vein of my left forearm, and a thick tube drained out of me into a tall white bucket. Another needle poked into my right arm—blood siphoned down the tube from the tank, straight into my vein. The sharp tang of copper mixed with magic filled the air as I struggled against the tight straps that held me, naked, against the gurney.

This is the famous Iron Ritual?

THIS is how they create Knight Mages?

It made perfect sense, in the same way a dire bear mauling an innocent person did. They were draining my blood and replacing it with magically polluted blood. Strands of silver glittered in the tube connecting me and the tank. Grotesquely simple; an alchemy of the flesh.

I had to survive the transformation.

"Squire?" I whispered, silver escaping my nostrils. Talons dug into my scalp as a yellow beak appeared and two bright yellow eyes joined it.

"Zora," Squire hooted upside down. "You are pretty as a moonlit winter dream."

I smiled through the pain. Our shared love of reading medieval poetry nightly before going to bed was the only warm thing left in the world. The chill intensified. Gritting my teeth, I fought through the agony. I was the closest I'd ever been to success, while balancing on the edge of failure.

"Zora, you my best friend," Squire cawed sadly as he pressed his feathers against my forehead, trying to warm me.

I jerked in agreement.

I will survive.

I will survive.

I will survive.

Long minutes bled away, time the cruelest bastard of all. I screamed, cried, and swore as magic filled me. It left a trail of frost across my organs. Clouds of silver burned as they streamed out of my mouth, nose, and eyes.

Squire curled up atop my head and fell asleep. Muscles cramping, bones brittle, I could do nothing but convulse with shivers.

Silver slithered away, and the haze slowly receded from my vision.

Drip.

Drip.

Drip.

No bubbling sounds came from the empty, stained tank.

The ritual was over.

Drip.

Drip.

With a herculean effort, I looked down at the tube attached to my right forearm. It was clear, and no liquid sloshed through it. I looked at my left arm.

Drip.

A single droplet hovered at the end of the tube, then fell into the bucket of my extracted blood. The room reeked of sweat and despair.

I will not give up.

A hazy veneer of emerald light formed the spectral outline of a being with long flower-filled hair, effeminate features, and an imposing masculine build. They smelled like . . . *fighting to the death for the greater good in the middle of a snowy forest*?

Sharp pain lanced down my face from eyebrow to lip; my silver scar was on fire.

Everything went dark as I passed out.

Something rocked beneath me. Coarse material scratched against my back, and wheels squeaked in movement. Eyelids heavy and raw, I scraped them open, eyes watering from the warm light filtering through burlap material and . . . a *zipper*?

What the hell?

I was in a bag, and *everything* hurt.

Talons pricked my shoulder as Squire's brown-and-white face came into view. "Zora?" he chirped.

Awareness hit me.

I really am too fortunate to die.

I rolled, caught in the bag, into a free fall. I slammed into the hard floor, unable to use my extremities to break my descent. Squire flapped his wings desperately in the confined space, hitting both of us. I tried to speak, but air just whistled through my open lips. Clawing at the fabric, I fought to get out.

"She's survived the unsurvivable Iron Ritual!" a muffled voice screamed, and all hell broke loose around me.

"How's that possible?"

"*Get the Marshal!*"

Boots pounded. Someone pulled down the zipper. Brightness scorched my eyes as scarlet uniforms leaned close, the soldiers' mouths open with horror.

"Me survive?" Squire hooted as he tucked himself into a small ball, hiding behind my hair. Mean-looking Shadow Swords shoved the soldiers away, glaring down at me as they parted like water, falling into perfect attention.

The Marshal approached, leaning over me. "You lived . . . *How . . . special.*"

Her eyes flashed with confusion, and she turned to whisper something in a Shadow Sword's ear.

I shouldn't be alive right now. Against all odds, my gambit had paid off.

I now had Knight magic.

I could calm a storm.

The old god might be dead, but I wasn't.

An eerie cold breeze whispered across my face. Neck aching, I lifted my head, searching through the sea of soldier legs, trying to find the source.

At the end of the hall, Tarantula radiated a terrifying capacity for violence. Expensive silver leather boots, covered in matching silver scales, gleamed different from the rest; prisoner chains draped across them, catching the light; *DANGER* was stretched across a wide chest.

His shackles were a joke.

Why is he staring at me like that?

He looked even paler than usual, which should have been impossible. He swayed slightly before he caught himself, shaking his head like he was coming out of a daze. Shadows sank into the deep hollows of his cheeks, giving him the appearance of a reanimated corpse.

As I held Tarantula's cruel gaze, another gust of wind blew across the front of my throat. His concentrated power caressed one spot.

When I was only fifteen years old, the then High Prince—the current reigning Emperor, Aleksander the Sadistic—bit my flesh and left a scar of his teeth. *Corruption leaves a stain.*

Tarantula smirked like something was funny. It was the same expression he'd worn after he'd murdered Aurora and chased me through the Barren Forest.

Purposefully I brought my hand out of the body bag and

rested my fingers across the coarse material over my stomach. Tarantula tensed with barely constrained fury. Satisfaction filled me. He knew it was the exact location where I'd shoved my bone dagger *deep* into his gut.

Two months ago, I captured Tarantula, Aleksander's strongest Royal Mage, and joined the Crimson Army so I could destroy the Draconis Empire; now I had the magic to make it happen.

The Marshal crouched down. "Don't get too excited. We'll see how you do on the test . . . before we dub you a Knight."

Wait. What test?

2

The Mage Behind the Wall

"Stand there." The Marshal pointed at a silver-capped drain in the center of the white floor.

On sluggish legs, I obeyed, stumbling into the dimly lit space.

With immense effort, I stood tall in the strange room nestled away in the lowest reaches of the base. There was no furniture. A dark mirror took up the entirety of one wall, with a wide silver spout protruding from the middle of it. A small porthole, cut out near the entrance door, connected the chamber to another room, which had oil lamps flickering against the walls.

After I'd gotten dressed, Shadow Swords had led us down a maze of stairs and endless corridors deep underneath the military base. Then the Marshal had taken over, leading me alone through the last few halls. I hadn't realized anything was below the palatial hangar that opened to the desert.

"Face forward." The Marshal gestured at the dark mirror.

Sweat poured down my forehead despite it being mild under the ground. I mopped it off with my sleeve. Since the Iron Ritual, I couldn't stop perspiring. *I want my mom.* My throat was sore. My vision blurred.

"Do you see this?" the Marshal asked as she patted the silver spout.

I nodded shakily.

"Verbal confirmation, soldier!"

"Yes, sir."

She rested her hand on the spout. "The storm magic is going to come out of here—and you're going to use your new Knight Mage ability to neutralize it. Stop the storm before it starts. That's how you pass. Simple."

A bad feeling twisted my gut.

"And if it doesn't stop?"

"It will. Form a Shield with your hands and hold it. Block the magic." She mimed making an X with her arms across her chest, the legendary Shield of the Knight Mages.

"But what if it does—"

"SILENCE, SOLDIER! Are you aware that . . ." The Marshal blurred, her voice drifting too far away to grasp. Strung out and raw, muscles quivering, I had nothing left to give. My vision wavered with tears, and I fought them back.

The girl in the mirror looked like a crone. Hunched and sheened in sweat. My silver scar was bright across my pallid, green-hued skin. Dark circles rimmed my amber-brown eyes, which were so light they appeared yellow. My long braid was half undone, a rat's nest of fine, straight hair hanging tangled to my waist.

I looked better than I felt.

"Give me the bird." The Marshal held out her palm, her voice cutting through the haze.

"No." I clutched Squire to my chest. He squawked with defiance, his head swiveling one hundred eighty degrees as he looked back and forth between us.

The Marshal's glare could strip paint. "It's not safe for him in here." She gestured with her fingers to the open door.

Not safe?

"Fly into the other room, dear," I whispered, lips trembling against his tawny head as I kissed him.

"Me wait for Zora," he chirped as he spread his wings and obeyed. He soared through the door and settled into the porthole. His tawny head tilted, eyes wide with concern.

"Do not leave the drain," the Marshal instructed as she crossed her arms over her chest. "Make a Shield."

"How is it possible to test magic . . . without a Royal Mage here to create a storm?" I blurted the question that had been bothering me since she said there would be a test.

The entire basis of the Storm Wars: Knight Mages nullified the destructive storm magic of Royal Mages.

"I'll be behind the glass, watching." The Marshal pointed at the mirror. "Do not disappoint me, soldier." She stalked out of the room, long cape fluttering.

She didn't answer my question.

The door swung shut, and locks clicked.

Squire stood in the porthole, a lonely, familiar face, pecking at the glass.

Crossing my arms over my ribs, I made a Shield like she'd demonstrated. Gravity pulled at my chest, my reflection looking more like a fairy-tale witch by the second. All I needed was a pointy hat, a broom, a hut deep in the forest, and the confidence to speak only in cryptic riddles.

My ragged exhales were too loud, air whistling from my parched throat. *Maybe nothing will—*

A muffled scream sounded.

Silence.

Another awful noise filled the shadowy room, even louder than the last. The wall of dark glass rattled. Agonized noises increased, and they sounded . . . male?

The Marshal is torturing someone on the other side.

Skin crawling, knees weak, I struggled to stand on the drain. Copper flooded my mouth, and I wiped at my wet lip; I'd bitten through it. In the mirror, blood dripped down my chin. As I rocked back and forth, my heart pounded against my rib cage. I blinked rapidly, struggling to keep my eyes open through the stinging sweat.

I stared at the innocuous silver spout.

The glass shook violently as a deep baritone voice *bellowed* with absolute agony.

I stepped back, flinching.

The Marshal said she'd be watching; it's a two-way mirror.

Shaking uncontrollably, I stumbled back onto the drain.

A loud scream was followed by a new gurgling noise. Pipes creaked . . . *Rushing water?* Hostile shadows stretched, and I curled low, steeling myself for certain pain. Strange vibrations mounted behind the rattling mirror.

I shuffled off the drain.

Don't be a coward, Zora.

I lunged back onto it.

Holding my stance, I braced myself, tired arms burning just from holding them in a Shield across my chest.

You can do this, Zora.

No, you can't.

You're blessed with freedom and strength. Lucky girl.

Sounds of someone being tortured echoed behind the glass.

I tasted bile.

Drip. Drip. Drip.

Water trickled out of the spout, dripping slowly onto the floor, streaked with glittering silver lines. Magic rose from the puddle in a smoky, metallic haze. The mirror stopped rattling.

Abrupt silence.

Is that it? The crushing pressure lifted off my shoulders, and I felt like Antichthon's biggest fool, blubbering and shaking over a tiny magical puddle.

A deep voice bellowed with agony, and the mirror clattered, shock waves rippling through it, nearly breaking it.

Gurgle.

Water exploded from the spout with intense pressure—straight toward my face and chest. Sputtering, I fell to my knees, arms shaking as I barely held them crossed. The arc of icy liquid drenched me, soaking me to the bone. It slammed painfully against my face, burning through my sinuses as storm magic hissed all around in a blinding haze.

Magic *burned* as it streamed out of my nose.

I squinted through the awful spray and burgeoning headache because my hands glowed a bright celestial silver. *Storm magic.* Awed, blinking in the watery deluge, I focused on the blurring shimmer.

I'd seen the only other living Knight Mages in action six years ago—Ella and Axel, the famous twins. Their arms had shone with a similar silver as their Shields redirected fire. The magical flames had never touched them, not once. *So why is the magic still intensifying as it touches me?*

Quaking from immense strain, I screamed through gritted teeth as the flow pushed me backward. Liquid quickly filled the room. It rose up, higher *and* higher, covering my knees and heading toward my waist.

I would drown at this rate.

The cold spray filled my nose, mouth, and lungs. I shook my head, lips pressed shut, desperately trying to get away from it, but there was nowhere to go. The drain on the floor was directly in front of the downpour. I teetered on my assigned position.

I will not fail.

Banging my fists against my soaking chest, I made a tighter Shield with my glowing hands, but it didn't stop the magic like it should have.

Liquid was at my waist.

A horrible throbbing pierced the right side of my head, and the muted light in the window was suddenly too bright. The overpowering scent of magic made me nauseous. The two-way mirror juddered, sending vibrations through the droplets.

You can do it. You can do anything. I imagined throwing the storm away from myself and diverting the torrent.

Nothing happened.

The icy liquid was at my chest—my chin—my nose.

Finally the spray stopped battering my face. I tipped my head back, inhaling raggedly. Pain throbbed deep inside my skull—like nothing I'd ever felt before—as my feet left the floor. I floated upward with the water, heading for the ceiling.

Hands splayed wide, I stopped pretending to make a Shield. They glowed bright silver in the swirling water, beacons of light in the darkness. Bubbles shimmered like glitter, rising off my fingers.

My nose bumped against the smooth stone ceiling. I inhaled deeply, strangely absent of panic as I was fully submerged.

Slipping under, I slowly drifted down through the blue; arms glowing silver, they shed rays of metallic light. Everything was quiet. I sank deeper, braid unraveling, long strands of hair floating all around. *Tap. Tap. Tap.* Squire pecked on the submerged porthole, yellow eyes wide and nervous.

I gave him a thumbs-up.

His head tilted with confusion.

I reached my hand out toward Squire to offer comfort. Shock waves of magic rippled through the water, exploding off my fingers. Senses heightened, I turned slowly toward the dark glass, hyperaware of a presence on the other side. I could sense . . . *another person*? They felt strangely familiar, like we were one and the same.

Save them.

Arm still outstretched, silver strands of magic tendrilled off my glowing skin. *Faster. Faster. Faster.* The mirror rippled, groaning as I sent water gushing toward it. A cyclone spun around me.

A scraping sounded, metal grinding against metal as the drain opened. Bubbles floated upward. A second, smaller spiral was forming near the floor.

Bang. Bang.

"*Stop.*" Through the watery haze, the Marshal stood at the window next to Squire, banging on the glass with both hands. Her eyes were wide, hat askew. "*Stop,*" she shouted, the sound muffled.

The drain groaned below.

My feet touched the floor, and suddenly the room was only half full. Liquid spun lazily around my legs, flowing down the drain. I coughed aggressively, the pounding in my skull unbearable. Arm still raised toward the mirror, I looked ridiculous. Soaking wet and wild, possessed, surrounded by whirling water, reaching for someone . . . *I don't even know who.*

The churning water was now at my ankles. Shivering, I sank to my knees with a loud splash, arms falling to my sides.

The water stilled, placid.

I keeled over.

Pain slowly receded from my throbbing forehead as I pressed it against the chilled floor. Exhaustion had never felt so catatonic. I tried to make sense of my surroundings. I was on my side in the fetal position, overtop the drain, as the last droplets of water emptied from the room.

Tiny silver flames danced mesmerizingly across my fingers.

Tap-tap-tap-tap.

Squire was pecking at the glass like he was trying desperately to get to me. I barely breathed, the raspy whistling too much on my very sensitive ears.

The door slammed open. Inching forward cautiously, the Marshal approached me with her sword drawn like I was a wild dire beast in a cage. Her blue eyes were frantic, cape hanging off with the clasp unpinned. "You . . . you . . . you . . ."

Squire flew over, settling onto my shoulder. "Zora swim!" he hooted with delight.

"Did . . . I . . ." Water exploded from my lips and streamed from my nose painfully. I propped myself up, gagging violently. "Pass?"

The Marshal straightened her uniform, inhaling deeply like she was steeling herself. "No," she said coldly. "You are *no* Knight Mage."

I collapsed back to the floor, unable to hold myself up, face pressed against the cool stone, stomach cramping with failure. The Iron Ritual hadn't worked.

"Somehow . . ." the Marshal whispered as she stared at my silver scar. "For some reason, the Iron Ritual made you into a . . . Royal Mage. You don't neutralize magic. You wield it."

Squire gasped. "Zora royal?"

What?

"You *created* a storm. This changes . . . everything."

I blacked out.

Clutching a towel around my wet clothes, I leaned my head against the red painted wall and tried not to pass out for the second time.

"Was there a Royal Mage . . . behind the mirror?" I asked slowly. "Was that their water magic filling the room—"

"Silence." The Marshal leaned into my personal space. We were in another dark room tucked away deep in the lower labyrinth of the base. Shadow Swords waited outside the door. "That is above your clearance level, soldier. *Never* speak of it again."

I opened my mouth to argue, then clicked my jaw shut. Miming a key, I mockingly pretended to lock my lips. Judging by the Marshal's blistering expression, she was not impressed.

A hanging oil lamp, the room's only source of light, cast ominous shadows across her pinched features as it swayed slightly over a circular table covered in model terrain: two continents separated by two oceans.

A map of Antichthon.

The Marshal stalked away and resumed pacing around the room.

I inched closer to the table.

Westmere was separated from the Empire's Azote by the great Moor Ocean to the east and the unfathomably expansive Glacial Ocean to the west. Both bodies of water were basically uncrossable, infested with dire killer whales larger than entire *Communes*.

The Moor Ocean was technically navigable if you had monsters at your disposal, which the Empire did. It was why they always attacked us from the east and why the continent of Azote was a blank. No Westmerean had ever visited and lived to tell the tale.

Within Westmere's three distinctive climates—modeled with frosted trees, expansive orange sand, and lush tropical forests—sat seven circular brick walls filled with play homes.

The isolated Northern Commune sat along the Eastern Coast among icy mountains. The four desert Middlelands Communes were nestled among sandy canyons, and the two Southern Communes were in a tropical rainforest.

In the middle of the Moor Ocean stood two figurines. One had a crown and a white fur cloak; the other had a blue spider tattoo. Dozens of boats were positioned behind them. Facing them were two Knight Mages, a helicopter, a plane, and a missile.

The Marshal twisted her cap in her hands, reciting complex statistical theories under her breath that I'd never heard of before. As she strategized about how to win a centuries-long magical war, I contemplated the best way to remove myself from her presence and get inside a hot shower. *Just tell her what you know so you can leave.*

I blurted, "I have something to say about Tarantula. He's—"

The Marshal froze and shook her head slowly, her blue eyes filled with paranoia. "Do *not* speak his name aloud." She glanced over at the door pointedly and stalked toward me.

"But we're alone in here . . . ?" I shivered as I looked around the empty, shadowy room.

She leaned close. "Do not underestimate the enemy. Royal Mage abilities are shrouded in secrecy because they are *more* than you can imagine," she whispered quietly. "There's a reason we still don't know exactly what the Emperor's storm magic is."

"What do you mean?"

"What do you think? Wait, don't answer that," she said coldly. "I don't want to know what goes on in your mind."

She whirled on her heel and stalked over to the board. She muttered to herself, staring at the map, lost in thought. I stopped trying to listen as I leaned against the wall, vision blurry.

I jolted awake, her scarred face hovering in front of mine—I'd fallen asleep standing upright. I blinked wearily. It was once again impossible to tell how much time had passed.

The Marshal leaned in, studying me intently. "Did anything happen to you during the Iron Ritual? Did you speak with anyone or experience any . . . revelations?"

An emerald figure shrouded in light. They were probably a figment of my imagination.

"No."

"Have you ever shown signs of possessing magic? Any mutations or abilities?" She peered suspiciously at my silver scar and then at where Squire snored loudly on my shoulder.

"No." I rubbed at the lines on my face. "It was a normal dire bear attack—I swear." Until today, my hands had never glowed silver with magical flames. I'd never felt anything *remotely* similar.

"Have you ever been to Azote?" Her eyebrow rose with accusation.

"Sure," I said sarcastically. "I crossed the *uncrossable* Moor Ocean."

"Watch your tone, soldier."

I sighed heavily. "I've lived my entire life in the North . . . What does all this mean? Why would this happen?"

"It means—" lines pulled tight around her mouth "—perhaps we *can* win this war. Maybe the old god isn't dead. Maybe we've been blessed." She shrugged, face pinching with frustration. "We do not and have never understood how magic works. *They* keep it cloaked in mystery. All we know is the Iron Ritual creates Knight Mages who can nullify it, and Royal Mages can have three storm affinities: snow, wind, or water."

My head spun with this new information.

"Isn't snow technically just . . . water?" I breathed out, dizzy with confusion.

She scoffed. "Is a blizzard the same as a *tsunami*?"

"No?"

"Try not to play the fool. You now possess the ability to wield storm magic—water," she whispered with gravitas. "Daily training is imperative for mastery, but *no one* on the base can know about this except me. No one. Do you understand?"

"Why can't I tell—"

"The fewer people the information can get tortured out of, the better. Do you *understand*, soldier?"

I nodded tiredly.

"I need verbal confirmation."

"Yes, sir," I muttered.

"Beginning today, *I* will tutor you in the military history of Westmere. Your lack of education as a Northerner is common knowledge." Her lips rolled with distaste, and I swallowed down my vitriol. "Shadow Swords will meet you at your room at high noon and escort you down here."

Is she calling me stupid?

"Do you understand, soldier?"

"Yes, sir."

"You will not reveal your new abilities under *any* circumstances, including but not limited to extreme physical and mental abuse. Do you understand?"

"Yes, sir."

"To everyone on this base, and in all Westmere, you are a novice Knight Mage who is struggling to control your defensive magic. If it comes to it, they are to believe the ritual failed and that you are *magicless*."

"Yes, sir." My voice cracked because I'd never been good at pretending.

She narrowed her eyes like she could read my thoughts. "Convince yourself that you are *actually* trying to gain Knight Mage powers, and act accordingly. Frustration . . . fear . . . annoyance—let yourself feel it all and then *show it*."

I nodded, sliding a little down the wall, trying to put space between us. Her intensity was overwhelming. She grabbed my face, stopping me from getting away. Her fingers were freezing.

She leaned forward so her mouth hovered right above my ear. "Tell me *everything* that has happened to you," she whispered, so softly I could barely hear her. "Quietly. I want to know every interaction you've ever had with them."

I didn't need to ask *who* she was referring to.

The tooth marks scarred onto my throat prickled as I brought my lips to her ear and obeyed. I'd been *dying* to tell someone for weeks. To get the crushing weight off my chest.

Her eyes widened, her pupils consumed her irises, and a sickly pallor spread across her face as I told the tale of a boy who became a man; the Great Siege of the North; Mom's kidnapping; Aurora's death; Tarantula's capture in the woods; and the threat that currently hung over my mom's head.

When I was done, she ripped away, shaking. For the first

time, the lines around her mouth and the scar above her eye didn't seem cruel. *Signs of trauma.*

"Why didn't you say something as soon as you arrived on base?" She raised her head, suspicion twisting her face. *Shhkkk.* She drew the sword from the sheath on her back and leveled the tip at my throat.

My scars reflected in the metal. "I thought you would immediately kill him," I said honestly.

The sword wavered.

She resheathed it.

"Why haven't you killed him yet?" I asked tonelessly, heat licking up the walls of my chest, heart pounding.

The Marshal turned and stalked over to the board. She slapped her palms onto the map, staring down at it pensively, head sinking below her shoulders; trees clattered as they fell over.

A manic sound escaped her lips, somewhere between a chuckle and a shriek, as she picked up the figurine of the cloaked Emperor. With her other hand, she raised Tarantula. She held both up to the light.

"Right now, we have a deadly Royal Mage in our midst, held on the *tiniest* of leashes. We have . . . leverage over him, and he's trading secrets with us, playing a role."

A creeping sensation made my limbs numb.

"Why would he—"

"The Storm Wars have not been raging." The figurines made a cracking sound as she clutched them in her fists. "We've been locked in a stalemate for centuries because we have . . . something they want . . . It is the only reason they haven't used their magic to wipe us off the face of Antichthon."

"Why don't we give them what they want?"

"Fool. Did you not hear your own story?" Her gaze bored through me. "If we did that, then they'd *murder* us all."

"And if we don't?" I whispered, shivering. Everything was

convoluted—smaller and bigger than I'd imagined, at the same time. *Messier.*

Her voice was steel. "Then they grow tired of waiting and massacre all of us."

"So we do nothing?" Thoughts scrambled, I was too exhausted to strategize.

"No," the Marshal said softly. "We beat them at their game and break the stalemate first."

"How could we—"

"By taking away one of their assets. Tipping the balance in our favor. Win enough battles and you win the war."

I scratched at my temples with growing frustration. "But you *just* said we can't kill him."

Sparks leaped in the Marshal's eyes. "The *man* is not the asset. Someone else would take his place. But we can use him and use what he—"

She froze.

"This is how we do it," she whispered, like she'd had a eureka moment. "Your new water abilities, the circumstances—it's perfect." She tossed one of the figurines, and it rolled at my feet.

I bent down for it, woozy.

"We use him to get to what we want." Her voice shook with excitement. "Then we're closer than we've ever been to winning this blasted war."

Feeling drugged, *out of control*, I grabbed the model of a man. My head filled with rushing white noise. Nothing made sense. The Marshal stood above me, legs parted wide. I didn't remember sitting down on the floor.

She crouched next to me, leaning close. Ruthless intelligence *burned* in her eyes.

Her face hovered beside mine. "Tarantula will be placed in your care. We'll pretend he's . . . training you. Yes—that will work," she breathed out almost silently. "You will be his *shadow*, day and night. You stay close to him, glued to his side, and then when the time finally comes . . . you make your move."

Doubt wrapped around my neck and crawled down my throat.

I shook my head no.

The Marshal nodded yes.

"Zora Ravenal, you are being issued a secret mission by all the power bestowed on my shoulders as the elected military leader of the one Democratic Commonwealth. Code name: *Quest.* Your mission directive is to keep Tarantula close and let him lead you to the asset. No one can know, besides the two of us, what your directive is. Not even the twins."

"That's a suicide mission. I don't think I can—"

Pain streaked across my face where the Marshal slapped me. "There's an active threat against your mother—or have you forgotten?"

I held her gaze, cheek burning, rage hot across my chest. "No, I haven't forgotten."

Her face turned blotchy red. "We have intel that the Empire is planning to *take* Westmere within the next few months. Do you want your mother, yourself, and everyone else on this damned continent murdered?"

"No."

"Do you *want* to win the Storm Wars . . . or do you want to give up because you're scared of the enemy? Do you want to avenge your friend . . . I believe you called her Aurora?"

My head jerked to the side, cheek throbbing as she slapped me again. *Harder.* I barely felt it. The pressure in my mind was crushing.

"Are you a coward, soldier?" she demanded.

Air whistled through my gritted teeth. "No, sir."

"Complete the quest."

"Yes, sir."

Standing up, she straightened her uniform.

Her hand, wrinkled from time and veined from combat, hovered in front of my face as she held it out for me to take.

I wanted to tell her no way, that I was going back home to the North. *Where everyone is starving because of the Storm Wars.*

I didn't want to die for any cause. *They've threatened Mom.* This was the very reason I'd joined the Crimson Army. *Aurora.*

My plan to gain magic had worked. *Damned lucky girl.* Stomach in knots, thoughts racing, I tried not to throw up because I was supposed to just be a Knight. *Is it possible to be too blessed?* I'd wanted magic, but not like this. The new sickening weight of responsibility crushed me.

The Marshal's lips pursed. "Either you're a coward or you're a hero—you can't be both. Westmere is counting on you."

With a resigned breath, I took her offered hand.

3

Knee-Deep in Deceit

"Zora Ravenal." The Marshal tapped a sword across the shoulder of my new armor, her cape flowing behind her as she knighted me.

I stood on a platform at the front of the military hangar. Hundreds of soldiers stood before me, the desert warm at my back.

"The Democratic Commonwealth is yours to defend," the Marshal said with gravitas. "The freedom of Westmere from the Draconis Empire's tyranny is now your responsibility." A heavy metal helmet was placed on my head. "So you are knighted, Mage."

Soldiers fell to their knees in unison, bowing as they lifted their right pointer fingers—the symbol that Antichthon's first democracy was still standing. Their hopeful faces were burned into my brain. No one grimaced as they looked up at my scars. Not anymore.

The pomp of the knighting ceremony still played on repeat in my mind a week later.

Now, I blinked rapidly in the hot wind, trying desperately to stop overthinking. Needing to get outside of my head and back into my body, I focused on the dizzying heights.

Chop—Chop—Chop—Chop.

Matte black helicopter blades spun overhead. This was my fifth training flight this week, practice for the Storm Wars and a new way to try to forget my quest. It had been two weeks since the Iron Ritual, and I was beginning to think I'd never be warm again.

Life had settled into a routine:

1. **Morning run or flight:** Sprint through the dunes. Try not to think about dire scorpions until I collapse and can't remember how doomed I am. Or, more preferably, jump face-first from a helicopter.

2. **Training at high noon:** Try, and fail, to conjure water magic while the Marshal whispers blistering insults about me, my ancestors, and my bird.

3. **Evenings:** Lie exhausted in bed and feel sorry for myself. Eat dinner with the other Knight Mages, the twins, and hide my tears from them.

"MIST FAILURE INCOMING," the Admiral bellowed over the intercom.

Our helicopter kept flying straight up—a steep ascent—into the violet sky. In the first light of dawn, silver streaks of magic shimmered, dancing in the atmosphere. I stood in the open doorway, balancing as the smell of fuel filled my lungs.

The worst part of my schedule was about to get infinitely *worse.* I had storm magic, but I could barely use it.

On top of that, the Marshal had quietly informed me yesterday, after I'd stared at a cup of water with my arm outstretched for *three* hours straight (nothing happened), that tomorrow my "quest" would start.

Today was tomorrow.

I stared numbly down at the sand, leaning forward into the wind.

"Me scared of heights!" Squire squawked as he shook on my shoulder, hiding behind my long braid. Apparently he'd developed a crippling fear of heights—five seconds ago. *Who am I to judge his fears?* Old god knew I struggled with my own.

I craned my neck, eyes watering as the temperature dropped. The desert flashed below us: orange sand rolled in endless peaks and troughs. Sunlight attacked, impossibly bright, cutting through the dark lenses of my goggles.

I miss Mom, and my snowboard, and the frosted Barren Forest of the North.

"T-MINUS TEN SECONDS."

Dry air whistled as my scarlet shorts and sleeveless shirt whipped vigorously against my exposed limbs.

Chop—Chop—

Long blue tendrils of the Mist rose up from the ground, chasing after us. A loud groan echoed, and the vehicle shuddered as the Mist attacked the helicopter's engine.

The propellers stalled.

We jerked violently, and my stomach rose like I'd flipped on my snowboard. Laughter burst from my lips.

"ABORT!" the Admiral shouted as he leaped from the open door with his arms and legs spread wide. *The dramatics of Midlanders never cease to amaze.*

The engine seized.

We banked to the right, the nose tipping down, straight toward the sand. "ABORT, KNIGHT MAGE," crackled disjointedly over the failing intercom. "KNIGHT, YOU MUST ABORT THE—"

I jumped forward with all my might, flipping straight out of the helicopter, tumbling through the open air with my knees tucked up. Squire plummeted with me, screeching.

Rule of survival: Have a terrifying amount of fun.

Eyes closed, I rolled head over heels. *WHOOSH.* Behind me, the helicopter deployed its oversized parachute, airbags exploding across the bottom as metal groaned, dramatically slowing its descent.

"ZORA!" Squire screeched into my ear, shattering the moment.

"Fly, darling." I pried him off my shoulder and gently tossed him up into the air. Squire plummeted like a rock beside me, spinning helplessly. He shrieked, magic sparkling around his beak.

"Fly!" I demonstrated, flapping my arms as I twisted and spun.

Squire unfurled his wings, catching air. I hurtled past him. He spun with happiness, then pulled into a nosedive and followed.

The great separator in nature: *When you see danger, do you run to it or away from it?* Sand in the wind burned my skin as exhilaration sparked in my soul. Laughing, I spun faster. *Why was I ever afraid?*

I saluted the Admiral as I spiraled joyfully through the whistling air. *Lucky, lucky girl.* Squire grabbed my braid with his beak and yanked as if trying to stop my descent.

Closer.

Closer.

Closer.

I could do anything I wanted. *The Emperor will never catch me.* I was too blessed to die. *He will learn.* You didn't mess with a girl who had fate on her side.

I deployed my parachute, and it yanked me upward. My spine ached, and the straps across my chest and thighs dug deep. No time left to direct the momentum. My stomach flipped, weightless, and then gravity won. I slammed down, rolling through the dune, ropes tangling behind me.

Unlike powdery snow, sand fought back. Coughing, I lay spread wide.

Squire settled on my forehead, his talons pricking my skin. "You alive?" he chirped aggressively. He'd never quite gotten the hang of proper grammar usage.

"No, I'm a ghost." I laughed.

Squire hooted, "A wraith!"

Just like that, my eyes burned with the pressure of unshed tears. Mom loved retelling the ancient fairy tales about immortal mermaids, witches, vampires, elves, keepers of the forest, wraiths, fae, and shifters with two hearts—one animal and one human. She said the epic romances about soulmates could teach us a lot about ourselves.

The ground vibrated as the helicopter bounced and slid to a stop a hundred feet away, surprisingly upright. The blue fog of the Mist dissipated from the now inert engine.

Two pilots clad in black climbed out as a dozen dire horses ridden by soldiers in scarlet uniforms galloped over. Layers of muscles bunched as the steeds' long legs easily navigated the sands, and their fangs flashed opal. Silver plumed from their noses as they breathed the magic in the atmosphere. The cavalry dismounted and attached chains to the helicopter.

"HAUL."

Whips cracked. The dire horses bolted, dragging the chopper back to the hangar. Other horses trotted out past them, fitted with empty tankards in sled beds. They were off to retrieve fuel from the stockpiles in the abandoned refineries out west.

Groaning, I stumbled to my feet, joints popping.

Carved lines bisected the dune, the only indication that a two-headed snake had recently slithered past.

Cobalt fangs flashed, silver magic wafting from its orifice as eight legs crawled beside my foot. I screamed. The giant dire tarantula was twice the size of my boot.

My feet tangled in the chute lines as I fell backward, kicking. Squire screeched. I scrambled away on all fours, the arachnid disappearing into the sand. Revolted, I hurried away. *Spiders are not animals. They're the spawn of monsters, and no one can convince me otherwise.*

Nauseous from the encounter with the arachnid, I trudged through the thick sand, back toward the hangar of the Scorpion Hole. Outside the entrance, two soldiers dressed in silver armor jousted—my fellow Knight Mages, the famous magical twins. *Crack.* Their long poles collided as they rode past each other, a variation of the crest of the Commonwealth: a Knight jousting at a golden-scaled, fire-breathing dragon.

I waved.

Ella pulled up her Knight visor, calling out my name as she raised her hand. Axel saluted me mockingly. Six years ago, they helped me during the Great Siege of the North, and now we were once again reunited, this time living together.

Half lost in memories, I returned my gear. Inside the hangar, swords clanged together as scarlet soldiers thrust and parried. Another group climbed ropes attached to the ceiling. Hundreds more stomped in formation, broadswords strapped across their backs. They bowed to me deeply, reverence on their faces. Shadow Swords nodded to me shallowly, their expressions indifferent.

Farther off in the corner behind the horse stalls sat a small mailroom for soldiers to send messages to loved ones. A row of blue-feathered homing dire falcons waited on the windowsill, silver wafting from their beaks.

Dozens of helicopters and fighter jets sat parked on wooden pallets. The jets had fusion-propulsion engines, the rotating silver mechanism sleek and shockingly large. The reusable helicopters were ready to be hauled out for training exercises, but the planes were saved for battle. There was no technology left that could prevent a jet from crashing once it broke the sound barrier.

At the far end of the hangar, seven missiles stood taller than people. Red button remote launchers and long metal arrows with tiny wires on the arrowheads—target designators—sat in a locked glass box on the wall. *They look just like I remember.*

Rumor had it, even *larger* missiles were located somewhere nearby, as well as a deadly atomic weapon rigged up to something important, and it was the only reason why the Empire hadn't massacred all of us.

The Atomic Paradox: *Would the atomic bomb explode first as the Mist attacked? Or would the Mist attack in the split second after it was activated, rendering it inert before it exploded?*

I shivered.

Stumbling, adrenaline draining away, I barely made it to the red door labeled *Knight Unit*. I slipped through the door and collapsed back against it, relieved to be away from so many eyes. Wherever I went, soldiers stared.

Cool air whispered against my feverish flesh in the inner hall, and I welcomed the change. A pinkish hue that hadn't been there this morning burned across my arms. The deep bronze of my skin had protected me from the sun for the past few months, but for some reason, I'd recently started getting burned. It always faded within a few hours, but each time it happened, it hurt worse.

"Squire's back!" Axel shoved the door open behind me, nearly sending me to the floor.

He'd changed out of his armor, and he sauntered after me as I backed away. Oil lamps swayed from the ceiling, drenching him in long shadows. He smiled wide, flashing two fang-like canines, like those of the fairy-tale vampires.

He'd sharpened them himself.

With a file.

"What—did you think the desert was going to eat him?" I asked as Axel tried to pet Squire, who hid beneath my braid. Apparently he had a natural distrust of men. *A spectacular display of advanced owl intelligence.*

Axel, realizing he wasn't making headway with my bird (read: avian genius), gave up with a dramatic sigh and turned to me.

"No," I said, but he'd already slung an arm over my shoulders.

His posture was casual, but his eyes had a hardened edge to them. The more time I spent around him, the more of an enigma he became. He was quick to anger, and even quicker to laugh. Lazy enjoyment hid simmering indifference, which masked bouts of inflammatory rage. Axel wasn't quite what he seemed, and you never knew how he would react.

I tried to yank away from his hold, but Axel flexed and stayed close, glued to my side.

Ella followed through the door, not hitting anyone with it. Unlike her brother, she wore her emotions on her sleeve. *I like her best.*

She joined us. "How was the parachute practice?"

"Amazing," I said honestly.

"I hate the heights." She shuddered. "They make me sick."

"They make me *alive*." I patted down my messy sandy hair while I still tried, unsuccessfully, to get away from Axel. "Your curls look pretty this morning." I shoved at her brother to no avail, admiring her with the genuine appreciation of someone who had pin-straight locks.

She slapped Axel on the back of the head. "Let her go."

"No." Axel pretended to gnash his fangs.

She hit him harder.

I fought free, pushing out from beneath their flailing arms. *Siblings.* With my newfound space, I leaned against the wall, knees weak from leftover adrenaline.

Ella patted my shoulder and made a soothing noise, apparently done beating her twin. She leaned forward and gave Squire a kiss on his head, and he preened happily. Axel made a noise of jealousy, but I understood Squire. Ella was warm and gentle, *just like Aurora.*

Grief hit me hardest at the most random times. The world appeared the same on the surface, but the tiniest details tipped the scales, and I remembered it was empty without her in it.

"*Soooo,*" Axel drawled. "Did you hear the big news? There's been an . . . addition . . . to your daily training schedule."

My stomach bottomed out. A part of me had still hoped the Marshal would realize she'd demanded too much of me and would change her mind. That she'd stay up all night tossing and turning, coming up with a new plan.

This can't be happening right now.

I wrenched my shoulders back, standing straight as I steeled myself.

Axel stepped away at my expression. "You're getting a new partner . . . sort of." He grimaced. "Apparently the Marshal's not happy with your progress and wants to give you more practice in the afternoons . . . with him."

Everything narrowed to a singular point.

It was happening.

Thoughts static, I backed away.

Axel continued, reciting the planned narrative mercilessly. "Rumor is, he agreed because of some bargain. A pardon for his crimes." He shook his head like he couldn't believe it. *Me neither.* "The diamonds dampen the strength of his magic, but they don't nullify it completely. Ostensibly he can still wield enough magic to . . . train you."

"But we'll be around to help," Ella offered softly. "You're not just stuck with him."

"He's in your room," Axel said. "Waiting for you." He pointed at my door.

Time moved like molasses, strange and suffocating, as I turned and walked stiffly down the white hall. I stared at the door handle. For some reason, I couldn't lift my arm. The door swung open from the inside before I could move. Bright morning light glowed around a towering silhouette. Sharp wind gusted my hair back.

"Hello, brat . . . or should I say . . . *partner.*" A familiar, bold accent butchered the words.

Aurora's murderer.

"Oh no, the spider whore," Squire screeched, hiding behind my braid (accurate).

The object of my demise leaned casually against the doorframe, his wide shoulders almost completely blocking the entrance to my room. The cyan arachnid tattoo spread across his hateful face. He smelled of decaying flesh, bloodletting, and—I inhaled deeper—*the complete absence of hope.*

Backing away across the hall, holding my breath, I tried to forget his distinctive scent—the *reek* of a ruined world.

"No," I whispered, and I wasn't acting. The panic was real.

"Yes?" Squire hooted.

"Yes—indeed," Tarantula purred, chains rattling as he raked his cuffed hands through his gold-streaked blond curls.

Morning light reflected off a profile that regularly haunted my nightmares: platinum mask, harsh jawline, malicious maroon lips.

A shock collar with diamonds stretched across a throat that I knew firsthand was *covered* in gruesome scars. Metal clinked together, a long chain hanging between the cuffs on his wrists and ankles granting him limited mobility.

"I am royal, and thou art a lowly Knight. *Bow* to me." His accent distorted each word, the corner of his lips twitching as if trying to fight a smirk. His use of *thou* and *thee* instead of *you* was just as jarring as the first time I'd heard it. He spoke with posh consonants and cruel intonations, like he'd learned dialect from archaic poetry.

"What?" I whispered, genuinely confused why he thought I'd obey such a ridiculous request.

He straightened, a muscle ticking in his jaw as surprise flashed across his steely gaze. The delusional megalomaniac apparently assumed I'd be engaging in some bizarre Mage hierarchy.

"On—your—knees, *Zora*," Tarantula ordered stiffly as he glared down at my legs as if waiting for me to buckle. "Now."

I stood taller.

He looked perturbed, like he'd genuinely expected that to work. *Is this man for real right now?* His audacity was almost inspirational.

"On your knees," Squire hooted back at him. "Wretched whore." (Helpful.)

"Silence, dirty bird," Tarantula said.

"Don't you dare speak to him like that."

Squire screeched louder. "Silence, dirty spider!"

"That's right, dear." Trying to act unaffected, I stroked his tawny feathered head with one trembling finger.

If an expression could kill, I'd be six feet under.

Tarantula stepped forward, and the tops of his curls brushed against the doorframe. He towered so much taller than I remembered, all lean muscles and jagged striations. Every inch of his flesh radiated deadliness. His heavy-lidded eyes were rimmed with dark circles, magnifying the sense of danger.

He's not blinking.

"BOW, vassal," Tarantula said quietly, magic glittering around him in a haze.

"No."

Vassal. Isn't it Knight?

"On your knees, hideous whore man," Squire squawked back, growing more verbose, and agitated, by the second (very helpful).

"*You* hideous whore man," I corrected him, forcing my voice to stay strong. "Unlike him, we're not living in the dark ages."

"Slut," Squire hooted.

"Close enough."

Tarantula's right eye twitched. "I order thee to bow to your royal liege, *serf*." His gaze flicked up and down my figure like he was remembering the patched holes in my well-worn clothes the first time we'd met.

A flush burned across my chest, ribs creaking with rage. "I order you to *silence yourself*."

I was done with everyone's judgment. Tarantula called me a serf because we had a cooperative land-based economy in the Northern Commune and were isolated from trade routes. We made do with apprenticeships, learning to sew our own clothes, growing crops in greenhouses, and, my specialty, hunting.

Tarantula considered all life on Westmere provincial and below him, especially Northern life. The Midlanders called me a peasant for the exact same reason.

"Never," Tarantula intoned, silver gushing from his pores like storm magic had found an endless source in him. The sharp scent burned my sinuses.

I gestured behind him at *my* room. "Get out." *Damn the Marshal's plan.* I couldn't do this.

Tarantula stared at my throat, and I raised my fingers to the tooth ridges on my jugular. His eyes narrowed, lingering, then slowly traveled up to my face.

"Have *you* not heard the news?" he asked slowly, like he was making a concerted effort *not* to use archaic language. "I have agreed to work with the Crimson Army for a full pardon . . . Say hello to your new magic trainer." He held his cuffed hands wide, chain glinting as his accent lingered, more guttural than I remembered.

I took another step back.

"No."

"Yes." Tarantula winked cruelly.

My skull slammed against the wall. *Aurora stared up at me with sightless eyes.* I choked, lungs spasming in panic as I gasped shallowly, barely staying upright. *She's dead because of him.*

If he had any mercy, he would walk away and give me space.

Tarantula stalked across the hall in two big steps and loomed above me. "This is a great honor for thee," he said coldly. "They are forcing this farce on me."

"I will kill you," I whispered. "For Aurora—for Mom."

He chuckled. "If thou wanted to, thou already would have, *Knight*." He said my title like it was a joke.

The world went up in flames. I lunged forward, going chest to chest, shoving him back across the hall with all my strength. "If you harm a single hair on my mom's head, I will not hesitate. I will *end* you—Empire scum."

"No, thou shan't." He bared rows of perfect white teeth. "Have thou not heard? The wicked live forever."

The raspy sound that escaped my lips would have made a sarcophagus-bound wraith proud. Cortisol levels spiking, I tensed, ready to fight for all our lives. Sensing the danger from down the hall, Axel pulled Ella behind him, blocking her with his larger body.

"Thou art weak," Tarantula said with a sadistic glint in his eye, his body bumping against mine. "We shall have to fix that first, partner."

"*You* are not my partner. You are my enemy. This is a disgrace, and I will kill you—"

"So dramatic. 'Tis an opportunity for us to—"

"—and if you try to hurt me, I will—"

"I will not!" he roared, magic exploding from his mouth, obscene, like dragon fire. "They have . . . *leverage* . . . over me."

"What do they have?" I asked, genuinely curious what his angle was in all of this.

His expression froze over, eyes dead. Leisurely he crossed his arms, the action carefully designed to look lazy and unthreatening, but his posture was too stiff. Each movement was far too purposeful to be anything but dangerous.

The skin around his eyes that wasn't covered by the platinum mask was covered in purple veins so dark they were almost onyx. *Signs of corruption.*

He had a violent, unsettling demeanor.

I waited.

He didn't speak.

Unwittingly my gaze dipped to the loose gray material that stretched across his striated torso, *DANGER* embroidered in garish orange across the prisoner garb. I could picture the exact place where my dagger had protruded from his stomach when I'd captured him. I'd left him impaled for weeks.

When I looked back up, the temperature in the air plummeted.

"Oh, I cannot *wait* to instruct thee, Zora," he said with a cryptic pause, the scent of magic intensifying. "It shall be . . . titillating."

He was in chains, and I was free. I wanted to escape him, but I wanted to destroy the Draconis Empire more. *I will complete my quest.*

"How magnanimous of you," I said slowly, gathering my courage. "But you'll want to be careful. You know, with your . . . unbecoming situation." I tapped my neck, then my wrists, baring my teeth like a fanged dire fox.

"A sexy situation," Squire sang (not helpful).

Silver-laced wind gusted directly at me, making my eyes water.

Tarantula's teeth ground together, neck tendons straining as his eyes rolled back in his head, the whites flickering like he was seconds away from losing all control. In the next blink, his features smoothed over—borderline serene—and the biting magic disappeared.

"Above all, I have allegiance only to myself," he said calmly, his accent changing into something palatable and less depraved. "The divine Emperor has abandoned me in this . . . wasteland named Westmere."

I couldn't meet his eyes. Instead, I stared at the wall beside his lying head. "Aleksander is just a pathetic little boy masquerading as a man. You have misspoken. We both know Aleksander is not anywhere near divine. He's just a coward who wants to enslave us all."

"Pathetic little boy," Squire crooned.

I laughed without humor.

Tarantula chuckled back.

I laughed louder.

He chuckled harder.

"Uh—are you okay?" Axel asked as he moved closer, waving a hand in front of my face. *No.* I realized how we looked to outsiders, me and Tarantula faking mirth, nearly manic with rage. Ella stood beside her brother, eyes wide with confusion.

"I'm fine." My voice cracked.

Axel didn't look convinced, and he raised the back of his hand to my forehead as if checking for a fever. I pushed him away, but he was persistent, pressing his fingers to my neck as if searching for a pulse.

Silver darkened to black as magic smoked off Tarantula, and behind him, posters were ripped off the walls by gusts of fierce wind. He pointed a finger at Axel and unleashed his storm magic.

Axel's hand fell away from my neck, his face turning an unnatural shade of blue as his eyes bugged from their sockets. His auburn hair whipped violently around his head as he clutched at his throat, collapsing to the floor.

"Look away, dear," I said, and Squire swiveled his head.

Rule of survival: Revolt against royals.

I lunged, throwing a fist at Tarantula. He took the punch to the face with a smirk, chains stopping him from retaliating. A strange shudder rolled through him.

Axel choked loudly on the ground. Ella shouted and formed a Shield in front of him. It wasn't happening fast enough. Blood dripped from Axel's bulging eyes as vessels ruptured.

I threw another punch. *Harder.* Just like he'd ordered the other day. My fist cracked against Tarantula's cheek, but his mirthful expression didn't change. Instead, he slowly wet his crimson lips, eyes hooded.

Changing tactics, I aimed low, slamming my knuckles against his old dagger wound. This time he froze. The strange light left his eyes. They went flat as he stared down at where I'd touched him.

Ella shouted, and Squire screeched in solidarity.

I aimed again for the wound. He shifted and spun, pinning me hard against the wall with his larger body. His hips pressed against mine, and magic poured off his torso, gusts of wind battering my face. His strange, dangerous smell had a heady note of black cherry.

The sweat dripping down my spine began to freeze.

Tarantula's nostrils flared wide where they peeked out from beneath his mask, like he'd scented prey. A flush crawled up his neck, covering his jaw.

"So improper," he muttered, but he leaned closer, teeth bared. I shifted, punching at his old stab wound with my limited mobility. He moved with deadly precision, hips flexing, pinning me harder.

SIZZLE.

Electricity exploded from his collar, and cobalt veins protruded from his neck. Long seconds passed. Then he fell onto one knee before me. Voltage prickled across my skin, barely noticeable compared to how his body had felt against mine.

The Mist gathered at our feet.

A yard away, a Shadow Sword turned the dial with a fierce scowl. He was a handsome, tall man with dark hair and vibrant green eyes. With expert dexterity, he withdrew his sword and leveled it at Tarantula's gut.

I rubbed at my chest, trying desperately to center myself as Tarantula convulsed on the floor. The Mist thickened, and the Shadow Sword turned down the dial. I recognized the soldier from the hall the day of the Iron Ritual. He'd pulled me behind himself protectively.

Axel coughed as he massaged his throat, eyes watering. Ella

helped him to his feet, and he leaned heavily against her, his face pale, expression shaken.

"Knight." The Shadow Sword bowed deeply, still holding his sword threateningly with one hand. He handed me the dial with the other. "The name is Ryse. I am at your esteemed service."

"The diamonds don't work." I gestured desperately at Tarantula, who seethed, panting in the aftermath of the electricity. "He can still . . . *choke people.*"

Ryse turned the dial back up, radiating calm assurance. "They're effective. He cannot conjure a storm. For all intents and purposes, he is neutered. He is now . . . handleable."

Tarantula slapped his hand against the floor, muscles taut with electricity. "How dare thou," he snarled.

He doesn't look handleable to me.

Sinking into myself, I imagined the white-tipped trees in a quiet, peaceful forest. Snow was falling all around. A chessboard was set up across a stump, and I played against myself. *Everything will be okay.* I was blessed with luck and an endless source of joy. The crushing pressure around my heart eased, and I forced my shoulders back, holding Ryse's gaze.

"Thank you, Ryse," I said, meaning it.

"Anytime you need me—" Ryse bowed once more "—I will happily serve." He turned on his heel and left. Ella nodded to me as she helped Axel turn to head back to their room.

Axel glared down at the monster as he passed, but Tarantula didn't seem to notice. His gaze was locked on me. *Still not blinking.*

Tarantula made a dark sound from the floor, eyes flashing with malicious intent as he stared. "*Thank you, Ryse,*" he said with a high-pitched mocking sneer.

"I loathe *everything* about you." I stomped into my room and slammed the door shut in his face. I opened it again and closed it harder just to make a point.

Tarantula snarled something outside, but I couldn't hear

through the rushing in my ears. Sliding down the door, I wrapped my arms around my knees and rocked. Tears blurred my vision.

~~I can't complete my quest.~~

~~I can't complete my quest.~~

~~I can't complete my quest.~~

Yes, you can.

On all fours, I crawled to the bag that held all my belongings: books, hand-sharpened dire bone daggers, and a few knickknacks.

I searched desperately for the thinnest book with a flowery gold cover. The one I'd impulsively stolen from Mom's room the day I left to save her, because I couldn't function without having a piece of her with me. *Mom's journal.* She'd told me to never read it, and I still hadn't broken my promise.

Sitting on the floor, I held it against my chest.

A few minutes later, afraid *he* was going to try to come inside, I moved to put it away. As I pushed it back into my sack, the pages fell open. I froze. They were covered in a strange, unreadable language full of *x*'s, *z*'s, and *y*'s. I held it up to the window light.

A tiny card fluttered out.

The portrait of a strikingly handsome man stared up at me. Startlingly pale, with short, light blond hair, almond-shaped crystal-blue eyes, and an ouroboros tattoo around his right eye—the snake that ate its own tail into infinity. He wore all black and possessed an aura of danger, tangible even in two dimensions. The worst part—he had the eyes of a killer.

I turned the picture over.

There is nothing in my black, cursed heart, but thou. My love is wider than the ocean, and fiercer than any storm. Every day, I wake up and drown for thee.

Mom barely spoke about my dad, or that horrible day when he disappeared while she was pregnant with me. The few times she'd whispered about my father, she'd called him dark and handsome. She said we had the same eyes. Mine were light amber, a far cry from this man's cruel blue gaze.

We weren't related. He was just a dalliance from before she met my father. A stranger.

I flipped gingerly through the book, pausing at a page with strange symbols.

The Marshal said Royal Mages had three possible storm abilities: snow, wind, and water. Three of those symbols were depicted here, as well as fire and lightning. *No, it can't be.* Was this some type of Royal Mage . . . *storm power hierarchy*?

Deeply unsettled, I gently shut the journal, hid it inside a larger book, shoved them into my sack, then tucked it all away under my bed.

The council elders of the Northern Commune always warned that hard times made monsters out of good men, but they never said what it did to women. I had a bad feeling Tarantula was going to make *far worse* out of me.

4

Stage of Grief: Denial

Lounging across from me, Tarantula asked, "What . . . art thou reading?" His voice was a deep rasp, the sound reminiscent of a dire wolf's warning growl. He was all throat and menace, looking deceptively casual.

A second bed had been moved into my already claustrophobic room. Our narrow beds sat across from each other on opposite walls, one arm's distance apart. Our headboards flanked a large window, which sat above a small end table.

I could hear the exact moment each breath escaped from Tarantula's lungs as he studied me. Handcuffs glinted around his wrists and ankles, and the diamonds on his throat caught the moonlight.

Squire snored beside me, tucked half under the covers like he didn't have a single care in the world.

Tarantula was close enough to reach out and strangle; close enough to land a killing blow; close enough to whisper a death threat and be heard; close enough to die by his hand; close enough to touch; close enough to maul; close enough that he would hear me if I sobbed into my pillow.

I clutched the poetry book protectively to my chest. "None

of your business." My voice came out too hesitant, *weak*, in the quiet bedroom.

"Thou do not need to pretend." He smirked, tucking his arm behind his head, biceps straining through fabric. "Westmere literacy rates are pitifully abysmal—a sad state of idiocy."

I lowered my book. "Excuse . . . me?"

"*You* suffer terribly—poor illiterate peasant," he drawled, the modern pronoun bizarre on his accented tongue, as if he was trying to appear different than he was.

It didn't work.

"Don't call me that," I said, fingers trembling.

"A poor serf? 'Tis what thou art. Do thou need me to read that book to help thee find sleep? I am at your impoverished service."

Crack.

Pages opened wide as the book fell from his thick skull, fluttering to the floor.

Magic hissed, steaming off his shoulders, a silver haze in the dark night. He touched his forehead with disbelief. "Thou . . . did *not* . . . throw a book at me."

"But I can't read. What else would I use it for? Is it not a weapon?"

He blinked slowly. "I detect sarcasm."

"I *detect* an egotistical, pompous pig."

He smiled lazily like I'd complimented him.

The sun had set hours before, and it would be hours until it rose anew. Our first night together. Darkness crept around his body, shadows multiplying as they crawled through the room. Evil thrived at night, Tarantula its perfect personification. No person, thing, or natural element would save me.

Not from him.

"Why the damned would thou risk your life in the Iron Ritual?" he asked abruptly.

"Isn't it obvious?" I bared my teeth. "I'm going to destroy you."

His glare could kill.

Four walls closed in around us—animals in a cage. Shards of light from the full moon pierced through the inky blackness, reflecting across his shiny platinum mask.

Neither of us had slept for a single second. A mutual state of aggressive stubbornness. The harder I willed him to fall asleep, the more he seemed to tense, his eyes bright and alert.

Without a book to occupy my hands, I clicked my fingernails together.

He pointed at me, his long arm nearly crossing the distance between our beds, magic rising off his finger like smoke. "Careful," he said threateningly, eyes flashing.

"Ryse was right," I said, needing to wipe the grin off his face. "You really are neutered."

"Thou art unlearned and rude, assaulting your betters." His accent roughened with rage as he gestured at the book on the floor. "Such a brat. Is there no such thing as education in this sewage pit of a contin—"

"Don't call me stupid!" I turned the dial for the first time.

Tarantula convulsed on the bed, blue sparks jumping as he tasted electrocution. Metal chains clattered. Whispered grunts escaped his parted lips as his body went taut. Only a ruthless monster could have created this collar. *I want to kiss the engineer.*

Blue strands of Mist rose from the floor in thick streams, attacking the collar. I turned the dial down. The Mist retreated. Pained masculine rasps filled the quiet room.

"Don't call me stupid," I repeated.

His arm shot out. Silver exploded from his hand.

Wind slammed against me, and my braid slapped my face. He pinned me with storm magic to the bed, arms spread. Metal dug into my palm where the dial lay in my open hand. I couldn't move my fingers—all five digits were spread wide, trapped by the invisible force.

How in the damned is this him neutered?

The sensation of being crushed by the gusts of punishing wind increased. I screamed silently through the panic, eyes watering as silver strands battered me. Sheets slapped loudly against the wall. I focused on reaching the dial as everything began turning black.

"How does *thou* like that?" he asked, smug with gloating. "Thou insufferable—"

I wrenched my pinkie finger through the magic and hit metal—the dial turned all the way up. Tarantula shouted expletives, thumping his fists against the bed as he kicked the wall and the electric light show resumed. Inches away, his neck tendons strained, spider legs twitching across his jaw. He made a retching sound as glorious sparks sizzled brightly in the night.

We suffered together for long, hideous moments.

The Mist gathered. Streaks of blue rose from the floor, gaining shape.

Frigid wind slowly dissipated as he lost control of his magic, and I turned the voltage off. I grabbed at my chest, faint with relief. "*Apologize* for calling me stupid."

He labored with harsh, pained exhales. "No." He coughed. "I shan't tell a lie."

The device rested heavy above my pounding heart as I struggled to calm my spiraling thoughts. You couldn't reason with evil. You couldn't tame a monster.

I can complete my quest.

I will complete my quest.

I won't fail.

A single tear streaked down my face. "You're an awful, wicked bastard," I whispered as I rubbed at my aching, bruised ribs. He wielded his power like a hammer.

"Says the heartless, *torturous* brat," he said with disgust as mutual hatred filled the air, tingling on my tongue.

Tense hours passed in restless hostility as we both refused to break.

When the golden haze of morning light drifted through the window—and Squire shrieked his morning song, *passionate, loud, and off-key*—nothing had changed. Tarantula had stopped pretending to blink hours ago, and my vision blurred from refusing to look away. You had to meet a predator in the eye. *Always.* Even if it felt like you were dying.

A frazzled ball of nerves sparked where my heart used to be as I debated pulling the covers up over my head. I wanted to pretend everything was fine; I wanted to tell the Marshal I was too weak; I wanted to refuse to go through with it; *I want to abandon my duty.*

Curling onto my side, I pulled my knees to my chest, making myself as small as possible, hiding from my cowardice.

Tarantula made a sound in the back of his throat.

Gathering my fear, pretending it was courage, I threw myself out of the bed, grabbed the dial, and ran to the adjoining washroom, slamming the door behind me.

Rule of survival: The only way to surmount danger is to keep moving through it. Don't stop.

Splashing cold water on my face, and then Squire's, I brushed my teeth quickly. It took everything in my power not to stare at the second bag on the sink, the one filled with masculine products. *Why does he get toiletries?* The door creaked, chains clanking. I spun around with a strangled shriek, holding the dial up defensively.

Tarantula held his hands up in a surrender gesture.

Squire screeched on my shoulder.

Tarantula's nostrils flared as he glared down at us. Long seconds stretched. He studied the scars on the side of my face, lingering where the silver one bisected the corner of my lip.

"Thou have toothpaste on your chin," he said coldly, but his ears turned scarlet, betraying his agitation.

I hastily wiped my face, feeling unmoored.

His lips quirked up. "Made thee check."

Dirty trickster. I held up the dial threateningly.

"Careful," he warned. "Someday I *shan't* be collared." His voice dropped an octave as he crowded me deeper into the washroom until my knees knocked against the toilet. "Thou will be defenseless against my wrath."

Long, graceful fingers rose up and flicked the end of my braid mockingly. "Thou art," he whispered, "in *grave* danger." A flush spread across his face, disappearing beneath his mask.

He took another step closer, body heat and magic pouring off him. His eyes flashed with a strange iridescent sheen. *Sunlight dancing across naked snow.* A masculine scent filled my nose, sharp and deadly—dark cherry mixed with . . . *grandiose delusions*?

I struggled not to breathe him in.

His lashes fluttered as he looked down at where I'd pressed my bone dagger to his chest. I always slept with it sheathed across my hip.

"*Careful*," I said, mimicking his deep voice. "I've taken down beasts far more dangerous than you."

He leaned closer, pressing himself into my dagger, and dragged his tongue across his upper teeth. "There is no beast more vicious than me in all Antichthon, because I will do . . . *anything* to get what I want."

I broke out in a cold sweat because he radiated grave seriousness. He wasn't lying.

I pressed the blade harder into the front of his jumpsuit, needing to hurt him, and put some space between us so I could breathe without feeling sick to my stomach. My fingers prickled. Silver gathered around the dagger blade, traveling off his chest and onto my skin.

We both stared down at where the storm magic swirled between us.

"What is the meaning of this?" I asked.

He hunched forward, leaning down to my level so we were

in a bastardization of an embrace. "Fate," he whispered darkly, his hot breath fanning across the sensitive shell of my ear.

I started to pull away, but he grabbed my forearm, his grip a vise, holding my dagger up to his stomach. His flesh was on fire; it was like touching burning coals. Both of us jolted as if electrocuted, and he released me, but I kept my blade pointed at him.

"Zora Ravenal." His accent butchered my name. "I finally comprehend thee."

Shivers trailed up my arm, the magic burning between us.

"And what am I?" I stared down at the glowing weapon, refusing to turn my face up toward his.

His warm lips brushed against my flesh, and I jolted.

"Thou art *feral*."

I threw my shoulder into his with all my might, pushing to give myself some space.

He watched me retreat from the room, eyes alight with enjoyment.

"Art thou afraid?"

"Never."

He hummed. Turning, he didn't bother to close the washroom door and went about his morning ablutions. Giving him my back, I hastily put on a clean training uniform like it was a race, making sure I kept the device in one hand and my dagger in the other.

Seconds later, he lazily emerged, a toothbrush hanging from his mouth, jumpsuit unzipped to show off the hard planes of his chest. The chains hanging from his wrists and ankles looked more like fashion accessories than constraints.

His eyes tracked me with predatory intensity as I backed out of the room. *If I'm feral, then what are you?* There was nothing to do but get away from him, because the Marshal had thrown me into a cage with a monster.

The twins were still asleep, as usual, and the sterile hall had an eerie quiet. Panic clawed at my subconscious as I ran-walked out into the hangar, toward the desert, focusing on my routine.

A routine was good.

Centering.

I needed space to pretend I was strong enough to complete the quest.

In total discombobulation, I jogged out into the sand at a much faster pace than usual. Squire bobbed his head back and forth on my shoulder as if riding a steed. Adrenaline mixed with cortisol, creating a jittery sensation that needed to be expelled before it exploded. I'd always had too much energy for idleness.

Dunes stretched in every direction, a darker orange in the glow of morning, as I ran like my life depended on it. It was deadly quiet, nothing but the whisper of sand passing over the undulating mounds.

The back of my neck prickled like a dire bear was chasing after me. *Impossible.* The predators of the North were miles away. *I miss them.*

Premonitions of terror multiplied.

~~*It's just in your head.*~~

~~*It's just in your head.*~~

~~*It's just in your head.*~~

"How far art thou running, partner?" Tarantula matched my stride. A red balaclava made of breathable material covered his masked face, hiding everything but his unmerciful gaze.

I shrieked, tripping in the sand, wishing it was a dire scorpion and not *him.*

Tarantula reacted quickly, grabbing my shoulder to keep me upright. His hand tightened, disturbingly rough against my skin, covered in hard calluses. He shuddered.

Sparks of hot awareness streaked down my arm while his shadow cast me in complete darkness. His fingers curled, nails digging into my flesh. *Why is it suddenly so hard to breathe?* I felt like I was on fire.

Tipping his head back, he inhaled loudly like he was in physical agony.

"Unhand my arm, creepy bast—"

He shoved me over.

Squire and I toppled into the sand.

Sputtering with outrage, I popped back to my feet, pointing the metal device at him like a sword. Squire flapped his wings with distress, then flew up high, circling a safe distance away.

"What are *you* doing?" I spit sand out of my mouth, gesturing to the endless terrain he could choose to haunt instead of me.

"Running," he deadpanned as he lazily crossed his chained arms over his chest. They'd left enough slack in his ankles that he could run. *What is wrong with the Crimson Army?*

"Find someone else to torment," I called over my shoulder as I sprinted in a different direction, away from him.

"No. I choose thee."

He fell in step beside me, casually matching me stride for stride. His heavy musculature moved across the sand in a way that defied laws of physics and *civility*. He breathed easily as he bounced on his toes, settling into a swift cadence.

I pushed the pace.

He sped up.

Squire soared above, screeching with understandable terror.

I ran with everything I had, gasping from exertion, but Tarantula's shoulders stayed perfectly parallel with mine. I tried to lose him, but he never left my side.

Cruel bastard.

We turned back around, both of us swiveling at the exact same spot, somehow in unspoken agreement about the length of our run. When the ornate brick exterior and sterile white of the hangar came back into view, Tarantula looked down at me.

He smirked tauntingly and broke into a full sprint. I matched him for a few seconds, pushing with everything I had, but his longer stride was impossible to keep up with. He started to pull away.

He can't win.

I lunged forward, and my shoulder slammed into his back. I shoved him over with a grunt but kept my feet. Not expecting the attack, he tripped and rolled down the dune.

"Thou wicked wench!" he shouted as he scrambled to get up while I once again sprinted past him with everything I had.

As I savored the endorphin rush of beating him, the crushing pressure of my task was forgotten.

When I got to the hangar entrance, I did a victory dance. Then exhaustion hit me, and I barely caught myself from falling over. Vision spinning, I staggered and collapsed to my knees, gagging from exertion.

"Am I the desert wench?" Squire asked as he landed on my head.

"Sure." I groaned in agony.

Squire preened his feathers, chest puffing up with pride. "Me *very* sexy."

"No comment."

I couldn't remember the last time I'd ever pushed myself so hard, and the heat made everything a million times worse. Dry-mouthed, I tried to swallow, but my lips cracked because I'd donated all my moisture to the desert.

Hands on my knees, I struggled not to be sick. Silver leather boots wrapped in chained ankle cuffs stepped near my face.

Tarantula stood over me, unmoving and silent as he watched me suffer. I clutched the metal dial in my hand so hard that my fingers cramped.

"Thou art a cheating, unmannered brat," he said quietly, his tone full of rage. "I shall teach thee decorum."

For a second, pure terror seized my throat, but the exhaustion crested, beating it out. With a pained groan, I hauled myself up straight, and Squire just barely kept his balance atop my head. Tarantula took a step toward me, and if his eyes were daggers, I'd have been skewered. I jerked backward, bumping into a soldier, head spinning.

The quest.

"Where's the Marshal?" I turned to the soldier I'd accosted, refusing to spend another second in Tarantula's awful presence. "I need to speak to her. *Now!*"

A few minutes later, I sat at one end of a wooden table with Squire perched on my shoulder in an austere conference room. Tarantula sat at the other end. He'd originally sat in the seat next to mine, but I'd moved until there was enough separation between us to avoid an incident.

The Marshal had walked in while I switched seats for the third time, her expression aggravated. Now she rubbed at her temples like she had a headache.

"He needs more chains," I said as I begged her silently to understand how serious I was.

"Request denied." Her blue eyes were cold, no recognition in them. "Sazha has agreed to train you for a pardon. He's already shackled and collared. You will learn to trust each other, and you *will* master your Knight abilities. This is an opportunity for both of you."

I stared at her in confusion. "Who . . . is Sazha?"

She pointed at Tarantula.

"You *named* him?" I asked.

Tarantula scoffed. "She did not give me anything—"

"He shared his real name as a gesture of good faith." The Marshal's gaze was shrewd, like she was trying to tell me something. "You *need* to put your personal prejudices and past grievances with Sazha behind you. For the good of the Commonwealth." She arched an eyebrow as if challenging me to disagree. *For the quest* was left unspoken.

"Stop calling him that!" I pounded on the table, debating the best angle to flip it and crush him.

"Sazha?"

"It's Tarantula," I spat, losing all semblance of control. "He's not a person. He's a slimy insect."

"*The* spider whore," Squire sang solemnly (helpful). Then added, "Slut" (too much).

The Marshal looked perturbed, but she recovered fast. "Sazha has undergone extensive questioning and has traded us . . . impressive intel. He has sworn an oath not to hurt you." She glared over at him. "He knows the *consequences*."

He stiffened in his chair.

The room was laden with deception.

I pointed at him, strung out from the sleepless night. "His face spells treachery, his mouth spills filth, and his eyes promise retribution. He's going to *kill* me . . . I can smell it." I paused, trying to articulate the unspeakable without jeopardizing the quest. "He needs more restraints—"

"Silence, soldier!" The Marshal banged on the table. With a deep breath, she shuffled her folders. "Sazha is your new partner. Drop it, Knight."

A metallic taste flooded my mouth as I bit down on my tongue.

"Your afternoons have been blocked out to train with him—at his discretion." She stood up. "You will meet with me at high noon tomorrow to continue filling in the . . . *gaps* in your education. Today you have off to acclimate to each other. Once you've obtained some level of mastery, you will both be sent on missions with the twins. We have intercepted intel that an Empire attack is imminent. *Remember* your duty. We need you."

I slumped over. "*Please*—"

The door slammed shut as the Marshal left the room, cutting me off.

We were alone.

Tarantula sat back lazily in his chair, kicking his ostentatious leather boots onto the table. "Thou art so transparent, *vassal*. Your anger makes thee weak . . . manipulable. Thou would benefit from etiquette lessons—"

"Why do you keep calling me that?"

The corner of his lips twitched as he fought a grin. "I call thee that because thou art my vassal—*mine*." He spoke like I was a *thing* to be owned.

"Silence, dirty scamp," Squire sang.

"Language, tiny bird," Tarantula reprimanded him with a posh, judgmental air.

"PICKLED HORSE," Squire squawked back at the top of his lungs, and I was unsure if he meant *whore*, but I was too afraid to ask.

With a deep, cleansing breath, I pushed my chair back, nodding calmly. I lunged across the table and shoved his chair over. Tarantula fell back with a shout of surprise.

Sprawled across the floor, he pushed himself up onto his elbows and glared daggers at me. Unsheathing my hidden bone knife, which, based on the Crimson Army code of conduct, I technically wasn't supposed to carry on my person—*desperate times*—I crouched beside him with the tip aimed at his face.

"No," I said as I rested the blade on his forehead. "You will never have a name to me other than the venomous, disgusting insect that you are. If you try to hurt me, I will do . . . *despicable* things to you."

He shivered like he was turned on. "Thou art a cruel, cold-hearted wench."

It almost sounded like he was giving me . . . a compliment? Squire chirped nervously.

Tarantula slowly smiled and pressed his forehead up into my knife. A tiny bead of blood welled.

"Beware, Zora," he said. "Thou move with cruelty—and there is naught I love more than to play *depraved* games." His gaze dropped to stare at my mouth, and he slowly licked his lips.

"No." I swallowed around the lump in my throat, forcing my voice not to shake. "There is nothing for me to fear because *you* could *never* best me." I pulled my knife away, wiping his blood off on my shorts.

"Thou art overconfident for an uneducated serf."

"And yet," I said slowly, "I'm not the one chained like a captive dire coyote."

He held his hand over his chest. "Your taunts sting—fairest lady," he drawled mockingly.

"There is no lady present."

"Obviously." His expression turned smug. "But I could . . . fashion a lady out of thee."

My blood ran cold. The conversation had taken a dangerous turn, and once again, his eyes were ravenous. His interchanging use of the archaic speech made me dizzy. *Nauseous.* He arched an eyebrow, looking down at where I was crouched low, nearly straddling him.

"How patronizing." I scrambled off him. "I will *never* be any man's lady—and if I commit such an atrocious lapse in judgment . . . it would be with any man but you."

He rose gracefully to his feet, looming above me. "Do not *dare* speak of other men in my presence."

"I'd have sex with every *guy* on this base before I ever touched you." I was startled by my own vitriol. I'd always considered myself a happy-go-lucky person. Blessed to live free. Despite all the hunger and tragedy, I still loved my life.

Tarantula's chest heaved, hands fisted as he glared down his nose at me. "Liar. Never speak to me of your hedonistic—"

"I'm not lying, and I'll speak however I want. I'm just a classless serf according to you, pompous prick—"

"Thou art a wicked liar. Saying thou would not touch me when—"

"It's the truth. I'd rather die."

He stilled, nostrils flaring as he inhaled loudly. "False. I can smell your deception."

He doesn't mean that, right?

"But alas, I was not offering," he said cruelly. "I have no

interest in the sins of any flesh." His lashes lowered, heavy with unidentifiable emotions. "I was raised with decorum."

"You have no interest in pleasure," I said, "because no one has ever had *any* interest in you. Whereas I have plenty of experience being desired." The lie tasted like ash on my tongue. The few times I'd had sex had been unremarkable at best, but he was flushing with rage, so I continued. "Many men have touched my *glorious* flesh—"

"SILENCE!" Magic flashed black around him. "Do not speak to me of your wicked follies . . . 'Tis distasteful how thou ruin yourself."

"Oh, I'm *far* from ruined," I whispered. "But you . . ." I stepped closer to him, and his chest heaved violently as if he'd been struck. "You're just a prude."

Long, elegant fingers slowly reached closer, and my stomach flipped over. He grabbed the door handle behind me and yanked it open, gesturing for me to walk through. "Torturous tramps go first."

"Thanks for noticing," I said sweetly.

As I stalked past, he breathed out noisily. The hand hanging at his side flexed like he had a cramp, and a red flush traveled up his neck beneath his collar.

No man acts like this.

He followed behind me so closely that his body heat burned the sensitive skin on the back of my neck. I tried not to breathe because his rich dark cherry scent was heady in the air.

The bite mark on my throat tingled, and I wished for the millionth time that I'd *never* met him or the Emperor all those years ago.

5

Before: Fate

Zora Ravenal, Fifteen Years Old
Eight Years Ago
Location: Barren Forest, Outside the Northern Commune

Blake kissed me, and it was all teeth and saliva, our frosty breaths mingling in the day's frigid air. Sighing, I squeezed my eyes shut and tried to enjoy it.

Oh nice, he bit me.

It didn't help that he was shaking, terrified to be outside the Commune's high walls, even though we were only a few paces away beneath the old bridge. Icicles hung jaggedly off the beams. The river was partially frozen, chunks of ice floating by.

"Only harlot girls kiss boys before marriage!" a boy's voice called out mockingly from above. The cutting foreign accent lingered in the cold.

It took a second for the insult to process.

"Excuse me?" I yelled back. "What did you just call me?"

I yanked away from Blake, glad for a distraction. *Does he think he's supposed to gnaw on my mouth? Genuinely bizarre.*

"Call me," Squire squawked nervously as he flew over and landed on my shoulder.

"Thou heard me," the stranger said sharply.

No one used *thou* instead of *you* outside of written poetry. *Nice, everyone has lost their mind—or I really shouldn't have thrown that third flip on my snowboard yesterday.*

"Zora, let it go," Blake whispered, and I shoved him away as he tried to hug me.

"Where I come from," the stranger said with a pompous scoff, "thou would be judged dishonorable and classless. A filthy serf. Thou need an education in etiquette."

"Oooh . . ." I sang sarcastically as I climbed up the bank from underneath the bridge. "Please, tell me more about this education process."

Squire ruffled his feathers. "Educate *me*?"

"Thou art steeped in ill repute." The stranger's voice drifted down, icier than the frosted pines.

"Wait, what was that?" I yelled. "Say it again?"

"Trampy woman," Squire squawked straight into my ear (unhelpful) as I jumped up high, grabbing on to the swaying bridge. My fingers throbbed inside my gloves, permanently bruised from opening steel traps all day.

I hoisted us both up over the rail.

A lone figure stood a few feet away. Bone reflected sunlight as I straightened and leveled my dagger at him.

"You're young," I said with a start.

"I'm aged fifteen," he said harshly.

"Exactly. We're the same age, so—"

"Where," he said, cutting me off, "did thou get that *magical* mark?" He pointed at my silver scar, but he looked more intrigued than scared. *Strange reaction.*

"None of your business," I said.

The boy sneered, somehow looking down his nose at me even though we were the same height. "Have thou never learned etiquette?"

"Why do you speak like an ancient crone from the fairy tales?" I countered, genuinely curious if he was trying to be pompous or if it just came naturally to him.

Shadows expanded as his features twisted with malice. "Thou speak of things thou do *not* understand," he spat.

A warning pounded in the base of my skull. A primitive instinct urged me to kill him while another whispered, *Run*. A strange scent clung to him . . . a sensation carried on the wind. I inhaled deeply, identifying the unusual smell: *certain death*. The boy reeked of mass murder.

Freezing wind whipped my braid, but his thick white fur cloak didn't so much as flutter.

His face was hostile in its symmetry; his skin pale as ice, so fine that a watershed of cobalt veins stretched across his sharp jaw and down his neck; his inky black hair curled at the ends, falling just above his bare ears; his aquiline nose was too big for his features; his maroon lips, a shade too aggressive.

Cruel features.

His eyes were the worst: an unsettling iridescent color with an icy blue ring, the shade of a frozen lake in sunlight. They were rimmed in ghastly dark circles, and the purple-black smudges made his features appear sunken. *Maniacal*. The dark swaths of his eyebrows contrasted unnaturally with his skin.

He was all harsh, jagged angles.

His posture was unnaturally straight, and his proportions were off. It was as if he'd just started puberty and his rib cage couldn't keep up with the expanding width of his shoulders.

His collarbone protruded grotesquely from beneath a fitted silk shirt that was completely impractical for the weather. His legs were disproportionately long, and his hands were too wide for his skinny forearms.

As I studied him, he stiffened with badly veiled scorn.

"Where *I* come from," he said slowly, his accent distorting the consonants, "extensive decorum lessons would be needed to save your tattered reputation."

I couldn't hide my huff of disbelief. He must be one of the strange desert folk from the Middlelands, or maybe he was a hedonist from the tropical South. Either way, he didn't belong in *my* forest.

"People *beg* just to speak with me." He continued his villainous monologue. "They fall to their knees, exultant, as they bask in my glorious presence."

"Wow. What a . . . vibrant imagination." I lazily twirled my knife. "You need to try harder to be threatening, sweetie. So far, it's *not* working." I flicked my gaze over him judgmentally. "Skinny and weak."

His features flickered between calm and catastrophic rage. Shivers of premonition crawled down my spine. *There's something wrong with him.*

"Look away, dearest," I whispered to Squire as I placed him on the railing. He obeyed as he always did during a hunt, swiveling his head around to stare pensively off into the distance.

The strange boy scoffed. "That abysmal creature needs to be put down. I shall do it for thee."

"Me pitiful," Squire sang in agreement, still not looking.

How dare he.

"Not if I kill you first." I took a step toward him, dagger high.

A long moment of silence stretched as he processed my threat, and then his pupils dilated, nostrils flaring, the same way a dire fox's did right before it attacked. The strange scent radiating off him intensified, and it smelled like . . . *murderous intentions*?

Rule of survival: Either you're the hunter or you're dead.

There was no third option.

One second we stared at each other. The next he lunged for my neck, but I was quicker and used to handling wild things. Dodging his grip, I grabbed his short inky hair with one hand and yanked his head forward while ramming mine up.

Bone cracked, cartilage popped, blood exploded as our faces slammed together. I stabbed down at the back of his neck, aiming for the space between his spine and skull.

He whirled and shoved me away like he was expecting me to go for the kill. We stumbled apart. Crimson gushed down his chin, and his nose hung at a gruesome angle.

Wetness dripped into my eyes where I'd split my forehead.

He brought long fingers up to his chin and looked down at the freezing blood in shock. "Thou . . . *broke* my nose?"

"I'll break your spine next."

"Beg for my forgiveness," he snarled, his words gravelly due to his smashed nose. "Uneducated peasant—kissing boys like a *trollop*."

"I bet you've never kissed anyone!" I saw red, loathing how he kept talking like I was dirty and beneath him.

He reared back with prudish outrage. "We are aged fifteen. That is *disgusting*."

Apparently kissing offended him, but his eyes said murder was acceptable. *Sociopath*.

A twig snapped, and we both whirled. Blake stood on the icy riverbank with his mouth hanging open, eyes wide with horror as he pointed between our bloody faces. "Zora Ravenal . . . I'm t-telling the elders!" he shouted, panting with the wasting sickness. For some reason, most people in the North tended to suffer from a severe form of asthma, but I was lucky, because it hadn't affected me yet.

The newcomer arched an inky eyebrow, his hard gaze penetrating. "Zora Ravenal?" His accent blended the letters of my last name into something foreign. "Is that your sire's surname?"

"No," I said proudly. "It's my mom's."

His shoulders relaxed as if he was relieved by something, and he sauntered slowly toward me.

The bridge creaked, and I raised my knife. "Take another step closer and I'll slice your trachea."

He rolled his eyes. "Thou do not scare me with your girlish posturing."

Excuse me? I flipped my knife back and forth. *I'll show him girlie.*

A gasp sounded. "You're both insane." Blake sprinted away.

"Me look now, Zora?" Squire sang.

"Not yet," I said. "I'm almost done teaching him a lesson—"

His leg shot out, sweeping mine, and air exploded from my lungs as he threw his full weight down atop me. Sharp teeth pressed against my jugular. I brought my knife to the back of his neck and pressed.

"Release me," I whispered with horror, hyperaware of how his teeth dug deeper into the sensitive skin of my throat. *Mauling me.*

Groaning wantonly, he bit down harder.

I screamed.

Icy water splashed over the edge of the bridge, spraying us in a fine mist.

A wet pop sounded as he withdrew, and his tongue slowly dragged over the throbbing wound. Shuddering, he whispered a strange word against my sensitive flesh. Pain pulsed behind my eyes. Claustrophobic, I shoved him away, kicking and punching, scrambling back as my neck stung.

Using the icy rail, I hauled myself up to my feet, one hand rising to my bleeding throat.

He was still on all fours, his head tipped down, eyes raised up with his hateful gaze locked on me. The white bottoms of his eyes were visible, glowing against his sunken dark circles. *Evil, wretched boy.* Lazily he wiped the back of his hand across his bloody lips, tongue sweeping out.

"Oh . . . Zora Ravenal," he practically purred as the bridge swayed gently beneath us. His heavy fur cloak lay askew, and his teeth were coated in scarlet. "How exuberant . . . What a *fateful* development. Thou art so much more than I could have ever anticipated."

He licked his lips again, face transforming with awe as he deliberately crawled toward me. Black consumed his irises, his pupils blown disturbingly wide.

I dropped my fingers from the ruined front of my throat: flat tooth ridges were covered in frozen saliva. *His* teeth were imprinted on my skin. I shuddered, queasy and deeply unsettled.

His arm shot up, pointing at me.

Silver strands exploded from his fingers. *What in the damned?* Clouds darkened overhead. Magic battered me from seemingly every direction at once, snow gusting everywhere. I could barely see. Unable to fight against the crushing force, I scratched frantically at my throat.

He stood up gracefully.

I fell to my knees.

Clouds spun, water turning to ice as it splashed over the railings.

Leaning forward through the blizzard, he grabbed my chin tightly with one hand, whispering darkly in a different tongue. His other hand stroked across my throat, thumb dragging across the bleeding divots of his teeth. Sharp sensations streaked through my flesh.

He pulled his hand away, hiding it behind his back, and a flush covered his cheeks. "I should not have done that." He shook his head like he was coming out of a stupor.

"I apologize for—" he stared hungrily at my neck wound "—my impropriety."

He can't be serious.

I gasped, still struggling to breathe. The bridge swayed faster as his magic continued to attack me. Splashing sounds echoed. It was everywhere and nowhere all at once.

"Come with me, back to Azote." His voice dropped to a whisper as he leaned so disturbingly close that I could make out each light eyelash tipped in snow. They say the eyes are the window to the soul, and his were dead. Future massacres unfolded within their hateful depths.

Save the world.

From him.

I slammed my fist into his groin, punching up with all my might, and he collapsed to his knees with a groan, cupping himself. The storm stopped, visibility returning. Jumping to my feet in one swift motion, I wrenched his inky hair back. He tried to stand, but I overpowered him.

"I would never go anywhere with the filthy likes of you," I said hoarsely, enjoying the fact that I stood taller than him.

"Thou do *not* mean that."

I yanked his head back harder. "I've never meant anything *more* in my entire life."

"Liar!"

"It's the truth." I could read animals and sense their intentions. He wanted to burn the world to the ground. "You're *despicable*."

The corner of his mouth tilted up in a smirk, confirming my suspicions. His eyes went flat, emotionless, like he'd dropped a mask of civility and was showing me his true irredeemable self. I brought the serrated edge of my dagger to his throat. Icy veins protruded, begging to be cut.

Rule of survival: Kill first. Worry about the consequences later.

I pressed the blade into his flesh, holding him captive. He smiled, neck flung back like he enjoyed being at my mercy. "My first official act," he whispered, voice husky, "will be to ruin your miserable serf life, Ravenal. It shall be my greatest pleasure."

"No. You'll be long dead," I whispered, meaning it, as I yanked on his hair and pressed the blade deeper.

Quiet seized the world, ominous whispers carrying on the wind. The sound of the rushing river intensified, and my fingers tingled, head throbbing. I'd sliced many animal necks before, and this was no different.

Right?

The bridge creaked and groaned as it swayed. "There is no corner of Antichthon," he said with gravitas, "where thou could hide from me. I shall find thee *every* single time. Your fate is already decided."

I inhaled deeper, his wicked scent burning my lungs: *Atomic bombs exploded. Blood fell from the sky like cursed rain. Eerie silence gripped the world, continents laid to waste.*

I'd never smelled anything like it before.

I pressed my knife, drawing blood from his pale throat.

He would die today.

"*No*, Zora!" Mom yanked me away from the boy who smelled like carnage. "What the damned are you doing?" she asked desperately, turning me toward her.

"Why are *you* outside the Commune?" It wasn't safe for her out here. She couldn't defend herself against a dire bear attack. Technically neither could Blake, but I'd made peace with his untimely demise.

"Aurora was worried sick trying to find you, and Blake ran back crying," Mom panted, voice thin with asthma. She must have sprinted from the Commune.

"Why is everyone so concerned?" I asked, genuinely confused as I glared back at the strange, hateful boy who was brushing snow off his knees with a scowl. *I should have killed him.*

"Didn't you hear?" Mom whispered into my ear. "The Marshal is meeting with the Empire today for peace talks in our Commune."

The *Democratic Papers*, the news regularly delivered by homing dire falcons, had recently elevated the Storm Wars threat level to five: *imminent violence.*

I remembered reading something about a summit in the North to try to maintain the fracturing Peace Accords. A desperate final attempt to appease the murderous Empire. Their unpredictable storm attacks had already ravaged parts of Westmere, and without food shipments from the South, hunger was becoming more common.

But the problem was, you couldn't reason with evil.

The Emperor Supreme, Aleksander the Fair, was rumored to be on his deathbed. His heir, the crown prince, was poised to inherit the Draconis Empire.

The prince had yet to reach magical maturity. He hadn't yet gained his full Royal Mage storm magic, but people in the Commune had already started whispering his name with fear. His reputation for violence preceded him.

High Prince Aleksander.

Strange colorless eyes flashed with magic as a fifteen-year-old boy in expensive furs glared at me with perfect, refined posture.

It's him.

The very first Emperor of the Draconis Empire—a powerful Royal Mage, Chriztoph the Raving—was infamous for his madness and unique iridescent eyes, which all of his descendants had; the lineage was known for its cruelty, magical strength, hostility, and excessive love of violence.

They were monsters, even among Azote's secretive elite class of deadly Royal Mages. That was almost all anyone on Westmere knew about the Empire.

Now Prince Aleksander stood before me with the famous imperial eyes, thinking I'd *willingly* go with him, the warmonger who wanted to conquer Westmere and enslave us all. Again. The reason I hadn't eaten in two days.

I lunged for him.

"NO!" Mom shouted, struggling to hold me back. I fought harder, pulling away from her. *I must save the world from him.*

"Please, I can't lose you," Mom whispered behind me. I froze mid-step, my bloody dagger raised at the cruel prince.

He smiled. "Ah, thou art both in . . . *awe* of my glorious presence."

My fingers cramped around the hilt as I desperately fought the urge to disembowel and skin him.

"Don't," Mom begged, grabbing my wrist as I raised my hand back, ready to throw my knife. Her fingers were warm against my chilled flesh.

Aleksander's smirk fell, a frown pulling down his mouth like he was beginning to fathom that I wanted him dead.

"Squire," I said softly. "Come here, darling." Then I leveled a blistering glare at the prince.

Squire chirped happily as he flew over and settled on my shoulder.

"Zora Ravenal." Aleksander tilted his head. "Thou belong to *me*."

"I belong to no man."

Mom's fingers tightened around my wrist. I let her pull me back so I stood beside her.

His nostrils flared. "Who said . . . I was simply a man?"

I rolled my eyes so hard my head hurt. "Go kill yourself in an Iron Maiden."

Aleksander jerked back as if struck.

"Divine Liege, art thou in danger?" a deep accented voice boomed through the Barren Forest. "Did that brat *dare* to attack thee?"

Shadows gathered around Aleksander as his expression iced over. "I am unharmed," he said with clipped authority.

Mom gasped, wrapping her arm around me.

A tall man with short, wavy white-blond hair emerged from the woods, corded muscles shifting beneath black cloth. A thin platinum mask concealed the top of his face. It started at his eyebrows and ended halfway down his nose. He'd taken the creed of the Royal Mages to never remove his mask. A cyan tattoo of a spider stretched across his chiseled jaw. Rows of platinum hoops and delicate chains dripped from both of his ears.

He was all translucent skin, maroon lips, and spider tattoo. Only in his twenties, his reputation preceded him; the infamous monster of the Royal Mages, he was named after the creature inked on his face.

Tarantula.

The world's most fearsome magic-wielding assassin had just called me a brat. He was rumored to have murdered *hundreds* on behalf of the Empire, but no one could prove he was behind the deaths. *Murderer.*

With each step Tarantula took, ice spread across the ground. The sharp scent of magic filled the air as a haze of silver glimmered around him, a tangible aura of death.

Tarantula zeroed in on me. "Thou art *begging* for death," he sneered, and I bristled. The silver haze darkened to onyx around his frame as he studied me. *Dark magic.* Clouds blocked out the sun, and the already freezing temperature plummeted.

It hurt to breathe, and the snowfall rapidly intensified.

"The skanky spider," Squire screeched at the top of his lungs (helpful?).

Aleksander turned to Tarantula with a scowl. "I have this handled. Your assistance is not needed. Stand down."

Tarantula looked between me and Aleksander. "The brat drew your blood . . . She will *die.*" Icy wind gusted through my hair as snow dumped down in thick flurries, painting the world in white. Tendrils of magic rose from his shoulders like smoke.

Aleksander's face darkened. "She is *not* your concern. Obey my order." A frigid wind gusted through the clearing.

Silence.

"Understood," Tarantula snarled, his tone indicating the opposite. He slowly bowed at his waist, turning his tattooed face to the side, exposing the side of his neck like a wild animal submitting within a hierarchy.

"Zora, we *need* to get out of here," Mom whispered, tugging on my arm. "Now. We need to get away from these . . . *men.* Quickly." She spoke like she knew something about them that I didn't.

"*Never* disobey me again!" Aleksander gestured, silver exploding from his hand as he battered the prostrated Tarantula. Abruptly he turned to me. "RUN."

I grabbed Mom's hand and sprinted off the bridge.

"Enjoy the ugly nose," I shouted over my shoulder as we retreated into the snowy trees, unable to help myself. In my peripheral vision, the edge of the river frothed with big silver bubbles. *How peculiar.*

"Zora Ravenal," Aleksander, the future Emperor, shouted with fury, his accented voice carrying over the howling wind. "Someday thou shall kneel before me *begging* for my mercy. It will be glorious when thou realize the extent of what has transpired here today . . . I look forward to that moment."

"False," I shouted back. "You'll be throwing yourself at my feet. You'll bend the knee for *me*, you sniveling coward of a—"

"How dare thou!" Tarantula cut me off as he stood up. "*Never* speak to my divine liege with such blasphemy."

"He's not divine," I singsonged back. "He's just a coward."

"Do not engage with them." Mom slapped my arm, horror in her gaze as she made an expression that said, *What the hell are you doing?*

Both men bellowed with fury.

Aleksander might have believed himself a god and Tarantula his divine assassin, but they were still just mortal flesh and blood. The Barren Forest was *my* home, and they were trespassers. I would never leave the great North; I'd never see them again. *Good riddance.*

"Zora," Mom warned as I pulled her faster through the trees, the Mist swirling in a light blue fog around our feet. "The Empire is evil, but we're not like them . . . You're a good person." Her eyes narrowed as she studied my face. "*Please*, don't forget that."

We passed my favorite spot, the one hidden among the trees. A single ruby rose defied the odds, perpetually blooming like freshly spilled blood across the snow; the petals shimmered with magic.

"I don't want to be good." I whispered the uncomfortable truth. "I want to be *free*."

6

Stage of Grief: Anger

Present Day
Location: Scorpion Hole Military Base

The day passed in a fugue of violence.

Now pale moonlight streamed through the window, casting fang-like shadows across the bedroom. Back aching, I sat stiffly in the wooden chair I'd moved into the corner opposite the washroom.

The dial sat on the chair's arm, pointed at where Tarantula lounged atop his bed. Squire slept peacefully on my lap as I turned the page of my book, but I didn't bother to look down. I nervously spun a fountain pen between my fingers.

Tarantula leaned lazily against his headboard with a book also open in his hands, *staring* at me.

Never had two people reading been more volatile. Each page flipped sent a knife point of dread trailing down my spine, and I prayed to the old god for strength in the face of evil.

"To love and to die," he said, and the deep register of his voice sliced through the tension. "I did not take thee for the blubbering romantic type."

I held the book up higher, turning it sharply like a weapon so he could read the full title.

"Ah," he said. "*To Love and to Die: A Hunter's Guidebook to the Wilderness.*" He cocked his head to the side as if puzzling through a problem. "What is it about?"

"I don't know," I deadpanned. "I can't read."

He smiled, and it was not a pleasant expression. He held up his book to show me the title, *The Creed of Kings and Democracies.* A history book about Westmere politics, very male-centric and a complete snooze-fest. Stolen from my pile. I read it to fall asleep.

He would enjoy that.

I rolled my eyes and focused on mine.

The page documented a fifteen-step process on how to slaughter, skin, and roast a boar. In the cramped margins, I'd annotated my favorite poems, each carefully selected for how they fit the moral dilemma presented at each stage of harvesting.

Contemplating the ethics of hunting brought me peace. You couldn't just kill an animal and walk away. You had to sit with it, bow to the forest, and thank the universe for your blessings.

I mindlessly scribbled between the lines: *Complete the quest. Complete the quest. Complete the quest.*

"Thou know . . ." Tarantula said slowly, with the tonal confidence of someone about to be extremely rude. "The Midlanders on this base think thou art uncivilized. It does not help, your consumption of such debased literature." He made a humorless sound. "I could give thee some recommendations, to help . . . *educate.*"

I counted to ten because the bastard wouldn't stop offering to teach me things. *If one more person calls me stupid.*

He slowly closed his book but kept his long middle finger pressed between the pages to hold his place. His hand completely dwarfed the cover. He cradled the book suggestively, his finger placement lewd. Images flashed through my mind of that same finger— *Nope, not going there.*

"Stop talking to me." A hot flush burned my face.

He slowly slipped his middle finger from between the pages, laying his book on his pillow. "I am going to the washroom."

"Don't care. I told you not to talk."

He gestured to the dial. "Just a forewarning. I know how much thou enjoy your power trips."

The mattress squeaked loudly as he stood, storm magic swirling around him like glitter. His shadow plunged a large swath of the room into darkness, myself included. I raised the dial high, and he eyeballed it as he sauntered across the space, stopping in front of my chair.

Ever so slowly, he leaned down so we were eye to eye, and the dial pressed against the *DANGER* written on his chest. His right hand spread across both pages of my open book.

"When I get out of this wretched collar—" his voice roughened, practically inarticulate as he hovered close enough to slaughter "—I am going to acquaint thee with a form of torment so personal—"

Zap.

He jolted with electricity and gritted his teeth, falling onto one knee. Eyes locked on mine, *not blinking*, he held on to the arms of my chair and leaned forward, caging me in. Voltage prickled over the wood, shocking me lightly.

The Mist rolled across the floor in a haze, gathering into tendrils. It rose toward the collar and dial.

I turned the knob down.

Tarantula pushed himself up, unfurling to his full height, muscles tense. With one last hateful glare, he stomped loudly into the washroom and slammed the door shut behind him. Immediately he opened it back wide like he'd remembered his only purpose in life was to torment me. The sound of his loud peeing filled the room.

"Very elegant," I called out, trying to hide my unease. "What a stand-up gentleman. You *clearly* have a lot to teach me."

The door slammed shut.

Water ran.

Seconds bled into minutes.

He was washing his hands for far too long. *Is he fashioning his toothbrush into a shiv?* Crap, I needed to sharpen mine. Time kept passing, and he remained inside the bathroom.

"Did *thou* fall into the toilet?" I asked, mimicking his accent as I tried to sound nonchalant.

Squire opened a bleary yellow eye on my lap. "No, me here," he chirped sleepily.

"Not you, darling."

He curled back into a ball and fell asleep.

"Did your sire ever teach *you* the concept of manners?" Tarantula yelled back mockingly, overenunciating the modern word. It sounded strange on his lips.

"No." I flipped the page. "I never met the man."

The door banged open, and Tarantula stalked out of the washroom. Sniffing dramatically, he smoothed and tucked in his sheets like the bed wasn't up to his high standards. Seating himself down elegantly, he lazed back against his headboard. My face prickled under his sharp scrutiny.

I will complete my quest. My pen ripped through the page as I steeled myself for his filth.

"'Tis probably for the best, for your sire's sake," he said slowly. "A headstrong daughter . . . not a womanly trait in sight. Controlling thee would cause any man consternation."

I snapped the book closed.

"Oh yes," I said quietly. "I'm sure the man who was taken hostage by the Empire, separated from his pregnant wife, and most likely mercilessly slaughtered would be *embarrassed* to have a competent daughter who could provide for his grieving widow."

Tarantula's jaw clenched. I stood, leaning over his bed with the dial leveled at his tattooed face. I didn't remember moving across the room.

He shook his head. "The Empire does not take hostages."

"Tell that to the man who was removed from his home in the middle of the night, never to return again."

His eyes sharpened. "Or . . . your sire just wanted to escape from your pregnant harpy of a mothe—"

He convulsed in a show of sparks as I turned up the dial.

Grabbing his curls, I wrenched his head back. He let out a guttural groan as he twitched, eyes twinkling with an emotion that looked suspiciously like enjoyment. *It can't be.* Electricity pricked my fingers, but I barely felt it through the burning rage.

He licked his lips, and the saliva sizzled.

"Say another word about my mom." I yanked hard at his hair, pulling him closer. He shuddered as I whispered, "And you will learn just how *feral* I can be."

Canines flashed as he smiled sadistically.

I slapped his face, sparks flying between us.

"Do that again," he ordered, voice gravelly as he convulsed, still grinning.

The collar sputtered.

Mist thickened around it in a thick blue cloud.

Turning down the dial, I dropped his silky hair, but I couldn't make myself back away. I stood over his bed, shaking. *"Zora, we are not like the Empire. We are good,"* Mom whispered in my head. His face blurred. I squeezed my eyes shut, refusing to let tears fall.

Two days stuck with him and I'd already become what they all called me—uncivilized.

When I opened my eyes, he stared up at me with an unreadable expression. "Thou art very loyal," he said quietly. "'Tis . . . becoming."

"My loyalties are none of your concern."

He folded his hands behind his head casually like he wasn't in chains, muscles still twitching with aftershocks. "I beg to differ."

"Say what you want. It doesn't change anything," I muttered.

He cleared his throat. "I can be very thorough."

"What?"

"It can be *immensely* pleasurable."

"Excuse me? What are you—"

"Do thou want me on my knees? Or on my back?"

"Stop speaking—"

"There are many ways . . . are there not?"

"*What* the damned are you talking about right now?"

"Begging."

I tried to find words, but there were none. Our gazes locked. *Oh nice, it feels like I'm on fire.* Time stretched peculiarly around us. My legs cramped from standing, but I refused to sit down as he kept his head tipped back, eyes hooded. *Raw, torturous domesticity.*

Hours passed, but neither of us moved.

I will not lose.

Never to him.

When dawn finally came, we exploded into action at the same time, jostling shoulders as we each tried to get to the washroom first. We brushed our teeth with violence, trading blistering glares.

I washed my face, and water sprayed out of the sink—splashing both of us. *Oh no.* I yanked on the faucet, pretending it was broken, then hid my glowing fingers behind my back. Pain thudded deep in my skull.

Accidental storm magic?

Is there even such a thing?

"Incompetent commoner." Tarantula rolled his eyes, looking exhausted as he toweled off, seemingly none the wiser to my slip-up.

"Pompous royal bastard. Get over yourself," I hissed, nerves strung out from the sleepless night.

He threw the towel onto the floor and stepped close. His rough thumb scraped heat across my cheek as he wiped off a droplet of water. We both froze in shock. His hand burned against my skin.

Danger imminent.

A flush slowly traveled above his collar, up the top of his neck, and settled across his cheeks, disappearing under his mask. His breath quickened.

He whispered quietly, "How did thou get this silver scar?" His nostrils flared as he leaned dangerously close. "It reeks of . . . *magic*."

"None of your business." I reared back, away from his wicked touch. "You smell yourself." I looked pointedly at the metallic flames steaming off his shoulders.

Raking a hand through his messy curls, he shook his head as if coming out of a daze. "That was . . . improper." His voice cracked. *Is his hand trembling?* "I apologize for my loutish behavior—"

"Not accepted." I pushed past him toward the bedroom—

He yanked me backward. He had my braid twisted around his fist and my head pulled back at a harsh angle as his face hovered inches from mine. Once again, he'd moved impossibly fast.

"What . . . are you doing?"

"Nothing," he said hoarsely, fixated on my mouth. His eyes were clouded over, unfocused, and the tips of his ears were bright pink.

"Release me," I demanded, struggling to concentrate with his scent polluting my nose: *dark cherry and magic.* It was masculine, rich, and drenched with tyrannical intentions.

Tarantula bit down on his overly full lower lip, shaking his head as he slowly untwined my braid from his wrist. Chest heaving, he dropped my hair and jerked back, shoulder slamming into the wall.

"Don't touch me *ever* again," I whispered, goose bumps on my arms as I backed away, dial raised. "Please."

"Then do not tempt me with your fire," he muttered under his breath.

"What did you just say?"

"Nothing, *Ravenal.* Nothing at all." He spat out my last name like it meant something to him.

A few minutes later, I hurried through the hangar with Squire on my shoulder. Dire horses neighed as I passed. A familiar face flashed in my peripheral vision.

I stopped in my tracks.

Whirling, I pointed at a soldier. "What is that?"

He handed over the newspaper with a low bow. The *Democratic Papers* had a bold headline: "The Birth of a New Hope: The Bear of the North Captures Royal Mage."

A masterful portrait filled the page below it.

On one knee, a woman held up a Royal Mage by his blond curls. A bone dagger protruded from his stomach. She had a long brown braid, and scars stood out stark across her bronze face. A pygmy owl sat on her shoulder.

Had there really been that much blood on the floor? I could still remember the day like it was yesterday—the day I captured Tarantula.

The Marshal had made it official. Every soldier in the hangar was reading it. Now everyone in Westmere knew our sordid history.

Frozen with shock, I barely registered when the bastard in question snatched the paper from my hands, prisoner chains clinking.

I stared blankly across the hangar.

Tarantula loomed above me in a white balaclava. "Thou—" He inhaled noisily, a cloud of silver expelling from his mouth. "*You,*" he corrected himself with quiet menace, "had a portrait session done with my unconscious body?"

"Unconscious ugly whore body," Squire hooted (helpful).

A magical wind gusted across my face, burning my eyes. Soldiers in scarlet backed away, looking between us like we were wild things.

"I wish I had just killed you," I said honestly. *For Aurora.*

"How *dare* thou, Ravenal." Tarantula stepped closer, cuffed hands rising.

"No—how dare *you*."

Squire bobbed his head. "How dare we?"

Tarantula grabbed my braid and yanked me to the floor, hard. Squire flapped away as I punched out, grappling. A glass jug of water on a bench nearby exploded into pieces, and he flipped to shield me as the shards scattered across the floor. *Crap, my magic.*

Kicking, I scrambled out of his hold, hiding my hands. I sprinted out of the hangar and into the desert. The dial was cold against my chest, tucked into the tight material of my exercise bra.

Squire cawed, soaring above.

Running across the dunes, I kicked sand, shrieking with frustration at the top of my lungs. The Middlelands sucked, and my quest was impossible. All my luck had run out. Sweat dripped down my neck as I half ran, half fell forward up the stupid sand, wishing it was a snow-covered mountain. I needed my snowboard and hours alone in the forest.

No, you're still lucky. You can handle him—

WHAM. Tarantula slammed into me from behind, throwing me down the dune. We rolled, his rough hands wrapping around my throat. He didn't squeeze, just . . . *held*?

I kneed him in the balls. He grunted and swore. I pounded my fists against his kidneys as we kept tumbling. He grabbed my wrists with a bruising grip. I slammed my face forward. He barely dodged the blow. We finally came to a halt.

I bucked.

He held my hands as if in a vise above my head; his fingers shook with rage.

He was splayed atop me. Our chests, hips, and legs were flush together. *Where does he start and I end?* Angry heat poured off him, more scorching than the sun. A pounding thud reverberated between us, and it took a second to locate the source: our hearts raced wildly in tandem.

His face hovered above mine, eyes narrowing. "Sadistic wench," he spat out, studying me like he was planning my execution, as he held me pinned to the hot sand.

"Spider," I said back coldly, hyperaware of the hardness growing between his legs, pressing against my core.

Damn him.

Scoffing harshly, he pressed my wrists down harder and ever so tantalizingly rolled his hips. *Languid torture.* We both made breathy, guttural sounds. Shivers traveled down to my toes.

White-hot pleasure streaked where our legs touched, radiating out across my flesh. His cloth-covered lips hovered above mine, minty breath *tingling* across my skin. His pupils blew out.

"What are you . . . doing?"

"What art thou?" he said roughly. Layers of sinew and taut, violent strength pinned me. It felt like he was trying to crawl under my skin. *I should be hurting him.* My back arched high. I desperately needed more friction.

"What is the meaning of this?" My head tipped back.

"Thou art ruinous." His chest heaved against mine. "Thou art temptation of the highest order. No woman has *ever* tested a man like this. Your violent temperament . . ." He turned his head to the side and buried it against my neck, inhaling loudly. "'Tis *perverse.*" With a tormented rasp, he pressed firmly against my heat, grinding against it through the fabric. "I detest thee."

My core spasmed, and I nodded in agreement. *The hatred is mutual.* He swore gutturally under his breath.

A whimper nearly escaped my throat. I choked on it, struggling to swallow around the putrid self-loathing.

Your quest.

I was lying beneath the enemy.

Kill him.

"Curse upon your house." I bucked my hips, bridging with all my strength, twisting to push him off. "Get off me."

"Too late for curses." He rolled away, landing on his back, spread across the sand. He pressed a glowing hand to his heaving chest, then stiffened abruptly and sat up, his eyes like thorns. "Such a *violent* woman."

I scrambled away from him, jumping hastily to my feet.

Posture perfect, he stood up gracefully like he'd taken decorum lessons on how to extract oneself elegantly from a brawl. He pulled his shoulders back, and the haze of silver around him flickered black. Dark clouds gathered overhead, blocking the sun. *Where did they come from?*

"Partner." He adjusted the balaclava over his face like a crown. "Since thou already got a portrait glorifying your success, thou art going to show me your impressive Knight powers . . . Your training starts—NOW."

Silver exploded, wind battering me from all directions. He *oozed* unrepentant predation.

I spun aimlessly in a circle, waiting for him to choke me, but it didn't come. Instead, a gust slammed into my stomach. Another rammed into my back. Then my legs. Grit abraded my skin, blood beading from fresh wounds.

He bludgeoned me with magic, and for the first time, it felt . . . personal. *Cruel.* He wielded storm magic like an ax, cutting me down.

I yanked the dial from my bra.

"Coward!" he taunted. "Use your powers—*Knight Mage.*"

Putting the dial away, I raised my arms into a Shield, steeling myself for his abuse. *Pretend you're like the twins.* My hands glowed as I tried not to flinch. His eyes narrowed, glaring at me across the swirling, silvery wind.

Raising his arm high, he sent another wave of magic straight for my face.

I held my Shield up.

Bang. It threw me back into the sand.

Groaning, I got up to my feet, only for him to send another gust that tossed me into the air.

I slammed down roughly, choking on sand.

He bellowed, stalking toward me, his pale eyes shining as metallic flames smoked off his skull. "Do something!" The wind gusted harder, pummeling me from every direction, and I gritted my teeth, taking the battering.

I leaned forward, refusing to drop my Shield, trapped in a tornado.

The gusts intensified, and my feet lifted off the ground.

I fell to my knees, hacking, sand gritty in my lungs. *Finally* the wind stopped, and I gasped roughly, still suffocating. Tiny dust devils extinguished all around.

Chains rattled. Bright desert light burned my eyes as silver boots stepped close.

"Thou art *pathetic*, Ravenal." Tarantula crouched down next to me, blocking the sun. "A disappointment of unimaginable degrees. And to think, thou could have been great. Instead, thou art . . . *this*." He was a cruel, vengeful god. *But he's not* my *god.*

I spit onto his expensive boot.

He arched an eyebrow. "Do that again . . . I dare thee."

I obeyed.

His eyes hardened. "Lick it off."

"I still remember—" I coughed violently, ignoring his depraved request "—that day on the bridge." I pounded on my sternum, struggling for air. "You were . . . a sniveling wretch of a man."

He straightened to his full height, staring down at me. The harsh planes of his face were completely expressionless. *Inhuman.* He was a block of cobalt-veined marble masquerading as a man.

"So don't you dare call me pathetic," I whispered hoarsely

as I got to my feet. Wiping sweat and sand off my face, I stumbled away from him.

"Thou know *nothing*, Zora Ravenal."

"I know you're chained and leashed like a pathetic dog."

Tarantula stilled. "Art thou asking me to bite? Is that why thou keep spitting on me?" He grabbed my arm, wiping his thumb across a bloody abrasion.

"Oh, get *over* yourself!" I shoved him away, then traced the tooth marks scarred across my throat.

He reached for me again, hand flaming with magic. I flinched backward before I could stop myself, preparing for another violent attack. He swore and looked murderous. Turning abruptly, he stalked away.

I stomped in the other direction. Staggering through the desert, I wiped tears of frustration off my face. *I miss you, Mom.* Time stretched as I fantasized about mastering my power and punishing Tarantula.

Wincing through a haze of white, I covered my eyes as a reflected light blinded me. Strange bluish-black panels covered a corner of the hangar's roof, mostly hidden from view by a row of immense gargoyles.

Stumbling, I tripped on something hard. I was standing on a rounded piece of metal. It jutted out from the base's foundation. The wind howled, and sand gusted, covering it. A dire horse neighed loudly off in the distance.

Deeply unsettled, I sprinted the last stretch back into the hangar, feeling like I'd been caught doing something that I shouldn't. I didn't stop until the cooler interior fully surrounded me.

I barely registered the waiting Shadow Swords, who immediately escorted me down under the base for my afternoon training with the Marshal. After an hour of watching me fail to move a cup of water, she threw it at me. Glass shattered across the floor.

"Do *something*," she ordered. "Concentrate."

Gritting my teeth through the throbbing headache, I *focused* all my effort on the water. I *needed* to be more powerful than Tarantula. A single droplet rose up from the floor. Streaked with silver, it hovered in the air between us.

I whooped with excitement.

It splashed down.

"Are you kidding me?" The Marshal's glare was withering. "A single drop and you're smiling like a loon. This is *war.* I haven't been able to visit my wife in *over* a year—"

"Just bring her here," I pointed out, too tired to mince words.

"No civilians are allowed on this base. It's the law."

"Make an exception—"

She threw another glass of water at me. "We're under a level five threat. *Train* like it."

I barely ducked in time.

We continued for hours, but the results were the same. No matter how many times she threatened or taunted me, the magic hovered just out of my reach. I was so exhausted I could barely keep my eyes open.

When the session was *finally* over, I went and cried in the shower, fully clothed.

Ella rubbed my back at dinner while I napped at the table, and Axel prattled on about his day. Tarantula took his meal in the bedroom.

Afterward, Tarantula led me out into the desert and *once again* pummeled me with his awful wind. Shaking with exhaustion, I made a Shield and pretended to be disappointed when nothing happened.

After another few hours of misery, he stomped away with disappointment.

Feeling like a wraith, I headed back through the quiet military base. Night's shadows stretched around the empty hangar. A door I hadn't noticed before sat innocuously behind the missiles.

I couldn't face the tension in our bedroom, so I didn't fight the inexplicable instinct that urged me toward the door. *Anywhere is better than with him.* I tried the handle, but it was locked.

Pulling out my newly sharpened toothbrush shiv, I jiggled it in the handle lock with my ear hovering near the mechanism. *Click.* It popped open. A long, empty hall greeted me. Rows of formal portraits hung on the white walls, illuminated by low lamplight.

I crept forward.

The First Illustrious Marshal, a gold plaque declared next to a portrait. The elderly male in the painting wore outdated clothes. He had severe features and bright blue eyes. The next portrait said, *The Second Illustrious Marshal.* A woman stared down at me with wide, strong features and lighter blue eyes.

I continued down the row. Each Marshal, man or woman, shared eerie similarities.

When I got through the long line to the final portrait and stared into the familiar eyes of Kalen Reeves, the truth hit me. I staggered back, gripping the white wall behind me like it could somehow save me.

They had the same unique blue eye color.

They had the same nose.

The same severe facial structure.

Each one of our elected Marshals was related to the others, something the *Democratic Papers* had never shared. Did any of the rest of the candidates ever have a chance? I opened my mouth to scream, to do something. *Does it matter?* My teeth gnashed together, lungs deflating.

Mom was still in danger.

The North was still starving.

Focus on your quest.

The hall opened into an expansive circular rotunda with oil lamps flickering along the walls. Life-sized bronze sculptures of people were displayed around the perimeter. The Mist rose in slow tendrils from the floor, a faint blue glimmer, barely visible. A dramatic mural of aquamarine skies and clouds filled the ceiling.

On the white tile floor, seven horizontal rows were decorated with black letters, and three were painted a bright blue, standing out from the rest. I crouched down, faintly recognizing the rows as something Mom had tried to teach me one night when I was too tired to pay attention. *Some sort of table?* The three blue tiles had the letters *C, N, O*.

What does it mean?

This was something Kane, Steelden's idiotic valedictorian, would recognize instantly and scoff at me for not understanding. I felt stupid. Bitterness expanded inside my rib cage.

Nerves on edge, I tiptoed up to the nearest sculpture of . . . the Marshal? All of her ancestors were spread around her, immortalized in bronze. *What in the old god is going on here?* In the base of each sculpture gleamed the alchemy symbol for blood. *A secret society?*

Heart in my throat, I spun in a circle as I remembered a line from one of my favorite poetry books—*they want respect, but you must suspect those with power.*

Metal doors sat recessed between the sculptures. I tried a gold handle. *Locked.* Moving to the next door, I tried it. *Locked.* The back of my neck prickled as I moved around this strange room, trying handles unsuccessfully. Buzzing panic clouded my head, mounting with each second.

Wait. I paused and listened.

A very real buzzing sound tingled faintly through the quiet room.

In the center of the rotunda, the noise was softer. I moved to the periphery, where it was louder. I pressed my ear to a locked door, the noise strongest behind the steel. *Something is on the other side.* Strange wires, which looked like copper and zinc, ran from the ceiling, down the wall, and dipped underneath the door.

A lock clicked.

One of the doors to the rotunda slowly creaked, opened from within by someone. Heart pounding out of my chest, I turned and ran as fast as possible back through the hangar, toward my room. In the doorway, I slammed into Tarantula. He stood in the middle of the space, blocking my path, oozing viciousness.

The hair on my arms stood on end.

"What . . . art thou doing, Ravenal?" he asked with a hiss of breath.

I feigned disinterest. "I was just getting some water."

He tilted his head down, staring at where my finger touched the *D* of the *DANGER* written across his jumpsuit. Warmth prickled my hand as silvery storm magic tendrilled off him and onto me. *Again?*

I yanked my burning finger away.

His jaw clenched. "Do *not* touch me."

"Gladly." I shoved my shoulder into him and stomped past, flinging myself at my bed.

"Rude."

"Better to be rude than a monster."

"Better a monster," he said roughly, "than just a man."

What? Fear seized my heart, and I opened my mouth to demand he explain, but no sound came out. Tarantula obliterated my ability to think.

No one was going to save me from him; I had to save myself.

Tarantula stalked over to his bed, silver-scaled boots reflecting moonlight. I'd faced down the beast that donated them: six years ago.

That night, I fell asleep instantly, but my dreams were filled with memories.

7

F(IRE) AND ICE

ZORA RAVENAL, SEVENTEEN YEARS OLD
SIX YEARS AGO

Teetering at the very top of the peak, I balanced on my snowboard, the Commune far below. Northern lights glowed overhead while the Mist gathered in blue tendrils around tree trunks. The night sky reflected off the white of the Barren Mountain Range, creating the illusion of an endless cosmos.

I inhaled deeply.

The crisp air smelled like *freedom*.

I leaned forward, plummeting straight down the mountainside, faster than the icy wind. Weaving between fir trees, I jumped. My stomach rose, then dropped.

BAM.

Snow exploded across my goggles, momentarily blinding me. Tiny notches covered both sides, a mark for every kill I'd made; I'd run out of space years ago. The dire fox carcass was heavy across my shoulders. I didn't *need* to carry the carcass all the way up the mountain while lugging my snowboard, but hunting made me jittery with existential dread, and today the crushing emotions were worse than usual. I couldn't stop thinking about the fear in the fox's eyes as I'd killed it.

Snowboarding helped me forget.

I ate adrenaline for dinner.

Rule of survival: Enjoy the rush.

Crouching low, thighs burning, I spread my arms wide as I flew down the mountain like a four-winged dire eagle. Squire raced above. A pack of dire wolves howled off in the distance. Hurtling off another icy ledge, I gripped the board and spun, smiling as my stomach went weightless.

Arms flapping, I pretended I was omniscient and *powerful*, like the old god, before he died, flying high on his wings of platinum. Squire hooted as he soared beside my face.

I stuck the landing.

Throwing myself off the last big jump, I tossed my legs overhead and flipped backward. Reaching out, I just barely grabbed the rising dire fox carcass before I slammed back down, but the added weight made me wobble.

Wham.

Clipping the edge of my board on ice, I tumbled violently, smashing through piles of snow. White everywhere. Rolling down the last bit of the mountain, I *finally* came to a stop.

A fox head rested on my snow-covered chest, staring up at me judgmentally as my muscles throbbed in tandem with my heartbeat. A faint silver steamed off its shimmering fur.

Old texts spoke of animals completely untouched by magic, and therefore they didn't have the dire beast classification. I'd never met such a creature. *Probably a myth.*

I held the fox's lifeless gaze and whispered an apology.

I'd be black and blue tomorrow.

A penance.

I pushed the piles of snow off my long-sleeved wool shirt.

The summer solstice was approaching, and the temperatures were hovering around freezing, the warmest they'd get all year. It was practically balmy. *Perfect snowboarding conditions.*

Squire dropped from the sky. "Me win," he cawed as he landed on my forehead.

"It was a tie," I said as I sat up, and he squawked with indignation.

Unclipping the leather buckles from the special hooks Mom had sewn onto my boots, I released myself from the snowboard and shook my head, sparkles of snow drifting all around. Centuries ago, snowboarding used to be popular in the North, but these days, not many people ventured outside the protective walls of our Commune.

I'd tried to explain to Mom the rush was worth hiking up steep terrain for hours. It was the only time my head was clear, thoughts calm. Sure, a hypothetical dire bear could maul you. You could hit a tree, spin out, fall into a ravine, or break your neck landing a jump. But that was the point—you were having fun.

Longingly I looked at the mountain as Squire flapped beside me.

Should I climb back up?

I stood, and a hunger cramp nearly sent me to my knees. There was a very real chance I'd pass out if I tried, and I had to get this dire fox home. *I'll come back another night.*

The Commune was depending on me, since the greenhouse harvest wasn't as bountiful this year. Responsibility was a constant crushing weight on my— *Don't think about it.*

I readjusted my board and stalked through the forest, forcing my racing heart to slow as I sank back into my role as a hunter.

Vision sharpening, ears listening, I focused on the calm. I'd eat when the job was done. Hunting was both a strange game and a form of dissociation.

Mind over matter. Limits were meant to be tested and surpassed. The weight of duty didn't diminish because you suffered personally. If anything, it just grew heavier. I'd learned to live with the constant pressure. Gareth had taught me how to *survive.*

Squire tucked his wings and rolled forward through the air, pretending to throw a flip on a snowboard.

Laughing at his antics, I chased after him.

ROAR. We both froze, turning to stare at each other as the bestial sound echoed among the swirling Mist and magic. In its wake, the quiet seemed to intensify. *No woodland creature makes that noise.*

A warning horn bellowed from the Commune walls—three times. In slow motion, I looked up. Squire landed on my shoulder. Beyond the dark green treetops, fire flared in the sky as a beast breathed flames. Screams were carried on the frigid wind.

The Commune is under attack.

Mom and Aurora.

I dropped my board in the snow. I'd come back for it later. The dire fox carcass joined it, and I sprinted through the trees with everything I had. Squire jostled on my shoulder, forgetting he could fly.

ROAR. Another ghastly sound reverberated, this one more high-pitched, as a second beast sprayed ice from its mouth.

Unlike the fictional monsters in fairy tales, these were flying in the night—and *very* real. They must have made the treacherous journey from Azote across the unpassable Moor Ocean.

Dragons.

One silver-scaled and ice-breathing, the other golden-scaled and fire-breathing. Battle saddles were strapped across their mammoth backs, a figure riding astride each one—Royal Mages from the Draconis Empire.

Heart in my throat, I pumped my legs faster, leaping over icy rocks. Spindly lower branches slapped across my face, and I batted them aside. High above, the silver-scaled dragon swooped down, a cloud of ice covering the city in blizzard conditions. Tarantula rode astride his infamous silver dragon: *Pestilence.*

The gray brick Commune walls neared as I ran past the single rose blooming lonely in the forest.

ROAR.

Golden scales flashed as the second dragon swooped low: *Plague.* Her stomach turned coal red as she opened her jaw and bright red fire exploded with impossible heat. She was one of the deadliest monsters in Antichthon.

A tall, lean figure rode astride her, wearing a golden Royal Mage mask that covered his entire face. A heavy white fur cloak fluttered in the air behind his crowned head.

It was *him*, again.

The High Prince was now the freshly crowned Emperor of the Draconis Empire. He rode beside Tarantula on the backs of their royal dragons. The new Emperor had already earned a name for himself, and people whispered it with fear.

Aleksander the Sadistic.

His bite mark marred my throat.

Heat exploded above my head. I dropped face down onto the snow, screaming into it. Trees were on fire above. I crawled through the ice toward the wall, hair sizzling around my face as the ground vibrated with dragon roars.

This can't be happening.

I stood up in horror, slamming my foot down onto the latch and stumbling through the Commune's gate. Waist-high snow covered the city, which was constructed with six main streets radiating outward from the central square like spokes on a wheel; five concentric rings of roads spread out from the middle, connecting it all.

Magic-laced snow glittered along the tree-lined streets. The bottoms of the pines were buried in ice, but the tops burned with dragon fire, and flaming pine needles fell like rain over empty roads. The warning horn had done its job.

I fought my way forward desperately, losing energy with each impossible step as I made my way through the magical blizzard. The Empire had no reason to target the barren North.

The moon glowed eerily in the smoky haze, reflecting off the few tiled roofs that weren't buried in snow.

They've come back for you. It's because of what happened two years ago. The Emperor was drawing battle lines with magical dragons' breath.

BOOM.

BOOM.

Two fighter jets from the south flew overhead, engines roaring as they broke the sound barrier. Modern relics in a medieval world.

The Mist chased after the jets in blue streaks, approaching the machinery that was famous for reaching speeds of up to four thousand miles per hour.

The mayor must have used the broadband radio to notify the Marshal that we were under attack. The Scorpion Hole was strategically located halfway between the Northern Commune and the Southern Communes, just close enough that jets could respond before they were overtaken by the Mist.

Parachutes deployed as four figures ejected from the planes directly above the Commune, floating through the air. Two of them wore stiff black uniforms and directed their chutes outside the city walls, away from the conflict. *The pilots.*

The other two headed toward the center of the city, their famous silver armor shining as they descended.

Knight Mages.

They were the only two people in the past century to survive the deadly Iron Ritual—the twins, Ella and Axel.

The Storm Wars had arrived in the North.

Luminous blue tendrils of the Mist rose up from the ground. A high-pitched sound echoed as the Mist shut down the first plane. It turned into a nosedive, arcing just past the Commune walls.

Kaboom.

The ground shook as it exploded on impact. A mushroom cloud of blue-and-white lightning ballooned high into the air as it reacted with the Mist, and then a red fireball snuffed out the electric show.

The second jet fell in an arc, heading toward Pestilence with impossible speed.

The dragon banked violently and just barely missed being hit. Caught in the wind, he spun through the air as the plane exploded against the forest floor, the Mist sparking in a cloud of blue electricity.

"ZORA!" Squire screeched on my shoulder as a flaming pine tree cracked in half, falling toward us. I dove out of the way just in time. "Me fire god!" Squire chirped, and I dumped snow onto his smoldering feathers. The flames went out with a sizzle.

Plague roared above.

Get to Mom and Aurora. I resumed fighting through the snow, leaping over the melting snowbanks with everything I had. Finally I made it to a main street, one of the six that led straight to the center square.

The famous Knight Mage twins, Ella and Axel, stood in the middle of the street with their arms raised into Shields—nullifying the magical blaze—as Plague hovered above them, breathing fire.

Axel fell to his knees under the magical onslaught, taking the brunt of it, but Ella stood tall, her long auburn hair blowing in the wind. A golden mask flashed as the Emperor turned his head abruptly and leaned low on Plague's back, staring straight at me.

Rule of survival: Know when to run for your life.

I turned to flee.

A flaming tree had fallen across the road, completely blocking my path. All the other paths were covered in snow piles taller than my head. The only way to move was forward, where Plague approached.

"Me scared," Squire hooted.

"Look away, dear," I whispered. He swiveled his head around as Plague maneuvered closer, her black talons wrapping around the jagged roof spires. Thin roof tiles cracked, bricks crumbling under her weight.

Old god bless my way.

I sprinted forward.

The twins screamed something, gesturing to me as they navigated between falling branches.

"ZORA!" Aleksander bellowed with the same pompous accent from my nightmares. He tugged on the reins, and Plague roared flames in my direction. I desperately flung myself out of the way, barely missing being scorched.

Crack.

I slammed into the brick side of a townhome headfirst. Everything blurred, and nausea choked me as I clutched at my skull, doubled over.

Lying in a snowbank, I lifted my throbbing head. Plague climbed along rooftops, settling onto the house directly across the street from me. Off in the distance, Pestilence rose from the forest, banking toward the city at top speed.

Plague leaned closer.

"Big *scary* bird!" Squire hooted with distress as I raised my hand in front of him protectively.

Plague lowered her long snout. Her predatory orange eyes glowed with heat. Her jaw unhinged as she breathed, and endless rows of opal teeth flashed. Magic surrounded her in a deadly haze.

"Zora," Aleksander shouted down, half hanging from his saddle. "Come with me!"

Pulling out a bone dagger with my left hand, ignoring the throbbing that made it hard to see, I raised my right pointer finger high into the sky—the symbol of Antichthon's first democracy. Mom always said our self-governance was the biggest threat to the Draconis Emperors, who wanted to enslave us all and rule the world.

"I will *never* go with you!" I shouted with all my might,

mimicking the fearsome roar of a mammoth dire bear. "Because I will *never* surrender to tyranny!"

Aleksander's cold laughter carried down on the frigid wind. "No one will defend thee from me."

Blood dripped down my face, stinging my eyes. I raised my dagger higher, flames glinting off the countless nicks in the bone.

"I WILL FIGHT FOR ME," I shouted, swaying with dizziness as I pulled myself up to my feet. *Lucky girls survive.* I wouldn't let him take me.

He shook his head violently. "Come with me now, or I will burn your Commune to the ground!"

Squire screeched.

Tears of frustration burned my eyes, but I refused to let him see how much he affected me. *What should I do?* He reached out for me, and Plague leaned closer.

"Then burn it all, Emperor!" I brought my dagger up to my throat, holding his gaze. I would never kill myself, but he didn't know that.

He jolted.

Hand steady, I held the blade to my throat. Destruction didn't offer him any leverage if I was dead, and we both knew it. We were locked in a stalemate.

The Emperor pointed an elegant finger down at me, magic gathering.

The twins threw themselves in front of me, their hands raised into Shields.

A third jet rumbled off in the distance.

Everyone froze.

The roaring engine thundered through the Commune, and both dragons swiveled their heads. Blue strands of Mist rose up from the forest.

Something vibrated, and Ella pulled out a thin remote with a bright red button on the end. "It's time," she said.

Axel's hand shot out, and he grabbed his sister's wrist. "No—

don't." His voice shook with rage. "If you waste it . . . *if I miss*, the Marshal will punish us."

Ella yanked her hand out of his grip, holding the device behind her back. "We must help the people, and this is the closest we've ever gotten to dragons. We have to try—"

"We *don't* have to do anything." Axel grabbed her shoulder, his knuckles white as he leaned over her.

Ella stared up at him and then back at me, where my dagger was still pressed to my throat. Her eyes were wide behind her helmet. She blanched, looking between us. The device vibrated a second time; the fighter jet was getting closer.

Axel gritted his teeth. "Don't do—"

"Do it," I said, cutting him off, my hunting voice deeper than normal as I listened to my instincts. A narrow window of opportunity was quickly closing.

Ella swallowed visibly as she held my gaze.

Axel's helmet rattled as he scowled over at me. "Stay out of this. You don't know what the hell we're talking about—"

"Use it," I ordered her louder.

"No, don't you dare—"

"Now."

Ella pushed the remote button behind her back. "Aim for the underbelly!" she shouted as Axel swore violently.

Five things happened at once: a pilot ejected from the fighter jet as the Mist attacked it; a long missile detached from the side of the machinery and hovered in the air; Plague and Pestilence pushed up into the sky, distracted by the missile; I lowered my blade; and there was a loud beeping noise on Axel's back.

"Target designator activated," said a mechanical female voice.

The third jet crashed into the forest in another fireball as Axel stepped forward. In one smooth move, he pulled a shiny bow off his back. I'd never seen a metal one, and no one used wooden bows anymore because dire animal hides were too thick.

Axel fit a matching long arrow into the bowstring and aimed it up at Plague.

A light beeped on the strange arrowhead. The Mist rose from the ground, heading toward it.

Axel breathed deeply, then unleashed his arrow. It arced through the air, and Mist chased closely behind in a shimmering streak. The arrow burrowed into a scale on the bottom of Plague's belly, and the shaft detached, falling away.

Ella pressed the red button again.

A high-pitched whistle trilled through the air. The hovering missile shot forward, straight for Plague. The Mist chased after it—close, but not close enough.

ROAR.

Plague shot up high into the sky, golden scales gleaming as the missile followed her vertical ascent. Clouds parted, revealing a full blood moon.

Her wings stretched wide. Aleksander looked small astride her back. With the missile mere feet from her tail—their shadowy outlines were framed by the blood moon—Plague abruptly pulled her wings in tight and plummeted toward the ground.

Spinning, she just barely missed clipping the missile.

It curved after her.

Aleksander yelled something into the night, and Tarantula yanked on his reins. Pestilence opened his maw, and ice exploded. It spewed over Plague, turning her golden scales a silvery azure as she nosedived past, heading straight toward the Barren Forest. *Why did they do that?*

The missile veered off course, slowing as it uselessly flew in a different direction.

My heart dropped.

Pestilence's ice broke the tracker.

Plague pulled up from her descent, branches clattering loudly as ice chunks fell off her body. Trees tilted in the rush of wind, and the forest groaned as she rose back into the air.

The Mist seized the stalled missile, and it plummeted, deactivated. Aleksander whooped loudly while Plague barrel-rolled, shaking off the last of the ice. Tarantula held both of his arms up in the air.

Axel screamed with frustration, slamming his bow down onto the icy road. It splintered into pieces.

Aleksander and Plague turned, flying straight back toward me. Once again, they landed on the rooftop across from me, casting the street into dark shadows.

"Come with me now, Zora!" Aleksander shouted. "Or I will take *everything* from thee, so thou will have no one . . . thou will crawl, *begging*—for me." The air carried the stench of his diabolical intentions.

As I asphyxiated on abject terror, sounds warped. My strength drained away as I fell to my knees, overwhelmed by the horror of it all. He had storm magic, and I had nothing. There were no moves left to make.

We'd lost the battle, and I was just a teenage girl, kneeling in blood-splattered snow before a monstrous Emperor who rode astride an unfathomably powerful dragon.

"NO QUARTER!" Ella screamed at the top of her lungs, Knight armor rattling as she threw herself in front of me. Axel swore. He lunged for her, grabbing her arm. She yanked out of his hold, face tilted up to Plague with defiance.

Aleksander went rigid in his saddle. "How dare thou!"

"Article II of the Storm Wars Peace Accords," Ella shouted. "*Safe* prisoners of war. If you take any soldier of the Crimson Army hostage, it will be a breach of the statute, and the Marshal will order no quarter . . . What you seek will be executed."

What does he seek that the Commonwealth has?

Aleksander shook his head, pointing down at where I kneeled. "She is not a member of your pathetic army!"

Ella looked back at me. "Zora Ravenal, do you accept a lifetime enlistment in the Crimson Army? Verbal agreement is sufficient for contractual obligation."

Aleksander's eyes widened as he leaned forward off Plague like he was going to throw himself at me.

"I do," I said numbly.

Aleksander bellowed with fury, magic rising off his shoulders in a steaming haze; he was on fire with power.

"She is now protected under the statute!" Ella screamed, raising her arms into a Shield.

Swearing loudly, foreign words falling from his cruel lips, Aleksander and Plague rose into the air. "This is *not* over, Ravenal!" They banked away, joining Pestilence high in the sky. Under the blood moon, they flew away east, back across the Moor Ocean toward Azote, the home of the Draconis Empire.

"Bye-bye, big fat birds," Squire cawed.

Aleksander had failed; I was still free.

Lucky, lucky girl.

Gasping with disbelief, unable to process my good fortune, I clutched my racing heart. "Thank you," I said to Ella. "Thank you *so* much."

Ella smiled sadly. "Of course—"

"How old are you?" Axel asked me as he stepped in front of Ella protectively.

"Seventeen."

He shook his head, eyes narrowed. "You're old enough to pledge enlistment but too young to join. We'll inform the Marshal . . . but the Crimson Army will probably forget to come back for you. They have no interest in the North."

"And if they remember?"

His expression wasn't encouraging. "I'd start praying to the old god. Your life is in peril."

It already was.

Someone screamed in agony as they staggered into the main street—on fire. Ella ran to help them, and Axel chased after her.

On my hands and knees, I crawled through the street like an animal, over the melting ice. Head spinning with concussed pain, stomach in my throat, heart full of gratitude, I fought to get to them—Mom and Aurora.

Finally I threw myself at our door, banging desperately.

It flung open.

Mom and Aurora pulled me inside. I collapsed into their arms. Together they smelled like stringent soap, vanilla, and the only people in the world who mattered. Their knees buckled as I grabbed at them, and down to the stone floor we all went, together.

Squire hooted, cuddling between us all.

I tried to speak but couldn't through my chattering teeth. Mom shouted with worry as she and Aurora patted out the flames sizzling the ends of my hair. I checked them over frantically for injuries.

"We're okay," Mom said as I grabbed them roughly. "We're *all* okay, honey. Breathe."

Aurora coughed as she hugged my back while Mom hugged my front. Squire pecked at my cheek, his way of giving kisses.

"I'm so glad you made it back," Aurora whispered. "I was so worried."

I held them tightly, shaking with strangled laughter as tears poured down my cheeks.

"I got you, sweetheart," Mom said. "I got you. No one will harm you—"

Aurora nodded. "We aren't going anywhere."

"I won't let them hurt you," I whispered.

Aurora rested her head on my shoulder as the three of us lay sprawled across the floor. "We're stronger than you think," she said. "Just because we don't venture outside the walls like you doesn't mean we're helpless."

Mom sighed as she brushed singed hair off my forehead. Her bronze complexion had a slight sickly pallor in the firelight.

I cried harder, because each day Mom got older and Aurora got sicker. Mom's voice had a slight rasp of asthma, but we'd both noticed Aurora's cough getting deeper, more rattling over the years.

I roughly pulled the furry dire elk pelt off the chair, nearly knocking over our chessboard. I righted a potato with wires sticking out of it—a school project Mom had made me do a couple years ago. The wires were connected to a tiny piece of silver; they created a zap when touched, powered by the potato—a model of lost artificial technology.

I draped the fur around Aurora's shoulders, and Mom helped me as my hands shook.

"We're *going* to survive," I promised them both, head aching. "They will not beat us . . . The Empire *will* fall."

"Sweetheart, please—don't worry about the Storm Wars," Mom said. "It's bigger than all of us. Just focus on keeping yourself safe."

Aurora nodded in agreement.

The three of us had positioned ourselves into a circle on the floor, sitting close like we always did when we played our dice games. It was why Aurora had been over in the first place. We'd all agreed to a round tonight.

As if sensing my tangled thoughts, Mom pulled the three six-sided platinum dice out of their box. She said they were a secret gift from my father and we could never tell anyone about them. How he had the precious, extremely rare metallic objects, I'd never understood.

"Just one quick round," Aurora said. "I know my parents don't care, but I'm sure they're worried with the attack."

"Of course they are, dear," Mom said, but the smile didn't reach her eyes. Aurora had four older siblings. Aurora's parents forgot about her at best and resented her at worst. It was why she spent so much time with us.

Mom tossed the three dice on the floor between us. She'd rolled a score of four—a two, a one, and another one.

"Lucky roll," Mom said with a smile. The game was simple. Whoever rolled the lowest numbers won the round. "See, it's a sign. Everything will work out for us."

I wrapped my arms around my knees, rocking back and forth. "We're not lucky," I whispered, remembering the rows of jagged dragon teeth. *We're being hunted.* Squire trembled on my shoulder, eyes wide with terror. I petted his tiny head.

Aurora clapped her hands, laughing as she rolled the dice and got a ten.

"We can't win," I whispered.

Mom's eyes crinkled as she handed me the platinum dice. "Life isn't about winning."

That's not true. After all, Mom and I played chess every night before bed because she said it would teach me everything I needed to know in life. I hadn't lost a match in years.

Rule of survival: Always win.

I rolled my turn. Three ones stared up at me.

111.

"Lucky, special girl," Mom said, and I felt sick.

8

Stage of Grief: (Seductive) Bargaining

Present Day

"Cease this, and go to sleep . . . *now*, vassal," Tarantula said coldly, his voice menacing in our dark bedroom. He'd moved in weeks ago, but nothing had changed between us.

Well, mostly nothing.

I snorted. "Nice try."

It took all my concentration to sound articulate and not high out of my mind. Axel had given me a pack of Southern cigarettes to cope with my "stress management problems."

Ironic, because he didn't know *half* of my struggles. He just knew that I kept falling asleep during dinner. The Marshal was growing frustrated with my magical progress—or lack thereof. She harassed me daily over my inability to control more than one drop of water at a time.

I spun the cigarette between my fingers. Long and thin, the burning white paper held a cooling spice that tasted like mint and forgotten dreams. They were popular in the Middlelands. Axel had told me earlier to "enjoy the buzz, and don't do anything

I wouldn't do." Confusing instructions because he seemed incapable of shame.

I'd also unpacked my cherished chess set—the one Mom had pushed into my hands when I left home. Smoking, I resumed playing against myself but grew bored and dropped the queen with a sigh.

I turned to the other occupant in the room.

Tarantula leaned against the wall beside his bed, with his legs hanging over his mattress, staring at me. He wasn't blinking. The silvery haze around his body mixed with moonlight. *Pretty.*

I blew out a cloud of smoke, and it lingered in the air like frost. Here lies Zora, homesick and high. *Highly homesick and . . . sick of his highness.* Chuckling at my devastating wit, I inhaled more deeply, tongue tingling with the minty coolness.

Tarantula glared at my mouth like it personally offended him. His ears were flushed bright red.

This is fun.

"Cease doing . . . that," Tarantula ordered loudly in his bossy, delusional tone.

"Stop doing . . . what?" Sticking my tongue out with the cigarette pressed against my top teeth, I tried to see how many seconds I could keep the long paper balanced on it.

Slowly I slid across the sheets, propped my legs up on the wall beside my bed, and hung my head over the edge of the mattress. I stared back at him, tongue out, cigarette still dangling where it was pressed precariously against my teeth.

"Ravenal . . . I swear to the storm spirits, if thou don't put your tongue back behind your tempting lips . . ."

"Has anyone told you that you look better upside down?"

"No."

"Wow, really?"

"Yes."

"Are you being serious right now?"

"Yes."

"No one . . . has ever told you? Not once?"

"No."

"Are you sure?"

"Yes."

"No one told you . . . twice?"

"No."

"In a row?"

"Ravenal, thou art such a lightweight. Put the cursed cigarette back in your mouth and go to sleep. Thou art courting my madness and tempting me with . . . *Never* in all the worlds has a woman sent a man closer to peril . . ."

"You're a weird guy," I said with honesty as I delicately held the long, smoking cigarette between two fingers.

Lazily I trailed it down my body and held it above my crotch. *Phantom phallic gestures.* Ella and I had painted our nails together yesterday, and I admired how pretty the onyx contrasted with the paper in the moon rays.

Tarantula swore viciously under his breath.

I tilted my head so I could see him better from upside down. "Wait—do you want to . . . taste it?" I wiggled my eyebrows, holding the cigarette above my hips. Even buzzed, I couldn't forget how weeks ago he pinned me into the sand and pressed himself wickedly against me.

Memories devour.

His face turned bright red, the flush crawling up his ears. "I'm *not* . . . answering thee." He yanked his blanket up so it covered his lap.

"Do it," I whispered as I rolled my hips, needing to rectify our power imbalance. "I'll let you have a smoke. The mint really . . . tingles the tongue."

He draped a forearm across his closed eyes, chains glinting. "Such impropriety," he grumbled. A dark, strangled sound escaped from his chest.

"Suck on it," I said louder. "You know you want to."

His shoulders stiffened, and I laughed because a person had never looked more uncomfortable on soft bedding.

"*Pathetic*, that's what you are," I whispered gravely, cigarette still smoking above my lap. "You're all bark, no bite. All you do is threaten and—"

The chain between his cuffs stretched across my torso, pinning me to the mattress. Tarantula had moved with impossible speed. He kneeled beside my bed, leaning forward, with his crotch directly in front of my upside-down face; magic glowed as it steamed off his thighs.

He pressed his hands firmly into the comforter beside my hips, pinning me with the chain between his wrists.

Ever so slowly, he leaned his face forward . . . *closer* . . . *closer*. I lifted my head to get a better view. His lips hovered above my lap. He tilted his face to the side. His jawline was sharp enough to slice your finger on. His tongue licked wantonly up the length of my cigarette, all the way to the burning tip.

Oh . . . myoldgod.

I never thought he'd actually do it. He was always blushing and muttering about decorum.

Trailing his tongue back down the lit cigarette to my hand, he wrapped his mouth sideways around the base, where I gripped it with two fingers. His hot breath wafted over my hand. Chills exploded as his tongue tasted my skin.

With hooded, evil eyes, he expertly plucked the cigarette from my fingers with his teeth, tilting it with his tongue so it hung properly from his lips. Chain digging into my torso, he inhaled deeply. He clenched his fingers, comforter bunching, and blew a cloud of minty smoke out of his nose, directly between my thighs.

I jolted, gasping.

He made a sound of pure masculine satisfaction.

Staring hungrily at my face, he leaned down with the cigarette between his teeth and slowly dragged the burning edge up across the delicate material of my sleep shirt.

He paused with it over the hollow of my throat, then pulled it away, dragging his hands upward in its wake. Gently he draped the icy chain over my neck like jewelry.

I froze.

Pleasure pebbled—*everywhere.* He cupped my jaw with long fingers, holding me tenderly in the deadly position.

What is happening right now?

I sucked in harshly as his thumb stroked over the column of my jugular, which, for the first time in my life, somehow felt *more* erogenous than my breasts. He lowered so his face hovered above mine.

Over the side of the bed, I tipped my chin back farther, boneless.

Tarantula held my upside-down face, cigarette between his lips, his chain chilly across my neck.

"Ravenal," he said huskily, breathing smoke directly into my mouth as he spoke, the minty coolness corrupted with the scent of dark cherry.

His calloused thumb dragged over my throat, down to my collarbone. *My* cigarette bobbed between his straight white teeth as he pulled the chain tighter across my jugular. "Thou art *incorrect* . . . I only desire to bite, not bark. My teeth *yearn* to mar your arresting flesh."

Oh.

Oh.

Not good.

Not good at all.

It took my sluggish, foggy brain a long second to process his reference to my earlier statement. "I think there's a translation issue happening here." My voice came out unnaturally high-pitched.

"No, there is not. I know *exactly* what thou meant," he said as he leaned closer to pull the cigarette from his mouth while keeping the metal chain pressed against my flesh.

He brought the cigarette to my mouth, dragging the unlit end back and forth across my lower lip.

"Uh, no. I don't think you do . . ." I cleared my throat. "Understand. Me."

He gently pressed the paper inside my parted lips, stopping when it rested on my tongue.

"'Tis thou who does not get it."

Cool metal disappeared, my neck uncomfortably bare as he rose gracefully to his feet and stepped away. With nowhere to go in the cramped room, he turned harshly, giving me his back.

Silence stretched between us.

"I think . . . you should stay away from me, spider," I said to his unbecoming butt. Very hideous. Not at all firm, juicy, and captivating. *I should bite it.*

Still facing the wall, he laughed, but the sound held no humor. "Go to sleep, Ravenal."

"No, I won't."

"Thou will obey me, vassal," Tarantula said harshly. "Retire, now."

"No."

He inhaled loudly through gritted teeth. Then his voice dropped an octave. "Who did thou say your sire was again?"

"Sazha sounds like a girl's name," I blurted. The realization had been killing me since I'd first heard it.

The sharp scent of his magic intensified. "Do thou *yearn* for my punishment?"

"Shhh, Sazha Washa." I held a finger up to my smoking lips. "He can hear you."

"Who?"

I made the spooky ghost sound Mom always made when telling stories about wraiths. "The Emperor. He's in this very room."

"Ravenal," he said darkly. "If thou don't find sleep in the next five minutes, so help me . . . I shall *put* thee to sleep. Permanently."

"No, you won't do anything." I waved the dial in the air and then realized it was just my cigarette. *Wait, where did I put it?*

"There is nothing in the world that can protect thee from me."

"I don't need protection from *any* man. I can take care of myself."

"Ah." He paused pointedly, still not turning to look at me. "Thou art plighted with delusions."

"You're afraid," I said quietly. "I can taste it in the air. I can sense it. I can smell it on you."

"Thou lie."

"You reek of death and the urge to destroy the world—"

"Retire in sleep now, vassal," he ordered. "Obey. This is a direct order from your royal."

I scoffed. "I don't obey any man. But *you'll* obey me, by the end . . . of this." *My stupid, scandalous quest.*

He laughed, but his shoulders didn't shake as he stood ramrod straight in the night. "By what cause would I? 'Tis a ludicrous proposition that I would take orders from a brat such as—"

"You're intrigued by my prospective . . . *domination.* You want me on . . . *top* of you." The buzz made me brave. "Do you not?" Still hanging off the bed, I raised the long cigarette to my eyes, studying it. "You're the one who just sucked on . . . *me.* I bet you want to do it again."

Tarantula jolted as if struck. The shadows in the room gained claws, silver thickening around his tensed shoulders, and then it exploded. A crushing sensation hit me.

"I AM YOUR SOVEREIGN. SLEEP, RAVENAL!"

I passed out.

Sunlight blinded me, and with it came a bucket of shame.

I shot out of bed, dial raised defensively. *What the heck did they put in those cigarettes? Southerners are crazy.* I whirled around.

The object of my hatred lounged casually on his bed with one cuffed arm relaxed lazily behind blond curls. Prisoner chains dangled across his platinum mask. *I'm never smoking again.*

Heat flushed across my face. "What the damned did you do to me last night?"

Tarantula stared back at me impassively, no recognition showing on his face. "Nothing. What art thou rambling about?" He tilted his head to the side and pointed to the extinguished cigarette lying half burned on the floor. "Thou were high on that stupid stick, and I—"

"You did something to me and I slept." I aimed the dial at him harshly, trying desperately not to think about the ridiculous way I'd acted. I'd flirted with the enemy while his chains were wrapped around my neck, and I . . . liked it.

"Thou retired from exhaustion," Tarantula said slowly. "I do not know what type of dreams have misled—"

I cut him off. "Stop trying to gaslight me. I know what happened."

"Do thou . . . *really*, Ravenal?" he asked with a cryptic drawl as he wiped his thumb across his lower lip suggestively.

Memories of his tongue against my fingers sent sparks of awareness down my frayed nerves. *He kneeled in front of me, holding my jaw as he licked vulgarly across my cigarette.* The hair on my arms stood up.

The Marshal would be pleased.

I wanted to *die*.

Metal refracted sunlight across the room as he tucked a curl behind his ear. The top of his jumpsuit was unzipped perilously low, revealing the chiseled planes of his hard chest. *Absolutely revolting.* I focused on his spider tattoo and tried to think about Aurora and Mom.

He smirked like he had a secret.

We both do.

"Why do you keep calling me a vassal?" I asked, changing tactics. "Explain yourself."

He sighed heavily. "Thou art a Knight Mage. I am a Royal Mage. That renders thee—" he pointed his finger at my throat "—my vassal." His smirk could strip paint.

"What are you talking about?" I asked. "Those are just names—"

"Art thou sure?" His frigid tone had a modern edge. "One of us is bred with magic in their veins, and the other is . . . *made*."

"What blood was used in the Iron Ritual?"

He flashed his teeth like a dire wolf but didn't answer. A pit expanded in my stomach, unease mounting.

"Where does the storm magic come from?" I asked louder.

"Not the right question."

"Where does the Mist come from?"

His eyes sharpened. "Thou would never believe me."

"What determines a Royal Mage's type of storm magic?"

His gaze shuttered. "Inheritance." A gust of silver-laced wind whipped through my hair, but he didn't expound.

"Stop being a cryptic bastard and just tell me what the—"

Tarantula unfurled fluidly off his bed, rising to his full height. The sharp scent of magic mixed with other notes. Dark cherry and . . . *nefarious schemes*? I discreetly sniffed the air, intoxicated by the danger; adrenaline pounded through my veins.

I inhaled deeper.

"Art thou done objectifying me?" Tarantula asked in a clipped tone as he wet his lower lip.

Fighting embarrassment, I shrugged like I didn't care. "It's just a scent. Am I not allowed to enjoy it?" I inhaled loudly, moaning dramatically to get a rise out of him.

The tendons on his neck strained under his collar with such force the metal creaked. He muttered something under his breath in his rough heathenish language. Chains clinked against his cuffs as he dragged both hands through his messy curls, stalking toward the washroom.

I shot off the bed, beating him to the door, and blocked his path.

He worked his jaw back and forth as he tried to incinerate me with his eyes. "Stop afflicting me, Ravenal."

Squire sat up on my pillow, feathers sticking up on his little head. He flew onto my shoulder. "Morning, spider whore," he sang sleepily (very helpful).

I waved the dial and closed the washroom door in Tarantula's face.

"Thou vexing, impudent wench." He made an unholy sound of agitation on the other side, and there was a crash in the room as if something had been thrown. He was somehow both the damsel in distress *and* the despicable dragon at the same time. *The duality of evil.*

I hastily turned on the shower. Fully clothed, and afraid to be naked within his proximity even with the door shut, I turned the water up to scalding.

Resting my forehead against the wall, I tried not to cry. Squire preened his feathers, chirping with delight.

My quest: impossible.

How did I ever think I could defeat the Empire?

Shaking, teeth chattering, I used my dagger to resharpen my toothbrush shiv—just in case. You could never have too many weapons. Gripped by the exhaustion of intense pressure, I dropped to my knees, hands clasped, eyes closed, face tilted up at the spray. I prayed for strength.

I am lucky and blessed. The universe conspires in my favor. What I desire desires me more. My quest is possible. I can do it. Please, old god, protect me.

A few minutes later, I pushed past Tarantula into the room with a towel wrapped tightly around me and my soaking clothes.

"So improper," he muttered, cheeks flushing red as he kept his gaze averted from me.

What's his problem now? I'm covered in clothes and *a towel.*

"You're pathetic," I said.

"I know." He stalked past me and slammed the washroom door shut.

After changing in a rush, I sprinted out of the hangar as fast as possible. The sand radiated heat, burning my legs, and I savored the exhaustion of pushing my body to the limits. *Freedom.* Squire bobbed his head while he balanced on my shoulder, urging me forward.

"I think we've finally lost him." I relaxed into the flow.

"Who art thou losing?" Tarantula asked.

I screamed.

"Hoo?" Squire squawked as he flapped his wings with fright.

"Where the damned did you come from?" I looked around with confusion. I'd been *sure* we were alone. *How does he keep sneaking up on me?*

Tarantula didn't answer as he easily fell into step beside me.

After an indeterminate amount of time, I lost my ability to pretend he didn't exist. "Have you ever heard of personal space?" I asked. "Get your own morning routine."

"Cease blithering, partner."

"Don't tell me what to do."

"Silence yourself, brat."

"Me speak," Squire offered (cute).

Tarantula rolled his eyes.

When we crested the final dune and the gothic spires of the base came into view, he pulled ahead of me.

For a moment, I contemplated letting him win.

Zaps echoed as electricity exploded out of his collar for a single second. *A little shock is good for the constitution.* He threw sand, bellowing with rage behind me. It was just enough to let me win. Heart in my throat, I leaped with all my strength, gasping with relief when I landed in the hangar first.

Rule of survival: Never lose, especially not to men.

After last night, I needed to reassert the balance of power.

I held my arms up and did a victory dance, savoring the rush. *You're still better than him. Winner, winner, dragon dinner—*

A heavy weight slammed into me from behind. *Not again.* Turning midair, Tarantula took the brunt of the fall. He rolled so I landed on his chest as he smacked down onto the cold marble floor. Chains jangled loudly, and wings flapped as Squire detangled himself. We grappled. His bicep wrapped around my head. He held me immobilized.

His balaclava hovered inches in front of my face. "Curse upon your house, Ravenal. Thou art the most exasperating woman on the face of the—"

"Good," I said, proud to be difficult.

He rolled, his heavy weight crushing. "Infuriating brat," he muttered under his breath. "Always arguing and hurting me with such impropriety . . ."

Closing my eyes, I went limp, pretending to be dead.

Tarantula felt my forehead. "Ravenal?" He sounded concerned.

I wrestled, twisting so I landed on top. Triumphantly I shoved my forearm into the side of his face. "Don't be such a *prude*," I gloated, enjoying the feel of him at my mercy.

A man's true place is beneath a woman.

"Are you two done?" the Marshal asked, her face severe as she stood over us. Dead silence filled the hangar. Everyone stared at us.

"Yes?" I said.

"No." Tarantula bowed his back, arching with impossible strength and rolling again so he loomed above me. "Now 'tis over." He released me and climbed to his feet as he poshly brushed off his prisoner jumpsuit. He still didn't pull up the zipper. *Someone should report him for violating the dress code.*

I pushed myself up onto my tired legs.

"Today's practice assignment." The Marshal glared at me with disappointment—a frequent expression these days—as she held out a piece of paper.

I snatched it before he could take it.

"No," I said, crumpling it in my fist. "Are you out of your—"

"Silence, Knight." She cut me off, refusing to meet my eyes. *She's trying to force us closer.* "Your pilot is ready for the training run."

"Silence, Marshal," Squire squawked as he finished hovering and landed on my shoulder (not helpful).

She glared at him.

I shook my head. "But why would we—"

"This is a *trust* exercise." Her glare was withering. I could practically hear her mentally screaming at me to be silent and obey. "You two need it."

In this moment, I hated her, almost as much as I hated him.

"So let me get this straight," I said. "You want us both to jump from a helicopter, and you want *me* to pull . . . *his* chute?" I pointed. "His—Tarantula's?"

"Wonderful, she can read." The Marshal clapped. "The Commonwealth is so lucky to have such a brilliant asset." She glared at me. "Yes—that's exactly what I want you to do. This is about you showing us that you're *mature* enough to work alongside him."

"No." I shook my head vehemently. "No, I'm not doing it. I refuse. That's taking this too far. You can't make me."

"You can make me," Squire offered (not helpful).

The Marshal held my gaze, a warning in the blue depths of her eyes. "Don't let me down. We're all counting on you, *Knight* Ravenal." She walked away.

A few minutes later, I sat in the open doorway of a helicopter with my legs dangling over the side. We were flying straight up as high into the air as possible, per the Marshal's directive.

It was a cloudless, sunny day. The desert stretched endlessly below.

Chop—Chop—Chop.

Squire trembled with fear on my shoulder, and I ignored the unsettling sensation of Tarantula's stare.

"I'm not pulling your chute," I said for the zillionth time.

Tarantula relaxed casually against the wall in my peripheral vision. "Thou shall, vassal." He spoke with the utmost certainty, like he knew for a fact that I would save him. "The Marshal wants a declaration of cooperation. Thou will gift it to her."

Delusion is a common character trait on this military base.

"T-MINUS FIFTEEN SECONDS TO ABORT," crackled disjointedly over the failing intercom.

The Mist approached.

We jerked.

Giddiness mounted like it always did before a free fall; my heart raced with anticipation.

"THREE SECONDS."

Propellers stalled. Lights and alarms flashed inside the machinery, and then everything went dark.

The helicopter tipped violently to the side.

I laughed as my stomach whooped.

Tarantula grabbed my shoulder. I glanced back. His covered face hovered inches from mine.

I asked him, "What are you doing—"

He shoved.

We were free-falling.

I twisted, but he kept a punishing hold on my arm as we spun through the air.

He yanked off my balaclava, and it floated away.

"What the damned!" I kicked at him with all my might. Squire squawked, his talons digging deep into my shoulder as he plummeted with me.

I kicked Tarantula harder, but his hand was an unbreakable vise. "Let me go, you stupid—"

"Calm yourself. Complete the objective!" Tarantula yelled into my ear over the rushing wind as we tussled, his grip so painful there would be bruises. *Wow, he's really committing to this.*

Sand approached fast.

He ripped off his balaclava and threw it aside.

"Pull my chute," he mouthed, grabbing my hips and yanking me closer to him. We were spinning through the air, upside down, chest to chest. I could feel his heart beating through the fabric pressed against my sternum. Magic crackled between us, metallic and glittering in the sunlight.

"NOW," he mouthed.

Squire screeched with terror as he released my shoulder and then caught wind, casually flying away.

Tarantula's masked nose pressed against mine as we spun faster through the air. His legs tangled with mine, his arms wrapping around me, his pupils dilating.

We plummeted.

Breaking his grip, I grabbed his messy curls with my free hand and *wrenched* his head back with all my might. "*Be gone, enemy,*" I shouted into his ear, trying not to notice how his locks were impossibly soft—silk between my fingers.

He inhaled roughly, shuddering against me as I yanked his head back farther.

Sand neared, and ridiculous laughter escaped my throat. Adrenaline made me weightless. Invincible. *I can do anything in the world.*

Tarantula's eyes widened.

He yanked his head from my hold, grabbed my jaw with a cuffed hand, and slammed his mouth against mine, swallowing my laughter. His lips *burned*, radiating a level of heat that shouldn't have been humanly possible.

I tugged on his silky hair, fever streaking down my open mouth, neck, and lower. His tongue battled mine, plunging deep. *Dominating.* His rough fingers cupped my face with reverence. Euphoria sizzled across my senses as he kissed me like we were both about to die.

"I *despise* you," I said into his open mouth.

He pulled away, releasing me.

I spun in a free fall, gasping for air. My head rushed with an overload of endorphins, and there was no doubt in my heart or weakness in my limbs.

Dear old god, please give me strength. My intentions were pure. *Curse the quest.* I'd had enough.

"Thou would kill us?" he mouthed, plummeting beside me a foot away, staring at me like he'd never seen me before.

"No. I would just kill *you*."

I pulled my release, and my spine yanked painfully as the straps wrenched me upward at the last possible second.

BAM.

Tarantula slammed into the sand, his chute untouched.

I gasped shallowly, mouth on fire, as seconds later I collided with a dune with a little less force. The chute collapsed behind me in a tangle of strings, and the sand burned warm against my throbbing, too-sensitive flesh.

Hand to my mouth, I slumped back against the desert sand. The tingling across my lips wouldn't stop, and I tried to lick it away. It was the taste of dark cherry and . . . *subjugation*; seductive evil. I felt my face flush. Existential dread scorched across my flesh, hotter than the bright sun.

No man had ever tasted so tempting.

Shivers of unease attacked my spine, streaks of awareness on overheated skin. Kissing him felt like kissing a deployed missile. We'd both exploded. Me metaphorically and him literally, because he was now dead.

I was free.

Murder has never felt so good.

Vines loosened around my heart, the thorns retracting. For the first time in weeks, I could breathe without wanting to cry. The pressure dissipated off my chest. The quest was over.

"How . . . *dare* . . . thou," Tarantula's deep voice boomed from the dune across from me. He brushed sand off himself, rising elegantly up to his feet, mostly uninjured, except for bloody scrapes, as if he hadn't just *fallen* from the clouds.

Oh.

No.

His shadow blocked the sun as he stalked over and stood above me with disheveled hair. The theater of the absurd. It was all too much to fathom. *How is this possible?* Royal Mages were more powerful than I had ever imagined. *I should have decapitated him while I had the chance.* That might have worked. *Maybe.*

Instead, I'd failed, again.

We were *still* stuck together.

"You should be dead," I whispered with crushing dread as I licked his taste off my dry lips, desperately parched.

Tarantula crouched down next to me. "Thou art going to *pay*—Ravenal." He reached out, grabbed the end of my braid, and slowly wrapped it around his fist until my scalp stung.

With a yank, he tugged my head back.

Once again, we were face to mask. His lips were so close to mine that I could taste his rough exhale as it left his mouth. Heat radiated off his skin. Pleasure mixed with pain.

"Thou art a *plague* upon me, Ravenal," he whispered with quiet menace. "'Tis *unseemly* what thou do to me."

I leaned closer, and his eyes widened, breath sputtering.

"You will feel far worse," I promised, desperately trying not to inhale his corrupt scent. "Before I'm done with you."

Tarantula grunted, and his gaze dropped to my mouth, then went back to my eyes, then lingered on my scars. His chest heaved. A muscle in his jaw ticked. He ground his teeth together. Silver turned pure black as it steamed off his skull. Magic and man seethed together.

His mouth hovered wickedly close, and I could taste his hatred. His lips brushed slightly against mine, and sensations exploded down my nerve endings. *Scorching heat.*

I froze, eyes wide, stars dancing.

"Thou cannot make me feel worse," he said hoarsely, brushing against my open mouth, the smallest, most tantalizing of touches, "than *this*, Ravenal."

He pulled away and dropped my braid, releasing me. He barely exerted any pressure, but I collapsed onto my back, boneless. Head spinning, I lay spread-eagle on the sand while he loomed over me.

"Why did you . . . kiss me?" I whispered.

"What art thou blabbering about, Ravenal?" He tilted his head to the side slowly, eyes narrowing with icy menace. "I have *never* . . . touched thee." He ripped his hands through his hair and stalked away, muttering in his strange, consonant-heavy language.

What in the damned just happened?

"KNIGHT MAGE, YOU FAILED TO COMPLETE THE—" the Marshal shouted across the dunes, stomping toward me. A dozen Shadow Swords marched with her in perfect formation. The sky was black behind her, a dust storm gathering on the horizon.

Squire landed on my forehead. "Me fail?" He pecked at my nose with concern.

"It appears so."

He squawked with indignation.

I rolled over onto my knees, chucked sand, and screamed at the top of my lungs until I tasted blood.

Memories welled up, haunting me.

9

Before: Reign of T(error)

Zora Ravenal, Twenty-Two Years Old
Four Months Ago

Aurora coughed softly and cuddled closer to me as we walked through the town's center toward home. I rested my chin on the top of her head, enjoying her warmth and her distinctive scent—*laughter and happiness.*

The tips of her blond hair shimmered bright pink, matching the dye streaked through her right eyebrow. All imports were impacted because of the Storm Wars, so she'd saved up for months to buy a bottle of dye from an old shipment, and I'd spent all morning painstakingly applying it. My fingertips were stained bright pink, but the result was worth it.

She looked beautiful.

Above, canvas flapped loudly against brick. A fifty-foot portrait hung across the civic center. *BEWARE, EMPEROR ALEKSANDER THE SADISTIC AND TARANTULA BRING THE STORM WARS TO THE NORTH.*

Below the warning was a detailed painting, the most recent portrait of the Emperor. The artist had captured his depraved likeness with remarkable exactitude. His face hadn't changed much since his teenage years.

Lifeless pale eyes rimmed in dark circles stared down at me from a face with angular features, hollowed cheeks, hateful maroon lips, inky hair, and shockingly dark eyebrows.

My favorite part: his big aristocratic nose had a large, discolored bump at the top, and a single scar stretched across the skin on the front of his neck. Every time he looked in the mirror, I hoped he thought of me and how I'd damaged him.

"Zora, Aurora—is that you?" Blake called down the street. Puberty had turned him from an annoying boy into a tall, handsome, and even *more* annoying man.

Aurora and I shared a look. Then we both ran down the street, giggling like teenagers. Blake shouted our names, but his voice grew distant as we crossed the snowy cobblestones.

"You'd think he'd take the hint by now," Aurora said as she struggled to keep up with me.

"Men are stupid." I leaped down the stairs where the street intersected with the first row of townhomes.

"Men *very* stupid," Squire sang with the energy of a scornful woman (accurate).

Aurora stepped down one stair at a time while I waited at the bottom. "Where are all the strong warrior men?" she asked. "Where are all the Knight Mages who slay dragons and *yearn* for women?"

"I think Blake is experiencing yearning," I pointed out as I grabbed her arm. She gave me a grateful smile and leaned against me for warmth.

Squire nodded. "Yearns for me?"

"Sure," I said.

"Yay!" Squire hooted.

Aurora playfully punched my arm. "No, I need a man who will *burn the world to the ground* with their physical prowess, murdering everyone, just so they can worship at my feet. They'll pine longingly for months, following me around, begging, doing anything to curry my favor."

She smiled dreamily.

"That sounds like stalking," I said. "And if a man did that to you, I'd kill him. For your own safety."

She winked, nudging me. "But what if someone did it for you? You're also dangerous. It would be . . ." She put her hands together and mimed an explosion.

"Disturbing," I said.

"Hot." She blew me a kiss.

I blew her one back. "I would *stab* this fictional man so many times he'd be begging for death as he bled out across my lap and—"

"Uh, never mind." She laughed. "Speaking of horrors, did you hear just last week the four Adams brothers went outside the walls on a dare and they were *all* killed by a dire bear? I swear, we're suffering from a masculinity crisis. Did you hear they were—"

"I heard."

I'd found their severed pieces and hauled them back inside the gate for the funeral pyre.

"Well then, let's discuss something positive," Aurora said, resting her head against me with a contented sigh. "The new wool lining technique we've been perfecting makes gloves extra-warm."

"I'll top that. I discovered a new snowboarding trail."

Aurora laughed. "That doesn't beat my obsessions. Have you seen the new wool shirts that are super thin and—"

BLARE.

We stopped. "Another magic storm?" Aurora asked. "Why do they keep targeting us—"

BLARE—BLARE—BLARE.

"DIRECT INVASION," Manto, the head council member, bellowed. His words traveled on the wind, loud and haunting through the Commune.

Aurora and I turned to each other in slow motion as chaos exploded. People screamed to their neighbors and stopped what they were doing. Parents picked up their young children and ran inside. Doors slammed shut. Locks clicked.

I grabbed Aurora's arm and sprinted, dragging her with me, running as fast as possible. My hackles rose when we got to my street.

Icicles the size of people hung off lampposts and porches, glittering with lines of silver. *A magical blizzard.* I searched the horizon, but unlike during the Great Siege of the North, there were no dragons, no roars, no flames. The sky above churned with dark clouds, but no sleet fell.

Has a Royal Mage somehow already attacked?

"Mom!" I screamed as I ran up the steps to our home, throwing myself inside.

Silence.

The central hearth glowed dark red with dying embers, my snowboard sat untouched beside it, and the chessboard on the end table was set up for tonight's game.

"Mom?"

I searched every room, rushed upstairs, but the house was empty.

"Mrs. Ravenal . . . ?" Aurora called out downstairs, her voice trailing off with confusion.

A neighbor would know. I sprinted out to the street and up the slippery steps to the house beside ours. I raised my fist to—

The door flung open, ice shattering. "Zora—they took . . . they took . . ." Mrs. Sheridan trailed off helplessly, tears spilling down her red face as she struggled to breathe. "They took your mother."

Aurora gasped behind me.

In slow motion, I grabbed Mrs. Sheridan by the front of her cape and shook her with all my might. "Who took her?"

She sobbed. "They were on horseback and—"

"*Who?*" I shook her harder. She coughed, hanging her head uselessly. I shoved her back, slamming her roughly against the door. "*Tell* me."

"Two . . . Royal M-Mages," she whispered.

I backed away, and she collapsed. After running back home and racing up the stairs to my bedroom, I donned my thickest layers and grabbed my goggles and bone daggers.

"You can't go out there." Aurora blocked me and Squire, her arms wide across the doorway. "The ice will kill you. Zora, you can't go out and . . ." She hyperventilated and reached for me. "Don't go!"

I shook my head. "There are *no* circumstances where I don't go after my mother right now." I shoved past her, and she didn't fight, collapsing back against the doorframe as I ran down the stairs and out into the street.

Aurora's voice screamed behind me, "*I love you! Be safe!*"

"Love you too," I whispered, disappearing through the gate in the Commune wall. Heading deep into the forest, I passed the mystifying spot where a single rose bloomed, edged with frost.

Mrs. Sheridan had said they'd taken Mom on horseback, but no true Northerner would ever ride them into the woods. One wrong step and you'd pitch straight into a tree well—never to be seen again. We mostly rode them within the Commune walls.

There was only one path they could've taken: the riverbank. I followed the river east, passing the creaking bridge where I'd had my first kiss and then broken the nose of the future Emperor. *Possibly my best work.*

I kept going, deeper into the wild.

In the river, branches were piled high into the sky, blocking most of the water's flow, creating a wide pond that protruded off to the left. Smoke billowed out the top of the structure through a natural vent. *Dire beavers.* They were as large as people, and I'd stumbled upon many of their engineering feats. I never hunted them, and they didn't bother me. We had different roles to play in this forest.

Hunching low, fighting through intensifying sleet, I continued forward as my fingers and toes went numb.

There were no shortcuts in survival.

ROAR. In the gray clouds, there was a snapping *whoosh* sound. Silver scales glinted. *Pestilence?* The dragon disappeared into the storm.

Why is he heading in the same direction? Why is he here?

Heartbeat pounding in my ears, I continued onward.

Hours later, a faint object shimmered dark on the horizon.

I dropped onto my belly, falling deep into the fresh snow, face down, as I held my breath. Snow burned against tiny slivers of exposed skin. Slowly I lifted my head, goggles half above the frozen line. Squire poked his feathery head out of my scarf to also look. Mist drifted around my face.

Shadows moved along the white riverbank. *A dire horse?*

I stayed as low as possible, belly-crawling into the forest and creeping quietly through the trees. Up ahead, a black dire horse traversed the bank and a person rode, draped in a familiar, expensive white fur cloak. A second person stalked beside the steed with something large draped over their shoulder.

I moved closer.

The one riding the steed, rocking perilously like they weren't used to a saddle, wore a full golden mask.

The Emperor.

Beneath him, the man leading the horse turned his head toward the trees. He wore a partial platinum mask and had a spider tattooed on his jaw.

Tarantula.

More imposing than I remembered, his height and musculature were staggering. His hair was also curlier and more golden than I recalled, the strands glowing like expensive honey in the streaks of sunlight that broke through the clouds.

Tarantula's bundle moved.

Slung over his wide shoulder like a sack of ice was a woman wrapped in furs. She lifted her head, and her strangled screams were muffled, distorted by a gag. *Mom.* I stifled a gasp.

Shaking with rage, I crouched lower.

Closer.

I pulled back my right arm, bone knife gleaming.

Rule of survival: To beat a predator, you must play its game.

I burst out of the tree line and flung my dagger.

Tarantula snapped his head around. *Crack-crack-crack.* A dozen icicles snapped off tree branches, magic pulling them up and around his shoulders. They pointed directly at me, sharpened ends twirling. I raised my arms up, shielding Squire.

The attack didn't come.

Instead, Aleksander slumped low in his saddle. My bone hilt protruded from the base of his neck. His vertebrae: severed.

That was too easy.

Apprehension built.

Aleksander toppled off his mount, limbs splaying as he hit the ground with a sickening crunch. The dire horse neighed as it bucked and kicked. A head rolled across the snow.

"Oh no," Squire hooted quietly. Mom yelled on Tarantula's shoulder, the sound muffled behind the gag.

It wasn't Aleksander.

A woman stared up at me.

The golden Royal Mage mask rolled off like it had never been affixed properly. Time stopped. Blond hair spilled out, the ends dyed bright pink. Pretty green eyes were frozen wide, blue lips open in a silent scream as a thick chunk of ice protruded from her mouth. She'd already been dead.

No.

Please . . . no.

Aurora.

White-hot relief filled my chest that they'd chosen her and

not Mom. Then a wave of anguish nearly brought me to my knees. *She didn't hear me say "I love you."* Hot tears streamed down my face, freezing painfully as I choked on uncontrollable sobs that exploded without thought. *I never got to say goodbye.*

Leaning over, I threw up violently.

Ice daggers hovered, spinning in a silver haze around Tarantula as he tilted his head to the side, watching me with confusion. Unidentifiable emotions flashed across his eyes. His rows of earrings clattered together.

Everything slowed as I comprehended their depraved deceit, starting back with Mrs. Sheridan. Tarantula had kidnapped Mom, knowing I would come after her, and Aleksander had stayed back with Pestilence, waiting until I left, to steal Aurora.

A setup.

Psychological warfare.

Squire panicked, shrieking as Tarantula took a step toward me, [illegible]les spinning lazily with magic. He opened and closed his mouth like he wanted to say something but couldn't find the words.

Rule of survival: When bested, change the terrain.

Turning, I sprinted deep into the cover of the forest. The trees were my only protection from his magical weapons. *They will not win.* They already had because Aurora was dead. *No, they haven't.* Mom still lived. I'd misjudged the parameters of the game we were playing.

There were no rules.

"Wait," Tarantula called out with a dark rasp as he followed me into the forest.

"*Murderer,*" I screamed, voice catching on sobs.

I glanced back at him through the tears. Ice hovered around his shoulders, glittering silver.

Grief sharpened into rage as tree branches smacked my face. Squire screeched where he balanced precariously on my shoulder.

Tarantula's stalking you.

Kill him first.

Long, awful minutes stretched as he followed after me while he held Mom hostage over his shoulder. His boots crunched against ice, and the biting scent of his magic filled the forest. He wasn't even trying to be quiet.

I ran faster.

He followed, gaining.

Squire cawed with terror.

"Fly away," I begged him.

"Me can't." Squire trembled as he pressed close, his voice small with fear.

That's it.

I was no creature's prey, let alone this man's.

Turning, I dug my numb fingers into my holster. The forest stilled. Tarantula approached, only a few paces away. He'd gained significant ground and oozed controlled satisfaction. Metallic magic glowed around him in a blinding haze.

No one man should ever wield this much storm magic.

I ran straight toward Tarantula, flinging my dagger. Squire screeched. A thick chunk of bark ripped off a tree and flew in front of Tarantula's neck, blocking my dagger, which sank uselessly into the snow.

But I'd already leaped.

Arms outstretched, legs straight behind me, I slammed into Tarantula's legs. He groaned with . . . pleasure? *I must have imagined it.* Mom screamed behind her gag as he dropped her, grunting in surprise as we plowed down onto the forest floor, rolling. Wings flapped violently. "Me a pacifist," Squire screeched (unhelpful).

Fists and knees flew in a white blur as we tumbled through the trees.

I stabbed down with another dagger, *for Aurora*, clipping Tarantula's thigh. Blood splattered. Long fingers wrapped around my throat, slamming my head back against a tree trunk. His fingers spasmed as he shuddered, inhaling loudly. Squire fluttered away, rising to the treetops.

Tarantula tried to straddle me, but I still had my knife, swiping. I stabbed, clipping both his arms as he bellowed and released my neck.

Dark maroon sprayed between us.

He stared down at me, chest heaving.

Magic replaced where his hands had squeezed, stealing my breath as I threw myself at him. I didn't need to breathe. I had rage.

He grabbed my dagger hand, twisting my arm behind my back, yanking me to my feet. I screeched, kicking and bucking. He roughly pried the weapon out of my fingers. I flinched, waiting for the blow. He threw my knife to the side, and it shattered against a tree trunk.

With his grip tight on my wrist, and my arm still wrenched at an unnatural angle, he stepped close into my personal space. His chest pressed against mine as he bit down on his full lower lip.

His platinum mask reflected my bloody tears. Flames of magic steamed off his head. Looming over me with his deranged size, he pulled my wrist down farther, arching my back at an awful angle.

"Tell . . . Aleksander," I said through gritted teeth. "Zora said . . . kill . . . himself."

"Do not worry yourself," Tarantula said quietly, his foreign accent straight from my nightmares. "Thou will get to deliver that message in the flesh."

My heart stopped.

"What—"

"He commanded me to tell thee . . ." Tarantula leaned closer as his other hand cupped the back of my neck. "This is his warning. If thou keep hiding behind walls in the North . . . he will take your mother from thee." Spider legs flexed on his jaw. "Do *not* try to deceive him. The Crimson Army's no quarter will not protect her. After all, she's too old to enlist."

"I'm not hiding," I said automatically.

"Leave the North," he ordered. "Leave her behind, and he *promises* he won't harm her."

"And where would I go?"

"*Anywhere* else."

"Why?"

"He did not say."

"Why would I trust his word?"

"It is all thou have."

I swallowed a scream of frustration. "Tell Aleksander . . ."

He waited for me to finish, leaning closer to hear better. I slammed my knee between his legs.

He swore and shifted, but I'd expected it and stomped my boot down on the top of his foot. He shouted, his grip loosening for a split second. I unsheathed a dagger with my left hand and stabbed.

We both stared down at the hilt protruding from the middle of his stomach. Tarantula took a step forward, lunging for me, but I'd already backed out of his range. He staggered, tripped, and leaned against a tree trunk as he heaved, staring at me, his blood melting the snow.

"Tell Aleksander I admire his royal picture." I tapped my nose. "His face looks *great* . . . Love the asymmetry. Now his outside matches his inside—*hideous*."

Icicles trembled as magic gusted. They broke from a tree branch, hovering dangerously in the air, but then they fell, shattering at his feet. His magic failed him. "Aleksander shall make thee *suffer* for this," Tarantula groaned, sliding down the tree and collapsing.

"No—he won't. Because I'll make him suffer first." I kicked him in the side with all my strength, needing to *hurt* him for Aurora. His head lolled, and he didn't even grunt in pain.

I screamed with frustration, turning in a circle, his threat ringing in my ears. Hopeless, tears still streaking down my face, I didn't know what to do.

A muffled sound echoed.

"Mom," I said as I turned and fell to my knees beside her. I cut apart the rope that tied the furs around her, then pulled down her gag, running my hands everywhere. Miraculously she appeared unharmed.

"Zora, baby," she whispered hoarsely as she coughed and reached for my face with a trembling glove. "Aurora."

"I know." My voice cracked as I pulled off my outer cloak and draped it around her shoulders, not listening to her protests. Quiet descended as the wind died. Sparkles drifted through the air. The magical ice storm had ceased like it never existed.

A twisted nightmare.

Tarantula sat slumped over, unconscious with pieces of snow drifting around him like glitter. Instincts screamed at me to grab Mom and run as far away from him as possible, but I hadn't survived this long by listening to fear. My thoughts raced. His capture could be useful to me, but I wanted his death more.

Creeping over, I unsheathed a dagger from my boot and studied his messy blond curls streaked with strands of gold.

I yanked his head up by his hair. His scarf unraveled. *What in the knighthood?* His neck was covered in an overlapping cicatrix of jagged scars.

He'd been mutilated.

Awareness dawned. I pulled him up higher, exposing his protruding Adam's apple. Up close, the incredibly detailed spider tattoo appeared to crawl across his jaw. With steady fingers, I pried off the top of his mask, which was practically welded to his face. *Royal creed be damned.* Finally it pulled away.

He had a crooked nose; a wide, angular jaw; razor-sharp cheekbones; full crimson lips; sunken eyes ringed in dark purple circles; and golden eyebrows, arched elegantly.

Curse it all.

Bark dug into my palm as I gripped a tree, holding myself

upright. Everything was so much worse than I'd originally thought. Leaning closer as if hypnotized, I inhaled his awful, deadly scent.

The face staring up at me looked similar to Aleksander's on the bridge, but it was so different at the same time. A much more *manly*, attractive version lay before me. Tarantula was rumored to be the Emperor's cousin.

The strongest of the elite Royal Mages were thought to be related, some families more powerful than others, but it was unclear how many Royal Mages the Empire had. Some estimated only a handful, since no more than two or three ever attacked at the same time; others hypothesized there were *hundreds* of them, but only the strongest warriors, related to the Emperor, battled in the Storm Wars.

Sharing the same bone structure and uniquely colored eyes, Tarantula and Aleksander were definitely cousins, maybe even brothers. *What strange, deceptive games they play.* Trying not to throw up from the intensity of sudden understanding, I pressed the mask back onto his face. His machinations were obscene.

I brought my knife up to an old ridge in the middle of his neck, choosing the best angle. *Enough is enough.* Time to end it all.

Beneath my hand, Tarantula's chest rose and fell, his heart beating strong, even though my other dagger was still buried deep in his gut. Royal Mages were notoriously hard to kill, but "heads will fall" was a popular saying because decapitation worked.

The blade cut through the top layer of skin like butter.

He deserved to die.

For Aurora.

It was just a throat, the same as a dire fox's, and all I had to do was push my blade clean through. *A little deeper.* I'd sever his windpipe, hack through the spinal cord. I'd done it countless times before, and it was practically muscle memory. *For her.* I pushed my dagger deeper, rage an endless static in my head.

My hand shook.

"Please don't do this," Mom begged. "You're not like them."

Tarantula was less honorable than the most rabid dire coyote and more monstrous than any growling dire bear. Ending him would be a service to all Antichthon. My facial scars tingled.

"Kill him, Zora," I whispered, tensing every muscle as I began to—

I shoved the unconscious body.

Swearing, I kicked snow and stumbled away. Heaving with desperation, I hung my head, clutching my pounding temples.

"Zora?" Mom said hesitantly as I gasped louder, fighting through a surge of raw panic.

"I can't . . . kill him." My voice cracked. The only friend I'd ever had was dead by his hand. I was a monster for not ending a monster, but doing so would surely make me into one.

Right. *Right?*

Mom shook her head. "You're *brave*, Zora. You have the heart of a dire lion. There is fierceness in justice, humanity, and kindness. You are not cruel like them . . . You are stronger."

Then why do I feel so weak?

Mom was too kind for her own good, and my inclinations were violent. One of us chased peace, and the other adrenaline. The spectrum of womanhood: she worried about my safety, while I hunted to ensure hers. Now, because of me, we were both damned.

Wiping desperately at the tears that hadn't stopped falling since I'd discovered Aurora, I tried to stop the tremble in my hands.

"We'll take him as a hostage," I whispered miserably, slightly mollified that I could still torture him.

A few minutes later, with blood and tears frozen across my face, Squire balanced on top of my head as I yanked Tarantula's heavy arms behind his wide back. I tied them together with the rope he'd used to secure the furs.

Grunting, I slowly dragged him by the feet out of the woods. The black dire horse stood at the edge of the rushing river, waiting. Panting, I positioned Tarantula with his back slung across the horse's wide flank, the hilt of my dagger protruding up from his stomach.

Gathering piles of snow, I packed them over Aurora, hiding her from the animals, while Mom sang one of the old god's hymns:

"Up the Mountain Ravine we travel,
Our souls drawn to the wondrous view,
But the rocks are jagged, not gravel,
And our bodies will fall, into the blue."

Squire chirped mournfully while I fell to my knees, head bowed, hands clasped with tears frozen on my cheeks. Mom laid her hand on my shaking shoulder, muttering prayers no one used anymore. She was the only person I'd ever met who believed the old god had not abandoned us, despite all evidence to the contrary.

The wind picked up, sharp and biting. We needed to get out of here before Pestilence came back from wherever he'd disappeared to. Mom insisted I take the saddle, but I wouldn't hear of it.

The entire way back to the Commune, I wondered why I couldn't kill a man who deserved to die, and I wondered if Aurora would ever forgive me.

When we finally got back and delivered Tarantula to the council, Manto was *ecstatic.* He insisted on immediately documenting the capture. Despite my protests and worry for Mom, he ushered me into the master painter's office, which was how I found myself posing while woozy with grief.

Marge battled the canvas with her brush as I kneeled on one leg, holding Tarantula's torso up by his tangled curls, my bicep straining. His platinum earrings clattered together as I bore his dead weight like a prize, dagger still protruding from his stomach.

There was no duty of care for the damned, but I wasn't sure which of us was worse off. I was gutted to the soul.

The rumor that Royal Mages were more difficult to kill than normal people was true, because Tarantula should have been dead from blood loss, but every time I touched his pulse, it beat strong beneath his feverish skin.

He was a corpse. He was a god. *A corpse of a god?* Iron flooded my mouth as I bit down too hard on my tongue.

Squire rested peacefully, snoring on my straining shoulder as my muscles cramped with despair.

Marge gestured with her brush. "Lift him higher."

I yanked harder, curls coming out in my fist, still despairing over why I couldn't kill him. His existence was a stain on my hands. An awful, wounded sound wrenched from my throat, and Squire peeked an eye open as he wobbled, chirping with distress.

"It's done," Marge announced.

Thud. I threw Tarantula down onto the stone floor, wiped my hands off on my pant leg with utter disgust, and spit on him. My mucus was bloody.

Numbly I headed back to Manto's office on stiff legs. I needed to arrange protection for Mom because the Emperor's threat was clear—I had to leave the North. Manto would have to find a new hunter.

They will not win.

I was now old enough to serve in the military; I'd reached the socially proper age to die, violently, for the Commonwealth. *Lucky damned girl.* Hurting one man wasn't enough for me, not anymore. I needed to scream while kneeling amid the ashes of the fallen Draconis Empire.

It was time to head south and join the Crimson Army.

Rule of survival: Fight.

10

Stage of Grief: Depression

Present Day
Location: Scorpion Hole Military Base

Hours after I jumped from the helicopter, Aurora's death played on repeat inside my head. Even worse, my mouth still tingled from where Tarantula had kissed me while we fell through the air.

He'd just walked away like it meant nothing to him. *It means nothing to me too, obviously.*

Spread across the low cushions that formed a small couch in the corner of the twins' room, I rested with my head on Ella's lap. She combed her fingers through my hair, running them soothingly across the new bandage on my forehead.

After the jump, during training, the Marshal had thrown a dozen glasses of water at me. I'd used my magic and diverted eleven of them. The twelfth had shattered against my head.

Shadows elongated in the golden sunset. Axel sharpened a shank on his bed with a pocketknife. Squire waddled across the room, his talons clacking as he peered into spaces, investigating.

For the past hour, we'd talked about the Iron Ritual, all three of us sharing theories about whose blood they'd poured into us, but we couldn't come up with anything that made sense.

"Why did you both have to do the Iron Ritual?" I blurted. The question had been bothering me a lot lately.

Axel's eyes went flat, no light in their depths. "Another recruit subjected Ella to his unwanted . . . amorous attention."

She tensed beneath me, her nails digging into my scalp, and my stomach turned over.

Axel spun his pocketknife. "So I disemboweled him."

"And I slit his throat," Ella whispered.

They stared at me, waiting for my reaction. A dark tension filled the room—*abuse and abusive consequences.*

"Good," I said. "I'm glad he suffered." Dark satisfaction blossomed as I imagined devouring those who dared to violate others. Satisfaction quickly bled away, curdling into shame. *Could I have disemboweled him in that moment?* My capacity for violence was conditional, but I couldn't articulate the parameters. Not even to myself.

In my mind, I could slit a man from throat to navel as easy as a dire elk, but in reality, my blade would probably shake—my conviction wavering. Murder was easier in theory. The twins were stronger than me.

Exhaling in unison, they shared a conspiratorial look. Ella resumed combing through my hair, and Axel bared his fangs, grinning. The conversation turned. I showed them the scars on my back. Ella revealed a jagged wound on her hip. Her leg had almost ripped off on landing the first time she jumped from a helicopter.

Axel stopped sharpening his shank and pulled down the neck of his exercise shirt. Two perfectly circular white divots stood out against his tan collarbone. "Vampire bite."

"Really?" My jaw dropped as I thought about the fairy tales Mom loved to share.

Axel's voice dropped an octave as he leaned forward conspiratorially. "We were just ten years old, playing in the caves beside our Commune, and a *stunning* woman emerged from the darkness.

She grabbed my face, her white-blond hair and light gray eyes sparkling in the dark. Then . . ." He slapped the bed. "She *bit* me, faster than a viper. As I lay on the ground, head spinning from blood loss, she attacked my precious Ella. We were both incapacitated for weeks and just barely survived."

Squire squawked with terror.

"That's how I got these." Axel bared his fangs again.

Deeply unsettled, I wiped my clammy palms across my thighs, trying to find my voice.

"Oh please, stop lying." Ella sighed loudly. "He filed them himself. I woke up in the cave to a dire viper slithering away and no memory of *any* attack."

"Ella!" Axel shouted with betrayal. "I know what I saw."

Ella shook her head. "He's prone to bouts of exaggeration and overimagination."

I laughed, weak with relief.

"No, I'm not," Axel argued, pouting with his arms crossed. He acted petulant and childish, but the sharp glint of intelligence didn't leave his gaze. *He's not what he seems.* But neither was I.

Ella slowly braided a section of my hair, and I focused on her calming presence. We were the same, but different. Her thighs were soft beneath my cheek, and she smelled like roses mixed with everything good in the world.

"Here's another funny story," Ella offered. "Pa made us eat a cup of sand once. Our stomachs hurt for *days*. I'd never seen him so mad."

Axel pointed at us and made a grumpy face, imitating an older man scolding children. "You listened to me, kids—that was your first error, and your second was swallowing the grit. Two snake bites and you're dead. The desert doesn't suffer idiots. It chews them up and spits them out."

"Then he told us to eat *another* cup of sand to atone for eating the first one," Ella said with a laugh as she brushed out another section and started braiding, lost in memory.

I lifted my head, confused. "So you ate *more* sand?"

Midlanders had a strange energy. They were true desert folk, molded by their empty land. We called the North barren, but the Middlelands was nothing but bizarre creatures, endless dunes, and punishing heat.

Axel grinned lazily, showing off his hand-sharpened canines. "Oh, I did, but Ella didn't. He refused to feed me for the next week . . . Not that I could eat, mind you, because of the intestinal pain. He said I was dumber than a roadrunner mating with a dire scorpion, and he was right."

"Pa was crazy," Ella said with fondness.

"I don't think I would have eaten it," I said. "Even the first time. Even if Mom had told me to."

Axel nodded. "Pa said it made sense. Boys pretend otherwise, but we all secretly like being told what to do. Girls are *far* more complicated."

Does Tarantula want me to tell him what to do? My stomach twisted, and for some reason, I couldn't get that strange thought out of my head. *Or do I want him to tell me what to do? Don't go there, Zora.*

Was it warm in here?

My mind wandered.

He would look good on his knees.

Pleading with me for mercy.

Naked.

Ella sighed loudly, lost in nostalgia, and Axel sharpened his shank while I battled deviant ruminations. Heat scorched across my chest, and a flush burned my cheeks.

Could he make me beg? Do I want to be under him or on top?

Eager to change the topic, I asked Ella what it was like being in a fighter jet and ejecting out of the cockpit. She described it as terrifying, the force of gravity pinning you back to your seat and then a horrible falling sensation as you tumbled through the air.

It sounded divine.

Someday I hope to fly.

"Here," I said, sitting up, needing to clear my head. "Let's change places. I'll braid yours now." Ella eagerly lay down and positioned her head on my lap. I sectioned off her waves and braided them tightly. "So, what do you do for fun?"

"I like to sketch," she said. "The quiet calm of drawing for hours grounds me. What about you?"

"Snowboarding, as *fast* as possible down the side of a mountain."

Ella grimaced. "I hate heights. I've gotten better at it, but it's awful every time we go up in the helicopters."

"No." I shook my head. "It's *exhilarating.* Flipping through the air . . . free."

She looked skeptical.

Axel arched an eyebrow. "Have you heard of dune surfing? You'd probably like it, but you wouldn't be as good as me at it, obviously."

Ella and I rolled our eyes.

"I also prefer hooking up with people," Axel continued. "There's this soldier named Kane. Highly disappointing bedroom performance. Stay clear."

I gasped. "That's the idiot I saved from the scorpion . . . You *hooked up* with him?"

"It was not good." Axel grimaced. "I cannot emphasize that enough. Whatever you're imagining . . . worse."

"Ew," Ella said.

I shook my head. "I don't want to know."

"Now, medic Sara, on the other hand." Axel kissed his fingers. "But I also love composing music. Thanks for asking about *my* hobbies, Zora. I really appreciate it."

"No problem," I said back sarcastically, matching his tone, still trying desperately not to think about Kane naked.

Eyes cold, smile mischievous, Axel pulled a small wooden instrument out from under his bed. He plucked a string. "It's a fiddle. You're welcome."

"You're welcome" for what?

He jumped off the bed, scissor-kicking, and landed on his knees in front of us. "Are you ready?"

"Me ready!" Squire hooted and flew over, landing on Axel's head.

"Uh—no?" I said.

Ella shook her head. "Please, not again."

"Too bad!" Axel shouted. "Hello, Scorpion Hole, thank you for coming out tonight!" He bobbed his head, and Squire held on to his hair for dear life. Baring his fangs, Axel sang in a deep, theatrical voice:

"Antichthon had two lands,
Oh, Westmere and Azote.
One Communes and sands,
The other castle with moat."

"Now the chorus!" Axel put down his fiddle and rose to his feet, swaying with his head tipped back.

"Modern-medieval times, how you test us all.
Battered and battling, you break us down,
Land of the poor versus the land of the crown.
Modern-medieval times, how you watch us fall,
From the helicopter, straight to the ground."

Axel swiped up his fiddle and strummed, head down as he angstily crooned in an even deeper baritone:

"Knights stop magic to save,
But Royals wield storms that kill.
These dark times birthed a knave.
A spidery bastard of iron will,
Oh, Tarantula, how you vex me, honey.

Sexy and cruel, you play me still.
Your smirk is richer than any money.
Your body so hard, like a pickle, dill."

"Now you sing the chorus," Axel drawled as he pointed at us, waiting.

Ella looked at me for help, and I shrugged. "I don't remember," I whispered to her. "I didn't know there'd be a test on it."

Axel shook his head at us with disappointment, his merry energy contrasting with the harsh look in his eyes as he sang in a low pitch:

"Modern-medieval times, how you test us all.
Battered and battling, you break us down,
Land of the poor versus the land of the crown.
Modern-medieval times, how you make us bawl.
Burning up in dragon flames, broken, we crawl."

Axel took a deep bow and smirked. "You're both welcome."

"No one said thank you," I pointed out.

His eyes flashed. "Exactly. You're both extremely ungrateful for the *charm* I bring to this miserable base."

Ella stood up and pulled me to my feet, ignoring her brother completely. "Let's go to dinner." We tried to leave quickly. Unfortunately, Axel, with Squire still on his head, followed closely behind us, humming.

Our usual chairs were set up at the dining table in our wing. Today an extensive spread of dire scorpion meat, beans, bread, and vegetables was already waiting for us.

I took large helpings of everything but the scorpion. I'd never been comfortable with eating animals I hadn't killed myself, because something about it felt intrinsically *wrong*.

The twins sat in the two chairs across from me like usual, and they dug in without reservation. Thankfully Axel forgot his fiddle on the floor. Leaning back in my chair, with a singing Squire now balanced on my head, I tried to breathe slowly through my mouth.

The door slammed open.

Tarantula stalked into the room, prisoner chains glinting.

"Where have you been all afternoon?" I asked, trying to act casual, like he hadn't kissed me right before I tried to murder him.

"Hi, spider slut!" Squire chirped (helpful).

Tarantula rolled his eyes. "Greetings, minuscule bird."

His curls were slicked back, a single lock hanging over his forehead. The zipper of his suit was still pulled down lower than respectable. He prowled silently around the table.

"Where were you?" I repeated.

His eyebrow arched. He pulled back the only free chair with a harsh squeak and gracefully sat down beside me. Posture rigid, shoulders and head pulled back, he even sat pompously.

"Answer me." I slammed my fist down on the tabletop, plates and glasses rattling.

He leveled me with a hateful glare. "I owe thee *nothing*, Ravenal."

"I thought you were my partner. Aren't we supposed to be working together?"

"Thou failed to pull my chute."

"What did you want me to do? Save you? You killed Aurora."

He tensed.

"You *murdered* her in cold blood," I continued. "Did you think it would make me like you? Ruining my life and taking her away—"

"*Silence*, Ravenal!" He pounded his fist on the table.

The twins startled, and a fork clattered to the floor. "Don't speak to her like that," Ella said, regaining her composure first. Axel bared his fangs.

"Thank you, Ella," I said calmly. "But please, stay out of this. He's *my* partner to handle."

Tarantula breathed out roughly. "Thou. Have. No. Power.

Over. Me." He bit out each word, his accent distorting the hard consonants.

I reached for the dial lying on the table, but his arm shot out in a blur, too fast to track. He pointed his metal fork at my neck before I could grab the device. The dull utensil hovered a hair's breadth away from my skin.

"I *dare* thee to try it," he taunted quietly. "We can both play murder—if that is what thou want." His cold smile said he'd stab me with the fork and happily cause grievous bodily harm.

I stared longingly at the dial.

He pressed his fork tines into the side of my neck—not hard enough to break the skin, but enough pressure that I froze with alarm. *Primordial panic.* Slowly I reached for my fork and jammed it against the top of his fabric-covered thigh. He grunted, and his fork scraped down my flesh.

The twins looked back and forth between us, matching expressions of concern on their faces.

"Don't worry." I cleared my throat. "I have him *handled.*"

Pain pricked as he pushed his fork deeper, and the old bite mark on my throat tingled.

"You should eat the food—not each other," Axel said with a lazy drawl. "But I understand how you might be feeling right now, Zora . . ." He winked at me and whispered dramatically, "About his . . . *pickle.*"

"Dill!" Squire hooted, remembering the lyrics (extremely unhelpful).

A flush traveled up Tarantula's neck, all the way to his ears, and we pulled our forks away from each other at the same time.

"I would never *eat* the likes of him," I said to Axel, not sure why my voice was so husky.

Tarantula bit down on the crimson pillow of his full lower lip. "Speak for yourself," he muttered.

"What?" I wasn't sure what was happening anymore. My heart was pounding in my throat, and my thighs were pressing together.

"I would eat *thee* . . . out."

My chair squeaked as I jolted.

Tarantula's heavy-lidded gaze shifted, ice turning molten, as he radiated cruel satisfaction. "Thou should be very afraid, Ravenal. The depth of what I desire is . . . untenable."

I arranged my fork neatly beside my plate, then chugged water greedily. The cool liquid soothed my ragged throat.

Axel narrowed his eyes. "What did he just say?" he asked Ella under his breath.

"He wants to *eat* her," she whispered back.

My knees knocked painfully against the table.

The twins turned their heads in sync, studying the two of us like we were scientific specimens. I drank faster, needing to quench the endless fire. Water spilled down my chin and across my throat. Hastily I wiped it away. Flushing with embarrassment, I felt like a fool. Bracing myself, I waited for a sneering comment about my lack of decorum.

Tarantula held himself still, chest heaving, like my affliction was contagious.

Ella covered her mouth as she tried to hide her laughter.

Axel smirked. "Oh, how you *vex* me, honey," he sang sarcastically, eyes flat.

"How stupendous," Tarantula drawled, matching Axel's scornful energy, but his gaze kept shifting back to me. "We have a jester. Art thou also the Groom of the Stool? I do love fresh towels and a helping hand for . . . other inconveniences."

"No." Axel bared his fangs. "I do not serve any man. I make art because it's my passion." He sang, "Sexy and cruel, you play me still, your body so hard, like a pickle . . ."

Ella and I both shook our heads no.

Axel, who apparently wanted to die, smiled. "Dill."

A splotchy flush covered Tarantula's cheeks, scarlet spreading up beneath his mask as he stared at Axel with horror.

"Jester, do thou want to live?" Tarantula asked slowly, radiating quiet menace. "No bard has ever—"

"Wait, you *know* actual real-life bards?" I asked.

"Oooh, I'm so scared." Axel rolled his eyes as Ella struggled to breathe.

Tarantula frowned at me. "Do thou not have personal bards? Are they not common on Westmere?"

All three of us gaped at him, and even Ella stopped laughing.

Squire chirped, "Zora has Squire!"

I reached up and patted his head. "Very true, darling."

Tarantula's eyes narrowed, his face still flushed bright red as he tried not to look at any of us. "'Tis just a personal jester," he muttered. "'Tis not a big deal."

"You are genuinely the most out-of-touch person I've ever met," I said.

His lips curled down into a scowl. "Of course, one cannot compare riches with churls. Royalty is not aspirational for the impoverished—my mistake. I forgot."

"And yet," I snarled, "here you are at a classless peasant's mercy."

"Ah, that is where your error lies." His canines were too sharp for comfort. An awful trick of the light. "Thou art at *my* mercy, Ravenal. I am in the process of educating thee."

"There is nothing the likes of you could ever teach me." I picked up the dial, fingers cramping. "I'm in control here, bastard."

"Maybe with your pathetic past dalliances, but not with me, *brat*." His tone dropped an octave as he leaned closer, invading my personal space. "Thou will be beneath me when thou . . . climax."

I choked on air, my enraged brain taking a second to process the meaning. *Wait, he's not talking about . . .*

Ella gasped loudly. Apparently I hadn't heard him wrong.

"Wait—what did he just say?" Axel asked. "Curse it all. I missed it."

"Extra food servings and drinks," a soldier stated loudly as he entered the room, slicing through the mounting tension.

He replaced the empty bean bowl with another. Legumes were a food staple in the Middlelands, and I'd grown to love them.

The twins and I dug in eagerly. Training with the Marshal left me ravenous, and these days it felt like my stomach was a bottomless pit. I could never eat enough to feel full.

"I'll bring out a third course," the soldier said to me.

"Thanks." I smiled back through a mouthful of food.

The soldier jumped, tray shaking in his hands as Tarantula glowered at him.

Three wooden tankards were hastily placed in front of me and the twins. They were sealed and had tiny wooden straws that somehow were built into the body of the vessel. They must have poured the liquid in through the tiny straw opening. The twins immediately started sucking down the contents, sighing with relief as they noisily gulped.

"What is it?" I asked the soldier.

"Special medical liquid for Mages. Enough time has passed since the Iron Ritual that your body can now digest it," he said. "It helps strengthen your magic and is specially formulated for—"

"Leave," Tarantula said. The soldier bowed and hurried away.

"That was rude," I said.

"Spidery man *very* rude," Squire agreed, lying belly up on top of my head. We both pretended one of his feathers wasn't hanging loose across my forehead.

I stared at the strange tankard, distrust rising. "Is it . . . good?"

Axel waved at me to drink, his eyes bright, cheeks filling with healthy color as he gulped. Steeling myself, I took a tiny sip and gasped. It tasted like sweet cherries, utterly delicious, but as soon as I took a deeper gulp, it soured. A horrible deathly aftertaste overwhelmed my taste buds. I gagged, covering my mouth with the back of my hand. *Rancid.* Whatever they'd given me had gone bad.

"What in the damned? That was disgusting."

Everyone stared at me. Even Squire leaned over my forehead, yellow eyes bright.

"What?" I asked.

Axel pushed his drink aside and grabbed mine, taking a long sip.

"It tastes delicious to me," he said with confusion, licking maroon off his lips.

"Like sweet cherries?" I asked.

"Yes," Ella said as she put down her empty tankard. "Do you not like it?" The juice stained her teeth as she spoke, and she licked it away.

"I did at first," I said. "But then it . . . soured, like it was spoiled."

Axel sucked down my drink noisily, shaking his head no.

"You're a Mage," I said to Tarantula accusingly. "Why don't you drink it?"

His eyes were wide behind his mask, and his lips were pressed into a straight line. He looked unsettled. "I also do not enjoy the taste," he whispered, as if perturbed by something grievous.

"So what—" I made air quotes "—'Mage juice' do *you* drink?"

He shook his head curtly. "I do not."

"Okay," I said. "Then I won't either. That settles it. I don't need to—"

"Drink, Ravenal." He cut me off, his tone more frightening than when I'd attempted to kill him via helicopter jump, or when he'd found out that I'd posed for a portrait with his unconscious stabbed body. *I have no regrets.*

Moving quicker than my eye could track, he reached across the table and grabbed the tankard from Axel's hand. He placed it in front of me. Axel looked sheepish, like he'd been caught doing something bad.

"Obey, Ravenal," Tarantula ordered. "Quench your thirst."

"Um, no. Why would I listen to—"

"DRINK, MY VASSAL!" he bellowed at the top of his lungs.

My braid whipped as gusts of silver wind exploded through the room. I picked up the half-full drink and chugged, gagging, struggling to get it down. When I finished, I paused, heaving for air, the empty tankard in my hands. I stared at it, then slowly looked up.

Tarantula's eyes were narrowed into slits.

"How dare you." I chucked it at him as hard as I could. His hand snapped up, and he caught it, a hair's breadth away from his face.

A long pause stretched.

He chucked the tankard back at me.

I ducked just in time. Wood exploded into shards against the wall behind me.

"You bastard, you almost hit Squire. *What* did you just do to me?"

"What do you mean, Zora?" Axel asked with sudden seriousness. "He didn't . . . do anything." Ella looked confused beside him. "He just yelled at you to drink, and you did."

I shook my head, looking down at the frost covering my skin. "No, the magic exploded from him. I felt it. I *saw* it."

"What are you talking about?" Axel looked disturbed. "We were here the entire time. There was no magic. We didn't see or feel . . . anything."

They looked worried.

I took a deep, steadying breath, nodding calmly. Shoving my chair back, I threw myself at Tarantula, fists flying. "Tell me what you did!" He grabbed my arms as we grappled, pinning them behind my back. I kicked his shin, and he smiled.

"Simmer down, Ravenal. Thou art embarrassing yourself, again," he said patronizingly, like he was talking to a child.

I spit onto his cheek.

He went dangerously still, breath hitching. Leaning closer, he brought his mouth to my ear. "Do that again," he said quietly. "I *dare* thee." Magic thickened around him.

"What are you—"

"Spit on me." He laughed with what sounded like genuine mirth as I froze. "Ah, I see. Do thou wish for *me* to do the spitting?

I shall oblige." His eyes hardened. "Stick out your tongue, Ravenal."

Excuse me?

I shoved him back, stumbling away while he stood rigid and heavy-lidded, swathed in satisfaction. *Or perhaps it's dissatisfaction?* Maliciousness took many forms, and he was impossible to read.

Shivering, cold to the bone, I backed away.

He cracked his neck loudly like he was preparing to fight, magic glowing as it gathered around his hands. Ella threw herself in front of me protectively, crossing her arms in a Shield. Axel stepped beside her.

Three versus one, the odds were not in our favor.

Hazy silver transmuted into flickering flames, gathering around Tarantula's skull as he glared at Axel like he was trying to incinerate him with his eyes. Magic acted strangely around Tarantula, clinging to his pores, darkening, *warping.*

"Step aside from *my* Ravenal, jester."

Axel scoffed. "No."

His Ravenal?

I pushed in front of the twins. "Hurt them," I said as I picked up the forgotten dial, regaining my wits, "and I won't stop until your skin melts from your bones."

Tensing, I waited for his retaliation.

His lashes fluttered, nostrils flaring. Vicious amusement flickered across his face. Long, painful seconds passed, and just when I thought he would strike, a coiled dire viper ready to explode, his shoulders relaxed.

"'Tis time for your evening training, Ravenal." His voice was clipped with cruel amusement. "Accompany me to the desert. Now."

The twins sighed with audible relief.

"All three of thee."

This time I wasn't the only one who swore.

11

Stage of Grief: Rage

"Halt my attack!" Tarantula shouted into the rapidly cooling night, his outstretched hand glowing in the darkness.

On the other side of a roaring bonfire, I stood beside the twins. Storm magic shot off Tarantula's palm, creating a flame thrower.

I gritted my teeth and mentally prepared for pain but held my stance.

Rule of survival: Never show your fear.

Heat licked at my face. At the last possible second, I flung myself backward away from it. The twins held their positions with their arms crossed in Shields, and the magical flames extinguished on contact with their forearms.

Tarantula put his glowing hand down, jawline sharp enough to slice, as his eyes flashed. I tried to remember the thud his body had made when he hit the sand, chute untouched. *Good times.*

The twins panted, dropping their Shields as they tried to catch their breath.

"Sufficient," Tarantula told Ella as she hunched over with her hands on her knees.

Tarantula turned rapidly, arm raised. Magic exploded, brighter than before, as he attacked an unsuspecting Axel. Straightening just in time, Axel made a Shield and flung the blast away. Sand exploded off in the distance as the fire was redirected.

"You missed," Axel taunted, sweat pouring down his face.

Tarantula sent more magic his way.

Axel tried to deflect it, but he was unable to throw aside the larger fiery blast; he bellowed as he held his forearms tighter to his chest, just barely nullifying the flames. Seconds bled into a long minute. Axel fell to his knees under the onslaught.

"STOP IT!" I screamed as I got back up to my feet.

Tarantula turned, directing a much smaller flame straight at me. I mimicked Axel's stance, legs spread wide, arms in a Shield, knowing it would do nothing. *Please, old god, protect me.*

My legs shook. Heat attacked me like an angry dire wolf, snapping at my neck, and I dropped to the ground, the end of my braid singed.

I rolled over and lay on the chilly sand, shivering as sweat dried across my limbs. A sea of stars twinkled above. My heart pounded painfully, existential exhaustion eating away at my tired bones.

The quest is impossible.

I can't do it.

Squire flew silently through the inky sky, wings spread wide as he enjoyed the coolness of the desert night. A tiny dire mouse struggled in his beak. He threw it up in the air and swallowed it whole. *Violence everywhere.*

"Again, Ravenal." Tarantula's voice cracked like a whip.

Lifting my head, neck aching, I observed the evil.

The bonfire danced between us, creating a shadowy silhouette. His eyes turned crimson, flames reflected in their glassy depths.

"On your feet. We're not stopping until thou get it."

I'll never get it. This is just torture.

No one is going to save me.

Not from this.

I hastily wiped at my eyes, trying to hide my tears. Logs shifted, crackling and popping; embers burst high into the night.

"Ravenal, on your feet!" He pointed his finger at me.

Save yourself. I scrambled back, flames just missing my bare toes. An hour ago, my boots had started to melt, and the sensation had been terrifying. I'd kicked them off.

The twins watched me with matching grimaces as I staggered upright beside them. All three of us raised our hands into Shields, but only one of us was pretending.

An hour later, I was missing half an eyebrow, the very tip of my nose was burned, and my feet were covered in blisters.

"We are done for tonight." Tarantula shot me a look of cold frustration. He stalked back toward the hangar.

Leaning against Ella, I limped beside her and Axel with Squire silent on my shoulder. What felt like forever later, we *finally* made it to my bedroom.

"Zora, are you okay?" Ella whispered with concern as I wiped at my eyes. Squire flew off my shoulder and tucked himself under the covers by my pillow.

I forced a smile. "Of course. I've had much worse. How are you feeling? You were impressive out there." A tiny dagger of jealousy stabbed me through the heart. Why couldn't I have been a Knight Mage like her? The Iron Ritual had cursed me.

Ella blushed at the praise, and I felt like the worst person who had ever lived. Axel exited the washroom holding a medical kit. His expression was solemn as he gestured for me to sit. He reached for the soles of my feet with paste on his fingers—

"Touch her, jester—" Tarantula appeared abruptly in the doorway "—and thou shall perish by my hand."

Axel's eyes went flat as he slowly turned toward Tarantula. "I told you . . . *not* to call me that."

Ella and I shared a look of concern.

"It's fine," I said as Ella grabbed Axel's arm and pulled him back. "I'll do it myself."

Axel smirked meanly. "No—I'm going to help you."

"I sense your impending demise, jester." Tarantula crossed his arms, leaning with deceptive casualness against the doorframe. He used his taller height to look down at Axel, who wasn't a short man.

Axel pulled away from Ella and stepped up to him. "*Loosen* up, spider." He smacked him on the arm, hard. Tarantula stared down at where Axel had touched him with narrowed eyes.

"Touch me again, bard . . . and I shall *remove* your fingernails, one by one." His voice had a wistful edge, like he'd done it before.

"I'm confused. Am I a jester or a bard?" Axel swayed his hips mockingly as he played an imaginary fiddle.

A gust of silver formed a noose around Axel's throat; he choked, face turning red.

Tarantula leaned closer and wrapped his long fingers around Axel's straining neck as the other man clawed hopelessly at his arms.

"Glad they're staying calm," I whispered.

Ella rolled her eyes. "*Men.* Do you want me to stay with you?" She glanced with concern at Tarantula.

"I'm fine, seriously. Go shower. You guys need to rest."

Axel fell to his knees, fury on his face. Tarantula loomed above him, magic pouring off his raised hand.

Ella looked down at her sweaty clothes, her hair sticking to her face, and nodded reluctantly. "Scream if you need anything. We're happy to hurt him." She shot Tarantula a blistering scowl as she forcefully ripped her brother from his grip and dragged him from the room.

Axel gasped loudly in the hall as Tarantula released his magical hold, and the twins' voices faded away.

Wincing, I grabbed the jar and smeared the paste onto my right foot. Tarantula stalked to my bed. He gently wrapped his long fingers around my ankle and extended my foot out of my reach.

"Hey, what in the damned are you—"

"Why do thou wave your ankle around for everyone to see?" He stared down at me with narrowed eyes, his touch burning hot. "Is it your goal in life to be looked upon in the *nude* by everyone?"

"Wait . . . what?" I felt as lost as Axel. "Are we talking about my nude . . . *ankle* right now . . . or something else?"

He inhaled loudly. "'Tis your ankle. It should not be exposed before all. Your flesh is far too precious."

"Calm down, princess. Don't let my ankle get you into a tizzy." I laughed at my own joke.

"Too late," he snarled, his thumb trailing over the top of my shin.

I choked.

With a cutting scowl, he dabbed the medicine onto the bottoms of both my feet and then carefully wrapped each one in thick bandages. He took *forever* tucking the ends until he nodded, finally satisfied that everything looked perfect.

I opened my mouth to thank him, and then I remembered *he* caused the damage in the first place. "Screw you, you weird ankle creep."

He dropped my foot like it burned him and stepped back, breathing far too loudly.

"No," he said as he climbed into his bed.

"No what?"

"Thou shan't *screw* me."

"It's just a figure of speech, princess."

He opened his mouth like he was going to say something, and magic whooshed out like fire. His jaw clicked shut. *Is he losing control of his power?* He made a frustrated sound and flipped over, giving me his back.

I did the same.

Time passed strangely.

"Why," I whispered into the night, unable to sleep, "do you keep calling me vassal?"

He didn't elaborate. Apparently my exposed ankle had finally rendered him speechless. Shadows stretched across the room as I tossed and turned restlessly, too exhausted to stay awake but too strung out to sleep.

When dawn approached, I raced Tarantula to the washroom, but my feet were injured, so he beat me. He smirked in the doorway, blocking my entrance.

Enraged after suffering a night in his silent, infuriating presence, I yanked the dial up. He gritted his teeth, glaring down at me as he held on to the doorframe.

Sparks sizzled as they leaped between us.

He bared his teeth, a vein protruding from the top of his forehead. His knees wobbled, but he withstood the electrocution; I watched him suffer, refusing to look away first.

Time stretched as neither of us backed down.

Blue Mist exploded up from the floor. *POP.* Metal sputtered. I tried to turn the dial, but nothing happened. The Mist had finally won.

Oh, this is not *good.*

Silence swelled.

Diamonds winked on the intact collar. *He's still contained.* Mostly. Probably? *Hopefully?*

I was royally doomed.

Tarantula's expression sharpened with triumph.

I tossed the useless dial away and backed up to my bed. I pulled the toothbrush shiv out from under my pillow and stalked back toward him, pointing the sharpened edge at his face.

"Try to hurt me and I'll gut you," I promised.

A mocking sound of disbelief escaped his lips, guttural and deeply depraved. My burned nose stung unmercifully as I accidentally wrinkled it.

"Thou art in *profound* peril," Tarantula said, his voice cold with delight.

"Anything else obvious you care to point out?" I asked, trying to hide my unease. "Or are we just stating facts? In that case, I'll go next. You're disgusting and weirdly obsessed with women's ankles."

His gaze shot down to my bandaged feet, and the tips of his ears turned pink.

"Misogynist," I spat.

He arched a golden eyebrow. "Says the *misandrist* . . . and I have nothing against women. Women are sacred and the only source of beauty in this cold world," he said poshly. "Any man who hates them merely hates himself."

"How positively unremarkable," I whispered, hating how I shivered at the intensity in his voice. "But you're correct, for once. I find most men disappointing, and you . . . *especially* so." I leveled my shiv at his masked face and then lowered it so it pointed at his crotch.

His eyes narrowed into slits as he stared down at the weapon.

"I used to think," I said slowly, "Chriztoph the Raving enslaving us all in the platinum mines made him the most loathsome person who ever existed. But congratulations—I think you're worse than him."

"Ah," he said. "My most illustrious ancestor. What a compliment. Every single wind in Antichthon trembles at his command. Thou could never understand what such power feels like." His voice brimmed with pride.

"*Was*," I corrected. "He's dead, just like you'll be."

"Art thou . . . sure about that?" He slowly licked his lips, staring at my weapon and adjusting the hardness growing between his legs.

Sick, cryptic bastard.

The tops of his cheeks turned bright red, and he casually placed his hands in his pockets, tenting out his pants to hide his inappropriately timed erection. *Too late.* He backed away and slammed the washroom door in my face.

"I despise you," I muttered under my breath.

"I can still hear thee."

"Good." Muttering expletives, I hobbled out of our room and down the hall on the sides of my feet, too stubborn not to go for my morning run. *No man will make me change how I live my life.*

In the hangar, I corrected course when I saw the Marshal. I shoved through Shadow Swords. They stiffened but moved aside as she gestured to let me pass, and then they fell back into position, blocking us from view of the rest of the base. Ryse caught my eyes, and I looked away.

"What do you want that can't wait until later?" the Marshal asked.

"I need a new shock collar," I whispered. "The Mist deactivated the electricity."

Her lips pursed, grooves deep around her eyes. "We'll work on another one. The diamonds and chains will be enough for now."

"It's not safe for me."

Her expression was unimpressed. "That's the point, soldier."

"Then I want to torture him more," I spat, thinking about the devices I'd read about in my favorite medieval poetry books. "Let me put him on the rack."

She blinked rapidly, genuine surprise on her face. For a second, I could see she was considering it. *Wait, does the Crimson Army actually have a torture rack?*

Her expression iced over. "No."

"What is the point of the military industrial complex if not to *torture* our enemies?" I whispered furiously under my breath.

She arched her eyebrow, scar pulling tight. "Are you getting enough sleep?"

I swallowed down a scream of frustration. "I *can't.* He's in my damned bedroom."

She rolled her eyes and stepped back dismissively. "Compose yourself. Master your Knight Mage powers," she said loudly for everyone else's benefit.

Curse you.

Shadow Swords brushed past me as she stalked away.

I swallowed another scream and went for a very short, agonizing morning run. *Highly therapeutic, and not at all a sign of madness.*

Later that day, my hands glowed bright silver, head throbbing as I raised a large stream of water out of a glass pitcher. I flicked my arm out. It drenched the Marshal.

Long seconds passed as she stared at me.

I flinched, waiting for her retaliation.

She grabbed a towel and calmly wiped her face. "Good," she said tonelessly. "Progress, finally. However, a puddle isn't going to defeat anyone. These sessions will be extended an extra hour daily. Until you're dangerous."

I blinked at her, exhaustion a crushing weight, not sure how I should feel.

"You're dismissed."

"Yes, sir."

A few minutes later, when I got back to my room, Tarantula gestured for me to immediately follow him out into the desert for training.

"Please," I whispered. "I can't right now. I'm too tired."

His colorless eyes narrowed as he studied my face. For a hopeful second, I thought he'd relent. I fantasized about melting in the heat of a scalding shower.

"Let's go," he said coldly. "My pardon is based on your mastery of magic." He stalked out the door.

I'm not following him. I moved toward the washroom but froze as I grabbed the handle.

"You're my best friend," Aurora said as she held my hand in front of the roaring fireplace. Snow drifted in a hush outside the candlelit window, falling dreamily. We were two twelve-year-old girls having a sleepover.

Tears poured down my face as I rested my forehead on the door, gasping raggedly. I clawed at the wood, wishing with all my heart that I could go back in time and save her.

"Ravenal—let's go!" Tarantula shouted angrily from the hall. "Thou have no work ethic," he muttered loudly.

I wiped at my face. My spine cracked as I wrenched my shoulders high and schooled my expression. The North was depending on me.

I'm going to complete this quest.

He will not win.

Without a word, I followed him out into the sand. I let him batter me with his magic while I made a Shield uselessly across my chest. Squire hid behind a tiny cactus that sprouted from a dune like a weed, unable to watch.

There was nothing I could do, even if I wanted to; no water in the desert; no hope.

Hours later, we walked in hostile silence through the base. I limped, grimacing with each pained step. Squire slept on my shoulder, his head tucked low. Beside me, Tarantula's gait was much slower than usual as he side-eyed me. His nostrils flared, lips pursed like he was barely holding himself back from saying something scathing.

Tension mounted.

I miss the good old days when I could electrocute him.

As we turned the corner, we both came to a stop. A Shadow Sword stood in front of our bedroom door, holding a folded prisoner uniform. She was a stunning woman with blond hair and arresting turquoise eyes. I recognized her as Jane, a member of the Marshal's cadre. An unforgettable beauty.

She had the type of soft features and large doe eyes that men went to war over. *What would it be like to be that pretty?* She also looked like she still possessed sanity, something I didn't have. Not anymore. Not after living with him.

I tried to wipe some of the dried blood and sand off my face. My features were sharp, *jagged*, beneath my hand.

"It's time for your shower and change of clothes," Jane said to Tarantula, her tone commanding as she held up a chatelaine, three keys jangling on the ring.

A vein pulsed on Tarantula's jawline, giving away his ire.

"Now?" I blurted, feeling strange and unsteady. I'd objectively known he was showering, his curls were always silky and his uniform cleanly pressed, but I hadn't thought about the specifics. Face burning, I ignored the sudden queasiness in my stomach. *Indigestion, that's it.*

Jane nodded. "We usually do it earlier in the day, but I had business—Marshal's orders," she said, mistaking the reason for my horrified expression. "Don't worry. I monitor him *very* closely after I take his chains off." She gestured to her sword and winked at Tarantula. "He hasn't tried anything . . . inappropriate." From her tone, she was hoping to change that.

Tarantula stiffened beside me.

"He should stay dirty," I grumbled, not knowing why my organs were suddenly in knots. "I guess I'll . . . go to Ella's room," I said quickly, neck hot as I focused on the floor. "Give you guys privacy."

Berating myself for making it weird, I willed my body to burst into flames. *Where is an attacking dragon when you actually need it?*

"Actually," Jane said, her tone clipped as her lips pinched together, "the Marshal recommended *you* monitor his shower." *Of course she did. Meddling bitch.* Jane shook her head like she disagreed, then smiled over at him. "I thought I'd let Tarantula decide who he wants to watch him—"

"Ravenal," Tarantula said immediately, cutting her off. "She is the one I want."

"Don't say it like that," I said automatically. "Creep."

Jane opened her mouth like she was going to argue, a flush of frustration covering her neck. She obviously hadn't tried showing him her ankle. *Devastating for her.* She shoved the keys and uniform into my hands.

"What?" I asked. "I think you should—"

"Just hold him at sword point, remove his wrist and ankle cuffs so he can take off the uniform, and let him shower. Then give him the new uniform and reattach the cuffs before you let him out of the bathroom."

I shook my head no, but she was already walking away.

Slowly I turned.

Tarantula stepped into my personal space, looking positively delighted. "Do not worry, Ravenal. I won't bite thee . . . unless thou ask me to."

"Some people shouldn't speak. *You* are some people." I wrenched open our door and gestured for him to go. "Bastards first."

He sauntered through proudly.

A few minutes later, after delaying as long as possible tucking Squire into bed and fussing over him, I stood in the washroom, holding an extensive network of prisoner chains in one hand. In the other, I clutched my sharpest bone dagger.

Tarantula stretched his hands above his head, popping his neck loudly, then untied his silver boots and pulled them off. Rolling his shoulders, he stood tall and pulled down his jumpsuit zipper.

I pointed my dagger at his chest, stopping the zipper's descent. "What are you doing?"

"Showering," he said slowly with a husky tenor.

A shiver whispered down my oversensitive spine. "Undress *behind* the curtain." I gestured to the tub.

"Jane had me disrobe first."

"I don't care what you and Jane did," I said, gagging as I thought about the two of them, alone, naked, and— *Not going there.* "Get in the shower, *now.*"

I pushed my blade into the *D* on his chest.

He tipped his head back, with his full lower lip caught between his teeth. His pupils slowly expanded as a red flush traveled up his cheeks. "Thou can hurt me . . . if thou want."

"What?"

"Hurt me."

"Excuse me—"

"I do not mind." He smiled lazily, lashes fluttering.

I pulled my dagger away from him. "Stop that."

"Stop . . . what?"

"Being yourself. Try for one second to not make it *weird*—"

"Thou art very officious."

"I don't *care* what you think about me—"

"I never said it was a bad thing." He wet his lips, eyelids heavy behind his mask. Slowly he stepped back into the tub, staring at me as he lazily lowered his zipper, exposing pale ridges—

I turned around, neck prickling under the weight of his heated gaze. My thoughts were scrambled. I must have hit my head harder than I thought during training today.

You *never* gave a predator your back.

He could snap my neck.

Rip out my spine.

Bite me.

Skin crawling with awareness, I refused to turn around as he chuckled under his breath, because *anything* was better than watching him undress.

Finally the shower curtain pulled and the sound of running water started. He made a deep sound of pleasure and sighed loudly. "Ah, that feels divine."

I placed his clean uniform on the sink with shaking hands

and threw myself out of the steam-filled washroom. After shutting the door loudly, I slid down it, clutching the chains and dagger to my racing heart with clammy hands. Heat burned my cheeks, and I refused to think about why.

"Thou can hurt me."

My imagination procured an image of him on his knees, sweating, teeth grinding together, blood dripping, as he moaned with— *Great, now I'm also a degenerate. Moral corruption really sneaks up on a girl.*

Half an hour later, he didn't fight me as I hooked his chains back on. He stared straight into my eyes, nostrils flaring like he was trying to inhale me.

"Thou smell like . . ."

I leaned closer, seeking his body heat unconsciously.

"Righteous integrity," he said with a hiss of breath, lips curling down like my scent *deeply* offended him.

I pulled away, too shaken to ask what he meant.

The next day, I told the Marshal that Jane had to monitor his showers. She must have seen the panic on my face, because she didn't argue.

The following weeks passed in a tortuous blur. I barely recognized myself in the mirror. Dark circles ringed my bloodshot eyes, and my cheekbones were sharper, face hollowed with stress. I had a permanent headache from magical fatigue.

Tarantula and I both read at night, flipping our pages with increasing hostility. We ran together in the morning. More and more, I improved the amount of water I could raise, but I could only make it spin slowly. The twins told jokes as we ate, and I forced myself to chug the awful cherry drink they gave us. Tarantula battered me with his magic out in the sands, growing more sadistic the longer I failed.

Exhaustion was my constant companion.

The only unforeseen development—my chessboard.

I'd left it arranged on the table between our beds one morning, ready to play another unsatisfying game against myself at night, but when I came back, a piece had been moved.

I'd countered.

The next day, another piece was played.

Tarantula and I didn't talk about it, *obviously*, but the game slowly progressed, day by day, as we outsmarted each other on the board, into a dead tie. Equal numbers of pieces were removed from both sides as we each hunted down the other's king without success.

We existed in a détente, but it wasn't peaceful. If anything, it felt *more* hostile than ever. We glared at each other in the bedroom with our books raised like weapons; we scowled in the desert, in the dining room, in the hangar, and as we passed each other in the halls.

Maddeningly mutual hatred.

Our second chess game ended in a draw, so he reset the board, and we started again. Fiery loathing mounted with each silent, tension-filled week, the displeasure fervently reciprocated by both parties.

The only positive part of my days were the hours I spent hanging out in the twins' room. Axel wrote more ridiculous songs, singing for me and Ella as she sketched and I read poetry to Squire.

One morning, Axel got special permission and took me dune surfing. We sailed down the sand for hours straight, the steel boards attached to canvas sails flying beneath the bright sun. Ella sat on a blanket sketching, cheering us on. We even saw a dire scorpion, disappearing off in the distance.

When it was time for my afternoon training with the Marshal, Tarantula stalked out into the dunes and threw magic at me and Axel, sending us both crashing. We whooped with laughter. Windswept and giddy with adrenaline, I didn't even care.

It was a rare moment of happiness.

The twins were my new forest. A safe place to retreat to. They made me feel like a living, breathing person and not a vessel for hate. They were vastly different from the rest of the soldiers on the base.

Men and women stared with interest at Tarantula as he walked by. They shot him coy glances and gossiped as he passed. A few grew bold, stopping us and asking if we needed anything. They were interested in him *sexually. Completely and unfathomably disturbing.*

Tarantula visibly stiffened every time, the tips of his ears turning bright pink.

Ryse approached me a couple times, his demeanor carefully controlled, and I appreciated the loathing in his gaze when he glared at Tarantula, but I wasn't sure I wanted to take him up on his offer. Exhausted and strung out, I was too tired to desire anything but *rest.*

One afternoon, the Marshal announced to the base that a stockpile of supplies in the South had been compromised and destroyed by dragon fire. "The Commonwealth is growing desperate. We need to take action," she announced. The next week, a fresh batch of recruits arrived on base.

A boy died on his first day of training when his chute didn't open. The body was carted through the hangar, wheels squeaking loudly. I hyperventilated in the shower, smacking the wall to muffle my sobs.

My quest had never felt more important, and it was still impossible. I was steadily being pulverized by the heaviness of impossible expectations. I'd gotten everything I ever wanted, and it was killing me.

When training with the Marshal, I controlled larger amounts of water, but it was slow progress and I struggled to direct it.

My third chess match with Tarantula ended in *another* stalemate. I threw his king across the room with a scream of frustration.

The next day, the board was set up again, ready for another round. I laughed maniacally at the thought of him on all fours, ignobly crawling under his bed, trying desperately to find his missing piece.

The twins and I also started jumping more frequently from the helicopters. It was the closest practice we could get to simulating a fighter jet ejection. I asked for more flight sessions, desperate for a hit of adrenaline to get me out of my head. The Marshal reluctantly approved my request. Ryse was always my pilot, and he watched me in the mirror of the helicopter as we flew.

I threw endless flips, plummeted face-first, and spun vertically with my arms wide. I also pulled my chute later each time, chasing the high of near failure. The relief was short-lived.

When I wasn't hunting, running, or snowboarding, I'd always been prone to existential despair and chronic overthinking. Madness courted my brain if my body stayed idle. *The joys of womanhood.* My time in the military was no different.

Desperately I tried to convince myself I was still lucky, but I didn't believe it.

Peculiar events were happening at the Scorpion Hole. Once while pausing behind a plane on my way out to the desert, I overheard soldiers whispering to each other about the atmosphere, aqua regia, and . . . *artificial air technology*? None of it made any sense. *Would I understand if I'd attended Steelden?* I tried, and failed, not to feel dumb.

I attempted to listen in on more conversations, but I never gleaned anything further, technical jargon flying over my head. Many times I debated sending a letter and asking Mom for clarification, since she was the smartest person I knew, but I'd heard rumors the mail was monitored.

The days repeated on end.

Our fourth chess match ended in a stalemate. This time I threw the pieces at Tarantula's face, one at a time, while he laughed at me. The next day, the board was perfectly set up. *Bastard.* We resumed playing.

A week later, the cycle finally broke.

12

TYRANNY'S PR(ICE)

I hurried through the hangar toward the desert for my morning run, my neck flushing as Tarantula followed closely behind. A gasp sounded, then a shout.

I turned.

Tarantula violently ripped the *Democratic Papers* out of a soldier's hand. His jaw clenched as he read, spider legs pulling. He opened the paper wide, disappearing behind it.

I inched toward him, tilting my head to see the story on the front page. Squire also tilted his head as if reading.

Aleksander the Sadistic Offers a Thousand Rubies as a Reward to Whoever in the Draconis Empire Can Capture Mage Zora Ravenal, Dead or Alive: The Commonwealth Gains Upper Hand with New Deadly Knight

Below it, a wanted poster took up the entire page: an old portrait of me and . . . Mom? She looked beautiful. We'd posed for the portrait when I was sixteen years old, and both of us cherished it. How did the Empire get it? Fear gnawed at my bones as I focused on the tiny caption.

> This portrait was published in the *Excelsior Gazette*, the Draconis Empire's corrupt propaganda news source. A homing dire falcon was intercepted at a port, carrying the paper. It is thought to be a failed attempt to strike fear into the Commonwealth.

Horror crushed my soul.

"I guess Aleksander is upset about his little royal spy being captured," I whispered tonelessly, a lump expanding in my throat.

Tarantula ripped the paper in two.

Then three.

Then four.

All the soldiers in the hangar turned to stare at him as he shouted with rage and shredded the paper into progressively smaller pieces. If I hadn't known any better, I'd have thought he cared about my health and safety.

I knew the truth. He'd snap my neck with a smile.

Finally Tarantula threw the tiny pieces to the ground and stalked toward the desert.

"What's wrong?" I shouted after him, wanting him to *hurt* like I was hurting. "Are you upset Aleksander didn't offer a reward for *your* return? Are you mad that he's forgotten about you, because you're just a little—"

"Silence!" He whirled around, finger pointing at my chest. "There are things at play beyond your understanding, Ravenal. And I am not little . . . *anywhere*."

"No," I said with a dramatic gasp. "I'm *so* heartbroken that you're upset." I held my thumb and pointer finger up so they were only an inch apart. "*Little* man."

He leaned down so his masked face hovered inches from mine. "Thou could not . . . handle . . . my endowment."

I choked. "How dignified."

"I was referring to my immense coffers. What were thou pondering?"

I stomped down on his foot, trying not to think about how Mom was in more danger and I was stuck with him.

Eyelids lowering, he stared down at where I'd stepped on him, unmoving. "Run," he ordered quietly. Tension thickened as it expanded between us, somehow defying all four states of matter at the same time: solid, liquid, gas, and magic.

"You don't scare me."

He turned his head slowly. "Thou art a terrible liar."

Frissons of fear licked up my throat.

Rule of survival: Listen to your instincts. They will keep you alive.

Backing away from him, I rubbed mindlessly at the tooth prints on my neck. "I need the Marshal." I turned to the soldiers marching nearby. "Someone get her for me!"

A few minutes later, the Marshal stalked into the hangar with a scowl. Shadow Swords flanked her in perfect formation; Ryse was at the front, his eyes locked on mine.

"What do you want?" she asked me.

"Let me go on a mission North to make sure my mom's safe. *Please.*"

She waved her hand dismissively. "I'm sure she'll be fine with—"

"I'm not asking." I grabbed her arm, stopping her as she started to turn away.

A sword point bit into my throat; Ryse moved between us defensively, his expression unreadable.

The Marshal opened her mouth as she stared down at where I held her, but it shut as she met my gaze. Whatever she saw on my face made her pause. Her eyes were shrewd. "You haven't . . . made any progress on your Knight Mage abilities," she said carefully, aware of our audience.

"I'm skilled with daggers."

"You could get gravely injured. Your loss would be . . . *devastating* for the Commonwealth."

"I am *strong*," I said through clenched teeth as I telepathically screamed at her that I was getting better at wielding storm magic. "It's just a routine checkup. I *need* to know she's safe."

Ryse pushed the blade deeper into my throat, just hard enough to hurt but not draw blood.

I leaned closer. "Please—let me check on her. I won't do *anything* rash."

The Marshal inhaled roughly. "Fine," she said, gesturing behind me. "But you'll take Sazha with you—for protection." Her eyes gleamed. *So that's why she's letting me. She wants us to bond.*

I internally combusted. "The only person I need protection from is *him*."

"Do you want me to rescind my permission?" she asked coldly.

"No, sir!" I fell into position, saluting her.

Upper lip curling at my insolence, she turned on her heel and walked away. Shadow Swords pivoted like water, flanking her. The blade at my throat disappeared as Ryse joined them, but he glanced back over his shoulder at me.

"BACK TO WORK!" the Admiral shouted from somewhere in the back, and the quiet hangar burst into activity.

A few hours later, Tarantula and I wore full Knight armor as we rode on horseback through fields of towering white cacti. Our steeds were heavily muscled, sprinting north with impossible speed. My holsters were also strapped across my thighs and waist, loaded with daggers. Sweat dripped down my face. Heavy fur cloaks, goggles, and gloves were in packs hanging off the sides of our stallions.

Tarantula's wrists were still cuffed, but the chains connecting his legs had been removed. *Not at all worrisome.* A tinny sound rang out as Squire repositioned himself on top of my head, pecking at my Knight helmet, creating a helpful beat for my inner voice, which was panic-screaming.

It was a little less than a two-day ride from the Middlelands to the North.

The sun dipped, and starlight rose, guiding our path along the canyon banks. A river rushed far below.

Thighs cramping, I startled awake, tightness in my lower back as the sun rose hot and punishing. Cacti became brush and then transformed into low trees. The canyon diminished until we were trotting along a dirt-covered riverbank. The dirt became pebbles, then slabs of wide rocks as trees grew in height, wide leaves slowly replaced with long needles.

The temperature plummeted as I drifted between rest and sleep.

Sweat turned into shivers.

A light layer of frost crept along the stone bank. It turned into ice, then crunching snow. White-tipped fir trees towered above, the Mist wrapping around their trunks in a light blue fog. Heavy clouds blotted the magic-streaked violet sky, and dire wolves howled off in the distance.

I relaxed.

At last I was back in the North.

A familiar gray brick wall loomed above the treetops. Nostalgia punched me in the gut. The Commune looked the same, but . . . different.

"Me home!" Squire hooted with excitement, and I went numb all over.

I dismounted before Tarantula could say something and ruin everything. As I staggered up to *my* gate, red flashed in my periphery. A rose bloomed, bright against the snow.

For some reason, its miraculous persistence made me want to cry. I stomped down on the gate's hidden latch like I had thousands of times before.

Dusk glowed on the horizon, so people should have been milling about after supper, gossiping as they prepared for bed.

The streets were eerily silent. Squire shivered on my shoulder, hiding behind my braid.

Glass lanterns flickered, hanging off the sides of ice-covered townhomes with decorative red bows tied to them. The oil would burn out in a few hours if not replenished. Someone had lit them this morning. Foreboding crawled down my neck. Long icicles hung from them.

The trees lining the streets were completely frosted over. Chimes tinkled ominously. Boot prints covered the snow as if people had trampled frantically.

I tried the nearest door—locked. I pressed my ear to the wood, and voices whispered inside. *They're alive, just hiding.* I staggered back, faint with momentary relief.

A hard object bumped my shoulder. Tarantula stood unnaturally still, his head cocked like he was listening.

Pulling out my longest knife, I ran.

Unease rose as I sprinted down my street. The first townhome door at the end of the row was already open. Fresh blood splattered the porch. I inhaled. A familiar sweet tang hung in the air, but as soon as I tried to place it, an overwhelmingly rancid scent overpowered the notes. It reeked of tyranny. *Of the Draconis Empire.*

Something thudded.

The open door banged noisily against bricks, half hanging off its hinges. A head with sightless eyes rolled through the entranceway, down the porch steps, and onto the street in front of me. I tilted my head to the side as it turned over.

It was Manto—or what was left of him.

My stomach dropped.

The Empire's designs on Westmere always ended in the same way: death, subjugation, suffering. An Emperor could conquer our lands only through the slaughter of innocents.

A door slammed shut three townhomes away. Two intruders, a man and woman with long, flowing white-blond hair, appeared on the porch—and froze. *Royal Mages.* Slim purple masks covered their pale faces.

Blood covered their hands. *Eight houses away from Mom.* "Please let her be okay," I prayed desperately to the old god.

The Royal Mages turned their heads in unison, staring straight at me. Their hands started to glow a bright silver.

Armor clattered against chains as Tarantula stepped up beside me.

A pernicious deathly quiet blanketed the street; colors leeched saturation; the world held its breath.

"Tarantula . . . is that thou?" the woman yelled, her posh accent jarring.

Tarantula's hand shot out in a blur. His cold prisoner chains moved against my throat as he yanked me back against his chest, fingers around my neck. His body burned behind me. Metal dug into my skin, my thoughts static as he held me hostage.

The man in the purple mask clapped slowly, long blond hair blowing in the wind, and the woman beside him smiled conspiratorially. "Great work, capturing her," she practically purred. "Aleksander will reward thee *handsomely.*"

I tried to yank away from Tarantula, but his grip was unbreakable. He held me hard enough to bruise. The chain pulled tighter, and I choked.

"Let me go," I whispered, voice cracking. I never trusted him, but still, this felt . . . *heinous.* Paralyzed with dread, I stared up with disbelief at his inscrutable expression. He didn't even glance down at me. All his attention was fixed on the Royal Mages.

They laughed as I struggled.

I tried desperately to think around my frazzled panic. "You promised the Marshal . . . The leverage. Your pardon."

Tarantula didn't say anything.

"*Please,*" I whispered, vision blurring as I stared down the road at my home. "You can't take her from me too." The door was shut tight. *Please let Mom be inside.*

He jolted behind me as if struck, but he didn't let go.

Carefully I wrapped my free hand around the hilt of a dagger strapped to my side. Tarantula's chain yanked down my torso. He squeezed my wrist painfully before I could grab it.

I spread my fingers wide, desperately searching for my magic, but there was no tingle of awareness like usual in water's presence. The snow was foreign . . . not mine to wield. *Curse it all.*

"Bring her to us!" The woman gestured. "We have a few more houses to check, and then we'll go back to claim the reward—"

"No." Tarantula's voice rang loudly in the quiet street, cold and assured.

Both Royal Mages stopped, their heads tilting to the side in eerie synchronization as they studied him with confused expressions.

Tarantula's heart pounded through his layer of armor, thudding against my spine. His cheek jostled my helmet as he leaned over me. "I order thee to stay behind me," he whispered under his breath. "Hide. Now."

Wait.

What?

One second I was constrained, pinned against his chest. The next he released me, pulled away the chain, and shoved me behind him.

Silver exploded from Tarantula's palm, flinging both the Royal Mages up into the air. They soared backward above the street but landed with a roll, deftly springing back up to their feet with their glowing palms raised high.

Icicles broke off from the townhomes nearest them, and a dozen spears flew at Tarantula.

Squire shrieked behind my braid as I sprinted off to the side, hiding behind the thick trunk of a tall pine tree. "Look away, dear."

His head swiveled around. "Me afraid," he chirped.

"Me too," I whispered.

In the middle of the street, Tarantula waved his hand. All

the icicles turned around midair, then hovered for a second. He waved his other fingers, and they shot back at the senders. The Mages reared back with shock, then hid behind a porch, and the daggers shattered against the side of a townhome.

Tarantula sent more gusting toward them, but the Mages split up. The woman ran across the street, and he aimed for her while the man sent a volley of icicles back at his throat.

Tarantula ducked low, avoiding all of them. At that exact moment, the woman threw more at his legs. He grunted mid-roll and staggered as he stood up. Two had clipped the sides of his thighs, and blood splattered across the ice.

Bellowing, Tarantula waved, and an entire snow-covered roof detached from a house, burying the man. He did the same to another roof across the street, hitting the woman. The man fought his way out first.

Tarantula pointed, and a tree branch broke off.

With a flick of his wrist, it impaled the man through the gut. It should have taken him down. But instead of falling, the Mage grunted and ripped it out, blood spraying. He raised his arms and sent more icicles flying at Tarantula. One grazed his side, and he stared down at the wound.

Magic hissed, rising in a haze around Tarantula's head. His eyes darkened. *CRACK.* The *entire* tree uprooted beside the Mage, plowing into him. He slammed against a townhome, hard.

The woman shouted with confusion as she burst out of the snow pile, gesturing angrily at Tarantula. She looked like she'd seen a ghost. "Who art—"

She also went flying, rolling across the road as the tree that hit the man swung into her.

"Who—" The man tried to speak, but no sound came out as he staggered into the street, waving his hands angrily. Silver glowed around his teeth. Tarantula had gagged him with his magic. *Why?* Icicle after icicle shot forward, and Tarantula batted them all away, redirecting them with his magic.

The man screamed louder, "How dare thou—"

A branch skewered straight through his open mouth.

Holy shit.

His brain exploded.

Pow. The woman flung an immense pile of snow down the street, and Tarantula stopped it in the air inches from his face, gritting his teeth. His smile was spine-chilling as he threw it back at her.

Boom. She jumped out of the way and shrieked as she sent another pile back.

He caught it again.

The ground shook as silver magic—ice and wind—flew back and forth in the narrow road, faster than the eye could track. *Pop. Pop. Pop.* Silver streaks lingered in the air like a fighter jet's vapor trail. My eyes watered, and the sharp scent of the occult burned my nose.

Both waved their glowing hands, moving closer toward each other. Instead of tiring, they picked up speed the longer they fought. *The art of war.*

Heart pounding in my throat, I felt like I was witnessing something I shouldn't ever have been privy to. Ducking low, I inched away from my hiding space, slowly edging forward. *Please stay distracted.*

Magic flung the woman back against bricks, and Tarantula stalked toward her. I took the opening, sprinting with everything I had toward my home.

Five houses away from Mom.

Four.

Three.

Two.

A scream echoed. The woman was back on her feet, directly across the road, staring me down. Tarantula had been hit by a pile of snow and was fighting to free himself.

She raised her glowing hands.

I chucked my dagger. It sank into her sternum, right above her heart—a kill shot. I waited. *Why is she still standing?*

She ripped it out of her chest and chucked it with magic straight back at me.

I dropped to the ground, but agony exploded as the blade buried itself in my dominant shoulder, inches away from my heart.

Groaning, I rose to my feet and dug into my holster. As best I could, I threw a second dagger. It also hit true, burrowing deeper into the open wound directly above her heart. She staggered back, blood pouring from her mouth as she screamed with outrage and raised her glowing hands.

I sprinted the last few feet, but a mountain of silver snow flew through the air in my direction.

"ZORA!" Tarantula bellowed. In my peripheral vision, he lunged for the woman with his hands spread wide.

The mound of snow cast me in shadow. *Lucky girl, you'll be okay.* I chucked Squire off my shoulder as hard as I could.

BAM. The avalanche plowed into me, throwing me violently onto the icy road. Crushing darkness everywhere.

A memory played, Mom singing softly:

"Into the frosty Barren Forest we travel,
For our souls know the best way to go,
But the twisted path is ice, not gravel,
And we'll lose our bodies in the snow."

13

IMPRECATION

Death was a freezing figure of malice and rage. He tore me apart with his icy fingers, shredding my anatomy in search of my soul. I fought against him. This would not be my grave.

Get up, Zora.

Save yourself.

Squire screeched far away.

A second figure joined Death. They were shrouded in an emerald glow, their long hair defying gravity like silk, effeminate features wavering in and out of focus as they hovered nearby.

They smelled like magic, pine, and a peaceful future.

Squire hooted with desperation like he was trying to communicate one last frantic time. In his panic, he'd devolved, forgetting that we shared the same language.

"SYXZAL!" Tarantula shouted.

Air gusted above with a shrill whistle, and the demolishing pressure slowly lessened. Snow creaked and groaned.

The emerald figure stepped away, dissipating.

Wind howled louder, blasting violently.

More pressure released.

I gasped as the crushing weight lifted, and I blinked through icy lashes. The mountain of snow rose up higher and higher, hovering in the air above me. Tarantula bellowed, and his magic flung it away. It boomed as it landed somewhere off in the distance.

Sweet freedom.

Hair whipped around my face.

Euphoric relief fired through my abused synapses. Unable to move, I lay in the street. Gray spires towered above, cutting into the endless sky. I'd never seen such a beautiful sight.

Squire hooted, tawny wings spread wide as he swooped in a big arc and landed on my forehead. He pecked at my nose, squawking with delight as he trembled.

A single tear dripped down my cheek, freezing in its path.

"Syxzal," Tarantula said in his strange language, voice and accent guttural.

He stepped forward, standing above me.

Flames of magic smoldered in his gaze, and as he stared at me, his golden lashes started to smoke. Blood was streaked in arcs across his platinum mask. Cobalt veins protruded from his forehead and jaw as he stood impossibly rigid, radiating malice.

Two fractured chains hung from his cuffed hands.

He'd broken free of his shackles.

How is that possible?

In slow motion, he crouched down onto his knees, reaching for my face with . . . red gloves?

Why are they dripping?

"Syxzal," he repeated, his voice more of an animal's rasp than recognizable speech.

Warmth splattered my face, and cortisol exploded as I realized he was reaching for me with fingers drenched in thick, viscous blood. He'd lunged for the woman with those same deadly hands.

You're in grave peril.

Time snapped back into place, and life reentered my body with an anguished gasp.

Rule of survival: Run.

Pushing up, biceps burning, I dug my broken nails into the cobblestones, shuffling backward away from him on trembling limbs.

Tarantula watched me retreat with flames where his eyes should have been. *Is this real, or is it in my head?* Pain streaked down my crushed muscles with each panicked movement through the empty, icy street. Hard stone jarred against my aching spine.

Blood-splattered boots stalked after me. The temperature dropped. It was getting harder to inhale.

Snow flurried down softly in a wintry kiss.

With measured, sinister steps, Tarantula continued to follow my scrambling path. Broken chains blew around him. Blood dripped off his drenched forearms, a bright trail of red across the ice.

He *reeked* of mass murder.

I backed away faster, desperation mounting.

An aura of unconstrained, predatory omniscience flowed around him. The old god was dead . . . *right*?

"Stop, evil spider!" Squire squawked with terror as he balanced on top of my head (helpful).

Tarantula continued following me like he was possessed, his armor squeaking ominously with each step. A helmet sat casually tucked under his arm, and the spider tattoo crawled across his jaw.

He was more intimidating than his dragon.

Depravity beyond comprehension.

Something slimy squished against my fingers. I yanked my hand away, looking around. I struggled to process what my tunnel vision had been protecting me from. Gruesome carnage *everywhere.*

I stopped and pulled my helmet off in shock; Tarantula froze a few feet away, observing me.

How is this even possible?

Numbness intensified as I tried to process the grotesque. The two Royal Mages in the purple masks were scattered all over the street in pieces, like a missile had exploded.

Tarantula watched me with an indecipherable expression as diamonds winked across his throat, catching the last rays of dusk.

He's magically castrated.

Right?

I closed my eyes to escape the horrors and whispered, "How did you . . ."

Warm lips brushed against the shell of my ear.

My eyes shot open.

Tarantula crouched on all fours above me like a savage animal, a hair's breadth away from my face.

He'd somehow moved impossibly fast in complete silence. A dark cherry scent wafted off him, mixing with the ever-present darker notes of . . . *sordid intentions*?

"What did you do?" I whispered.

"What had to be done. When the snow . . . *hit* thee—" he clenched his jaw, head rolling on his neck like he was struggling for control "—I *ripped* them apart with my magic . . . and my hands."

"But the diamonds . . ." I trailed off, trying to swallow around the sudden blockage in my throat because the carnage on the street was extensive. "You're supposed to be . . . *contained*."

His heated mouth whispered across my icy flesh, burning.

"I am compromised."

"But are you contained?"

"Obviously," he drawled.

I'm not so sure about that. I shuffled away from him, but he crawled with me. Following. Hunting. A sharp pain lanced through my arm, and I couldn't contain my gasp.

"Do *not* hurt yourself." He grabbed my shoulder and stopped my retreat. Wetting his lower lip, he flashed the corner of a . . . *fang*? He dragged his blood-soaked finger across the side of my face intimately, tracing my jawline.

He smirked, and his teeth were normal, no fang to be seen.

Strange illusions. My mind was slipping away from me, endangered by the proximity to his madness. Tarantula wasn't on the edge of sanity. He was fully gone—nothing but predatory mania in his eyes. *Royally corrupt.*

"What—" air whistled from between my lips in barely a whisper "—are you . . . doing?"

Tarantula leaned closer, chest above mine, his magic hissing as it reached for me. Wind shrieked as it blew through the street, screaming as if trying to tell me something. Silver glittered amid the falling snow.

Squire rebalanced on my head, his beak in Tarantula's face. "Scary spidery man," he squawked at the top of his lungs.

Tarantula didn't so much as flinch. He remained obsessively fixated on my face.

Trepidation mixed with self-preservation. "Get *off* me," I said, disturbingly aware of his proximity. His gaze lowered, and we both stared down at where the dagger hilt protruded from my shoulder. It was a testament to how overwhelming his presence was that I'd *forgotten* about the knife skewering me.

Dots sparked in my vision, nausea making the street spin. My arms trembled. I fought the urge to collapse as a wave of weakness overwhelmed me. Sensory overload.

"Now who is the liar?" Tarantula asked with a glare.

"It's nothing."

"No. Thou art *stabbed*." Air whistled loudly through his flared nostrils.

"Wow, really? I didn't notice the dagger sticking out of my—"

"Careful. I do not appreciate the sarcasm." A vein pulsed in his forehead. "*Syxzal*."

"What does that mean?"

He stared at my lips. "Vexation . . . damnation . . . duty . . . honor . . . *fate*." He leaned closer as he whispered each word, his lips brushing against mine, then pressing as he spoke them directly into my mouth.

I'd never thought of my lips as particularly sensitive, but they were now on fire, tingling with a sharp heat that streaked down my face and neck.

"Oh," I said eloquently.

Tarantula pulled away and stood up, running his fingers roughly through his curls. His arms dropped, hands clenched and fisted as he struggled for control.

Another wave of nausea hit, and I collapsed backward, spread-eagle, teeth chattering. Squire hooted, sitting beside my head as I lay pathetically on the cobblestones. *Get up, Zora.* I urged myself to act, but I couldn't. Nothing was left of me. Adrenaline had drained away, and my body wasn't cooperating. The full-body contusion from being crushed wasn't helping.

Tarantula made a harsh growling sound.

"What is actually *wrong* with you?" I asked as I stared up at the gray sky and tried to ignore him. He stepped into my vision, studying my face with an inscrutable expression. "Why are you acting so . . . wild?" I whispered.

Tarantula's eyelashes lowered. "What is wrong with *me*?" he asked with disbelief. "After thou have tested my nerves and plighted my soul, thou dare ask about . . . me?" He whipped his arm out, violently pointing his stained finger down at me. Blood splattered on the snow between us. "Next time, use your damned magic, *Knight* Mage."

"I tried."

Rule of survival: Deceive your enemies, always.

"Thou failed," he said accusingly.

"I just need more practice—"

"The indigo siblings *crushed* thee directly before me." His rage boiled over. "And thou ask me what is wrong . . . with me? THOU DID NOT EVEN TRY TO HALT THEM!"

"I stabbed her twice. You're being dramat—"

"Oh please. Thou put on a pathetic display of—"

"Calm down and get out of my face."

"—weakness. Thou art supposed to be strong and not—"

"I *am* strong enough."

"No, thou art not. Instead of using your magic, thou made *me* save thee—"

"I didn't *make* you do anything," I said slowly, voice shaking. "I never asked you to help me."

He inhaled sharply, nostrils flaring as silver gathered around his hands in a burning haze. His arms shot forward.

WHOOSH.

Squire screeched as wood panels ripped off the nearby townhomes and glass exploded down the street, shards flying everywhere. People screamed inside. The shattering crescendoed as Tarantula methodically decimated every window in the vicinity.

Flinching back, I raised my arms protectively around Squire, but the glass diverted around us like we were in a protective bubble. Tarantula bent over, eyes closed, chest heaving, with his hands on his knees. Silver magic *gushed* off him.

I scrambled backward, hyperventilating.

While he was still bent over, his eyes shot open. Tarantula tracked my every move with unblinking fervor. Glass clattered as a gust of chilly wind carried the broken pieces across the icy cobblestones.

Concentrate, Zora.

I staggered woozily to my feet, shards crunching beneath my boots. *You're here for a reason.* It took a long second to sort through my befuddled thoughts, and then it hit me.

"Mom," I said hoarsely, guilt eating me alive. *How had I forgotten?*

Squire flew up and settled on my shoulder. "Mom?" he squawked with confusion.

"Stop moving," Tarantula said as I hobbled past him before he could read my intentions. He hurried after me. "Thou art hurting yourself."

"Mom!" I yelled, ignoring the pain in my arm as I ran toward my home.

"Sit back down, right now. Thou art the most bullheaded—"

A familiar door flung open. "Zora, sweetie! Is that you?"

"Mommy," Squire hooted with delight.

Tears flooded down my face before I'd processed what was happening. I was on my knees, and she was running toward me, wrapping her arms around me. *Holding me.*

Long, wonderful seconds passed as I embraced the only family I had left.

"You're not safe," I whispered into her ear when I finally found my voice.

"Shhh, sweetheart, it's okay. I have protection." She gestured to where a man stood on her stoop. He was covered in muscles, and I recognized him as Vale, the most competent man in the Commune. Manto had kept his promise to protect her when I left.

Everything blurred.

And now he's dead.

"Sweetheart, please." She cradled my head, gasping as she saw the dagger sticking out of my shoulder. "Who did that . . . ? Why . . ." She trailed off as she took in the carnage all over the street.

"I'm fine," I said reflexively. It was a testament to how much I'd suffered in the Crimson Army that I wasn't lying.

She yelled as she caught me just before I face-planted.

"Just a light passing out," I whispered. "Nothing to worry about."

Mom held me cradled in her arms. "I'm *beyond* worried."

I laughed, so grateful she was alive I could happily die. She smacked me lightly on the back of the head.

"Wow, beat a woman while she's down."

Mom wiped hair off my forehead, whispering something about "fairy's tales" and "all my fault," as if saying a prayer.

"It's *fairy tales*, and it's not your fault," I promised her. "It's mine."

"No." She shook her head, eyes crinkling. "It's fairy's tales."

"I've never heard anyone else call it that. You're definitely wrong."

"No, I'm not." Both of us laughed, and I tried to nudge her but gasped with pain.

"My Zora." Her fingers trembled as she cupped my face. "You need medical attention. I don't . . . We don't have any supplies in the North . . . to help this."

Her eyes were wide and panicked. We both knew the only thing our local "medic" did was prescribe bark soup. People didn't get gravely injured in the North. If they did, they were dead.

"I need to take her back and treat her." Tarantula stood above us, long shackles blowing in the wind.

Mom's jaw dropped as she glared up at him, cradling me protectively. "I thought the papers were m-making up stories," she said, her voice thin with asthma.

"It's fine," I said weakly. "He's my . . . *prisoner*?"

His severed chains clattered loudly as if making a mockery of my statement. Mom shook her head, not looking convinced. *Understandable.* It didn't help that the last time she'd seen him, he'd kidnapped her, and now he'd just murdered two Royal Mages with his *bare* hands.

I glared at Tarantula, gesturing with my head across the street. He rolled his eyes but turned his back to give us some privacy and walked a few steps away. He picked up my Knight helmet and busied himself hanging it off his armor belt.

"We should go and report this to the Marshal," I whispered to Mom. "Come with me. I can keep you safe—"

"My life is here." Mom shook her head, mouth tilted stubbornly. She always acted like this whenever I'd mentioned leaving the North. "Plus, I have Vale." She gestured back at the man, who was now sharpening an ax on our front stoop. The sight made me feel only marginally better.

"Please," I begged, unable to let it go. "It's not safe. The threats against you are—"

"Like I've told you before," she said harshly, "I will *never* leave the North." Her expression softened as she saw my devastation. She leaned down and gently kissed my forehead. "I heard you've become a Knight Mage . . . I always knew you were destined for greatness, my sweet, lucky girl."

I was breaking at the seams.

"Please," I repeated as I cried, wishing I could tell her about my impossible quest and how the Iron Ritual had malfunctioned, making me into a Royal Mage. *They want me to do the unthinkable.* I glanced at Tarantula, trying to tell her with my wide, panicked eyes what I'd promised the Marshal I would never speak out loud.

Mom's breath hitched, fear flashing across her face like somehow she'd understood me perfectly. She masked her surprise quickly.

Cheeks tight from frozen tears, I leaned my head against her shoulder. Squire repositioned himself so he was pressed between both of us.

"Everything is not as it seems," I whispered.

She gently stroked my hair. "And yet you and I are real. Hope is where the divine enters, and you know what that means . . ." She trailed off, waiting for me to finish her favorite saying.

"Our souls are free, old god turn us toward the light," I whispered, throat impossibly tight as a wave of inarticulable sensations washed over me.

Mom always felt that way to me. *Divine.* She believed in everything, *in me*, so strongly that it felt sacrilegious to argue with her limitless faith.

Long minutes passed as the three of us embraced, and I wished with every aching beat of my heart that the moment would never end. Squeezing my eyes shut, I tried not to notice how brittle, *starving*, her frame felt beneath my touch.

Sharp pain shot up my shoulder. I tried to hide my wince, but it was too late.

"Please, go get help, Zora. Write to me." Mom's smile was steeped with melancholy, lips wobbling as she tried to be strong for both of us. "Remember, please." She placed a hand over her heart, the meaning clear.

"I love you," I whispered, tongue numb from the weight of everything I wanted to say but could not. "I'll be back home soon. Keep my snowboard polished for me."

She rolled her eyes as I laughed. "Oh please, you and that death trap." We hugged each other tighter. "I love you *so* much." She kissed my forehead. "Old god, please protect my lucky girl."

No one can save me.

Not from this.

Feeling like I was dying, chest cavity filled with dirt, weeds growing from my decaying flesh, I inhaled deeply and wrenched away from her embrace. She smelled like kindness and hope for a better future, but her temples were sunken in, mouth too large for her skull. I swallowed down bile.

The North was still starving, and she smiled at me like she believed I was going to save them all.

I can complete my quest.

"Please remember," she said. "You don't have to be perfect all of the time. You just have to be good."

I will complete my quest—for her.

I nodded jerkily, pretending like my heart wasn't separated from my body and beating on the cobblestones at her feet.

Please, old god, let me complete my quest.

Tarantula reappeared beside me, once again moving with eerie silence. If Mom's spirit was pure light, then his was the gaping darkness between stars.

He bent low and lifted me beneath the knees. Squire hooted, wings flapping as he balanced atop my head. Closing my eyes midair, I tensed. *Oh, it's not an attack.*

He held me cradled tenderly against his chest. *Even more unsettling.* He turned and began walking away.

"You better not hurt her!" Mom called as she stood on the street, face twisted with concern.

I waved back, trying not to give off *I'm terrified right now* energy, which I was, clearly. Hating how scared she looked, I said quickly, "He's harmless once you get to know him."

Tarantula made a choking sound.

"Practically docile," I added just to annoy him.

From the way he missed a step, it had worked.

Mom tilted her head to the side as she watched us like she was studying something puzzling.

"Let me down. I can walk." I squirmed. "You're making me look *weak* in front of my mom," I hissed with annoyance.

"How devastating, partner." His arms felt like steel as they flexed, pinning me gently against him.

"Oh, shut it. I'm not your anything," I whispered furiously. "Smile and pretend to be nice. I don't want her to worry."

He turned back to Mom, lowering his head in an imitation of a formal bow. "I will keep your daughter safe, I promise," he said with gravitas.

Wait, what?

Mom arched an eyebrow, looking more intrigued by the second.

He turned to continue forward.

"I don't need your protection," I said. "Now she's going to think I'm pathetic and need a *man* to save me." I gagged dramatically at the ridiculous notion.

Rolling his eyes, he pointedly looked down at the dagger in my shoulder. "Cease fighting me, syxzal."

"*Tell me* what that means."

"I shan't."

"Cad," I muttered.

"Spidery man *very* rude," Squire chirped (helpful).

Tarantula's jaw clenched, but he didn't elucidate. The quiet was maddening, and I needed a distraction from the grief of leaving Mom. We were walking away from her when all I wanted to do was run toward her.

"Family traitor," I spat, wiping at my eyes as I tried to get a reaction out of him.

"First thou condemn me for my loyalty to the Draconis Empire. Then thou slander me for protecting thee from them. Which is it, Ravenal?" He scowled as he easily carried me through the Commune, waiting for my answer.

"Both," I said, not needing to think about it. "I hate you for both. Either you have loyalty to something or you have nothing. No character. Just cowardice."

His lips pulled up, face hardening with hostility. "And what art *thou* loyal to?"

"The Emperor's demise, the fall of the Draconis Empire, the freedom of Westmere, my mom." I ticked off each item on my fingers. "Ella and Axel," I added. *My quest.*

"Death to the Emperor," Squire crooned in agreement (extremely helpful).

"Yes," I said. "*Exactly* that."

Squire chirped happily.

"Also, Squire." I put down another finger. "Obviously."

Tarantula's warm breath fanned across my cheek. "I possess more fealty and devotion than thou could *ever* imagine in your wildest serf dreams."

"Better a serf—" I held his gaze, refusing to let the word get to me "—than tyrannical scum."

"Better a tyrant than oppressed."

"Better to fight oppression than to revel in it. An autocrat *always* falls."

"Art thou sure about that?"

"Those who kill for power," I said, reciting one of Mom's favorite speeches, "are already dead inside. There's nothing left of them to save. Tyranny is an atypical state, and nature *always* corrects itself."

Tarantula scoffed loudly, the sound vibrating through his chest. "A serf would say such to justify their inability to survive."

"Careful," I whispered. "You're starting to sound like you believe in divine providence—in Aleksander and the Draconis Empire. Playing with other people's lives is a *mental* illness."

Squire cooed in agreement. "Bad, *bad* man."

Tarantula snorted.

"The soul of a killer degrades with each murder; what is sowed is always afflicted back," I whispered. It was a line from one of my favorite poems, and my stomach ached because it also applied to me. Hunting was a grisly endeavor, and no amount of self-awareness was going to save me from what I'd become.

Tarantula rolled his eyes, boots crunching through the glass-covered snow. Wind howled louder, Mist swirling blue around the tree trunks as we stepped back out into the Barren Forest. "Ah, brat . . . that is what thou art not comprehending," he said sotto voce. "I have *never* once claimed to possess a soul. That is for your people."

My people?

Dread crawled up my esophagus.

14

Deadly Embraces

Tarantula held me against his chest—like a dragon clenching its prey in its jaw—and then placed me on my saddle. He quickly unlaced the armor on my calves and thighs.

When I was down to my uniform, he dug through the packs and pulled fur gloves onto my hands. He yanked a hat gently down over my head and repositioned me in the saddle like some helpless doll.

I slowly reached for the last dagger in my holster—*need to stab him.* Every movement sent sharp agony exploding through my shoulder.

"Cease moving," Tarantula ordered coldly, and I stilled. "Thou can stab me later. Do *not* hurt yourself."

Wait . . . what did he just say?

He rummaged through the packs with increasing frustration. "Why in the damned did no soldier pack a medical kit?" he shouted, and three-eyed dire ravens cawed as they rose from the treetops. "We cannot take the knife out until we get back to the base."

"I don't take orders from you," I whispered hoarsely.

He mounted behind me on *my* steed.

"Scoot up." His hands wrapped around me, and he manhandled me forward, pressing against me in the too-small saddle.

I would have struggled, but the throbbing in my shoulder had become unmerciful. Sweat dripped down my face even though my breath frosted and I shivered. His masculine thighs pressed tightly against my body. He gripped the reins with his unshackled hands, caging me.

The other dire horse neighed as we cantered forward. *When did he tie them together? When did he remove his armor?* I was losing it.

Darkness beat along the edges of my vision. A warmth draped over my front, and I sighed. The intoxicating scent of dark cherry and even darker magic filled my tired lungs. It took a second to process that he'd placed his cloak over me.

We rode forward at a punishing pace.

Snowy trees blurred, growing shorter, as time moved strangely. The world tipped to the side, gravity pulling me with it. A firm hand splayed across my collarbone, and the top of a calloused thumb pressed against the tiny notch at the bottom of my neck. He held me upright.

"What . . . doing?" I whispered through the haze of pain.

A hard chest shifted behind me. "Do not speak, Ravenal."

"Why?"

"Why *me*?" Squire hooted from where he sat on top of the dire horse's head. From the way the steed's ears were swiveling back and forth, it did not consent to the extra passenger.

"Why?" I repeated louder, annoyed by his silence as I tried to lean forward and put space between us.

"Hoo?" Squire chirped (unhelpful).

"Do thou ever listen or give up?" Tarantula's thumb pressed harder into the divot of my throat. "I have never met anyone so *difficult*. Can thou do anything but argue?"

"No," I said. Boneless, I collapsed back against the enemy's chest, staring up at his face as I was cradled between his thighs. *Vile and wholly unacceptable.* I couldn't find the strength to move.

"'Tis like thou exist, Ravenal, to test my patience and drive me mad."

"Oh please, you're already mad." My head lolled as I lost the ability to hold it up.

The corner of his lips quirked up into the smallest of smiles. "Thou know me so well. But I have never claimed to be anything else. Madness runs in my lineage. Thou should give up now."

His mask reflected starlight, and our mouths were once again perilously close together. *We have to stop finding ourselves in this position.* His cupid's bow was surprisingly pronounced, and up close, the color of his lips was more of a red wine than a crimson.

"Never," I promised.

He searched my face.

Memories of severed heads, teeth digging into my neck, and two men riding dragons twisted through my subconscious. *Madness runs in the family.* Of course it did. The world was in shambles because of it.

Tarantula nodded like he could see the terror in my eyes. "'Tis what I'm afraid of," he said calmly. "Thou do not know how to give up. It would almost be admirable if it were not so vexing."

I tried to look away from his marble-sculpted features, but I was transfixed by the danger.

"Why . . . your throat . . . scarred?" I whispered through numb lips as the moonlight highlighted the diamonds on his collar.

"Do not ask questions that thou do not want the answers to."

"I want . . . to know."

"No, Ravenal . . . thou *really* do not."

"Tell me."

"Thou could not handle it."

"What game—" I coughed weakly "—are you playing at?"

His lips curled with cruelty. "The type where *no one* makes it out alive."

Warning horns sounded in my mind. I tried to pull away, but his hand pressed harder, holding me forcefully against his chest. His calloused thumb slowly stroked.

"Let . . . go." I coughed as I struggled, my flesh burning up where he touched me. Butterflies sharpened their knives inside my stomach, and heat flared.

His rough hand slowly trailed higher, warm fingers wrapping around my throat in a tender, obscene gesture. "Never, syxzal."

The butterflies went to war.

"If you won't tell me what it means, then why? Why did you just start calling me that? Why now? What changed?"

Darkness plucked at my vision, distorting the world into shades of exhaustion as the horse galloped. With each forward motion, Tarantula's hips pressed into mine. His stomach burned like a furnace, radiating warmth.

We were sealed together. *In damnation.*

"I realized," he whispered, "what I was willing . . . to risk." His fingers tightened around my throat, just enough to make me gasp. "And what I was not."

Streaks of pleasure exploded down my neck, to my chest, deep into my core. The saddle provided exquisite friction. He smirked with primal satisfaction, and I could see it on his face. He thought he had me beat.

Over my dead body.

With a surprised grunt, he jerked violently.

His fingers spasmed around my jugular, muscles tensing as we both looked down. My bone knife protruded from the middle of his thigh.

I gripped the hilt, hand steady.

My last weapon, forgotten in its holster, had now found its home. It had not gone to waste. Pain streaked down my side from the effort it had taken to wield it, but a rush of victory lightened my chest. *You're a hunter. Don't forget it.*

"Release me," I demanded as I tensed, preparing for his retaliation.

A raspy baritone sound escaped his lips.

He's laughing?

Now?

Fear gained teeth as he squeezed my neck, not hard enough to hurt but hard enough to make a point. "Thou will have to do *far* worse than that . . . my Ravenal."

I plan to. Don't worry. The quest hovered in my mind's eye, never far from my thoughts.

"I just stabbed you," I said, feeling numb. "And I'm not *your* anything."

"Thou art just flirting with me. Also, thou dost protest . . . too much," he taunted with humor.

"I *stabbed* you," I repeated. Because he should have been upset. No man could be this delusional. *Right?*

Head tipped back, I lolled in and out of deep sleep with him holding me the entire time while he directed the horses.

When we finally arrived back at the Scorpion Hole, Tarantula still hadn't released his grip on my throat. A crimson stain had spread across his thigh, and a normal person would have been in pain, but he seemed to barely notice the knife jutting from his flesh.

The twins ran out of the hangar as we approached. Alarm transformed their faces as they took us in.

"Release her," Ella said as she stalked through the sand toward us.

"No, Ella! Don't go near him," Axel ordered harshly, running after her with worry on his face. *Smart man.*

"Set Zora free," Ella demanded, ignoring her brother's concern. "Right now."

Axel pulled his sister behind him protectively and focused on us. His eyes flashed. "I agree—let Zora go."

Fingers pressed firmly around my sensitive neck, and I could feel the tremor of anger as it rolled through Tarantula. "She is *Knight Ravenal* to thee, jester," he said slowly, his tone caustic. "Never speak her name on your lips again, or I shall rip off your face."

The twins shared a look.

He's not joking.

The scattered remains of the indigo siblings were seared into my brain.

Axel's eyes narrowed, his expression flat. "Her name is *Zora*." He bared his fangs. "I can call my *friend* whatever I want to."

Ella pushed past her brother. "Let her go right now." She unsheathed her sword and aimed it up at Tarantula.

"Release *Zora*," Axel drawled again. "Or I'll go alert the Marshal—"

Tarantula slowly lifted his glowing hand, and it was still streaked with dried blood. He pointed it at Axel. Silver shot off him in a haze.

Axel raised his hands into a Shield and threw the gust aside. Sand exploded high into the air. He shouted, "I told you to let Zora—"

"Zora is *my* partner. Not yours. *Stop* saying her name, bard."

More magic streamed from his fingers, but Axel whirled expertly, deflecting it. Sand sprayed down atop him.

Axel spun, a bright metallic light casting off his fingers as if his skin was lit from within as he absorbed the next burst.

And the fourth.

And the fifth.

On the sixth attack, Axel blocked the frontal assault, but a second gust of magic wrapped around his back. He was thrown upward, high into the air. Ella screamed as he crashed into the sand. *Hard.*

"Go to him," Tarantula ordered Ella, sneering down at her sword as dozens of magical dust devils swirled around us. "Or I'll make sure your jester brother never walks again."

Ella sheathed her weapon and ran to help her twin.

Tarantula chuckled darkly as she retreated. At that moment, soldiers swarmed out of the hangar, shouting directions.

Nails scraped across my jugular.

Tarantula released me and dismounted onto the sand.

My muscles liquified. *Finally free.* Gravity pulled me sideways off the steed, toward the dunes, and I let it win. Steel arms wrapped around mine, catching me.

With uncharacteristic gentleness, Tarantula pulled me out of the saddle and helped me stand. He acted like I was a defenseless damsel in distress, but my knife still protruded from his thigh.

He's toying with you.

I tried to push him away, wincing with pain.

"Cease hurting yourself," he ordered in a clipped tone.

I kicked at the hilt, jostling his wound. He grunted but still didn't release me.

Ella ran over, snaking her arm under mine. "I got her," she snapped, pulling me protectively into her embrace as she glared at him. Tarantula hesitated, clearly shocked that she'd come back and defied his order, even though *he* was the prisoner.

"I said—I *got* her," Ella repeated.

Just when I thought he was going to rip me away from her, Tarantula's posture stiffened. He straightened, pulling his shoulders back, and stepped away.

"Thank you," I whispered to Ella gratefully as I leaned limply against her, trying not to throw up from the frissons of agony shooting down my arm.

She brushed hair off my face. "I have you. Did he do this?"

I shook my head no. "It was a different Royal Mage, but he . . . killed her." *With his bare hands.*

Ella sagged with relief.

She wouldn't be relaxed if she'd seen him in action.

"My mom was okay," I whispered, voice catching. "I got to hug her."

Ella held me tight. "What happened?" she asked as she resumed leading me to the hangar.

Vision blurring, I leaned close and relayed everything about my meeting with Mom. When my throat started to close up, emotions suffocating, Ella hugged me and changed the topic. "I thought Tarantula was going to incinerate me with his eyes when I pulled you out of his arms."

We both glanced back at him. He stalked smoothly through the sand, not even a hitch in his step.

Ella studied my face. "What's going on with you and him?"

"We hate each other."

She nodded like she could see the truth on my face. "Careful—strange rumors circulate down in the South. Royal Mages are known for their—"

"The madness," I said with a nod. "I know—"

"No, that's something else." Her voice was uncharacteristically firm. "Their *passion* is also infamous. Rumor has it, Azote is the land of *intense* romance, if you know what I mean."

I blinked through the mounting pain.

"Uh. No. What? Wait, what did you hear?"

"They're *very* possessive of their . . . lovers." She choked on the last word. "They'll do *anything* for them. Wars, riches, *sexual proclivities*—nothing is too extreme. At least . . . that's what the Southerners say."

I tripped, and she barely stopped us both from tumbling into the sand.

"What?" I struggled to exhale. "I'm not . . . No . . . We would never. He's my enemy."

She didn't look convinced.

"Ella, I *loathe* him."

"I know. I know where your allegiance lies. Don't worry. I just mean . . ." She chewed on her lip. "You're both very intense. I wouldn't fault you if you did."

"I just *stabbed* him."

"I think he liked it."

We both grimaced. I had no counterpoint.

Ella nodded like it all made sense. "You're both more aggressive than everyone else. And you both have streaks of . . . ferocity. It would make sense if you needed another outlet. And you're both very attractive."

I rolled my eyes, gesturing to my awful scars.

She arched an auburn eyebrow. "Zora, you have to see how people on this base look at you?"

"With fear," I deadpanned, but I knew what she meant. I'd seen the longing glances and attempts at seduction. People loved to play with dangerous things. They thought it made them brave. *It makes them stupid.*

"Well, no one's arguing with that," Ella said, and we both shared a knowing look. "It just seems like you should explore other options when it comes to Tarantula—"

"Did you hit your head?" I asked, because the stunning woman who looked like a fairy-tale princess was the one lecturing *me* on toxic romance. "You know you're the prettiest person I've ever met in real life. You could have a dalliance, if that's what this is about—"

"No, it's not that," she said quickly. "I'm just pointing out the obvious."

"Nothing is obvious anymore," I grumbled.

"With that, I agree." Ella nodded with concern. "No matter what you do, remember to be *very* careful. His passion is . . . spilling over. Tarantula is not a normal man, and there are going to be consequences."

Agony streaked down my arm as I nodded solemnly.

"Did you see that?" Axel asked as he stomped over, brushing sand off his training uniform. "That spidery bastard threw me across the sand. You both need to stay away from him . . ."

"I'm *trying* to stay away," I whispered miserably, thinking about the quest and the Marshal's impossible expectations.

Off in the distance, Tarantula slowly traced the hilt protruding from his thigh, a flush trailing up his jaw.

Heat filled my cheeks, and I hastily looked away.

It was going to be a *long* night.

A few minutes later, I debriefed the Marshal alone. The model map of Westmere stretched out behind us. I was shaking, clammy, and nauseous. The dagger still protruded from my shoulder because she said removing it had to wait.

"Two Royal Mages eliminated," she whispered quietly. "This changes everything. He's actually *compromised* . . . by you." She sounded shocked that I'd pulled anything off.

Her confidence is truly heartwarming.

The dagger pinched every time I breathed, sending hot streaks of pain down my torso as I struggled to listen to her.

"He's shown his intentions." She vibrated with intensity. "It's time for the second part of your quest. I'll send you all on a mission South. Complete it. Keep doing *exactly* what you're doing. When you get back, it will be time for the final move. I've made contact with a new . . . player who is also aligned with our cause. When you return, a series of . . . *events* will unfold."

"What events?"

"Only I can know."

I started to pull away, but she grabbed my shoulders and held me close, jostling my wound. I yelped, eyes rolling back in my head. Knees weakening, I started to collapse. Her tight grip held me upright.

"Come to me," she ordered. "That is all you must do when you return from the mission. I will give you the previously discussed *materials*."

She released me, and I staggered out of her hold, swaying precariously.

"Complete your quest, soldier. Save the world."

"*Obviously*, sir."

"You've done well," she said, ignoring my sarcasm. "Keep it up. Your sacrifices have not gone unnoticed."

I covered my mouth, holding back the awful words I wanted to spew as I left the room. She stayed behind, head bent low, studying the map.

In the hall, Shadow Swords fell silently into formation behind me. Ryse offered me his arm, helping me up the stairs. When we got to the hangar, he bowed low, green eyes lingering on my face. Then he disappeared with the rest of the Shadow Swords.

"Let's get thee back to the room, partner," Tarantula drawled lazily as he stepped out of the shadows. *He was waiting for me?* Moving gingerly, I tried to pass him.

He lifted me up, clutching me possessively against his chest, taking care not to jostle my injured shoulder.

15

Venomous Tension

Tarantula carried me through the hangar.

"Help," I said. "I'm being kidnapped by a raging misogynistic, homicidal, despotic megalomaniac who's afraid of a lady's ankles."

No one in the Middlelands cared.

Typical.

He brought me back to our dark room.

"Curse you," I said.

"Curse on the spider slut!" Squire added (helpful). He sat on top of Tarantula's head, plucking curls from his scalp. He waved his beak around excitedly, showing off his new prizes.

From the way Tarantula flexed his jaw, he deeply regretted his past choices. *Good. He should find a new partner to torment.*

In front of my bed, Tarantula came to a stop. I flinched, waiting for him to drop me. He gently lowered me onto the bed, tucking the covers around me, all the way down to my toes.

"Curse you," I spat, wishing he'd just thrown me down.

Squire plucked another strand and squawked with distress, "Curse *me*?"

"No. Not you, dear."

Squire chirped with relief.

"I'm already cursed," Tarantula said stiffly. "Try harder to be threatening." He rubbed his sternum like he was having chest pains.

"Darling," I said as I pulled the shimmering strand out of Squire's beak. "You don't want to touch the Empire filth. He's probably diseased." With a dramatic gag, I dropped his hair onto the floor.

Tarantula looked shrewdly between me and Squire as if studying a mystery he didn't quite understand. He opened his mouth to speak—

The door burst open.

He whirled to the newcomer.

Medic Sara practically fell into our room, looking harried. Her auburn hair, a common Midlander trait, hung freely around her shoulders. Her uniform was wrinkled and half on, as if she'd been asleep with no time to get fully dressed, and she clutched a medical bag overflowing with supplies.

Squire rustled his feathers with annoyance. "Not you!" he hooted (helpful).

"The Marshal wanted me to tend to your wounds. I just heard what happened!" Sara said hastily as she hurried over to my bedside.

Tarantula worked his jaw back and forth, tattoo pulling.

Sara pushed him aside, oblivious to his wrath, and leaned over me.

"Zora," she gasped. "Damn, that wound is horrible. They told me, but I didn't believe it. We need to remove your uniform." She rustled through her bag, then brandished scissors with a blunt tip. She immediately got to work.

Squire hid under the covers.

Sara worked quickly, pulling away strips of fabric, careful not to disturb my shoulder.

"Are you feeling okay right now?" she asked. "Be honest.

This is a pretty extreme injury." She rested her wrist on my head. "I think you're getting a fever. What's your pain scale right now? Zero is nothing. Ten is astronomical."

"Zero," I whispered.

"Me ten!" Squire chirped nervously (not helpful).

Sara looked between us like she didn't know what she was supposed to do with that information. "Go to sleep," I whispered, and Squire closed his eyes obediently.

"Really—a zero?" she asked as she focused on me. "You don't feel *any* pain?"

"No. I feel nothing."

A long, awkward pause stretched as she studied me with empathy. "Listen, Zora," she said with a friendly smile, "I think we got off on the wrong foot."

Jittery dread twisted my innards, but her mouth kept on moving.

"I know the last time we met, we were both overwhelmed . . ." Sara trailed off. "I know you're not *really* a stupid peasant. And you didn't mean to drop Kane when he was injured. Friends?"

Uneducated Northern peasant.

My stomach bottomed out, and I looked away. *How does one ever really know if they are stupid?*

"Get out."

The heavily accented words were spat so quietly it took a moment for both of us to process what Tarantula had said.

Sara turned to him with confusion, pulling away. I relaxed with relief as she put some distance between us. She was a physical reminder of how the Midlanders had all treated me before I became a Mage.

Chest tight, I tried to breathe through the heavy emotions rising like the living dead in the graveyard beneath my breastbone. *Maggots in the soil of my flesh.* Old shames lingered.

Sara frowned. "The Marshal ordered me to—"

"I order thee . . . Get the *fuck* out." Tarantula pointed to the door, the profanity sounding strange from his lips.

Her eyes widened as he turned and she got a good look at the knife sticking out of his thigh, his pant leg stained with dried blood.

"Did I stutter?" Tarantula took a menacing step toward her, broken chains hanging uselessly from his wrists. "Medic." His tone made her title sound putrid.

Paling, she dropped her bag with a clatter. "Sorry, Zora. Let's talk about this later." She barely spared me, her patient with a *stab* wound, a glance as she bolted out of the room, desperate to get away from Tarantula.

"It's number Six, not Zora," I whispered back on instinct, but Sara had already left. *Thanks for all the help.*

Bang. The door slammed shut, and fresh agony throbbed along my arm.

Squire poked his head out of the covers and chirped with relief, "Me a *one* now."

He settled himself contentedly onto my pillow.

Tarantula tipped his head to the side, his mask shadowy in the umbra of night. He stepped to my bedside. "She insulted thee . . . yet thou said *nothing* to defend yourself." He scowled. "But thou scream at me . . ."

I shrugged. "It's different with you. You need to be put in your place."

A strange light sparked in his eyes. "So I am . . . special to thee?"

"Especially *annoying*," I mumbled mockingly.

"How does one know," he blurted with uncharacteristic haste, "if a person is . . . afflicted with attraction?" A pink flush colored the tops of his sharp cheekbones.

I blinked, whiplashed by the change in topic. *He's not asking me about that right now. No. He can't be* that *unwell.*

His eyes held mine as he stood beside my bed. So much heat radiated off his skin that I began to sweat.

"I have never desired in the past," he whispered hoarsely, accent thickening. *Oh, he is.* "But how would I know if that . . . changed? How does one interpret inclinations of a carnal nature? What are the signs?" As he spoke, he leaned over my bed, his hands resting on my pillow, trapping me.

Inclinations?

Carnal nature?

His breath wafted across my skin as my wide eyes were reflected in his approaching mask. Maybe it was the blood loss and pain, but this conversation had taken a turn I'd never seen coming.

"You just feel it," I whispered. "Your pulse races, and there's a tension that builds inside of you. An . . . awareness for the person, the object of your desires. You're drawn to them, like cold dire beasts to a warm fire. It's inexplicable but overwhelming."

He wet his lower lip. "'Tis singular?" He exhaled roughly.

"What do you mean?"

"Thou have touched many a person." He scowled at me accusingly. "But what if a person *hungers* for a single individual . . . and no one else will do?"

He fixated on my mouth, looming above me, larger than the night. My head spun. His proximity made it hard to think.

"Uh—yes." I cleared my throat awkwardly, wincing as I shifted. "Some people are only interested in having—" I choked, struggling to get the word out "—sex, with one person, many, or even no one at all," I said in a rush. "It's specific to you. Everyone is different, and there aren't rules. It's just how you feel."

"But the *hunger*," he said forcefully. "What if I desire to . . . *ruin* . . . the object of my attention?" He inhaled roughly, his gaze glittering with magic as his eyes mapped my face. "What if I *yearn* to consume her whole and I cannot . . . avoid the dangerous inclinations? This hunger is devastating, a constant ache—the *darkest* of compulsions."

He pressed one hand to his chest, fingers spread wide across the *DANGER* on his jumpsuit, inches from my own heart. Our noses touched, and my senses came alive like I'd thrown myself face-first into a bonfire.

Why are we talking about this while I'm skewered?

Silence stretched as he waited for my answer.

"Um, maybe . . . don't. Yeah. No. *Nope.* I don't think you should do that." I cleared my throat, shaking my head. "Do not ruin anyone with your, um, devastating hunger. It's probably best if you keep to yourself."

He frowned, fingers flexing against his skin, clawing at his heart. Silver came off him in tendrils, sizzling as it wrapped around my skin.

I nodded, sinking lower into the bed.

"Try not to feel anything," I said louder. "Ever. For everyone's safety. I think abstinence is an important thing for you. Some people are meant to die alone."

He frowned.

"*You* are some people . . . the one who's dying alone," I said. "In case it wasn't clear—"

"Not all pain is wicked. There is pleasure in torment," he said slowly. "Is there not, Ravenal?" His breath fanned across my cheek, the lightest caress. I felt it in my core.

"What are we talking about right now?" I asked.

"I am special to thee."

"*Not* what I said."

"And . . ." He pulled away, unfurling to his full height, looming above my bedside. "Fleshly relations," he said with a prudish air.

I scoffed at the archaic descriptor, then groaned as a wave of pain made it hard to see.

"Why are you asking me . . . about fleshly relations?" I blinked slowly, feeling increasingly clammy and disoriented.

"Because . . . 'tis repugnant."

"No, it's not." Confused by the conversation, drugged by the agony in my shoulder, I asked something I'd been dying to know. "Have you had sex before?"

"Sex with Zora," Squire chirped in his sleep (*extremely* unhelpful).

Tarantula inhaled loudly. "Do not use your twisted tongue on me." Magic danced atop his head like a corrupt halo.

What is happening right now? I shook my head weakly, determined to end the conversation.

"You know, people on this base are interested in you . . . Don't ask me why, but I could give you some pointers. I've been with some men. It's not a big deal if you just—"

His calloused hand clamped down on my mouth, covering the lower half of my face. "Silence yourself," he ordered stiffly. A shudder rolled through him, his ears bright pink.

He looked *agonized.*

I tried to speak, but his hand pressed down harder.

Oh nice, now he's smothering me.

"Such bratty rudeness, Ravenal." He tsked. "How much do thou despise me?" he asked abruptly. "Focus on that."

So much. But what does that have to do with—

I screamed as unholy fire attacked my shoulder. White exploded between my eyes. I banged my fist on the bed, spine arching. Tears fell as agonizing streaks shot down my arm and my fingers cramped. Bile filled my throat.

The dagger dropped to the floor with a loud clatter. Warm blood gushed down my arm, ruining the sheets.

Tarantula released my face and knelt beside my bed, ripping open the medical bag. Then he leaned across me, pressing gauze into my hemorrhaging wound with both of his hands.

I screamed.

His eyes were filled with torment as he kept applying pressure. Air whistled through his clenched teeth. "'Tis almost done," he said quietly as he wrapped my shoulder tightly with bandages. "Thou art so strong, syxzal."

"Stitches," I gasped out as I clenched at the covers, desperately waiting for the stinging to abate.

He shook his head, putting supplies away. "Thou do not need them. Your body shall heal on its own in a few days."

"Because . . . Mage?" I asked weakly as I shivered.

"Something like that," he muttered under his breath. His tone made alarms go off deep in my subconscious.

My teeth chattered as I lost blood, but horrible memories from the Iron Ritual strangled me, and I sat up, leaning against my headboard. Tarantula tried to stop me, but I pushed his hands away because I needed to clear my head.

He muttered under his breath but pulled his comforter off his bed.

"What are you—"

He draped it over me, tucking it gently around my shoulders as I sat frozen, watching him.

"Why?" I asked.

He didn't answer. Instead, he sat down on his bare bed, grabbed the hilt protruding from his thigh, and yanked it out in one swift motion. "I have not a clue," he said as he inhaled noisily. "Nothing is clear, because of thee."

"Of course. Blame the woman."

He opened his fingers, and my bone dagger clattered loudly to the floor. "Correct—I shall blame thee. Wicked, perplexing . . . *princess*." He shook his head with frustration. "'Tis complicating my plans."

I'm no princess. But the way he emphasized the title made my stomach clench. Everything spun as tiredness pulled me under.

"Well, you're not a stroll in the forest yourself," I mumbled. "If I was you, I'd focus on *personal* improvement and stop fixating on me."

"I cannot." His glare sharpened, frigid and unyielding, as he dug through the medical bag. He expertly wrapped a bandage around his gushing wound.

"So, what . . . plans have I complicated?"

"Thou art cruel, spiteful, and completely unreasonable," he muttered under his breath, as if I hadn't spoken. "I have never met someone so stubborn. Thou never let anything go. Thou art dangerously impulsive, quick to start a violent fight . . . distrustful, skeptical, obnoxious—"

"Thank you for noticing."

"—and all-consuming," he said. "A hunger rages for only . . . thee."

I must have been losing more blood than I realized, because it sounded like he was insinuating something *extremely* dangerous for both of us. Quiet stretched as we both breathed heavily, sitting on our beds, fighting through pain.

Tarantula gestured to the chessboard arranged between us on the table, pieces positioned mid-game.

"Your turn, Ravenal."

Grunting through the agony, I leaned over and pushed my bishop diagonally across the board, clacking against one of his pawns and knocking it off. I'd already spent *hours* ruminating about my next move and didn't need to think about it.

I winked at him tauntingly.

Tarantula elegantly arched a golden eyebrow and leaned forward. He moved his knight three spaces, knocking my bishop off the board, then leaned back against his headboard with his fingers laced behind his head. A challenge burned in his gaze.

Smug bastard doesn't think I'll do it. He doesn't think I'm smart enough to play him all out.

Without hesitation, I leaned forward and moved my rook.

His face transformed with unadulterated excitement. Wounded, sweaty, covered in dried blood, and grunting with barely controlled pain, we leaned across our beds and played chess in the moonlight.

An hour later, the game ended in *another* stalemate.

I would have thrown the board, but it hurt too much to lift my arm.

"Play me again," Tarantula demanded. Eyes glittering, he reset the board and gestured, even though I never agreed. "Ladies first."

"What a gentleman," I said dryly as I moved my pawn. "Not."

"I was always the *most* genteel, but my decorum . . . evaporates around thee." He flushed like he was embarrassed by his admission. "Still, I aim to serve, Ravenal." Long, graceful fingers flicked out, dragging his pawn forward.

Blood rushing in my ears, vision wavering, I felt each heartbeat as it slammed against my breastbone. "Ha, scoundrels don't serve. They *manipulate*." I focused on the board. "You're just saying that to trick me."

"No." His voice dropped to a silky baritone. "I shall service thee . . . *thoroughly*."

I moved another pawn and glanced over; his expression was unreadable.

Stomach twisting, I scooched toward the wall, putting more space between us, wrapping his comforter tighter around myself. His eyes flicked down to it, then back to mine. He wasn't blinking, again. Dizzy from holding my breath, I turned away from the game and mumbled something about falling asleep.

Darkness swiftly yanked me under.

In the purgatory between dreams, I could feel him still watching me.

16

D(ANGER)

Every day, the Marshal pushed me harder to master my magic. We trained even though the wound on my shoulder was still healing.

She filled a long room with water—piped all the way from the river—and had me stand in it for hours on end, shivering. Unlike during the test, it was *my* job to infuse it with magic. An arduous, exhausting process.

It was a few weeks since the stabbing, and I could finally lift my arm without almost passing out.

"One," the Marshal bellowed, holding the wooden target with a *1* printed on it in front of her face.

"Two?" Squire hooted on my shoulder (not helpful).

Head throbbing, I raised my glowing hands. Pulling the water high, I directed it at her target. She sprinted across the room, trying to get out of the way. I sent the magic after her, concentrating. *Splash.* It hit true.

"Five!" she shouted, unimpressed.

Squire chirped, "One?"

I threw magic at *5*, which hung from the ceiling. A wall of water rose up between us, straight to the target.

"Ten!" she ordered.

"Nine?" Squire called out (really not helpful).

Without turning, I pointed my finger over my shoulder and threw a stream behind me, hitting the *10*.

We kept going for what felt like hours, only stopping for a few short breaks. Squire squawked numbers louder, getting into the spirit while completely missing the point of the exercise.

By the end I could barely stand up, head aching from exertion. "I win," Squire hooted. The Marshal dismissed us both, lips pinched, eyes narrowed. I immediately collapsed to my knees.

Nothing I did was good enough.

She left me kneeling in the water, feeling sorry for myself.

Teeth chattering, I finally gathered my courage and staggered up after her. In the map room, I dried myself off, and then Squire, before I quickly changed clothes to hide the evidence of my magic, while the Marshal studied the table. Sighing, I stumbled out into the hall, where a different Shadow Sword waited each day to escort me back to my room.

Gentle hands caught me; Ryse studied my face, interest in his calm green eyes. For the first time, we were alone.

"Shadowy man!" Squire hooted.

Almost alone.

Ryse cleared his throat, a smile on his lips. "Hello, Zora—and Squire," he said softly. I glanced away, hyperaware that my eyes were bloodshot and ringed with the purple-black hue of dark circles. On my shoulder, Squire rotated his head from one side to the other, uncomfortable with male attention.

"Let's get you both back," Ryse said, understanding in his voice.

We walked together in a pleasant quiet. He opened doors for me and offered his arm when I tripped going up the stairs, but I didn't take it. When we got back to my room, I grimaced, gingerly pushing open the door—*peaceful, blessed silence.*

No one was inside.

Tarantula must still be at his daily afternoon meeting with the Admiral, aka negotiations where they traded intel. Squire eagerly flew over to my bed, tucking himself under the covers, settling in for a nap.

Ryse exhaled behind me.

The moment stretched.

He didn't leave.

"Zora," Ryse said quietly. Masculine fingers brushed my braid aside and trailed down the back of my neck. A full-body shiver rolled through me, reminding me that I was still alive. I was so tired of feeling nothing but suffering.

Without looking back at him, I nodded and entered the room. In my peripheral vision, he followed.

The door shut behind us.

Click.

He turned the lock.

We were safe—no one could interrupt us.

Safety is good.

I stopped right in front of my bed. He came up behind me, his face even with mine. We were the same height. There was a buzzing in my stomach, an awareness, but it was faint . . . peaceful. Ryse was warm and gentle. *Everything I should want.*

Fingers trailed down my sides, and his lips pressed against the back of my spine. Sweet, soft kisses.

I shivered and turned, pressed flush against his chest. He gently cupped my face, and his lips found mine.

Ryse didn't exert pressure. Instead, he held me against his body and kissed me tenderly like I was glass that would break. His arms wrapped around my shoulders as he pressed his torso against me. My mouth opened wider, tongue sliding against his. Tenderly he explored deeper into my mouth. He smelled like sand and sunshine. *Pure goodness.*

Tension melted from my shoulders, and my tired legs gave out. I leaned against his chest, savoring his warm scent.

Ryse gently guided me back so I was sitting on the edge of the mattress as he bent toward me. His arms settled around my shoulders, a comfortable, *calming* hug. He leaned in and kissed me deeper.

I tilted my head up, eager for more. I wrapped my arms around him but pulled back when I hit his broadsword. Not wanting to take liberties, I awkwardly rested my hands on the front of his muscular chest.

He stooped lower and deepened the kiss.

A warm thumb brushed against the side of my neck. His fingers stilled, then drifted curiously back and forth against the divots. *The Emperor's bite.* Suddenly there wasn't enough air in the room; he was stealing it all from my lungs. A wave of fresh exhaustion hit me, and I wanted to curl up in bed and take a nap.

No.

Eyes squeezed shut, I refused to pull away, trying to lose myself in the moment. Trying to forget what I had to do—who I was hunting, and who hunted me.

I kissed Ryse, *needing* this gentle moment. He groaned into my open mouth, *finally* pressing his tongue harder against mine. I tilted my head eagerly, accidentally biting his lip.

"Sorry," I whispered.

He chuckled. "Don't worry, beautiful."

Such a nice thing to say.

I fought the urge to sigh with boredom.

Hinges groaned.

My eyes shot open—Ryse's were still closed.

The washroom door lazily swung open.

Someone.

Kill.

Me.

I was officially beyond worried.

Tarantula stepped into the room and froze. *Deathly still.* His gaze locked on mine, nostrils flaring. *What was he doing in there?*

His eyes iced over, colder than the frozen Barren Lake. The air around him shimmered, and the sharp scent of dark cherry and magic filled the room.

Ryse kissed me harder.

My pulse raced.

I whimpered—from terror.

Emboldened, Ryse cupped my neck with both hands, thumb stroking the divots on the side of my neck like he was trying to soothe away old pain. "You have no idea how long I've wanted to kiss you," he said, still with his eyes closed.

Please stop speaking.

Tarantula's gaze widened with mania. He lasered in, not blinking, on where Ryse was touching my jugular. My blood curdled, and my legs opened wider as I prepared to flee. Ryse leaned in for more.

Tarantula sauntered over. The new chains connecting his wrists were completely silent as he moved with lazy, sinister precision. Ryse didn't notice. Not even as Tarantula loomed behind him—*directly* in front of me.

My hackles rose.

Ryse kept kissing me.

I tried to pull back, to warn him, but his fingers were steady on the back of my neck, holding my tilted face up to his. There was nowhere to go. I banged my hand against his shoulder. He groaned, dark lashes resting against his cheekbones.

I gasped messily into Ryse's open mouth, trying desperately to speak between kisses. "He's—"

He groaned deeply. "Mmm-hmm."

"—*behind* . . . you."

Ryse chuckled. "Who?"

Tarantula leaned forward, setting his chin on my hand—the one that rested on Ryse's shoulder. Awareness exploded across my flesh. Ryse stiffened, eyes snapping wide at the new head beside his.

"Ravenal's *partner*," Tarantula purred, like it meant something, which it definitely didn't.

The moment stretched between the three of us with terrible stillness.

All hell broke loose.

Ryse ripped away from me, spinning. He threw a fist. Tarantula dodged and came up swinging. *Crack.* Ryse's head snapped to the side, blood exploding from his broken nose, onto me.

Squire woke up. "Hi, spider!" he chirped happily on my pillow (really not helpful).

In slow motion, I brought my fingers up to my wet face.

Tarantula bellowed as he leaned low and charged, plowing his shoulder into Ryse's torso, ramming him backward. Ryse punched blindly, hammering his back, but Tarantula didn't seem to notice.

Crash.

Tarantula chucked Ryse's body *through* the window.

And he says I *don't have manners?*

Chest heaving, Tarantula turned and stared at me. His lips were in a flat line, and his eyes flashed—*still not blinking.* He shook his head and jumped through the now missing glass, out into the desert, chasing after Ryse. There was a thud and a shout like someone had been tackled.

Glass crunched beneath my combat boots as I ran to the window.

Fists flew.

Tarantula straddled Ryse, bludgeoning him. It wasn't a fight; it was a massacre.

"*Stop it!*" I screamed, jumping through the window. Running across the sand, I threw myself onto Tarantula's back, wrapping my hands around the top of his stupid diamond collar. I squeezed the exposed sliver of his neck with all my strength.

Tarantula stilled, sitting up straight, straddling an unmoving Ryse. Legs wrapped around his torso, I hung off him, strangling with all my might. He shuddered. A deep sound escaped his lips as he took a long breath. It took me a moment to register that it wasn't a noise of pain. It was . . . *pleasure*?

Tarantula chuckled darkly.

"Get *off* Ryse," I snarled into his ear, exerting more pressure, desperate to hurt him.

Tarantula froze, muscles flexing beneath my touch.

"Ryse, is it . . . ?" he said softly. "Thou art on a first-name basis?"

"Yes, now get *off*."

"No."

I reached around, smacking at his face from behind. He lazily tipped his head back, lips parted as he rested his head against my shoulder and turned toward me—his eyes locked on mine. I slapped him harder, and his eyes rolled back in his head like he enjoyed being hit. *Never a good sign.*

"Let him go!" I demanded.

"No. Thou let *him* kiss thee." We both glanced down at Ryse, who was lying beneath us, unconscious. His face was covered in blood and swelling with bruises.

"And I'd do it again," I said.

Chains rattled.

A hand shot out.

"Take it back." Tarantula squeezed my cheeks, yanking my head forward, pulling us close. With me hanging off his back, the angle was awkward. I tried to speak, but I couldn't move my jaw in his tight grip.

Clambering off him, I ripped my face out of his grasp, stumbling sideways across the sand, needing to get *away*.

"Zora fight the spider," Squire hooted from the empty window frame. "Me help?"

Tarantula rolled off Ryse.

I waved at Squire. "No, dear, look away. I've got him handled." Squire swiveled his head, staring back into the bedroom.

Tarantula crawled toward me like a venomous arachnid.

"So, thou *desire* . . . to be kissed?" His arm snaked out lightning quick, and he wrapped it around my ankles. I fell back, landing on my butt. He crawled closer, up and over my legs.

I felt drugged.

Maintaining blistering eye contact, Tarantula slowly lowered his head to the top of my right shin where the edge of my boot ended. "Thou want . . . to be *touched*?" His warm lips brushed against my skin. I jolted as if electrocuted. "By *any* man?"

His lips parted, hot breath fanning up my leg as his tongue flicked out. He slowly dragged it up and over my skin, from my shin to the bottom of my shorts. Entranced, I fisted his curls—silk between my fingers. I bowed, back arched, pleasure exploding from my legs straight to my core.

Slowly he dragged his tongue up my other leg. Tendrils of cool magic leaped off his shoulders and wrapped around my calves.

"Thou taste promiscuous."

Is that an insult?

I tugged harder on his hair. "More," I begged, mindlessly burning up with need.

He groaned, hips jerking into the sand as he continued to climb up my legs, licking them like I was water and he was parched. Face unbearably hot, I collapsed back, staring up at the darkening violet sky. The flush traveled down my neck, over my tender breasts, straight to my core.

"Zora?" Ryse groaned in pain a few feet away.

I looked over.

Green eyes were wide with betrayal, the color stark against his blood-covered face.

Shame pierced my lungs.

"Get off me." I pushed at Tarantula's shoulders. His smug expression melted away as he glanced between me and Ryse. He slowly tilted his head to the side, holding eye contact, and opened his jaw wide.

He bit my thigh.

Hard.

Sensations exploded.

I swung at the back of his head, and he groaned as if he liked it, licking my skin. "Hit me again," he demanded against my leg.

I grabbed his curls and yanked his head away from my thigh. "Get off—now."

Rolling his eyes, looking offended like *he* was the one being attacked, he pushed up onto his hands. Instead of backing away, he crawled forward, caging me with his body. Inadvertently my hips lifted as we brushed together.

"Thou didn't even taste good," he said with vitriol as he rose up to his feet and stood above me.

"Thou art a *liar*," I mocked, bite mark throbbing with pleasure on my thigh as I lay limp in the sand.

Ryse groaned again.

Tarantula's eye twitched.

"WHAT IS THE MEANING OF THIS?" The Admiral appeared from around the side of the base, stalking toward us. His voice was like a face full of ice water, startling me out of my stupor.

Tarantula cracked his bloody knuckles and walked backward to the open window, his gaze never leaving mine. He jumped inside.

I closed my eyes as the Admiral ordered soldiers to aid Ryse.

It was going to be a *long* night.

That evening in training, Tarantula and I parried with wooden practice swords. He'd refused to let me rest after the kissing *incident* with Ryse.

A loud crack vibrated up my tired arm as he swung in a blur, pushing me back through the cavernous space. The Marshal had granted us use of the room because of the heat wave. It was spartan in its bareness, just a gray stone floor and three white walls.

Tarantula was an evil silhouette in front of the fourth wall: a floor-to-ceiling glass window that looked out on the violet sky and endless desert. Orange dunes stretched in waves, the setting sun a ball of red on the silver-streaked horizon. It cast long, dangerous shadows.

Sweat poured off my flushed face.

In one quick step, Tarantula wrenched me down by my braid to the hard floor. For some damned reason, it was his *favorite* move.

He stood over me and tapped his sword against my forehead. "Thou art dead. *Again.*"

His scowl was fierce.

He was punishing me for Ryse.

I grunted and swiped my sore leg out, but he easily jumped over it. Rolling to my feet, I feinted left, then thrust right, digging deep for every ounce of strength.

"Thou need . . . my *direction.*" His lower lip glistened as he wet it, glancing down pointedly at the fresh bite mark on my thigh. Thankfully it wasn't too deep and it would heal. *How dare he.*

"Go kill yourself." I spit blood onto the floor.

"I could not . . . even if I tried." He pressed the point into the side of my neck and dragged it forcefully across the front of my throat. "And just like that, Ravenal," he said coldly, "another loss."

"You got this, Zora," Ella shouted from where she sat in the corner, watching us.

Axel whittled a shank on the floor beside her. "She probably doesn't," he drawled lazily.

"Go, Zora, go!" Squire chirped encouragingly (helpful). He sat safely next to the twins, pecking greedily at the seeds someone on base had acquired for him.

I rolled over and gave them all a shaky thumbs-up.

Tarantula moved, blocking my view.

He was dressed in a scarlet training uniform. Despite his misconduct with Ryse, the Marshal had just granted him new clothes for "ease of training" because of the sweltering heat. *She should have made him wear* more *clothes, not less.* She was trying to cage us together, half naked. The only consolation was at least they'd reshackled his wrist chains.

The setting sun cast a devilish crimson glow across Tarantula's skin as he strutted around me in a circle. *A dire vulture salivating over a carcass.* For some depraved reason, he'd tucked the side corners of his loose shorts up into his waistband, revealing a lewd amount of chiseled thigh. To add insult to injury, the sleeveless material of the barely there top revealed his leanly muscled upper arms; cobalt superficial veins covered his forearms in a deadly network, and silver boots laced up his striated calves.

He looked . . . *slutty.*

I pushed his sword away and got back to my feet, gripping my own practice weapon. He tossed his casually back and forth between his hands, twirling it in an expert display of ambidexterity. *Not attractive at all.*

I raised mine and charged, pouring all my rage into the attack.

He countered easily, knocking me aside.

Spinning, I aimed for his knees.

He parried.

I thrust.

He raised his hand. A gust of air threw me halfway across the room. I rolled just in time to avoid hitting my head. I'd be covered in bruises tomorrow.

I screamed with annoyance as I gritted my teeth and got back to my feet.

"*Use* your magic!" he shouted with frustration. His eyes were molten.

Axel's water jug exploded in his face as he tried to drink

from it. *Curse it all. More accidental magic.* Ella rolled her eyes, muttering about her twin's dramatics. Thankfully none of them seemed to notice the glow on my fingers. I tucked them behind the sword hilt's guard.

I charged at Tarantula, trying to keep everyone distracted.

A wall of silver pushed me back.

I tipped my shoulder down and fought against it, stuck in the middle of the room, bellowing.

"You can do it. You've almost got him," Ella yelled, clapping her hands.

"DESTROY HIM!" Squire squawked with all his might (very helpful).

Boots scraped against stone as storm magic shoved me back helplessly.

"Be better, Ravenal," Tarantula taunted.

I'll show you better.

The magic stopped. I thrust my sword forward. Our wooden blades locked together. I shoved with all my force. He stumbled backward with surprise, slipping on my sweat. I leaped after him, landing a blow on his arm.

"Ha!" I yelled with excitement. "I got you."

Ella jumped up, clapping.

"*Finally,*" Axel said, oozing boredom.

Tarantula stared down at where my sword had left a red mark on the pale ridge of his bicep. He attacked in a blur of speed. It took all my concentration not to drop my weapon as I just barely parried each time. He was relentless, shoving me backward across the room.

My spine slammed against the hot glass wall. He leaned forward. His blade hovered inches from my throat. A rivulet of sweat dripped down his face, off his chin, and onto my cheek.

"Thou shall *never* dominate me, Ravenal," he said quietly. "I will always end up on top."

"False," I spat.

His nostrils flared as he inhaled roughly. His pupils blew wide as they focused on me. "Art thou . . . menstruating?" he asked slowly.

I froze with primal terror and looked down between my legs. No blood stained my shorts. He shouldn't have been able to tell. When I'd asked for cotton supplies, Ella had given me a Midlander period cup—a life-changing invention—that I hadn't needed until now because my periods had always been extremely infrequent and irregular. One of the many gifts from a lifetime of starvation.

When I looked up, he'd leaned so close that our noses touched.

"That's none of your business," I whispered. "Ankle-obsessed degenerate." I shoved against him with all my strength, but he barely twitched.

He was an immovable force.

"*Thou* art my business."

I tried desperately to shove him away. His leather boots slid back an inch as I pushed off the glass with everything I had. He smirked and flexed, pressing me back. I whimpered as our clashed swords pressed against my jugular.

Abruptly the pressure disappeared. He stepped away, putting space between us.

I sighed with relief and lowered my sword.

He lunged and drove his shoulder into my stomach. Twisting, he threw me to the floor, knocking the air from my lungs. *Cheating bastard.*

Arms splayed, I stared at the ceiling, struggling to breathe.

"I dare thee to touch another man—" he lay atop me, his weight crushing "—and see what happens. I was *merciful* today, but I shan't be in the future."

I brought my sword up to the back of his neck. "You're dead."

"Am I really?" he asked cryptically.

Ella whooped and clapped. Axel whistled mockingly.

Tarantula rolled off me, and we both got to our feet. Outside the sun disappeared beyond the horizon, and long shadows stretched across the hollow planes of his angular features. He cracked his sword down over his thigh, and it snapped in two. He threw the pieces away and stepped into my personal space, using his size to try to intimidate me. "*Thou* art dead." He glanced down.

The twins' cheering died off with confusion.

"Stop looking at my legs," I ordered.

"Then cover your distracting knees."

I sputtered. "It's just knees."

"No." His eyes narrowed to slits. "It's *your* knees."

"Then do not look in my vicinity." I stumbled toward the twins, the fight draining out of me in the face of his prudish perversion.

"*Then* do not look at me with that tantalizing light in your eyes when in *my* vicinity," Tarantula called back over his shoulder.

"I can't hear you!"

Axel threw a towel at me. "Zora, try not to get us all murdered." Ella hid her smile behind her hand.

"I know thou can hear me!" Tarantula bellowed.

"Oh, look, you angered him, again." Axel slapped my shoulder. "Nice work."

Tarantula stood across the room by the exit door with a hostile expression on his face as he glared at me.

"Leave," I ordered.

He dragged his hand roughly through his hair, chain clattering. "Thou art so . . . *bossy*."

I clapped mockingly. "Took you long enough to notice."

Shaking his head, he turned and stomped out of the room, slamming the door behind him.

"Ha." I turned to the twins. "Isn't he ridiculous."

Axel pursed his lips.

Squire squawked as he landed atop my head, seeds falling out of his mouth and bouncing off my forehead. *Who keeps taking them from the mailroom and giving them to him?* Ella led us out of the training room with a tired sigh.

That night, I just couldn't sit comfortably in bed, period cramps destroying my innards as I tried to focus on my favorite medieval book on war strategy. Squire chirped softly in his sleep, his tiny head resting on my pillow, the sheets tucked around his neck.

"Here," Tarantula said quietly, breaking what had been hours of silence between us.

I flipped over. He stood beside my bed, holding out a glass jar of a thick yellow substance.

"'Tis paste for your menstruation cramps." His ears turned pink. "For the pain. I got it from Ella—"

I snatched it from his hand, sniffing it suspiciously. The minty scent made my eyes water, and I had half a mind to throw it back at him just to be spiteful, but another cramp seized my organs. Grunting through the pain, I quickly rubbed the paste over my abdomen.

Tarantula made a dark sound, and I looked up.

He stared wide-eyed at the strip of exposed skin where I'd pulled down my pajama bottoms. It shone with the paste. His hands fisted, chest rising and falling, inhaling harder than when he sprinted.

His gaze shot to my face, and he backed away.

"What art thou reading?" Tarantula asked breathlessly, clearly trying to change the subject. "Instead of playing me," he finished with annoyance under his breath as he gestured to the chessboard frozen mid-match.

Huffing, repositioning his blanket over me for maximum comfort, which I refused to give back because it was cozy, I held up the book title so he could read it. The paste tingled coolly on my stomach, and for the first time in hours, I could think through the pain.

Tarantula read aloud, "*A Gentleman's Guide to Slaughtering.*" He froze. "Why the damned . . . art thou reading that?"

I shrugged. "If I'm going to defeat the Emperor, I need to beat him at his own game."

Tarantula sat down on his bed like his knees were weak.

I flipped the page and read the passage on deception closely, even though I could have recited its contents with my eyes closed. The author wrote at length about the importance of having multiple aliases.

"How do thou know?" he asked with a deadly tenor. "*Who* told thee that he reads that book?"

I peeked over the top.

He sat rigidly on his bed, his posture hostile. The acrid scent of his malefic intentions filled the room, and Squire coughed in his sleep.

"What are you talking about?" I asked slowly.

He didn't answer.

Focusing on the page, I resumed reading about deception. *How intriguing.*

17

CON(DESCENSION)

"I win, again!" I said as I jumped out of the hot sand and skidded to a stop inside the slightly cooler hangar.

After pulling off my soaking wet balaclava, I tucked it into the waistband of my running shorts and sighed with relief. Squire chirped as he balanced on my shoulder.

The heat wave was oppressive. For some reason, Antichthon was having more extreme weather events. My clothes clung to me like I'd jumped into a river, but my morning run was still the best part of my day. My period had also finally ended, and I'd conjured a whirlpool for the first time with the Marshal since the Iron Ritual.

Things were finally looking up.

Sweat dripped from my lashes, coating my mouth in tangy salt. No matter how many times I licked it, it wouldn't go away. Annoyed, I lifted the hem of my shirt and scrubbed at my face.

Tarantula made a guttural sound as he fell into step next to me, still in his white balaclava.

"No, thou did not win," he said, his voice deepening. "It was a tie."

"Incorrect—I leaped across first," I argued, wiping at my stinging eyes.

He swore under his breath.

"You're just jealous," I said through my shirt. "That you can't keep up with my impressive physical prowess—"

"Ravenal, put your shirt down," he ordered stiffly. "Now."

"What?" I blotted all around my face because the stupid sweat kept pouring from my forehead.

"Put it down," he said through gritted teeth. "Right now. 'Tis beyond indecent."

I held the hem up and wrung moisture out of it. "What's wrong with you?"

Tarantula stared down at my torso, his lips pressed into a flat line, jaw clenching. "Don't be a brat."

"You're so odd," I said as I dropped it, covering up my abdominal muscles. I was proud of all the new definition I'd gotten recently, and I wasn't going to let him make me feel bad about it. "First the ankle, then the knees, now this. Has anyone ever told you that you're a *very* abnormal person?"

"Yes."

"Well . . . maybe work on yourself. Self-improvement is important."

"I shan't."

"Loser mentality," I muttered. "*Extremely* unattractive."

He huffed, his boots silent against the stone. Heat radiated off him in tangible waves, and the corners of his shorts were once again tucked indecently into his waistband, exposing his thighs for all to see. *Absolutely disgusting.*

"Do not speak to me about what is attractive," he grumbled. "Everyone was feasting their eyes on your glorious flesh, Ravenal. Have some decorum. 'Tis embarrassing."

"No, they weren't," I said, and his eyes narrowed. "Ohmyoldgod, you're *such* a princess."

"Thou have no idea," he mumbled under his breath. "A single glimpse and I am . . . distraught."

I barely avoided banging into a workbench and spun, tripping into a solid wall—Tarantula. He reeked of dark cherry, darker intentions, and sweaty man.

"Ew," I said as I bounced off him. "Foul. Ick. *Grimy.*"

He stared down at me silently.

"You need to shower," I said.

He didn't answer, his eyes sharp through the holes of the hood he still hadn't removed.

"You smell," I added.

"Zora, you protest a *lot*," Squire sang on my shoulder in a shocking display of critical thinking skills (unhelpful).

I glared at my tiny owl.

He tilted his head, staring at me with wide eyes.

"I'm going to write a letter to my mom," I whispered, mostly because I needed an excuse. Pushing away from Tarantula, flushed and off-kilter, I ran away.

"New intelligence has come forward," the Marshal said with a satisfied smirk, Shadow Swords flanking her.

She stood at the front of the austere conference room. She'd called the emergency meeting an hour ago, and I still hadn't changed out of my soaked running clothes.

Pouring water from a pitcher on the table, I filled a glass and greedily gulped down the cool liquid.

Ella and Axel sat next to me on one side of the long wooden table. Tarantula sat on the other. He stared at me, as he had the entire meeting. He'd taken his balaclava off, and he was flushed from exertion, his curls disheveled.

Hyperaware of his gaze, I made a point of looking only at the Marshal. Unlike him, I wasn't *obvious*. I could be subtle.

I'm going to outplay you.

I'm going to complete my quest.

I'm going to win.

The Marshal's posture was rigid, her eyes blank. She gave nothing away as she spoke. "We have credible intel that the Draconis Empire has two Royal Mages acting as spies in the Commonwealth. This is a huge development and threat, not one but *two* enemies within our walls. All four of you must go. This must be neutralized. *Failure* is not an option."

The Southern mission she's talked about.

I focused on my glass of water.

"They're both located in our Babilon Commune." She pointed to the Westmere map that stretched across the wall behind her. "The first Mage is a male going by the alias Sibrain Cortz. He's running a high-end wine tavern. The second Mage is a male going by the alias Arcturus, no last name, and he runs a famous bathhouse. The four of you will head out today. Your mission is to eliminate Sibrain and Arcturus by *any* means necessary."

She paused, then held up one finger. "All the Royal Mages must be destroyed if democracy has a chance of defeating the Empire. Any questions?"

A loud squeak sounded as my knee knocked against the table.

"How did you obtain this intel?" I asked, genuinely curious.

"That's classified." Her gaze flickered over to Tarantula.

Interesting.

Every day he was acting more cooperative.

The Marshal pursed her lips, glaring down at me. "Your Mage training is not progressing as anticipated. Bring your daggers. We will focus on your magic when you return."

I nodded, catching the unspoken orders.

She turned to the rest of the group. "Southern clothes have been obtained for this mission. They are waiting for you in your rooms. You'll want to blend in with the locals. Good luck, Mages." Shadow Swords stood at attention, surrounding her as a seamless unit. Ryse tried to catch my gaze, but I looked down, guilt heavy in my chest. Tarantula roughly shoved his chair back across the stone, making a loud noise, and stood up.

The door slammed shut behind them.

"Thou art powerless and pathetic," Tarantula said coldly, leaning forward with his hands on the table, clearly incensed over Ryse. "I've never met a Mage so lazy—"

Water hurled across the room, splashing Tarantula as glass shards exploded against the wall next to his head. *Not again.* I waved my arm. "Uh, oops—I didn't mean to throw it," I said, quickly covering the fact that I'd never actually touched the glass.

Tarantula shook his head, water flying off the ends of his drenched curls. From the way he seethed, he hadn't picked up on my error. *Thank the old god.* The quest was still intact.

I stood up stiffly and headed for the door, but Tarantula blocked my path. "Do *not* throw things at me."

"Or what?" I asked with a scoff, still trying to hide my glowing fingers.

He crowded me. "I'll have to . . . discipline thee."

I slapped his face. *Just because I'm distracting him.* I definitely did *not* feel an intense rush of satisfaction as Tarantula jolted, lips parting with outrage. A gasp of shock burst from his throat as he brought his fingers to his reddening cheek. *Why was that so satisfying?*

He pushed me backward so I was flush against the wall. "Do *not* strike me," he said.

I slapped him again.

His jaw dropped as he gaped down at me. *Nice, I can see my fingerprints.* Our chests bumped. My nipples were hard, and the friction sent sparks down to my core. *I'm just cold, that's it. Nothing else is happening here.*

He jerked backward, chains clinking as he tugged at his curls with frustration. "Improper," he whispered with a hiss. "Inappropriate." The tips of his ears were now bright red, matching my handprint on his cheek.

He took another step back.

This time I took one forward. Emboldened, I crowded him toward the table. He stopped as his legs knocked against the wood.

"What was that about impropriety?" I asked, shoving at his chest. "Careful—I might show you my . . . *ankle*," I whispered dramatically.

He flinched as if struck.

"Or maybe my knee . . . cap."

He fisted his hands.

There is no other man in all Westmere this prudish.

"Ravenal," he breathed out, every line of his body taut with tension. "Cease this. Thou do not want me to snap."

On my tiptoes, I leaned forward so I could laugh mockingly into his face. "Maybe *I'll* snap first?"

Intrigue flashed in his gaze as he froze. "And . . . what would thee snapping . . . look like?" His voice brimmed with curiosity.

I patted his cheek (slapped him for the third time).

His eyes flashed.

"Wouldn't you like to know."

He scoffed like I was just a nuisance and not the person who was going to *destroy* him. Emotionally and physically. I leaned my hands on the table and caged him in with my body.

He practically sat back on the table, still trying to get away. We were pressed together, so close that I could feel the exact moment a shiver ran through his chest. Magic poured off his flesh, burning my skin.

"Hmm, maybe don't do . . . *whatever* this is," Axel drawled. "Soldiers are waiting to use the conference room, so I think you should stop—" he waved his hands at us "—this."

The twins sat in their chairs, gaping at us. Squire stood on Ella's head, happily eating seeds. Heat burned my face. *How did I forget they were also here?*

I stepped away from Tarantula and straightened my clothes. "We're done anyway," I said with a confidence I didn't feel.

Tarantula, who was still awkwardly bent backward across the table, didn't look convinced. "Are we?" he asked pointedly.

"Yes." Ella draped her arm over my shoulders and steered me out of the room before I could reengage.

Axel followed close behind us. "I've heard a *lot* of things about Babilon," he said ominously as we separated to our rooms.

"Uh, guys," I said as I stepped back into the hall.

Axel stuck his head out and held up silky white material. "Why is it transparent?" Ella stepped out holding similar fabric. It was the same sheer material that was waiting on my bed.

All three of us swore in unison.

18

THE JOURNEY TO BABILON

A few minutes later, the four of us lingered outside the hangar, standing in front of the largest dire horses from the stables. Packs were slung across their wide backs, full of the sheer material the Marshal had ordered us to wear and first aid kits, which medic Sara had made a show of packing.

Sara gave Axel a kiss on the cheek, then sidled up next to me. “Good luck on the mission, Zora.” She showed me a thumbs-up, nudging me like we were close friends.

I tried to smile back, but my face had gone stiff; shame killed.

Just another disagreeable Northern peasant.

Sara stumbled away, her hair blowing on a strange gust of magic. Looking around with confusion, she fell back into formation beside the rest of the soldiers who were watching us leave. I exhaled with relief.

The culprit smirked beside me.

“Chug the Mage juice before you leave,” the Marshal said as soldiers handed each of us a wooden jug, including Tarantula. “You all need your strength.”

The twins greedily sucked on the straws.

I stared at the jug in my hands, and next to me, Tarantula

did the same. He slowly brought it up to his lips. So did I. He drank, hollowing his cheeks, and I sipped as fast as I could, trying not to gag.

The twins placed their empty canisters down on the soldier's tray, wiping the scarlet cherry juice off their lips with contented sighs. Trying not to throw up, I sucked harder on my straw, and judging by the way Tarantula's face turned green, he felt the same, but he kept drinking.

"Done," he spat as he dropped his canister.

"Same," I said quickly as I took a big gulp and put down my empty tankard, trying not to puke. "A tie."

His nostrils flared. "No, I clearly won. Thou were slower than me—"

"No, you're mad. I just beat you."

A muscle in his jaw ticked as I gloated.

He'd finished first, but if I could make him think that I *really* thought I'd won, then that would enrage him and would therefore technically be a win for me. *Mentally tormenting men is surprisingly enjoyable.*

"You both winners," Squire chirped, and seeds fell out of his mouth onto my saddle (not helpful).

"Quiet, miniature bird," Tarantula snapped.

"Don't you *dare* speak to him like—"

The Marshal clapped her hands loudly, cutting me off as she looked between us with a pointed expression. "Good luck on your mission, Mages. *Remember*, the freedom of Westmere depends on you." She made the symbol of the one Democratic Commonwealth and stared at me, shaking her head, trying to convey a silent message.

Yeah, I get it. The quest.

Grabbing the saddle, I jumped up. My horse neighed, tossing its head back, silver snorting from its nose as I patted its sleek muscles. Squire chirped with excitement and flapped over, standing sentinel on top of its head, ready to lead the way on another grand adventure.

We cantered as a group at a quick clip out into the desert.

My braid bounced while I struggled to adjust to the brutally fast pace. We were practically flying. Lightness bubbled up inside my stomach, and I laughed despite all my worries. My heart raced with adrenaline as I leaned down low to be more aerodynamic.

Chains reflected light as Tarantula galloped beside me, close enough to reach out and touch. *Or kill.*

I steered my galloping horse away from his.

He followed.

Squire swiveled his head around, feathers fluttering as he looked back and forth between us, our horses neighing with discomfort at the proximity.

"Get away from me." I kicked in my heels and tried to lose him, the world blurring.

I needed space to plot.

"No," he said coldly and matched my pace like he could read my mind. Apparently his sole purpose in life was to annoy me. He was a *master* of his craft.

The twins spurred their steeds ahead, kicking up sand behind them as they charged forward. They were the only ones who'd traversed to the South before and knew where we were going. They led the way across the sand, toward the canyon.

We settled in for a long, hard ride, but the side of my face prickled as I felt Tarantula's blistering stare. Gritting my teeth, I forced myself to keep my eyes forward.

When we got to the steep canyon, the twins guided us south. The river rushed *far* below, and magic tingled along my fingers. Pure relief. There was something reassuring about rushing water. The world wasn't just a barren desert, even if that was how the Scorpion Hole made it feel.

We rode along the smooth stone of the canyon edge for hours.

On each side of the river, stone buildings were carved up into the cliffside, torches lighting the windows. Rope bridges hung long and dangerous across the canyon, connecting both sides. I peered over the neck of my sprinting horse. The desert Communes were like nothing I'd ever seen before. They didn't have to build walls like the North because the rock naturally enclosed them.

I leaned farther, half off my saddle as I squinted at the awe-inspiring architecture.

"Sit up straight, Ravenal." Tarantula pulled forcefully on his reins as he herded my horse away from the canyon's edge.

I made a mocking face at him. *What is his problem?*

He rolled his eyes at me as the sun dipped lower.

"Let's play a game," Ella called suddenly over her shoulder. She rode a couple horse lengths ahead of us. "I spy something pink."

"The sunset," Axel drawled.

Ella nodded. "I spy something white!" she shouted.

"That cloud," I yelled, and Ella looked back. I pointed at the only one in the sky.

She nodded sagely. "Exactly—you read my mind."

"I spy something evil," I said dryly.

Ella furrowed her brow with confusion, and Axel looked meaningfully back at Tarantula.

"Thou fail to amuse me, jester." A gust of silver wind exploded from Tarantula.

Axel made a Shield and blocked it just in time, twisting in his saddle, expression annoyed. "So damned rude," he said.

"You get the point," I said to Axel.

He smiled. "I know."

"Stop talking to each other," Tarantula ordered as he rode closer to me.

"Oh, get over yourself." I subtly pulled on my reins and led my sprinting steed away from Tarantula. He immediately followed, staying close. The short distance was unsafe at this pace. All it would take was one horse to stumble and we'd be thrown to the ground.

I fingered the hilt of my bone dagger, holstered around my thigh, and debated the merits of stabbing him.

"Try it," Tarantula shouted over the wind, still way too close. "I *dare* thee."

I unsheathed the dagger and flung it at him because I wanted to.

A metal chain flashed in my periphery as his shackled wrist shot out with impossible speed, catching it easily. Bone glinted. "Oops," he drawled as he lazily flipped my dagger one-handed with disturbing agility. "Thou missed."

I sat up straighter in my saddle, hips rocking as I faced forward, and refused to give him my attention. *Maybe he'll forget I exist.* He shouldn't have been able to react quick enough to catch it from such a short distance away, on a moving horse, but he did. *He's an abomination.*

Ella leaned over her horse's neck, her auburn hair whipping behind her as she glanced back at me with a furrowed brow. She blanched as she saw Tarantula casually spinning my knife.

Axel maneuvered his horse so he was between Tarantula and his sister.

"Are you okay?" Ella mouthed silently at me, even though Tarantula could definitely read her lips.

I started to shake my head no, but my steed jumped over a boulder and my stomach rose with giddiness.

Laughter bubbled up my throat. Just like that, I struggled to remember why I was upset.

Rule of survival: Remember to enjoy the ride.

"I'm wonderful!" I shouted, putting both of my hands in the air, relishing the adrenaline rush as my braid whipped behind me, stomach swooping. Head clear of thoughts, I was back in the moment. *What a glorious time to be alive.* This was almost as fun as snowboarding or falling from a helicopter. I tipped my head back and laughed louder, savoring the distraction. I kept forgetting that freedom was a state of mind, and I wasn't living in a cage.

We're flying.

Everything blurred as we picked up speed.

A hand wrapped around my arm like a vise. *What in the damned?* Tarantula rode beside me, powerful hips rolling as he leaned over and held me in a punishing grip. "Stop playing around. Grab on to your reins!"

"Don't tell me what to do." I kicked, urging my horse to run away from his.

We veered together.

"*Now*, Ravenal!" He pointed my dagger at me threateningly.

Our horses neighed, snapping at each other.

Ella shouted something, and Axel cursed.

I gripped my reins with both hands. Tarantula scowled, reluctantly relinquishing his grasp on my arm, putting some space between us.

"What's wrong with you?" I asked.

"Thou!"

"I'm not speaking to you."

"Thou just did."

Is it really *wrong for women to murder men?*

Time passed as the desert sand thinned out, low cactus plants sprouting from dirt and rocks. They grew taller as we headed farther south along the steep canyon. Hooves pounded in the night. Darkness fell, and starlight filled every inch of the sky. The temperature dropped as space glittered down on us. A full moon hung large and red.

"Are you done, spider?" I snapped.

Hours had passed, but Tarantula smirked as he continued to play with *my* dagger. Diamonds winked from his throat. He spun the knife dexterously between his fingers, his hips still moving with graceful power as he easily matched the rhythm of his steed. In contrast, sweat dripped down my spine, and I struggled to keep the pace, my lower back burning as my muscles cramped.

"Art thou done being difficult?" he asked.

"You're a blight on Antichthon," I said.

"That's actually a good song title," Axel added.

"Jester, I told thee not to speak," Tarantula said coldly.

Axel raised his middle finger.

Tarantula saluted him back.

"You're the worst," I mumbled.

Tarantula cracked his neck. "Once again, Ravenal, thou do not have a *singular clue* of just how unpleasant I can get." He sounded amused.

I clenched my reins so hard my fingers cramped, inner thighs burning as we plowed forward.

In the darkness of night, the path along the ravine grew less steep until the river rushed directly beside us. Cacti transformed into low, spiky plants and then into tall trees with long palm leaves. The path became a stone road demarcated with rocks on one side and the river on the other. Dry air became thick with humidity as strange birds sang above.

We'd entered a tropical forest, nearing our destination.

Lush greenery, vines, and large rocks transformed the landscape around the now loudly rushing river. A verdant, alive world. The wilderness seemed to breathe, humidity rising into clouds, and rain showers ended as quickly as they began. A symphony of foreign animal sounds grew.

The scent of magic thickened as hundreds of dire monkeys larger than people with strange silver markings moved above our heads.

We headed deeper into the rainforest, and the dry sand of the desert became a distant memory. It was disconcerting how dramatically the landscape could change with just a day of traveling.

"We're at the Commune," Ella said as her horse skidded to a stop on the road, detritus spraying beneath its hooves. Neighing, mine also came to a jarring stop. Stomach churning, I struggled to adjust to the sudden lack of motion. *Oh nice, everything's spinning.*

Axel gestured forward.

Green foliage grew in and around a towering wall that stretched before us to the treetops. Tiny waterfalls ran down the stones, gathering into pools. The Commune was built around the river, and the rushing water flowed *through* the stones, disappearing under the walls.

The forest and city were one.

Axel dismounted, groaning as he stretched. He stomped over and pushed aside long palm leaves, revealing a wooden door covered in vines, while the rest of us dismounted.

Knees shaking, my legs gave out, and I barely stopped myself from crumpling to the ground. Soreness radiated down my lower spine straight to my thighs, and it took everything I had to stay standing.

Ella groaned next to me. She teetered, and I caught her just before she fell over. Together we limped pathetically.

Tarantula looked down his nose at us as he stood ramrod straight, his posture perfectly rigid like he hadn't been riding for hours without a break. *Bastard.*

"Welcome to the Babilon Commune—the jewel of the South," Axel said as he opened the towering wooden door and pushed through strands of vines covered in bright pink flowers. He spoke with someone on the other side of the wall.

Axel peeked his head back through the door at us with a lazy grin. "Bring the horses in," he said. "They know that we're just visiting and want to sample their accommodations." He winked conspiratorially at us, reciting the plan the Marshal had outlined.

Babilon had to believe we were there for innocuous reasons. Otherwise Sibrain Cortz and Arcturus would make a run for it. The Marshal had said they were both men with a taste for power and they wouldn't be able to pass up meeting us.

The plan seemed tenuous at best, but who was I to argue? I was just a lowly soldier. The weight of my responsibility—*crushing.*

We followed Axel inside, guiding our steeds through the oversized door.

Flowered vines parted.

A walled Commune stretched before us, similar to and yet so different from the one I knew. Hundreds of times I'd walked through the snowy gate, entering an icy street of gothic gray stones.

"Ravenal," Tarantula said, and I snapped back to reality.

Tears were streaming down my face. There was no ice, no snow, and no familiar faces, except Squire, who perched on my shoulder, nuzzling my ear with his beak. Wiping the tears away, I swallowed the pain. Homesickness wasn't supposed to hurt like this.

Tarantula's jaw clenched as he loomed beside me. "Art thou okay?"

I flinched away from him. "Get away from me."

I stepped aside, needing space.

We approached a clover-covered street lined with wide banyan trees. Tall, strangely built wooden buildings sat in neat rows. Trees grew out the windows and roofs, thick vines crawled up the walls, and long strings of colorful flowers hung from their chimneys. The treetops created a canopy over the street, shading it from the bright sun.

Colorful birds sang down at us from the branches.

"Friends?" Squire chirped to them from my shoulder. The birds called back, and Squire dipped his beak in my hair nervously.

A tall man in a scarlet uniform nodded to Axel, then raised a long curling horn to his lips. A deafening blare exploded, and I covered my ears. His skin was a dark bronze, gleaming with health, and his lungs seemed strong.

"He said to mount our horses," Axel said. "He's going to announce us."

We all followed his lead, climbing back into our saddles. My lower back screamed in protest. The horn's sound was different from the warning horn in the North. *Don't think about it.*

Doors opened, and people flooded onto the canopied street. They wore colorful dresses and loose pants. Men, women, and children alike all had flowers behind their ears.

They streamed out in seemingly endless waves, neatly forming a line beside the banyan trees, flanking either side of the clover lane. A few coughs rang out, but the wasting sickness appeared to be milder down here, just like in the Middlelands.

Perhaps my father was of Southern heritage and that is why the wasting sickness never affected me?

The soldier yelled into the horn, "Babilon welcomes the twin Knights to our Commune—thank you for defending the Commonwealth!" His voice carried.

People clapped and cheered loudly all around. The horn waved as he gestured for us to head forward down the lane. We obeyed, riding through the exultant crowd. I scanned the faces, unable to stop myself from searching for some distant relative who had a face like mine. None shared similar features.

Axel winked and waved his cupped hand back to the crowd, while Ella smiled down at her fans. The twins acted like they'd done this before, which they probably had. The Marshal loved her publicity.

The world was just a stage, and we were all performers, dancing for our lives.

"And special welcome to the BEAR OF THE NORTH, ZORA RAVENAL, AND HER ROYAL HOSTAGE!"

The horn blared louder.

People screamed at the top of their lungs and jumped up and down. Some of them were crying. They bowed low as my horse passed, some falling to their knees. Their expressions twisted as they saw who rode beside me, chained and collared. They spit at him with hatred.

Tarantula scowled, teeth grinding together. Magic glimmered in a silver aura around his body. People held up the symbol of the united democracy as if they were warding him off.

"Knight Zora—Knight Zora—Knight Zora," they chanted all around.

I tried to keep a straight face, but my lips curled up as I basked in how much they loathed him. *This is the most beautiful thing I've ever seen.* They yelled insults at him, and I nodded in agreement as I pretended to wipe a tear off my face.

Tarantula shook his head at me.

If looks could kill, I'd once again have been dead.

"We love you, Zora," a child screamed as she reached out and touched my leg. She held her hand up and turned to her friends, who jumped with excitement around her.

"Save us from *them*," an old man sobbed as he reached for me, then broke into rattling coughs. "You *have* to save us."

The grin slipped from my face as ice trickled down my spine.

But who will save me?

Sound warped and my vision tunneled: far away, screaming men, women, and children were reaching for me with hope on their faces. In my mind's eye, they were crying out with the same zeal as they burned and then froze in dragons' breath. A vision of Death reached for me, tangling his corpse fingers in my hair as he breathed ice down my neck. I was petrified.

They believed in me, and yet most days I didn't even believe in myself.

I must complete my quest.

Please, old god.

Please.

I'd known the Marshal had spread propaganda about me throughout the Commonwealth, but knowing and seeing it in real life were two very different things. The pressure was crushing.

Existential obliteration. I clasped my shaking hands together, silently suffocating on my prayers.

Pink petals floated in the air as citizens threw them high, their cheers rising. Sunlight reflected dreamily through the canopy as I disintegrated.

Soldiers gestured before us to a tall, lopsided building with *Babilon Traveling Inn* written on a sign out front.

People clapped as we dismounted, calling us heroes. Young boys grabbed our horses and said something about a stable in the back. The innkeeper greeted us and led us inside, giving us keys to our four individual rooms. We followed him through hallways filled with flowers and bubbling fountains.

Bright colors were everywhere, but I felt frozen, drenched in shades of gray, a creature of the North, far from home. I didn't belong in this Southern world of hope.

Tarantula swatted a vine out of his way, shackles refracting light as magic glittered around him. He turned his head abruptly, eyes heavy-lidded, soft lashes lowered. Neither of us blinked.

Who will save me from him?

I was a creature of violence, shaped by survival in harsh circumstances, and that was the exact problem—so was he.

The Storm Wars had us both by the throat.

19

DANGEROUSLY (UN)DRESSED

Outside the open window, insects chirped as the sun set over Babilon's tree canopy. Squire stood on the ledge, his head cocked to the side, yellow eyes wide as he looked at me nervously.

A decorative fountain gurgled in the corner, and a humid breeze fluttered the sheer curtains. I sat on my canopied bed and debated the merits of deserting from the military and living alone in a Northern ice hut. Some things in life were not worth fighting tyranny over.

Mainly, my current outfit.

Doors banged, voices rising as the others stepped out into the hall at our agreed-upon time. Steeling myself, I stood up and caught a glimpse of my reflection in the corner mirror. *No way, I can't do this.*

I sat back down on the edge of the bed, cradling my head in my hands.

Squire chirped.

Stop acting pathetic. It could be worse.

I stood up. "Don't be a coward. It's not that bad," I said to myself as I paced back and forth. "You're just being dramatic." Stretching, I started to feel better. "I *can* do this."

Tawny feathers billowing in the humid breeze, Squire watched, eyes wide. "Zora," he hooted. "Are you a harlot?" (Not helpful.)

Stomping over, I pushed him out the window. He flew back up, hovering outside.

"The *slutty* harlot mad," he sang (really unhelpful). His situationally appropriate use of vocabulary was equally offensive and impressive.

"How dare you," I said, pointing my finger at him. "After everything we've been through together. It's just an outfit."

He chirped and flew away to hunt, soaring up above the rooftops.

"Don't you run away from me, mister!" I yelled.

Squire squawked back with attitude, disappearing into the trees.

Knock. "Zora?" Ella called through my door. "Did you say something? It's time to leave. Do you need help getting ready?"

"No!" I turned away from the window and girded myself. With a fresh pit in my stomach, I stepped out into the hall.

Water gurgled as it trickled down the inn's vine-covered stone walls. *Magic.* I could *feel* it with all my senses. It was a steady pressure behind my eyes and a faint tingling in my fingertips. Flowers hung from the ceiling, creating a soothing ambience. *Peaceful calm.*

The lack of danger set my teeth on edge.

I enjoyed frigid, austere things.

"Someone made a mistake," I said as I tried to cover my exposed skin with my long hair, which I'd left down to help the situation. "Somehow it looks way *worse* on."

The twins blinked at me, their jaws open.

"Wow," they said in unison.

I pointed to Ella's chest. "How come you get clothes beneath yours?" Under a white chiffon dress that hung to her knees, she wore shorts and a sleeveless top in the same color.

"I requested it before we left," Axel drawled.

"Why didn't you tell me?" I asked, folding my arms across the tiny *scrap* of fabric that was pretending to be a bra.

My long-sleeved white button-down shirt was completely sheer atop it. The only consolation was that my matching pants had a nude liner, so you couldn't see *everything*; it just created the illusion that you could.

Axel shrugged. "You didn't ask."

Ella covered her mouth, a laugh escaping from behind her hand as she wiggled her eyebrows at me. "You look . . . dreamy. Very ethereal."

"I look naked."

"*Ethereally* naked."

Axel arched an eyebrow as he lazily looked me over from head to toe. "He's going to *love* this," he said sarcastically. None of us needed to ask what prude he was referring to. "I helped him change with his shackles a while ago. I don't know what's taking him so long."

"He's probably primping," I muttered, cognizant of my own exposed state. "This is a disgrace to the Commonwealth," I said, moving my hands over my torso protectively. "The Emperor is murdering everyone, and they put me in *this.* It's blasphemy. I will be filing a detailed report about these . . . inappropriate working conditions."

Ella nodded along. "To whom will this report be addressed?"

"Everyone in the military," I said. "The Marshal. The old god."

Ella rubbed at the sheer material on my back, her touch burning through the silky fabric. "It's just for the mission. If anything, it will help us complete it quicker. How bad can it be?"

A lock clicked.

The sharp scent of dark cherry mixed with . . . *the desire to rule the world*? Chains clattered against priceless decorative platinum cuffs.

An icy shadow stretched out into the corridor, and colors lost saturation. The sound of falling water grew sharper, less bubbling and more aggressive. Flower petals ripped away as vines rustled. An unnatural wind gusted sharply as his hostility poisoned the air.

A man or a maleficent monster?

Both.

Tarantula stepped into the hall and halted mid-step.

The tips of his ears turned pink, light glinting off the rows of piercings as he purposefully stared at the space above my head.

"Absolutely *not*," he said. Maroon lips pressed into a flat line, and a vein pulsed along his jaw. His mask did nothing to conceal his displeasure. He loomed stiffly in the hall.

I choked.

He'd been given a golden chiffon fabric, the color matching the lowlights in his blond curls. His pants draped with perfect tailoring down his long legs. The worst part—he'd left his long-sleeved sheer button-down shirt undone.

Layers of lean striations flexed across his bare abdomen. His Adonis belt formed a razor-sharp V line, framing a tattoo of a silver butterfly—the bottom of which disappeared below his beltline. The sheer shirt emphasized the shocking width of his shoulders and narrowness of his waist.

Diamonds glinted at his neck, and his prisoner chains looked elegant, like purposeful accessories.

He seemed . . . *royal.*

Filthy rich.

Untouchable.

Despicable decadence.

The chiffon material pulled taut around his crotch, near bursting. His butterfly tattoo should have looked feminine and not so devastatingly *masculine.*

Shivers scraped down my spine.

Axel had more skin exposed. He wore only white flowy pants, no shirt over his chiseled chest, but he wasn't the one making it hard to breathe.

"What the damned art thou wearing, Ravenal?" Tarantula's

guttural accent made me jump out of my skin. Chains clinked as he lifted a long finger and pointed at me accusingly.

"Oh, look," Axel drawled, "they match."

I backed toward my door, laying more of my long hair across my torso as I tried to hide.

Chest heaving, Tarantula turned away from me and gripped the doorframe, muttering expletives under his breath.

Oh.

My.

Old.

God.

The sheer material slid luxuriously across his inked, muscular back. His expansive, ornate tattoo had unusual markings, and I leaned closer, trying to get a better view because the circular design seemed . . . *familiar*?

A noise of horror escaped my lips, and I slapped my hand over my mouth, too late to stifle it. *The same five symbols in Mom's journal.* The snowflake, fire, lightning, wind, and water icons were arranged within the intricate circle. *Storm magic.*

Tarantula whirled around, glaring daggers at me—well, trying to. Cheeks bright red, he stared at the space above my head as he struggled to compose himself.

"I think Zora looks perfect for our mission." Ella had far too much glee in her voice. "Sibrain Cortz won't know what hit him."

Tarantula's upper lip curled. "And how shall she *stop* him without magic?" He infused each word with maximum cruelty.

"Worry about yourself," I said as I pulled a dagger from the sheath in my combat boot and spun it between my fingers.

His smile was sardonic. "Ravenal, we both know thou art *not* going in public like . . . *this.*"

Just like that, I liked my outfit.

It has a certain flair.

"Yes—I am," I said coldly, matching his tone. "We're dressed the same. Are you changing?"

Axel raised his hand and blurted, "I vote for Zora."

Everyone turned to him with confusion.

"She wears it best."

Tarantula's gaze was knifelike. "Don't thou dare look at her." He pointed at Axel, who rolled his eyes and turned around, swaggering down the hall.

"That's my cue," he called over his shoulder.

Ella couldn't hide her laughter as she chased after her brother, and both disappeared around the corner.

Wait, guys?

I followed after them.

"Ravenal." Tarantula's voice cracked the air like a whip.

I froze.

"Who left those . . . *terrible* marks . . . on your back?"

Slowly I turned around.

We faced each other in the hall, an arm's distance between us. I recoiled, horror washing over me like a bucket of ice water. His mask of decency was obliterated, and in its wake was . . . *death.* I'd thought I'd seen his madness before, but I was wrong.

The entity before me was a force of nature, as moral as the dark side of the moon.

Total annihilation.

Murderous was too tame a description for him, because there were no words to define his capacity for destruction.

"Who?" he repeated quietly, voice frigid.

"It was a dire bear," I said, shrugging because I always forgot about the scars on my back. "Same as my face, but I'm fine now, so it doesn't matter—"

"Which dire bear?" he asked harshly. Silver turned black, magic rolling in waves off Tarantula's wide shoulders as he tensed; the exposed planes of his body went impossibly rigid, face contorted with wrath. "*What* did he look like?"

"He looked like a bear, because he *was* a bear." I laughed awkwardly. "It was just a wild animal—"

"What were his markings?" He enunciated slowly, "I. Want. A. Name."

Sanity is not his strong suit. Animal growls echoed in my darkest subconscious. I closed my eyes and clutched my head, emotions churning, struggling to stay calm. Memories played, each faster than the last: *the Barren Forest, a bear standing with blood-covered paws watching me stumble, excruciating pain; waking up healed in bed with no memory of how I'd gotten there.*

An ache throbbed behind my eyes.

When I opened them, a gasp tore from my throat. Tendrils of water sparkling silver with magic had drifted off the walls behind Tarantula and swirled slowly in a spiral—a mini-cyclone.

I dropped my glowing hands. *Not again.* Quickly I clutched them behind my back.

Tarantula didn't seem to notice, focused intently on my face.

Mentally I concentrated on the pressure in my head, on releasing the magic. Nothing happened. Exhaustion mounted, and more water gathered, a glittering whirlpool, spinning in the air behind him. I didn't know how to control my magic without gesturing, but if I brought my glowing hands up, it would give me away and Tarantula would know.

He'd realize my deceit.

Protect the quest.

"Ravenal," Tarantula said with quiet danger, shadows stretching across his face. "*Describe* the dire bear." He reached for my chin, long fingers extended, hovering a hair's breadth from my flesh. "Right now."

Heat and silver seeped off him, onto me.

"Uh . . ." The watery cyclone grew larger. "It had black fur," I said in a rush. "And I think there was a white marking on its nose?"

Tarantula inhaled sharply. "Bruce." The butterfly on his stomach slowly flapped as his striated abdominal muscles flexed tightly. He visibly shook from the force of his ire.

"Bruce?" I asked. "The dire bear's name is Bruce? That's—"

"The man." He bared his teeth, and for a second, his canines looked sharp, like Axel's. "I shall rip out *both* of his hearts for leaving such marks on thee." Black flames leaped higher, the scent of magic burning.

Water spiraled faster in the air behind him, a blur of glistening droplets, defying gravity.

"Wait . . ." I whispered. "Are the dire bears people . . . who transform into . . . bears?" *Are shifters real?*

It sounded so ridiculous saying it aloud that I almost laughed, but then I remembered how so many people who ventured outside the Northern Commune walls were attacked by dire bears. Almost as if . . . they were purposefully patrolling, keeping us inside the city.

Tarantula didn't deny it. Silently he seethed, still flushed, unable to meet my gaze.

Horror rose sharply, and I fought the urge to be sick. "The dire bears attack us on the Emperor's orders." I backed away from him down the hall. *Please don't look over your shoulder,* I mentally begged him.

By some miracle, Tarantula kept his gaze forward and followed me as if entranced.

Please.

Please.

Please.

I crossed my fingers behind me for luck, drawing Tarantula farther away from the cyclone of sparkling water still spiraling in the air.

"But that means . . ." I said, thoughts sluggish, head throbbing from magical exertion as I struggled to connect the dots through my panic. "They let me live. The dire bear . . . it stopped attacking me. Why? Why me?" *Why am I always so lucky?*

Tarantula slowly tilted his head, tendons straining beneath chiffon as he followed me. A predator locked on its prey. *Hunting.*

I backed away faster, almost to the corner.

"I do not know," Tarantula said. *Whoosh.* Silver exploded around his body. My hair whipped as wind gusted, ruined flowers and vines filling the air. Diamonds winked mockingly on his throat. *He's not contained in any way.*

His shredded debris joined my cyclone.

A sound of fear escaped my throat. He froze at the noise and closed his eyes, head tipped, nostrils flaring like he was struggling for control.

Hastily I waved my glowing hands at the water behind him, and the cyclone stopped, droplets raining to the floor, taking flower petals with them.

Turning, I sprinted.

I glanced over my shoulder; Tarantula's eyes shot open. He chased after me. Leaping down the stairs two at a time, I swallowed a scream. Bursting into the lobby, I nearly ran into the waiting twins.

"Did you try singing to him?" Axel suggested. "I find it helps."

I panted with my hands on my knees.

"What helps?" Tarantula asked as he came to a stop behind me.

All three of us ignored him.

"It's not your fault that you're pitchy." Axel winked at me. "Not everyone can be talented like me."

"How do you put up with him?" I asked Ella.

"Excessive corporal punishment," she deadpanned, and I forced out a laugh despite the abject terror clawing at me. Phantom pain laced down the scars on my spine.

The dire bears are people, and I almost just revealed my magic.

Breathing shallowly, I focused on Ella. I was playing a dangerous game, and I kept forgetting there were no rules.

Ella and Axel stiffened, both looking at Tarantula behind me, and I refused to glance back. *He will not intimidate me.*

"Let's go," I said, trying not to ponder any of the new revelations. There'd be time to panic later.

Ella linked her arm through mine and led us out into the street. "So, we're looking for a tall man with pale skin, long light blond hair, and colorless eyes," she whispered as we walked, reciting the description the Marshal had given us about Sibrain Cortz.

"Hideousness must run in the family," I said loudly with disdain, hiding behind bravado.

My spine *burned* under the weight of his intense scrutiny. His fury seethed, a violent tangible energy. I fought the urge to cover up and scream at him to look away. It didn't help that for some reason I couldn't stop thinking about his butterfly tattoo. *Why does he have it?*

Thoughts spiraling, I barely noticed as we traversed down a narrow stone path wedged between row homes. We came to a stop at a tall wooden door with two burly men guarding it, dressed in similar chiffon fabric. The building was completely concealed by thick vegetation, with torches hanging in its shadows.

"We're here to sample your *wine*," Axel drawled as he stepped forward, his chest puffed up.

The guards barely spared him a glance. "The Bear of the North," one said with awe as he stared at me, enraptured, then at Tarantula, who loomed behind me in cuffs. "The first Knight Mage to capture a Royal Mage in all of history . . ." The guard trailed off like he'd lost the ability to speak.

He gestured to a large painting hanging on the wall beside

the door. The canvas depicted *me*: I held up Tarantula by his hair, my knife protruding from his stomach, with a fierce scowl on my scarred, blood-covered face. Candles surrounded our notorious portrait. *Some sort of shrine?*

"It's our greatest honor," the other guard said as they both bowed low to me, "to be in your illustrious presence."

"It was my privilege to serve the Commonwealth," I said awkwardly. "It was truly my *pleasure* to stab him."

In my periphery, Tarantula huffed and rolled his eyes.

"Frankly," I continued, suddenly enjoying the moment, "I'd do it again, *right now*, just for the good of the—"

"Alright, thanks for having us," Ella said as she grabbed my arm and cut me off. "May we enter? The Bear of the North has heard *many* great things about Babilon's wine taverns."

The guards made sounds of half worship, half shock, as they nodded at her with wide eyes, transfixed by her beauty. They hastily pulled open the door for us to pass, still unable to speak.

Nothing could have prepared me for the inside.

Dark, seductive, and leafy.

Mystically enchanting.

Immense windows were being pulled closed by muscular men yanking ropes attached to a pulley system, ushering in darkness. The ceiling towered so high up that I couldn't see it among the dense foliage. The entire structure had been built around an impressive banyan tree; thousands of lanterns hung from its sprawling leafy branches and hanging vines; lights glittered like fireflies in the darkness.

The lanterns weren't the only things hanging from the tree.

Male and female dancers twirled from colorful silk ribbons that dangled from the towering branches, silky chiffon fabric shimmering. They were upside down, their long legs contorted into impossible positions as they lowered and raised themselves up on their scarves.

Down below on the floor, within the tree's thick roots,

couches were spread around and filled with people in similar outfits. The patrons smoked long Southern cigarettes and laughed as they savored ornate glasses of wine.

A melody played from the glittering foliage. Musicians sat atop the high branches, playing various instruments, and the tinkling sounds were falling from above like rain.

Male and female servers in richly colored chiffon poured wine into elegant flower-shaped glasses.

"The Knight Mages!" a voice shouted. The music stopped, dancers paused mid-twirl, and the people on the couches sat up straighter.

Everyone gawked at us.

We waved awkwardly.

Murmurs filled the room, and cheers exploded.

The music resumed, and the dancers went back to twirling among the lanterns. Hyperaware of how much clothing I *wasn't* wearing, I shifted my hair over the front of my torso, covering my chest. Of course, that left my scarred spine exposed, and a magical gust of air wafted across it.

Tarantula's gaze *burned.*

A waiter appeared with a tray full of wineglasses. "Fairy wine." He winked. "Compliments of the house."

Axel grabbed the rose glass and threw the shimmering red liquid back in one gulp. Ella took the stem of a hibiscus delicately, and to my surprise, Tarantula accepted the jasmine glass.

The waiter gestured to the last artful glass, a bougainvillea. "And one for the Bear of the North," he offered in a playful tone.

"That's okay," I said. "I don't drink."

Mom had said someone wrote a story in the *Democratic Papers* that fairy wine, named after a fictional drink from the fairy tales, was secretly a dangerous import from the Empire. But the author died mysteriously, and the next paper renounced all their findings. It was all very suspicious.

Mom had warned me never to drink fairy wine because of the danger: the censorship.

The waiter winked. "Don't worry. I have something we procured *just* for you today." From a velvet pouch, he pulled out a skinny glass tube in the shape of an iris, full of sparkling silver powder. "They call it magic in a bottle. Just pour it on your tongue for a special . . . *experience*."

He held it out for me to take, tipping it back and forth so the substance glittered in the shadowy light. I blinked, shaking myself out of a trance. As much as it was tempting to take, I needed to keep my wits about me.

The waiter leaned toward me. "The owner of this establishment told me to give it to you," he whispered conspiratorially. "He's watching us right now and wants to talk to you about how you *feel* after you take it." He licked his lips suggestively.

Sibrain Cortz is the owner.

I tamped down the urge to look around for him, not wanting to give myself away and appear suspicious. The waiter pressed the iris into my hand. "He wants to know if the Bear of the North is *strong* enough to . . . handle its effects."

"How magnanimous of him," Tarantula sneered behind me, condescension dripping from his mouth as he whirled the liquid slowly in his jasmine petals, clearly trying to blow our cover. "She won't be taking it—"

I dumped the sparkly powder onto my tongue. It was chalky and a little sweet.

"Tell him thank you," I said coyly as I leaned toward the waiter. "And that I'd *love* to give him my gratitude . . . in person."

The waiter breathed raggedly as he stared down at my partially exposed chest. "Go get your owner." I swiped a napkin off his tray. Pretending to dab my mouth, I discreetly spit the drug into it and shoved it into an empty cup. The taste still lingered on my tongue. *Hopefully it's not that potent in small doses.*

Nodding absentmindedly, the waiter turned and disappeared into the darkness of the room.

I motioned to the twins, feeling triumphant.

Ella had already wandered away. She stared glassily up at the tree lights like she'd never seen lanterns before, sipping her wine. Axel had moved across the room, leaning against a hanging root, two handsome men close on either side of him.

How did they move so fast?

A faint buzzing tickled my ears from the small amount of the drug that had lingered on my tongue, but otherwise I felt fine. Or did I?

Sighing, I debated, *Should I wait or explore?*

"Ravenal, what was that?" Tarantula's face hovered next to mine. A gust of icy wind blew down my spine, and my skin pebbled. His breath smelled sweet, like sun-ripened grapes and . . . *deplorable sins.*

"That was me completing the mission," I said as I studied the room, fantasizing about a world in which he didn't exist. "Or have you forgotten why we're here?"

I stepped forward.

Tarantula followed, looming behind me like a possessed shadow.

"Did thou enjoy having his filthy eyes all over your flesh? Was it enjoyable, how he debased thee with his attention?" he asked darkly, breath wafting across the side of my face as he leaned hazardously close. "Do thou enjoy cosplaying as a common tramp?"

"I'm in long sleeves and full pants."

Wind whispered across my neck, down my chest, stomach, and then brushed across my sensitive inner thighs. Pleasure exploded, heat burning in its wake as Tarantula caressed me with his dark magic.

He's taunting you.

I whirled to face him, finger raised.

"Don't talk to me about *decency* when you took a creed that aspires to nothing but slaughter," I whisper-shouted in his face, still not over the fact that the dire bears could be purposefully murdering Northerners. "I'm here to complete a mission . . . so be a good little hostage." I looked pointedly at his shackled wrists. "And keep your violent presence, *and* your magic, away from me."

He stared down at where my finger pressed into his bare chest, buttons open on either side, and then dragged his eyes up to mine.

"Thou cannot *fathom* the sacrifice that my creed entails," he said coldly as he leaned forward, pushing his bare skin against my finger. "At least I know what I'm fighting for. Thou live in a house of glass, Ravenal, propped up by spoon-fed propaganda." He exhaled roughly. "Do thou ever tire of your misplaced righteousness?"

Chemicals rushed through my bloodstream.

Scents sharpened and colors swirled in geometric patterns; Tarantula's face congealed, curls melting, rivulets mixing with his mask; the cobalt spider crawled slowly across his jaw, fangs snapping at me; a butterfly flew up his chest.

Apparently the drug had a very high potency even in tiny doses. *Why am I always surprised by the disastrous events of my life?*

Tarantula's eyes widened as he studied my face, like he could tell something was wrong with me but wasn't quite sure what.

I leaned closer so our lips ghosted across each other. "You can pretend with everyone else," I breathed out into his mouth. "But I'm the only person who sees you for exactly *who* you are."

He slowly turned his head, his warm lips grazing the side of my face, leaving a trail of heat. "And what have thou condemned me to be?" His magic brushed across my throat, caressing my scar.

"A prude."

His teeth ground together as he flushed.

Bullseye.

I turned on my heel.

He grabbed my arm, voice dropping to a gravelly rasp. "The hedonistically inclined *lower* classes chase pleasure anywhere they can get it." Wind slowly trailed up my calves, flowers of pleasure blooming in its wake. "Zora Ravenal, art thou a hedonist? Is that what thou want . . . from me?"

"I want *nothing* from you." I tried to yank my arm out of his grasp, but he stepped closer.

He bent forward at the waist so we stood eye to eye. "Tell me, Ravenal, do thou believe in soulmates?"

"What?"

"Do thou believe?" he said coldly.

"Why . . . would you ask me that?"

"It's a yes or no question."

"No."

"Good." He dropped my arm, his eyes sharper than broken glass as he stood tall. "*Very* good."

I walked away.

This time he didn't follow.

Colorful flowers bled into streaks of pastels as the leafy vegetation morphed into endless kaleidoscopic patterns. The lower I sank, the higher I flew.

20

(MISSION)ARY

Shadows stretched in the smoky din. I slunk around the hanging roots of the banyan tree with blue Mist swirling around my ankles. Everything glowed with a silver shimmer, and I couldn't tell if it was real or a drug-fueled hallucination.

Dancers spun above on their silks, and whispers followed me as I floated past, coalescing into a buzzing drone.

"It's her."

"The newest Knight."

"The Bear."

"She captured a Royal Mage."

"Savage Northerner."

"Dangerously attractive."

"Did you see her silver scar?"

Southerners watched from all around, laughing, drunk on their fairy wine. I observed it all from afar, detached, high out of my mind, as they basked in the rush of seduction.

On the surface, it was just a normal establishment, but I could smell it on them—they were drinking their way through the Storm Wars. They were either idiots or geniuses, *maybe both.*

It was getting harder to maneuver through space and time. Bones congealing, I melted away, *splendidly, sluggishly scintillated.* Petals drifted softly through the fragrant air, and I reached for one, but my hand was empty.

Are they real?

Nothing was clear.

Surrealism mounted as gentle, sublime sounds filled the humid air. High above in the leafy branches, the musicians played a delicate tune. Movement flickered, and I pivoted with maximum effort—pale features and blond hair flashed in the dark. *Perfect. Just as I planned.*

The man turned, unmasked face exposed.

I made a show of stumbling sluggishly and ducked behind a thick hanging root, collapsing back against the bark.

Sibrain Cortz thought he was stalking me.

But I was luring him in.

From the quick glimpse I'd gotten, his platinum hair hung long down his back in soft waves, at odds with the harsh planes of his facial features. He'd abandoned his creed, and the face of a Royal Mage was unsettling to see in all its glory. It had felt voyeuristic, wrong, to peer so freely upon the mysterious Empire elite. *He's definitely a spy.*

The scent of his magic hit me first—*cowardice?*

"Why are you hiding, beautiful?" a masculine voice purred as Sibrain raised a light eyebrow and stepped into my alcove, invading my personal space. Just like I planned. He spoke with a modern cadence and a hint of an accent. He wore nothing but silky white shorts; his attire should have been attractive.

He inspired . . . *boredom*. Droll ennui.

Nothing about him startled or provoked my thoughts. No adrenaline rush stole my breath. We stood eye to eye and had similar builds, but he was devoid of all contrast, bland, a washed-out man who would never reach the terrifying glory of his contemporaries.

Sensations whispered across my throat.

Silver flashed.

Oh.

His fingers were outstretched and pointing at my neck. Realization dawned like molasses. Unlike when Tarantula used his wind powers, I barely noticed it happening. Sibrain was asphyxiating me with his magic, and I hadn't even realized.

I tipped my head to the side and studied him up close. This was a good chance to practice my hunting. *It's been too long.*

His eyes narrowed as if he was confused why I wasn't making a Shield and fighting back like a Knight. Lantern lights warped into halos backlighting us in a warm haze of magic.

"So . . . *this* is the girl our illustrious Emperor was *so* obsessed with. How intriguing," Sibrain said softly, his accent nonexistent if not for a tiny inflection on his consonants. His oily gaze fixated on my silver scar. "Did you know, he used to go *on* and *on* about you? He even had a portrait of your face, hanging above his royal bed. We all thought he'd lost his mind. How could he be so bedeviled by a *peasant* girl? It didn't make sense then."

He took a step closer.

"And then . . . you dared to reject him." He held up two fingers. "Twice."

I leaned away from him, trying not to inhale his putrid scent of cowardice.

He pursed his lips mockingly. "Did you know, it's all your fault? You broke his heart, left him devastated . . . hopeless. And he grew more . . . *sadistically* inclined by the day."

Men loved to blame women for their evil, like it would absolve them. It didn't. I held my breath, which was surprisingly difficult, since he was also trying to choke me.

"How did you get this magical scar?" He reached for my face. "You've been marked. Do you know you're being . . . *watched*?" He looked around as if searching for someone.

I batted his hand away.

He's just trying to scare me.

Unconcerned, Sibrain continued his villainous monologue. "All that tender obsession became dark. *Tainted.* It didn't surprise me when he put a bounty on your head—you broke him." His freezing fingers wrapped around my neck. "There's something . . . *despicable* . . . dangerous about you. How impressed he'll be when I claim the bounty on your head." He smiled wider, his light blue eyes deranged.

His nails dug into my sensitive skin, closing my already constricting throat.

"First—a taste."

I let him come to me.

Closer.

Closer.

Closer.

Wetness brushed against my lips, and I jolted as Sibrain dragged his open mouth across my chin and lower to my neck. His gross tongue swept out, licking.

Wait for the right moment.

My temples throbbed. A sound creaked above.

Water poured over us like an irrigation pipe had burst above in the tree. It rained down, drenching both of us in my magic. My hair was soaking wet, sticking to my skin. Puddles grew at our feet. *Oops.* I tried to pretend it wasn't me, hiding my hands behind my back.

Sibrain pulled away from my neck and looked up with confusion, searching for the source.

I leaned forward, falling into him as if I'd passed out.

Now.

He took a step back, staggering for a second under my dead weight. I kicked my leg up to my butt as I leaned, grabbed the dagger in my boot, and thrust. I stabbed upward, straight through his gonads, and pulled the knife back.

"Filthy scum." He shoved me away, slamming my head back against the tree with a wet crunch, and I saw stars. He lunged, teeth bared, eyes manic, long blond hair soaking.

I might be suffocating, drugged, and partially blinded from pain, but I was no man's victim. Hand cramping from fisting the hilt with all my strength, I shoved the dagger up into his stomach with everything I had.

Blood gushed between us.

He grappled for the slick hilt, trying and failing to yank it out of my steady hand. He was gravely injured but still alive. Pulling the knife back, arm straightened, I flung my hand up in an arc.

Sibrain gurgled, blood spraying from his lips onto my face as my dagger speared through the side of his neck. Fighting, he threw me back harder, and my head cracked loudly against the tree trunk for the second time. *Damn him.* Sharp pain radiated down my neck, but I held on to my dagger and yanked him with me.

He leaned against me, lips sputtering crimson, nails clawing at my wrist in a perverse embrace as I pressed my dagger deeper into his neck, trying to sever his spinal cord. *He deserves it.*

I pushed the blade—

The world abruptly changed.

Cold replaced humidity, and I was leaning against the wide trunk of an ice-covered pine tree. Needles clattered in the wind high above where the branches started. Snowy flakes drifted lazily, covering the Barren Forest in a solemn hush. The world was white, cold, and mystical.

My teeth chattered.

Sibrain was skewered in my arms, his blood covering both of our chests and necks. Red splattered obscenely across the pristine snow at our feet. Nails dragged painfully along my wrist.

The flares of agony brought me back to the man who stared at me with wide eyes, struggling to dislodge my dagger from his neck. Snow gathered on his hair and bare shoulders. His breath came out as a frosty cloud, while mine was basically nonexistent, still partially strangled by his magic. *He's so pathetic.*

Icy branches clattered above. I pushed Sibrain away and looked around, desperate to figure out why this kept happening.

There has to be some reason— A single red rose glistened in the snowflakes.

Why the rose?

Using my distraction, Sibrain seized my throat much harder than before with his magic in a last-ditch effort to avoid certain death.

Humidity and music returned, and the lantern-covered branches of the banyan tree twinkled above our heads. Sibrain stumbled back into the smoky darkness. A pile of snow melted atop his head. *How is this possible?*

Bark scraped my spine as I slid down the tree trunk to the floor, clutching my neck, lungs burning. My skin was ice to the touch, prickling painfully as it adjusted to the sudden heat. I stared down at my bright red hands with confusion.

"Today I'll be the one with *all* the satisfaction," Sibrain said through gritted teeth. Snarling in agony, he ripped my dagger from his neck. In slow motion, he stabbed it toward me—

I started to roll away, but his arm stopped, the blade inches from my cheek as he struggled against an invisible force. His hair blew straight back from his head as if he stood in a wind tunnel.

I clutched at my blocked airway.

The scent of murderous delights filled the air, mixing with the floral aroma. My vision blackened at the edges, and the world warped in a silvery haze. Sibrain stood frozen above me with my dagger still outstretched, blood pouring from his neck wound. His eyes flicked down to mine, hatred seething in their depths.

Snap. Sibrain's raised arm broke back at a gruesome angle. Magic wrapped around my dagger, pulling it out of his hand, and it drifted down slowly like a feather, lying gently on my lap as I clawed at my neck.

Need air. Need air. Need air.

Silver exploded, whipping forward in a stream of punishing wind, and the gust was contained to an impossibly small radius: Sibrain's face. An odd slurping rip grew in intensity as the magic blasted his facial skin back in endless ripples. It slowly tore away. Sibrain opened his mouth to scream. A chunk of bark detached from the tree and flew into it, grotesquely impaling him.

I inhaled greedily, fresh oxygen flooding my starving lungs as Sibrain *finally* lost control of his magic and fell to his knees, grunting in pain.

Silver boots stepped silently from the shadows, a dark figure looming above an agonized Sibrain. A glowing hand lowered, long elegant fingers clenching.

"Do thou feel . . . *satisfaction* . . . now?" Tarantula asked casually.

Sibrain stopped struggling.

In a bewildering display, he lowered himself forward, bark still protruding from his lips, and pressed his skinless face to the ground at Tarantula's feet. He prostrated himself as if pleading for forgiveness, quivering in his presence.

Wind gusted, petals and branches thrashing. With one swift motion, Tarantula grabbed Sibrain by his hair, picked up the dagger in my lap, and decapitated him. He lazily dropped the severed head and wiped the blade on his chiffon pants.

He pointed the hilt down, lips thinning as he turned the full weight of his attention toward me. He pressed the hilt into my palm. It took me a couple tries before I could slide the dagger back into the sheath inside my combat boot. My hand shook violently.

With the knife finally secured, I stared blankly at the floor. A hand with neatly trimmed nails extended down to me. I took the offered palm.

Tarantula hoisted me to my feet.

"Did he . . . do anything?" he asked in a peculiar voice.

"Just kissed my neck," I said numbly, shivering at the memory of the unwanted advance but glad my plan had worked. *Well, kind of.* I shook my head, trying to reorder my addled thoughts. "What should we do with the—"

"Stop speaking." Tarantula held up his hand and cut me off. Silver hissed as it steamed off his palm.

"What's wrong with you?" I asked.

Tarantula grabbed my shoulders in his steely grip. The sweet scent of fairy wine wafted from his breath. "What is wrong . . . with *me*?" he asked slowly. "Why did thou allow yourself to be taken by surprise?"

"Uh, no. I was hunting *him*. I stabbed him three times," I pointed out. "In case you missed that."

A vein jumped across his jaw. "I lose thee for five seconds . . . and find thee suffocating and covered in blood with . . ." He trailed off like he couldn't finish the sentence. He roughly dragged his hands through his curls, leaving pink streaks.

"I had a plan," I said quietly, unable to articulate that I'd been transported into the Barren Forest. *I've fully lost my mind.* Drugged surrealism mounting, I tried to find reason. "We need to get rid of the body and—"

"Leave the pieces. I'll handle it later—"

"Southerners will see the body. A dereliction of our duty. I don't think that's what the Marshal—"

He laughed loudly, an icy, severe sound. "I shall handle the Southerners too. Do thou really care what she wants of us?"

"The mission is . . ."

"The mission?" he mocked, voice tight with barely constrained violence. "Is that all thou can speak of after he—"

"Stop." I pushed him back weakly, trying to make space between us. "You're acting . . . strange," I whispered. "Is it because Sibrain's another *precious* royal elite—"

"Don't thou dare speak his name." He flexed his fingers like they ached. "Thou do not know how close I am to . . . *killing* every single worthless person in this entire Commune."

"Ah, a massacre. How original." I was unsure if I was flying, falling, or standing on the ground. "Do you want an award? Perhaps another continent to terrorize—I know that's a big thing for your people."

He smiled slowly.

"You're a tyrant." I pushed away from him weakly, side-stepping around Sibrain's body.

Tarantula's arm shot out, chain taut, as he blocked my retreat. "Thou art not going *anywhere*, Ravenal."

I tamped down a wave of trepidation. "You're running out of moves, spider," I taunted, feeling odder by the second. It was getting harder to speak normally.

"Oh, I have plenty of moves left. Do not force my hand. Thou will have *regrets*."

I stood on my tiptoes. "I—already—regret—you," I said with intense concentration. In the shine of his platinum mask, my eyes glowed with rage, the usual amber an eerie shade of yellow.

He wet his lips. "So, thou admit it—thou art *mine* to regret."

"Not what I said."

"Careful. Semantics is a slippery slope, *Ravenal*."

"Truth is nuanced, *spider*."

He clicked his tongue. "And what . . . is the truth?"

I stood taller as he leaned lower, and I pressed our noses together. "The world is in ruin. It's. All. Your. Fault."

His smirk dripped with sin. "Exactly—so do not test me, vassal."

Vassal.

Vassal.

Vassal.

~~*It means nothing.*~~

I had a bad feeling his secrets were *far* more dangerous than mine.

He reached up and cupped the back of my head. His fingers returned covered in blood. Long seconds passed as he pulled away, looking between his hand and my face.

"Thou art injured." His tone was glacial.

Fear morphed into something more perilous, and I pushed past him, driving my shoulder roughly into his to make space. *Ouch.* I might as well have rammed a brick wall.

He must have seen something in my expression, because he

slowly stepped aside and he didn't stop me as I retreated into the buzzing room.

Ignore him.

He doesn't matter.

I glanced over my shoulder. Tarantula sauntered through the room, stalking after me with a rigid, refined posture. In slow motion, he brought his thumb to his mouth, the one covered in *my* blood. His burning eyes held mine. He licked his thumb wantonly from base to tip. Eyelashes fluttering, he visibly shivered.

I walked into a hanging root.

Masculine laughter echoed.

Whirling around, I turned to scold him and— *What in the damned?* Drugged, concussed, confused, I backed away from him through the maze of hanging roots and couches.

Tarantula smiled, and his canines were sharp. *Predatory.* Curls framed his mask, swirling with falling petals. He was like one of Marge's oil paintings—the type you stood in front of for hours. His appearance seduced the primordial subconscious.

Wind whispered gently across my neck.

A faint glow illuminated the smoky shadows. Strange silver lines flowed across Tarantula's exposed skin.

I stumbled, still moving backward.

My senses were betraying me.

This isn't real.

It can't be.

Tarantula's eyes blazed behind his mask. Every inch of his skin glowed with silver occult lines, as if he'd shattered into a million separate pieces and each shard had been melded back together with molten metal; a spider crawled across his jaw, and a gorgeous butterfly flapped low on his abdomen; opal fangs hung lower than his full bottom lip.

I turned and sprinted away from him.

Wait, are vampires real?

21

ATTR(ACT)ION

TWO DRUGGED HOURS LATER . . .

I leaned back on a low couch, head spinning, and the luxurious emerald material melded to my aching body.

When did I sit down?

Sibrain's blood caked my throat and chest. *My* blood itched across the back of my head and neck. A migraine throbbed in sync with my heartbeat. My lungs still burned from a light strangulation, and my concussion fueled the drugged cognitive dissonance.

I wanted to leave, but I could barely move my fingers. Too much effort. Easier to just melt into this couch.

Vines, roots, and flowers hung low, brushing against my head in the darkness; dancers twirled above in the haze, lanterns twinkling around them in starbursts; instruments crooned from the canopy as musicians played exquisitely.

On my right, a man and woman leaned together, giggling as they flirted. I stared at them, feeling . . . *nothing.*

The plight of a lifelong adrenaline junkie—there were only so many dangers that created enough of a rush. Decorative fingernails clicked against glasses as my couch companions sipped fairy wine, laughing with glossy eyes.

The humidity left me uncomfortably warm, and I missed the inhospitable cold of the freezing North.

Someone gave a toast, and flower glasses clinked together as Southerners cheered. I sank deeper into the cushions. All my energy—*exhausted.*

Staring up at the twinkly leafy canopy, I pretended the starbursts of light from the lanterns were galaxies in the night sky, winking down at me.

At some indeterminable point, someone pushed a long, minty cigarette between my lips. With intense concentrated effort, I held it lightly between my teeth. Smoke curled around my face, cooling my eyes, but I didn't inhale.

I tipped my head forward.

Big mistake.

Directly across the room, on a similarly situated plum-colored couch, a lone man sat with perfect, elegant posture. His cut, tall figure contrasted violently with the soft jewel-toned fabric. Golden chiffon was draped across him.

Tarantula stared at me through the din.

He held the neck of a crimson fairy wine bottle, bringing the drink lazily up to his lips.

Images niggled at the back of my mind, and I could have sworn he'd transformed earlier, but no one around looked alarmed. *I must have imagined the silver lines and fangs.*

Lids lowered, I oscillated between observing the branches above and watching the danger—him.

Patrons made eyes at Tarantula, but he ignored them all. Slowly he licked droplets of wine off his glistening lips. Visibility was low in the haze of cigarette smoke. Sultry laughter intensified.

A cool gust of wind, sharp with magic, blew underneath my chin, lifting my head up to look at— Tarantula stared at me, head lowered, the white bottoms of his eyes visible. *A dire wolf crouched low in the brush, hunting its prey with single-minded intensity.*

Another gust of wind trailed slowly down my feverish neck, and I hummed with pleasure, pondering sluggishly where the nice breeze came from.

Tarantula's mouth quirked up with amusement, magic dancing off his shoulders. He leaned back, powerful thighs parted, and his long-sleeved shirt fell open. His chest was obscene, covered in streaks of blood. He leisurely brought the wine bottle back up to his lips.

Head spinning, wind blowing coolly down my chest and across my stomach, I relaxed back on the cushions.

An upside-down dancer twirled on a scarf straight above me.

His head lowered slowly. I blinked, and the stranger's face hovered above mine. Legs tensed, wrapped in silk, he held himself upside down. His gaze traveled across my stomach and then fixated hungrily on my exposed chest. From his expression, he didn't mind the gore. Time crawled, but the dancer never looked at my face, not once, and I didn't know why it mattered, but it did.

I sighed out a puff of smoke as the dancer lowered even closer, hooded eyes still on my chest.

The people next to me kissed sloppily. The woman's eyes were wide open. *Not everyone has chemistry.*

I dragged my gaze forward.

Tarantula's lips had thinned into a straight line as he worked his jaw back and forth. His eyes were blazing, snow on fire, and a new tension corrupted his posture—a deadliness. His profile sharpened. Forced proximity had bred familiarity with his many moods, and there was no denying it. He was *boiling.*

The telltale cobalt vein pulsed along his jaw just beneath his spider tattoo. Lantern light danced across the side of his face smeared in fresh blood. Crimson stained his long fingers and was splattered across his chest and clothes.

A crime scene of a man.

Tarantula brought two bloody fingers, his pointer and middle finger, up to his pillowy lips and pressed them slowly inside his open mouth.

Silvery wind gusted softly across my two fingers, mimicking his actions. I felt flushed and shaky all over. My heart raced beneath my ribs. *Adrenaline overload.*

Tarantula smirked as he dragged his saliva-covered fingers down his chin and neck and over the striated ridges of his blood-covered abdominal muscles. Delight quivered across my senses as the whispering magic mapped the same path down my tender flesh.

Minty smoke cooled my lungs as I gasped raggedly. He brought his graceful fingers lower to the butterfly ink right above his beltline. His tongue flicked out, dragging across his mouth, and he cupped himself through his straining pants.

Dark hair obstructed my view. I leaned to the left, trying to get a better look. The upside-down dancer was shimmying lower. *Get out of my way.* I tilted my head, neck aching, not wanting to miss a second of the show.

Tarantula lifted his hand from his pants and saluted me as he leaned lazily back into the cushions, his thighs parting wider, fingers loose around the neck of the bottle.

He flexed his stomach as he drank, and the butterfly half disappeared where the silky material between his thighs cupped his obscene bulge.

He's just a man.

His lashes lowered.

An extremely handsome, diabolical man.

I struggled to breathe. It felt like we were the only two people alive, playing in a never-ending game of chess.

Silver streamed out of his nose as he exhaled. *Like the dragon he rides.*

The upside-down dancer slid lower, fully blocking my view.

We were face-to-face. He reached forward and tangled his hands in my hair as I tried to dodge out of the way. He pulled my head toward his, eyes closed. I watched him go in for the kiss with morbid fascination, rolling my cigarette nervously back and forth with my tongue.

Branches clattered on a sharp breeze, and lanterns rattled. The corner of the dancer's mouth pressed against mine. Silk ripped violently. His mouth disappeared as he went flying across the room.

I blinked.

Tarantula loomed above me. *How did he move so fast?*

What is he waiting for—

Pop.

A lantern exploded.

Pop-pop-pop-pop-pop-pop-pop.

In the tree above, one by one, every lantern shattered. Flames whooshed, growing horrifically fast, fanned by storm magic. All music stopped, replaced by shouts of terror.

Tarantula smirked. "Fire!" he yelled at the top of his lungs, infusing fake fear into his voice. "*Fire!*"

A momentary pause stretched, and then the place erupted with sheer panic. The couch dipped as it was vacated, Southerners converging into a screaming stampede. *Wait for me, guys.* No one waited. I didn't move a single muscle, because I couldn't. Dancers and musicians fell from above. The fire spread.

Tarantula and I were the only ones untouched. Sweat poured in rivulets down my chest as the temperature skyrocketed. He observed me with smug satisfaction.

Breezes caressed my face, trailing across my cheekbones.

He leisurely mapped my features with his magic while the building burned around us. Southerners cried out. Tree branches cracked loudly, and the couch vibrated as the giant banyan tree's foundation shook. The fire raged, flamed by his magic, and it felt like there was nothing that could stop him.

Diamonds glowed brightly around his neck as if fighting, *and failing*, to counteract his awful power as it streamed from him in waves.

I sucked on my cigarette.

"Get *up*, Ravenal," Tarantula ordered.

"Die," I ordered back.

Wind shrieked, a rapid intensification of magic. "Now," he said coldly.

"No?"

People screamed; branches crashed down everywhere; the entire banyan tree uprooted, flaming and falling, crushing people; jagged chunks of ceiling dropped like missiles.

Nice, another massacre.

He plucked my cigarette from my lips and brought it up to his crimson-stained mouth. Instead of smoking it, he turned it to the side and licked slowly across the paper, eyes never leaving mine.

His pupils dilated, black devouring the holographic sheen of his irises.

"What are you doing?" My voice was impossibly hoarse.

"Tasting thee."

Awareness prickled down my flushed neck, and I struggled to catch my breath. With every ounce of strength I possessed, I ignored the butterflies in my stomach and pointed my finger up at him. It glowed a stunning silver, steaming with magic, bright in the darkness.

"E—vil," I sounded out as pressure expanded inside my head. "D—ie."

A loud rumbling shook the floor. *Crack.* Silver-streaked water spurted up in thick streams, drenching both of us. He threw the cigarette down.

Crack.

Crack.

Crack.

Pipes exploded deep under the floor. Magic-infused water shot up and rained down hard, combating the flames.

Damn it all. I tried to hide the fact that my magic *yearned* to combat his. I tucked my hands under my thighs, hiding the bright glow. Head pounding, I fought against the pressure. Exhaustion intensified, draining me of life.

"You broke the pipes," I said, trying to come up with a cover.

Curls clung to the sides of his face, and he shook his head, warm water spraying off him. His eyes were locked on mine, simmering with heat, and he seemed fully unaware that *I* was the reason for the deluge.

Fires dissipated with a sizzle; his wind promptly flamed them back to a roar; the scent of burning intensified; water gushed into the air, fighting back the flames.

Bending low, Tarantula pushed wet hair off my face and tucked it gently behind my ear. Butterflies played guerrilla warfare in my stomach, and a strange new exhaustion made everything spin.

Tarantula frowned and pressed his inner wrist to my forehead. Blood exploded in an arc nearby as a falling branch impaled a Southerner. *That's not good.*

"Do thou have a fever?" Tarantula asked with concern.

"*Go* . . ." I trailed off, struggling to speak as I battled dizziness and magical exertion.

He squatted, leveling his ear near my mouth so he could hear me. "What art thou trying to say? Art thou okay?" He gently cupped the back of my injured head with his palm, prisoner chains clinking together.

". . . screw yourself," I said straight into his ear.

Rule of survival: Never swallow arachnid venom. Always spit it out.

"I think—" he sighed "—I shall screw thee instead, Ravenal." Our cheeks were pressed together, his mask feverish against my face, heated by his unreasonable body heat.

"You don't mean that," I said, voice shaking.

"Oh, but I do . . ."

"Please . . ." I leaned closer into him. "Stop sharing your feelings. No one asked."

He pulled away, shaking his head as if I was a lost cause.

Pipes exploded like bombs; water poured from above, sizzling over flames.

"Ravenal, thou art by far the single most annoying woman I have ever met."

I held my breath, refusing to inhale his masculine insolence. "I can be *way* worse."

He nodded curtly like he'd come to a decision. In one swift motion, he tossed me face-first over his shoulder and carried me through the wreckage. "I told thee earlier that I would handle the Southerners," he said casually. "But thou *never* listen. Never has a woman been more impatient, belligerent, sanctimonious, obstinate, or dangerously . . . beguiling."

Head bobbing helplessly, I scowled at the dimples on the bottom of his muscular back and pointed my glowing hands at a woman who was caught between two burning tree branches. I directed a jet of water, and it drenched the area. The fire dissipated. Praying, she pointed up to the sky in gratitude while she climbed free. *You're welcome.*

Wetness dripped from my nose, and I brought my glowing fingers to inspect it—*blood?* I pinched my nostrils, trying to stop it.

Ash fell in the smoky din, people screaming as they sprinted past.

"How did the fire start?" a woman asked as she helped people to safety.

"An accident!" a man replied. "The lanterns fell!"

Another nodded. "A *horrible* accident."

Can't they see the monster prowling through their midst? Why was

I the only one who could smell the world-dominating corruption leaking from him? He *reeked* of it.

"Thou drive me to horrible madness, Ravenal," Tarantula said conversationally as he stalked out into the humid night, oblivious to the fires I was putting out.

"Don't fool yourself," I said. "We both know you were *born* mad, Sazha." The name tasted strange in my mouth, like truth in the middle of a grand deception.

He stopped abruptly. My forehead knocked against his spine. Back muscles hardened as he tensed all over.

"*Careful* . . . Calling me that name . . . does things to me." His voice had a strange lilt to it, and his breathing turned ragged. Sharp scents intensified.

Aw, the megalomaniac is triggered.

"How about don't tell me what to do, *Sa—zha*." I slowly enunciated his name. The pungent scent of his dark intentions oozed off him in a sudden overwhelming wave; my hair whipped around my head; goose bumps of premonition pebbled my arms.

BOOM.

I coughed, choking on magic and abject horror.

The ground shook as the building collapsed behind us in a cloud of debris. Water and fire battled, flaring from the wreckage high into the sky. Dust burned my eyes. Southerners screamed as they ran to safety.

He'd razed the building.

Completely normal, nondisturbing behavior.

The Marshal's assessment was wrong. We should have killed him.

There were priceless diamonds around his neck, and they were supposed to be stopping him. If this was him magically castrated . . . I couldn't fathom what he was like unconstrained. *His full magical prowess must be inconceivable.*

The worst part was, the ruined building wasn't his most heinous crime of the night. His hand had moved upward during the explosion, holding me steady, and his fingers were now spread possessively across the very top of my thighs. He pressed me against the front of his shoulder, his thumb hovering at the juncture between my covered legs.

The calloused pad scraped slowly upward, and a whisper of wind followed in its wake. A two-pronged attack. Every nerve in my body quivered, desperate for him to do *more.* The chain from his shackle dug into the back of my thigh.

"I detest thee, dear." He dropped his hand. "Thou tempt me with corruption."

"I assure you that—" I punched at his kidneys with my fists, but he didn't miss a step "—I abhor you more. You are a *Plague*, just like your stupid dragon."

"Coming from the brat herself. And my dragon is Pestilence—get it right."

"Better a blight than a monster."

He laughed, putting his hand once again across my thighs like he couldn't help himself. His calloused thumb rested dangerously across the apex, pressing the chiffon material into my core.

All five of my senses came alive, and then a sixth. He pressed his thumb deeper, and I clenched around it. I'd never known flesh could be so fevered.

Blood rushed straight to my head, and I squeezed my thighs together, trapping his thumb inside of me. He made a harsh sound in his throat as he muttered under his breath about vexation, fate, and damnation.

I squirmed, and he exhaled raggedly as he walked faster through the now abandoned street, destruction flaming behind him.

His words said one thing, but his body was saying another. Even worse . . . *so was mine.* The unthinkable had come to pass. He'd caught me in his malevolent web.

22

One Bed

Upside down, concussed, and drugged, I mimicked a sack of flour as Tarantula stalked back to our inn, smoke rising behind us. Neck aching, I peered up at the canopy of spindly branches, shadows crawling toward me under the moonlight.

His thumb was still clenched between my thighs. A flush warmed my face, and it had nothing to do with the tropical climate.

"Zora, we've been looking everywhere for you!" Ella appeared out of the dark as she hurried through the street.

Tarantula shifted his hand away from my core.

Ella's arm was draped over the shoulders of an injured Southern man. A wood shard protruded from his calf, but he seemed unconcerned, staring down at Ella with hearts in his eyes.

Axel followed close behind, disheveled and covered in dust but otherwise intact. He ripped the injured man out of Ella's embrace and shoved him away. The man tripped, shouting in pain as he landed on his wound.

Ella gasped and moved to help him, but Axel held her back. "He's *fine*."

The man moaned in agony on the ground.

"Focus on Zora." Axel pointedly directed Ella toward me, and she smiled with delight, cheeks red, clearly still drunk on fairy wine.

"How are the drugs feeling?" she asked as she poked at me.

"Nom," I gurgled unintelligibly.

"Wow—that good?" Axel patted my back. "Do you happen to have any more on you? I want to try the—"

"What have I told thee about touching her, jester?" Tarantula cut him off as he shifted, moving me away.

I pointed at Tarantula, the razed building, and then myself, trying to discreetly convey the nuances of evil.

"Is she having a hallucinogenic episode?" Axel asked as he missed the message.

"Yes," Tarantula said.

Someone cried out for help, and Ella turned to go to them, but Axel once again grabbed her arm and steered her attention back to me. "Did we get Sibrain?" Axel asked, grunting as he fought to hold on to a struggling Ella.

"The first mark has been handled," Tarantula said coldly.

Axel nodded like this made sense. He had no idea Tarantula had skinned his face off with his magic, then decapitated him with my dagger. I tried to explain with my eyes.

"Do we know *why* the building collapsed?" Axel asked Tarantula, his gaze shrewd despite inebriation.

"An accidental fire," Tarantula said, picking up his pace.

Axel scoffed as he followed, but he didn't say anything. People screamed nearby, and he resumed pulling along a fighting Ella, who was desperate to get to them.

I nodded in agreement with her. "We should go help the Southerners—"

Tarantula cut me off. "We should rest for the night and go to the bathhouse tomorrow for Arcturus." He paused thoughtfully. "Or we could raze the rest of the city and flush him out now . . ." He stopped like he found another massacre alluring, and I could practically feel the bloodlust thumping through his veins. He straightened like he was fantasizing about the carnage.

Axel rolled his eyes. "No. We'll sleep."

Squire cawed as he flew down from the trees and landed on my butt. "Zora, you dead?"

"Mmm-hmm," I confirmed.

"My tragic heart mourns you," Squire hooted solemnly, and I appreciated the dramatic phrase. He was the only one who understood me. *Probably not the best sign.* In a brave display of solidarity, he pecked my butt and screeched to the moon.

A disorienting indeterminate amount of time later, I still tasted colors and saw smells while Tarantula carried me into my dark room at the inn. The twins had already disappeared into theirs for the night.

"Put me down now and *leave*," I demanded, hitting his hard muscles, hating how warm they were beneath my fingers.

"Thou art drugged . . . I would never leave a lady alone in her room in such a state. 'Tis dangerous. Thou could asphyxiate on vomit."

Charming.

A fountain gurgled pleasantly in the corner as long shadows stretched across the single canopied bed, barely big enough for one person. *Two people alone, stuck in an inn, I wonder what could happen?*

The peculiar thoughts were chased away as Tarantula leaned forward and, with shocking whipcord strength, repositioned me. He held me in his outstretched arms, high over the bed. Somehow Squire ended up standing on my forehead.

"Hello, spider," Squire said, ducking his head bashfully.

Tarantula nodded back. "Greetings, mini fledgling."

I shook my head at him. "*Don't* you dare—"

Tarantula dropped us both, and we bounced roughly on the mattress. Squire fell, his rotund body smushing against my face.

Before I could get up and fight, Tarantula yanked the sheets up to my chin, covering me completely.

"Thank you," Squire chittered, climbing under them. He curled into a ball beside me (not helpful).

"Sleep," Tarantula ordered.

"Yes, spider sir," Squire squawked happily and closed his eyes. Shocked at this unfathomable betrayal of friendship, I gaped at my already sleeping owl.

"Wait a second," I said as his sudden turn in allegiance hit me. "Have *you* been the one giving him the seeds?"

A flush traveled up Tarantula's neck from under his collar. "Maybe," he muttered, looking away from me.

How dare he try to corrupt my most faithful ally?

Overheating, I kicked the smothering layers off, leaving them all for Squire. Magic nipped at my sweaty skin, silky material sliding gently, and I sighed with relief. My limbs spread wide.

The flowery vines hanging from the ceiling caught the moonlight in shades of pink and green. *Beautiful.* I tipped my head back, savoring the spinning euphoria.

"Ravenal," Tarantula said hoarsely. "Cover your shoulders."

I turned my head, and it felt like lifting heavy bricks. *Wait, he's still here?*

Pearlescent eyes glowed eerily. He loomed above me, chest heaving, lips slightly parted as he stared at my . . . *clavicle*?

"It's just my shoulders?"

Eyes widening, Tarantula turned abruptly. He stalked a few steps to the wall and brought his arm up. Mumbling in his strange tongue, he hit his forehead against his forearm.

Squire hooted happily in his sleep.

"Are you having another . . . ankle episode?" I asked cautiously, not sure what was happening but knowing that I needed to bully him for it. "I think you need to look at me and get over this—"

SLAP.

Tarantula slammed his palm against the wall above his head.

"No," he said with a predatory baritone, still not glancing at me. "I shall never look . . . 'Tis disrespectful." The archaic magical symbols moved on his muscular back as he tensed—*snowflake, fire, lightning, wind, water.*

A low, tortured sound escaped his throat. Distant screams sounded far off in the humid night, traveling through the open window. I inhaled deeply. The strange scent of ruination mixed with yearning filled my lungs.

"Just to be clear," I said tentatively. "You're completely losing it right now over my shoulder—right? This is about a . . . shoulder. Two of them—"

"Ravenal!" *SLAP.* He hit the wall harder, my name falling from his lips like a desperate prayer. "Do *not* test my control right now."

Undoubtedly this was the funniest thing I'd ever experienced. Also, the man had lost his mind, and he needed to die. All three things were true at once.

SLAP. His fingers flexed, nails digging into the stone wall.

"You can touch one of my shoulders if you want—but only one," I blurted. *Why did I just say that?* I blamed the drugs.

Tarantula went impossibly still, frozen like a statue, elegant fingers convulsing where they were spread against the wall. "Thou . . . do not mean that." Nails scraping, he turned to face me. "Take it back," he whispered darkly.

"Uh—no?"

"Take." A long, elegant finger rose, glowing silver. "It." He pointed at me accusingly. "Back."

"Still no."

He prowled toward the bed, shadows gathering around him like dire moths to a bonfire. Asphyxiating, I choked on the peril—*him.* Panic mounted. I had to do something. I had to save myself from this man. *I have to save the world from him.*

I lunged and twisted.

CRASH.

He paused, staring down at the shattered glass and the single flame dancing around his boots, then back up at me. "Ravenal, did thou just *throw* . . . a lantern at me?"

We both looked over at the empty space on the right bedside table. The lantern on the left no longer had its mate. I *might* have panicked and thrown the oil lamp. Fire slowly spread across the wooden floor.

"I did, and I'll do it again," I said as I inched across the bed toward the remaining lantern.

"Don't thou dare, Ravenal."

In slow motion, we both glanced at the remaining lamp, then back at each other. The corner of his lips curled up, and we lunged at the same time. Air whistled through my empty fingers. He snatched the lantern away and chucked it. I threw myself off the bed as it whooshed past my head.

CRASH.

The lantern exploded against the wall above the headboard, shattered glass and fire raining down. The artful canopy caught flame.

"SQUIRE!" I screamed with horror, diving toward him, but a shimmering silvery bubble of magic appeared around his feathers, shielding his sleeping body from the falling debris.

Whoosh. I backed away as more of the bedding caught on fire. The pillow Squire rested on was the only part completely untouched by the chaos. He chittered happily in his sleep.

I turned, fists raised. "How dare you! You almost killed him!"

"I would never hurt the ugly, useless bird." Tarantula looked genuinely outraged at the accusation.

"You ignorant cad. He is *beautiful*."

He didn't look convinced.

"So," I continued. "You would spare him but harm me?"

His ears turned pink as he ripped his hands through his still-wet hair. "I *never* would have damaged a single hair upon your glorious head. I would have shielded thee too."

I pointed back at the growing blaze. "Then why did you throw a lamp?" Pink petals slowly fell from the vegetation on the ceiling, catching fire.

"Thou threw one at me." He held his head.

"Of course I did, *Empire scum*—and I'll do it again." I punched at him. Air whistled as he leaned back, just barely dodging the blow.

"Do not do this, Ravenal. I have no control after the events of tonight." He aimed a blood-covered finger at my face, and I swatted it away, but he brought it back up.

"You should have thought of that," I said with frustration, "before you threw a *lamp* at me."

"Thou did it first!"

I'd officially had enough of him. I threw myself at him, fists flying. He caught me mid-leap and easily tossed me back onto the bed. *Tempestuous bastard.* I sat up, sputtering, expecting to feel burning heat, but the area around my body glittered with silver. Just like Squire, he shielded me. *How dare he use his powers on me.*

Standing tall on the bed, canopy flaming all around, I jumped up high and threw myself straight at him. He rolled his eyes, like my falling body was a minor inconvenience. I slammed down atop him.

We crashed onto the hard floor, rolling. My fists landed glancing blows. He wrapped his powerful legs around me, twisting as we grappled. I bucked and punched with everything I had, but he ended up on top.

I was immobilized.

"Careful. There is broken glass," he said, grunting as I dug my heel into his kidney. Fire danced around, growing higher but still not touching either of us.

I grabbed one of the glass shards and lifted it high above his back. "I'll kill you right now," I promised.

His gaze sharpened, and magic shot off him, wind wrapping around my wrist so tightly that my forearm cramped with pain.

"Drop it," he ordered.

I clutched the jagged shard tighter, warm blood dripping across my palm, down my forearm, and splattering onto him.

He made a debased sound. The icy pressure on my wrist increased. Bone creaked as I struggled to hold on to my prize. "Thou art hurting yourself!"

"Your presence," I said quietly, "is hurting me *more*." Fighting through his magic, I pulled my hand down, closer to his skin.

Something shifted in his gaze. Suddenly he stopped fighting me. No pressure held my wrist, and nothing prevented me from stabbing him through the spine.

He brought his face close. "Do it, Ravenal—kill me." He inhaled loudly. "Or do thou . . . not have the conviction?"

I brought the glass down so the point pressed gently into the exposed skin at the base of his neck.

The room vanished.

Not again.

Humidity disappeared, replaced by biting cold, the gentle swaying of pines, and the soft hiss of falling snow. Tarantula lay atop me on the snowy ground of the Barren Forest, trees surrounding us. Flurries drifted thickly, sparkling in the copper light of a full blood moon.

I turned my head.

A rose peeked above the snow, a single icicle hanging off its petals.

It must mean something.

I swiveled back to him, breath lingering in an icy puff between us. Snowflakes gathered on his golden lashes.

"Are you seeing this?" I asked.

"Seeing what?" They displaced as he blinked, drifting down onto my face.

My fingers were numb in the sudden cold. The glass burned where I held it to his neck. Icicles, hanging jagged overhead, reflected the two of us.

Tarantula shuddered, his thighs wrapping tighter. He rolled his powerful hips, pressing himself against me. Heat streaked straight to my core, and we both groaned in unison.

A dire fox screamed in the night.

My back arched up, seeking more pressure.

"Don't move, Ravenal," Tarantula ordered. He flexed his hips again, pinning me to the ground, rubbing the ridges of his chest against mine. "Or I shall ruin us both."

My brain went blank, streaks of pleasure firing. I'd had sex a few times, but never had anyone fully *overwhelmed* me like this, and we weren't doing anything.

Icy branches clattered together.

"I am fighting—" his stubble scraped against the sensitive skin on my neck "—wicked inclinations to possess thee in a carnal manner."

Sweat streaked down his face, dripping onto my now freezing skin as the trees watched me. "Go to hell," I whispered, my bloody fingers slipping against the glass.

"Already there." His harsh, gravelly voice mixed with the hush of the forest.

Shouting with frustration, I chucked the shard away, unable to sever his spine.

The Barren Forest winked out of existence.

We were lying on the floor of the inn. The glass shattered into pieces against the stone wall.

Pain burned across my frozen flesh, Tarantula's body excruciatingly warm against mine. I tried not to, but I bucked against him, needing the friction desperately. He tightened his hold, pinning me so completely that I couldn't move.

Knock.

Knock.

Knock.

"Zora, the innkeeper got a noise complaint!" Ella shouted through the door, voice slurring. The door creaked, and her voice got louder. "Apparently someone thought there was a murder going— *Ohmyoldgod.* Uh . . . Zora?"

We both turned toward the open door. I flushed with embarrassment. Axel's eyebrows rose as he stood beside his sister, staring down at us, blinking rapidly.

Flowers fell flaming from the ceiling, where the fire had spread. The bed was ablaze, the curtains hanging around it burning bright. Squire still chittered peacefully in his sleep. Glass covered the floor. Distracted by Tarantula, I'd somehow forgotten that the room had turned into a bonfire.

"It was his fault," I said, uncomfortably aware of how hard his heart pounded, the beats vibrating against me. Instead of letting me go like I expected, he tightened his hold, shielding me with his body.

"Leave us," he ordered as magic coiled in dark tendrils around him.

I scoffed. *They're not just going to leave me with—*

Axel slammed the door shut, voices echoed, and there was a thumping like he was pulling his fighting sister away. I closed my eyes, wishing the old god was here to save me.

"Get off me," I said as I pushed at him, head throbbing with a contusion, a tension headache, existential dread, *and* a concussion.

I had no energy left.

Tarantula gathered me into his arms and stood up, cradling me tenderly against his naked, sweaty chest like I was something precious that needed saving and not the person who had stabbed him *repeatedly.*

The last thing I remembered was a gust of freezing magical wind filling the room. The flames winked out, and the room fell dark. In the scorched quiet, my archnemesis laid me gently on the ruined bed.

"Sleep," he whispered against my forehead with far more tenderness than a monster should have.

23

D(IRE) BEARS

I woke up in a ruined, tattered bed.

Head spinning, spread-eagle, I stared up at the shredded canopy and blackened plants hanging from the ceiling. A rough, masculine sound echoed below. Rolling with a tired groan, I leaned my head over the side of the bed.

Tarantula lay on his back.

Stretched across the scorched floor, surrounded by broken glass, he was still *very* alive. He didn't have a pillow or even a sheet, and I knew from living with him how much he fussed over his bedding.

Tarantula stared straight up at me, gaze hooded, lips slightly parted like he wanted to say something but couldn't find the words.

Silence stretched between us, and a flush of defeat mixed with something I refused to identify crawled up my neck. I rolled away, unable to stomach his knowing gaze. Unsavory emotions intensified as I realized my change of clothes had been burned to ash in the fire.

We got ready in silence.

On our way out, we stopped at Ella's room to raid a saddlebag, and I holstered my extra daggers around my thighs.

An hour later, I leaned against Ella, our arms linked together as we headed through the verdant Commune streets. If not for her support, I wouldn't have been standing upright. The harsh morning light burned too brightly because residual drugs still coursed through my system, making it hard to concentrate as I struggled to regulate my breathing.

Axel walked on my other side and reached out periodically to pat Squire, who sat happily on my shoulder.

Squire pecked at him hard enough to draw blood. "No touchy!" he chirped.

Axel laughed.

"This way." Tarantula pointed down an alleyway and stalked ahead of us. He glanced back at me, eyes hooded. His unbuttoned, scorched shirt fluttered around his torso. In a strange display of solidarity, he hadn't changed out of his ruined clothes. *He's probably taunting me.*

Awkward tension simmered.

Ella squeezed my arm close to her body. "Are you okay?" she asked as she searched my face, clearly alluding to the events she'd walked in on last night. Her gaze was knowing, and there was no judgment, just concern.

"Do you think there's something wrong with me?" I asked, hating how unsure I sounded. "If I can't—" I flexed my stinging right hand, wincing, a long red slice healing across my palm where I'd clutched the glass shard "—kill those who deserve to die?"

"No," Ella said confidently, her eyes still slightly glazed from the fairy wine. "Do you remember when the dragons attacked the North all those years ago and I looked back at you?"

"Of course."

"I was shaking with terror. I'd never felt so conflicted in all my life. The Marshal had threatened to have my head if I misused the missile, and I couldn't make the decision. *Everything* was on fire. Dragons were staring us down, their teeth larger than our bodies . . . and then I looked back at *you.* A stranger I'd never met. A teenage girl covered in blood." Everything quieted as she held my gaze. "Do you know what I saw?"

I shook my head.

"Strength," she said. "It was like you were a beacon in the middle of the carnage . . . a bright, blinding light. I swear, voices were whispering at me to trust you. It was what standing before the old god was supposed to feel like—"

"Ella, I don't know if I was—"

"—and *you* made the call when I was too afraid to, even though *I* was the Knight Mage."

I shook my head. "It wasn't like that. It was your quick thinking."

She leaned closer. "It was *exactly* like that. I think—" her voice dropped "—you're always shrinking yourself because your intensity scares people. You can be a good person *and* dangerous. Stop hiding, Zora."

Pressure burned my eyes.

"Let's go," Axel said loudly, startling us back to reality. He gestured at the bright pink flower arch that led to a tall door covered in hanging grasses. *Bathhouse* was written above in cursive script. Tarantula stalked through the blossoms and disappeared inside.

Ella and I reluctantly pulled away from each other, standing straight on our own. The distance stretched too far, too soon. I reached over, and she took my hand; her eyes were also suspiciously glassy.

I hadn't felt this supported since Aurora.

Girl friendships are proof that soulmates exist.

Axel draped his arms over both of our shoulders.

Squire squawked with outrage, "I said no touchy, vampire man!" He bit his finger, hard. Ella and I laughed.

Axel made a kissy-face at Squire, who screeched and hopped onto the top of my head.

"Ladies," Axel said. "What are we waiting for?" His voice was casual as he pushed us both forward through the green strands, but his eyes sharpened as he studied our faces with concern.

Inside the building, oversized flowers in glorious shades of purple hung from the high ceiling on thick vines. Below, dozens of small pools bubbled where they were built into the ground.

Cloudy humidity filled the air, and leafy plants surrounded the pools, providing privacy. An almost naked man stood up, water coursing off his— *Oh wow.* Who let him wear that in a public pool? *Male chastity belts are a crime against humanity.*

I squinted. Dozens of men and women in bathing outfits lounged in the waters, a pleasant buzz of conversation filling the fragrant air.

"Jester," Tarantula said coldly.

Axel rolled his eyes and stepped back with both hands raised above his head mockingly. Tarantula bared his perfect straight white teeth, and Axel flashed fang.

"How may we h-help you?" A pretty young woman in a silky white dress approached, looking harried. She held up a serving tray with four tiny trumpet flutes. "Please enjoy a sampling of the complimentary fairy wine."

She eyed us with blatant suspicion as she offered the drinks. Rumors were probably spreading about the wine tavern, and it didn't take a genius to put everything together. The first time we visited, it burned to the ground.

Tarantula's ripped shirt is stained with blood.

I glanced down at my chest.

Great, so is mine.

Ella and Axel each grabbed a glass, bowing their thanks to her as they politely drank the contents. Tarantula followed suit.

She waited for me to take one, but I shook my head no because a pounding had intensified behind my eyes as soon as we'd stepped inside. *So much water everywhere.* Magic tingled across my fingers. Her face blurred as I focused on not losing control. She pushed the tray toward me. "Please have a—"

"I'm good," I said.

"We are here for Arcturus. Where is he?" Tarantula asked, drawing her attention away from me. Flowers rustled as wind whistled ominously through the room. Hair whipping, Ella and Axel stepped nervously away from him. *Why is he suddenly so worked up?*

The young woman jumped with a start. "He's in the back, in a private pool." She pointed to a green door on the other side of the room. Her eyes darted around, and she dropped her voice to a whisper, glasses clattering on her tray. "I would advise *not* going back there. You should all leave, *please*."

Tarantula placed his empty flute back on the tray and stalked through the cloudy haze toward the green door. People in the pools gaped up at him as he passed.

The twins hurried after him, but I couldn't take my eyes off the woman, who could barely hold her tray. She seemed sincere and genuinely terrified.

Icy foreboding washed over me.

I started to follow the twins but stopped. Instincts sharpened. I halted next to the woman. "What . . . is it?" I asked quietly, the pressure in my temples intensifying.

Her eyes darted to where Tarantula had thrown open the green door, disappearing inside with the twins, then back to me and the remaining full flute on her tray. The other three sat beside it—the empty glasses were coated in a light green residue.

Everything warped, blood rushing in my ears.

Her mouth moved in slow motion. "Poi—son."

At that exact moment, a low growl vibrated through the air, and every hair on my body stood on end. I'd heard that sound before. *In the Barren Forest.*

Something crashed against a wall. *GROWL.* The loud, terrifying noise exploded from the back room.

"I'm sorry," the woman whispered as she backed away. I grabbed her, pulling her face close to mine.

"Do you know where the antidote is?" I asked in a rush.

She squeezed her eyes shut, flinching away. I shook her, and she nodded yes.

"Get it," I ordered coldly. "Now. This is an order from a Knight. The *Commonwealth* is depending on you." I shoved her away. "Do *not* disappoint me."

She opened her mouth to say something, but I was already pushing through the crowd of screaming people as they jumped out of the pools, some grabbing towels, others running toward the exit.

I fought to get to the green door. The scars on my face and back tingled with phantom pain.

More growls and crashing noises sounded from the back room. Palming two of my bone knives, I took a deep breath, sinking deeper into myself, and stepped through the green door.

Blood-splattered purple flowers covered the small room. A round pool bubbled untouched in the middle of the tiled floor. And against the far wall, Axel was slumped in front of Ella protectively.

They were both unconscious.

Next to the pool, Tarantula staggered back with his glowing hands held high. Diamonds glinted on his collar as silver wind exploded from his palms, pushing against a fully grown dire bear.

The beast towered as tall as the ceiling, with grotesque fangs, shaggy brown fur, and deadly green eyes; layers of thick hide formed an armor around its neck, back, belly, and head.

A dire bear's only weakness was its chest. When the bear was on all fours, that region was naturally protected from attack, but this beast stood upright on its hind legs, silver wafting from its nose. Razor-sharp claws flashed as it swiped a paw.

Gently I pulled a shaking Squire off my shoulder and placed him on a hanging vine.

"Look away, dear."

Squire swiveled his head to stare at the wall. "Me *no* want to look."

ROAR. The dire bear lunged, and the wind flowing from Tarantula just barely stopped him from being ripped to shreds. His magic faltered, the glow dimming around his hands. *He's been poisoned.*

One of Tarantula's legs gave out, his face blue under the strain . . . and then his other leg. He kneeled beside the pool, shirt fluttering, shaking with effort as the beast roared above him. A thick sheen of sweat covered his face.

Please let my blades be steady and my aim true.

"No, Zora." Tarantula's eyes widened as I leaped past him with my daggers extended. "*No!*"

Claws swiped. I tilted my head to the side, and the very end of my braid sliced off, hair unraveling as I slammed both blades *deep* through layers of fur, going for the heart. My aim was true, but the pelt was impossibly thick.

The dire bear howled as we careened around the room. Its maw angled down. Long teeth snapped in my face, a hair's breadth away. I flinched and closed my eyes, expecting to feel the blow of claws against my back, but it never came.

Magic hissed, and the dire bear growled as its paws were yanked above its head, pinned together by silver tendrils of power. The bear craned its head down, fangs gnashing as it tried desperately to get to me. With its arms held up, I was just out of reach.

With all my might, I held my daggers in place. Struggling for purchase as we careened, I glanced over my shoulder. Tarantula was slumped with his back against the wall, his legs slack on the floor.

His head lolled to the side, and his eyes were barely cracked open. But his hands were still raised high, silver pouring off them. His decorative platinum wrist cuffs glowed brightly beneath his shackles.

Tarantula's slitted gaze promised me a deadly retribution if I didn't stop my current course of action.

I held tight.

The dire bear charged forward. *BOOM*. We exploded through the wall, wood splintering around us, and I was violently thrown off its body, my daggers dislodged from its chest.

Bathhouse patrons screamed. Groaning, I slowly got up to my feet, body *aching* from the blunt force trauma. The dire bear looked bizarre, front paws trapped above its head. Leaning its neck forward awkwardly, it roared, spit flying from its awful maw.

A boy cried out, his back against the side of the large pool right in front of the monster. *He can't be more than ten years old.*

The dire bear focused on him.

Pointing my bloody daggers, I ran.

Screaming, I tried to distract it, but the dire bear was already lunging forward. In slow motion, the boy closed his eyes, hands covering his head.

I jumped, arms outstretched.

Halfway above the pool, I collided with the dire bear. We smashed down into the hot water. I stabbed as the mammoth body kicked out. The claws on its foot clipped the side of my leg, scoring deep.

In a blur of violence, we sank downward, *finally* coming to a stop at the pool's surprisingly deep bottom.

I stabbed at the dire bear's chest, twisting to get a better position. Crimson floated up in inky clouds, turning the heated water red. The beast twitched and roared as Tarantula's magic somehow kept its paws pinned.

Temples pounding, I pointed a glowing hand at its head. The water slowly spun around us, forming a whirlpool. Silver streamed into its open mouth as I drowned it.

Heart in my throat, I willed the water into its orifices as I tried not to pass out. Silver pinned the monster against the bottom of the pool, but exhaustion made it hard to think. I had only a few seconds, sustaining so much magic. My headache intensified as the dire bear kept fighting, thrashing and kicking desperately. My lungs burned unmercifully. Panic mounted.

I need air.

Air.

Air.

Air.

I was running out of time.

End it now. Sinking deeper into a hunting headspace, I dug my daggers farther into its chest and ripped them with all my might in a square formation, yanking off the thick layer of fur and then blubber. The pieces drifted away, up to the surface.

Kicking desperately to stay low, I brought my knives down, breaking through the thick rib cage with a loud crack. Blood gushed out, fully blinding me as the dire bear twisted.

Eyes squeezed shut, I skinned it by feel, just like I'd done with other beasts a thousand times before. Despite its larger size, the anatomy occupied the same general positions.

I sliced the four thick vessels of the heart as it contracted against my hands. Next I dislodged the broad windpipe, severing the breathing tube from the back wall of the rib cage.

I dropped one of my daggers, and it sank to the bottom of the pool as I reached in with a free hand and ripped the heart clean out of the exposed cavity. A horrible bubbling growl rolled through the water, and the dire bear went still.

Air.

I kicked toward the surface with everything I had.

Gasping, I sucked in oxygen greedily as I threw the still-beating heart onto the pool deck. I clutched a dagger in one hand and the edge of the pool with the other. The boy huddled in the corner, staring at me with an open mouth. Shock and awe on his face.

Coughing up water, I clung to the edge, resting my throbbing skull against the cool tile.

Lucky girl—

Fingers wrapped tightly around my ankle and wrenched me down. I screamed, bubbles exploding upward.

A snarling man with long, dark hair hung suspended under the water; a human heart beat within his open chest cavity. *Shifters have two hearts.* Blood turned the water red between us, and my fingers cramped around my last weapon. Light glinted off bone in his hand. *The dagger I dropped.*

Time slowed to a horrible crawl.

He lunged.

With everything I had, I drove my knife deep into his exposed chest. He sliced his blade clean across my neck.

Everything went eerily still. *Peaceful.* My body was—*gone*—detached from my soul as I hung suspended in the murky water. The man's eyes widened as his heart stopped.

Darkness; nothing less.

Eyelids heavy, my lashes fluttered open. Ice-covered branches swayed above, snow sparkling in the bright light.

A haze of emerald light took the shape of a tall person as they bent over me. The willowy figure had long hair, soft effeminate features, and a muscular build.

Every time I tried to focus, they disappeared. It was like trying to stare straight at the sun.

"Zora Ravenal," they said, voice vibrating with the might of a blizzard. It came from every direction all at once. "Your soul has been judged. You have been found worthy and have earned the title Keeper of my forest."

Like the fairy tales? I thought, exhausted with certain death.

"This is no tale," the emerald figure boomed, somehow hearing my thoughts.

Who are you?

"I am Barren, one of the great."

Great?

"Elves."

Oh.

"I tasted your soul when you were ten years old," Barren said with gravitas. "I marked your face with silver—a *warning* for all to stay away and not interfere, because you have been under my trials. I have been watching you."

Unmerciful pain burned down the longest scar on my face as if it was being opened anew. I screamed through gritted teeth.

"You have passed your trials. You have been found worthy."

I didn't do anything?

"You sacrificed your soul for a helpless child," Barren continued. "Zora Ravenal, you are now bonded to my forest—to me."

What does that . . . mean?

Barren's voice intensified, howling like an ice storm. "You must fight for those who cannot help themselves."

With great effort, I turned my head. Blood was splattered across virgin snow. A few feet away, icicles hung delicately from a single rose, sitting lonely in the white, aflame with magic. The bloody droplets on the snow vibrated, coagulating together, and slowly traveled toward me. Warmth burned across my throat, skin knitting itself back together.

Barren shimmered in and out of focus. A faint memory played of Mom describing elves as worlds unto themselves and more magic than people. In rare instances, elves used their powers to create Keepers, who were granted a secret strength—a power—and Mom always spoke of Keepers with great reverence.

What is the power of a Keeper? I thought wearily.

As if reading my mind, Barren said, "Your power is to act for those who cannot."

But how does a Keeper do that?

Barren shook their head like they were disappointed in me. "That *is* the point. You act on behalf of those who cannot help themselves . . . Good luck to you on your quest. I have foreseen. You are going to need it." Barren paused cryptically. "Before you go, you may have your memory back."

A glitching emerald finger pressed against my forehead. Barren's touch felt like snowboarding down a mountainside, jumping high, and landing a backflip perfectly . . . But then time warped in a blur of white as a bizarre falling sensation stretched me in different directions.

Abrupt stillness.

I blinked.

It was summertime in the Barren Forest, and I was ten years old, screaming in agony.

A dire bear's claws had just slashed down my face. Turning desperately, I covered my head, pain streaking across my back as the beast sliced me open. I collapsed face-first onto the ground. Choking, I stared at a tree, smiling sadly. *To the forest, I return.*

I coughed out blood. Snow melted as a silver puff of magic rose into the air. Droplets sizzled as they sank through the frozen dirt as if pulled by a force below.

The ground shook, and trees rustled together. Pine cones rained down. A burning warmth reached through my chest, straight into my soul. The shaking intensified, and my teeth rattled.

A green stem sprouted from the exact spot where my blood had disappeared, a splendid rosebud unfurling with delicate red petals.

A sheen of emerald light materialized. Barren's long, feminine fingers reached down and stroked the ruby petals. "The forest tastes your potential," they said. "*Goodness* lives in your blood—and you have been selected for my trials, just like your kin before. You come from a strong lineage of sacrifice. However, age corrupts the lesser creatures. You must prove yourself worthy of a higher righteousness, not fleeting, but true."

I gasped.

"I will be watching," Barren said. "If you fail, my blessing will be removed. If you succeed, it will be granted—forever."

I will not fail, I thought fiercely, knowing I could be a good person.

Barren shook their head. "It does not matter what you want now. These memories will be gone. It is not your mind but your soul I judge."

My eyes shot open. I was floating underwater. A man hung suspended nearby, my dagger hilt protruding from his exposed heart. Only one of us was still alive.

Luck? Something far worse.

Kicking, I surfaced with a ragged gasp. I threw myself out of the pool, scrambling, knees and ankles banging as I clambered out as fast as possible. A gross squelching sound followed as my hand hit a bear heart. On all fours, I looked around the empty bathhouse.

Pools bubbled.

The boy was gone.

Blood was streaked across the tiles, everywhere. I grasped at my throat, fingers shaking horribly. The ridge of a single scar sliced across smooth—whole—skin.

It was real.

Keeling over, I threw up water and bile. I dragged my hands across my face, fingers lingering on my longest scar.

Reflected back in a puddle of bloody water, it glowed metallic.

Thick and raised.

Magical.

The fairy tale was real; I was one of the fabled Keepers of the forest. "You must fight for those who cannot help themselves," I repeated hoarsely as I violently coughed up more water. "Easy. A simple directive." Digging my palms into my eyes, I tried to physically push back the tears.

Not like I don't have enough on my plate right now.

A body with long, dark hair floated in the red pool. I stared down at it, numb all over. Holding my breath, I staggered to my feet, knees shaking.

Am I blessed or cursed?

I turned in an unsteady circle, waiting for something to make sense. Nothing did. For the first time in my life, I wasn't sure of a single thing in the world. *Is anything real?* The bear heart stared up at me, and I refused to think about who the man in the pool was. *They were the same.* Or what it meant for the state of Antichthon.

Fairy-tale creatures can't be real? Obviously not.

Right.

Right?

I looked up to see the hole in the wall of the back room. In a fugue, I stumbled back through it. Inside, Tarantula lay slumped against the woodwork with his eyes closed. Across from him, the twins were also unconscious. *I need to help them. I need to . . . I need to . . .* I still couldn't think.

Hand on my pounding chest, I clawed at myself, desperate for air. It felt like I was still underwater. *Is anything real?* There was no order or sense to the world. I was having a metaphysical meltdown.

Too much had happened too fast.

Footsteps squelched. Baring my teeth with a growl, I whirled and raised a glowing hand.

"Here." The woman from before stood in the doorway, holding

a vial of liquid in her trembling fingers. "I f-found the antidote in his office. Like you asked."

She blanched as she stared at the missing portion of the wall. Then at the man floating in the water and the oversized dire bear heart.

"I . . . I . . . I . . ." She backed away from me.

"Stop." My voice came out deep and harsh. She froze. "Give it to them, now. Ella first." I gestured over my shoulder at her.

"Yes, Knight." Half bowing, half curtsying, she scurried across the room, pressing the vial to Ella's lips and then Axel's. Long seconds passed. *Finally* the twins gasped, spitting up green fluid as they coughed violently. Axel immediately grabbed Ella, checking her for injuries.

The woman walked hesitantly toward Tarantula, looking at me and then back at him, waiting for me to tell her to stop. That he didn't need saving. The words burned on the tip of my tongue, but I couldn't make myself say them. *It's just because of the quest. That's all.*

Still staring at me, she tipped the vial into his mouth, then backed away.

"You did well," I said, still speaking in a baritone unfamiliar to my ears. "The Commonwealth thanks you for your service."

Shaking, she bowed to me. "Thank y-you, Bear of the North."

Tarantula made a harsh rattling sound.

He inhaled roughly.

The girl ran, disappearing through what was left of the door.

Tarantula's eyes shot open. "How . . . dare . . . thou . . . put . . . yourself . . . in . . . danger."

"Typical," I muttered, too shaken to come up with anything witty.

Barren touched my forehead.

I died at ten years old and then again just now.

A single rose bloomed. It was on fire.

All this time, I'd been in grave peril. Every time I'd almost committed cold-blooded murder, the forest had watched me, ready to take my second chance at life away. I'd been so close so many times, and yet I'd survived against all odds. *So lucky, lucky, lucky, lucky.* Shaking, vision blurring, I staggered toward Ella.

"Where is Arcturus?" Tarantula demanded.

"Dead."

"How can thou be sure thou killed . . ." His voice trailed off as he turned to look where I was pointing—through the gaping hole where the wall used to be.

A bubble popped loudly in the steaming pool, and I jolted, stifling a scream. My nerves were shot. I was strung out. My head was frazzled.

"Is that his . . . severed heart?" Tarantula asked slowly. "Ravenal—did thou fell the beast . . . by *yourself*?"

I shrugged.

Tarantula brought his hand up to his chest, fingers clenching. "It cannot be." His eyes devoured me, burning with a wild obsession.

I opened and closed my mouth, but no sound came out. Antichthon was not what it seemed, and perhaps neither was I.

24

Executioner Style

I leaned against the twins as the three of us walked together. For once, Tarantula didn't say anything. He'd recovered quickest and stalked ahead of us through the Babilon streets, glowing with magic. *You'd think he'd thank me for saving him.*

I was a mess.

Death had left my legs unsteady.

When we *finally* made it to the inn's stables, the twins separated to saddle their steeds. Tarantula tethered my dire horse to his, and I meant to protest, but I couldn't remember how to speak. He grabbed my shoulder tightly.

"What?" I mouthed.

He shook his head with a fierce scowl, turned back to his horse, undid the pack, and pulled out one of the canteens of water. Uncorking it, he turned—water drenched my face. *Apparently I haven't drowned enough for the day.* I swore as I sputtered, wiping the liquid off my eyes and face.

"I am testing a theory," he said calmly, studying me with crossed arms.

"I'll show you a—"

He dumped the rest of the water over my head. "Do thou feel any different?"

"No." I hid my hands behind my back, hoping they weren't glowing. *He can't find out.*

"Seriously, how do thou feel?" he asked.

"Like I want to strangle you with my bare hands—"

Tarantula picked me up and placed me in his saddle. Before I could move, he mounted behind me and flexed so his thighs trapped me. They radiated heat like a furnace and had no business being so . . . overwhelming. *Dying has damaged me.*

Squire perched on the saddle, singing nonsensically off-key, and Axel quietly hummed the chorus.

"Are you okay?" Ella asked sluggishly as her body still recovered from the poisoning. "I love you, Zora."

"Love you so much," I said, meaning it.

Ella sniffled, and we reached between our dire horses for each other. Our fingers touched, and we shared a smile, a moment of peace amid the horrors.

"That is enough." Tarantula (the horrors) pulled me back in the saddle so I was pressed against him. "We need to leave."

Ella frowned. "Don't speak to her with that tone."

I opened my mouth to agree.

"Stop them!" someone shouted, and a horn sounded.

"Go!" Tarantula smacked the reins.

The twins kicked their stirrups, and our horses exploded forward, thundering through the street and out of the gate into the rainforest. Warm wind whipped through my unbraided wet hair, sending it straight back into his face.

Tarantula brushed the tendrils to the side. His rough finger pads scraped across the front of my neck, and shivers attacked me.

"How did thou get this scar?"

"I've always had it. You just never noticed."

"No." Fingers flexed against my throat as his breath made

my skin pebble. "'Tis impossible. I notice everything about thee. Always."

"Not this," I whispered, chilled to the bone.

I'd evaded death for the second time.

Tarantula's hand slowly fell away as if he sensed my melancholy. For once in his life, he didn't press. We rode in silence. Long hours passed. His hips rolled in powerful motion behind mine, expertly matching our horse's rhythm. The hard planes of his chest radiated intense heat beneath my spine. We were moving in tandem.

Unlike the last time we'd ridden together, no one was bleeding out. Instead, I was soaking wet and we were both in sheer clothes. We were indecent at best and downright vulgar at worst.

My thoughts veered into depraved territory. *It's because of the trauma. No other reason. None at all.*

As our carnivorous steeds picked up their brutal pace in the open desert, Tarantula pressed himself so flush against me that our sweat mingled, and I couldn't tell where his evil began and I ended. Nothing made sense anymore. Antichthon was a lie. There was only anarchy, magic, and the Mist. We were truly living in dark modern-medieval times.

"What is it?" Tarantula asked coldly—*a venomous arachnid in the body of a man*. Sand blurred around us. "Why did thou just tense?"

He stared hungrily down at me, his mask shining brilliant in the sunlight. A silver scar reflected back, glittering across my face. *"You must fight for those who cannot help themselves."*

"I'm afraid," I whispered, peeking up at him through lowered lashes.

Tarantula tensed, jaw working back and forth. "Thou . . . should be."

He held me closer than my own shadow, every inch of my body painfully aware of him. *I need to get away from this man*. He cracked the reins, his arms flexing as he caged me against his wide chest.

Eventually I passed out.

Axel crooned softly in a deep baritone. He was an exceptionally talented singer, and his morbid song created a dreamlike ambience.

Delicious hard warmth pressed against my cheek. Blinking, I took a second to get my bearings. My face was pressed against an armpit. Biceps flexed, holding me upright. I jolted straight and wiped drool off my chin, glancing up nervously.

Tarantula stared down at me. His hooded, piercing eyes studied my face.

I glanced away.

A hazy sunrise glowed on the horizon. Squire hooted as he perched on the horse's head, beak raised while the desert rushed around us. Dry air scratched roughly at my nose as the alien world of sand stretched endlessly in every direction. The twins rode beside us, a trail of dust billowing behind our steeds. Ella rubbed at her tired eyes, hunching low, riding half asleep while Axel watched her with concern.

From the veracity of my clear thoughts, critical thinking had returned. The scent of dark cherry filled my nose, and a hardness pressed against my lower spine. I jerked forward, nearly falling out of the saddle. He pulled me back upright.

Tarantula made an angry sound that vibrated through his chest.

Squire swiveled his head around and stared at me with wide, perpetually surprised eyes. "Morning, Zora!" he hooted with delight.

"Good morning, darling." I blew him a kiss and tried to scoot forward in the saddle.

"Hello, slutty spider." Squire tucked his beak bashfully (not helpful).

Tarantula waved. "Hello, little bird."

Squire chirped and turned like he was embarrassed.

Tarantula chuckled as he shifted his hips forward, still straddling me. Beads of sweat dripped uncomfortably down the side of my neck. He watched their descent. His tongue snaked out, wetting his lower lip.

I opened my mouth to tell him off but caught sight of the deep canyon to our left. We were close to getting back to the Scorpion Hole. *What is the Marshal's grand plan?*

Time stretched with painful slowness.

Finally our horses thundered to a stop in front of the base's hangar. We dismounted tiredly, all of us worse for wear.

As soon as our feet hit the sand, a dozen Shadow Swords leveled their weapons at Tarantula.

Axel pulled Ella behind him and backed her away from the scene. I inched toward them.

"What is the meaning of this?" Tarantula demanded.

A biting breeze slapped my hair across my face and blew through the Crimson Army.

Ryse lunged behind Tarantula. *Click.* He fitted a thin new shock collar around the very top of his neck.

Tarantula froze, jaw tight. The metal glinted in the sun, with even *more* diamonds than the last one. In one smooth motion, Ryse pressed a key into the latch and removed the old collar. He didn't meet my eye.

Tarantula stood with an unnatural stillness.

The Marshal stepped forward, cape billowing. "Your agreement was based on you remaining . . . neutralized, always. A shock collar is part of that. This is merely a housekeeping matter . . . for Knight Zora's protection." She pressed a new dial into my palm. Then she turned to Tarantula. "Knight Zora will escort you back to your private quarters. I will debrief each of you individually."

Ella mouthed something over her shoulder about coming to check on me, but Axel shielded her with his body, blocking my view as he led her back to their room. Shadow Swords bowed deep, falling into perfect formation around the Marshal as she also left.

Just like that, Tarantula and I were the last Mages in the hangar. Soldiers in scarlet milled about, but they all kept their distance.

Silence mounted.

Tarantula didn't say anything, but his lips curled upward and his eyes promised retribution. He didn't need to speak. A gust of wind whispered across the front of my jugular.

"Don't thou *dare* try anything," he warned.

I turned up the voltage and ran.

Tarantula and I were back within four walls, our beds far too close together. Electricity tingled across the tip of my tongue as he twitched on his mattress while I watched.

Night had fallen, but no moonlight softened the tension in the shadow-drenched room. Squire snored in my bed, tucked under the covers with his head on the pillow.

I will complete my quest.

I will complete my quest.

I will complete my quest.

My hand was steady as I periodically turned the dial.

Rule of survival: Never make a moment of peace with evil, only war. Don't let the darkness in.

Sparks burned brightly as Tarantula, still half naked, grunted in pain, fists thumping against the wall, chains rattling. His headboard rocked rhythmically. Silver boots kicked where they hung off the too-short bed.

"Despicable woman," he spat.

The meek didn't survive. Not these days, and especially not with *him* haunting the world. Sadists didn't deserve mercy. I stood next to his bed, legs spread wide for balance, still in my dirty clothes.

I needed answers, and he had them.

"Why do you call me vassal?" I asked again. "When will the Emperor attack Westmere? Why do you want to enslave us all?"

His lips pressed together, eyes promising pain.

"Why did you kill Aurora?"

Neon-blue lights jumped through the air. He somehow still looked posh and elegant, shirt parted, stomach clenching, while he was being *tortured*. Life wasn't fair.

I turned the dial down.

"Tell me something," I demanded for the fifteenth time, refusing to quail under his blistering expression.

"No." His eyes were murderous.

Electricity resumed its dance.

"Tell me *why* you killed my best friend."

"Thou shall get nothing from me . . . Ravenal," he said. "Thou art going to beg on your knees beneath me—"

The cycle resumed.

We were still the same two poles in ultimate opposition: Commonwealth versus Empire; poor versus rich; powerless against the powerful. We should have been Knight versus Royal, but only I knew the truth.

The script ended now. I'd already flipped it.

I should have been outmatched in every way, but his disdain could never hold a torch to mine. Poverty, hunger, hunting, survival, and constant terror for Mom hadn't broken me. They had made me *better* than him.

I *was* the North, and I was superior to him in every way that mattered. Sometimes, to be good, you had to do . . . *unseemly* things.

Minutes trickled into hours, but Tarantula refused to answer a single one of my questions. He smirked up at me tauntingly as he convulsed. He called me every horrible name in the book, spewing obscenities and insults.

He didn't fold, but neither did I.

At some hideous hour of dawn, I turned off the device because the blue Mist almost rendered it inert. His eyes promised me retribution. Backing up to my bed, emotions raw, I grabbed a dagger and pointed it down at him. "Move a muscle and I'll gut you."

Long seconds passed as his chest rose and fell. Muted light mixed with shadows, and the hushed golden rays of dawn filtered through the curtains.

His lips pressed into a straight line, polished platinum mask gleaming, unmarred by the voltage. The very reason why the Draconis Empire had once enslaved us. It all came back to a single element, stripped from the ground. None of the precious metal was left.

As he lay eerily still, his eyes were *far* too sharp; no delirium or befuddled agony clouded his gaze. A normal man would have long ago passed out from pain. *He's never been normal.*

Dark red marks crossed his torso where his chains had scalded his skin, and bruises marred his knuckles where he'd hit the wall.

His gaze dropped from my eyes to my mouth, then moved back again.

"Stop it, Ravenal," he rasped, his eyes molten. "Thou art aggravating me."

"Stop what?" I asked as I leaned closer, entranced by how his long golden lashes lowered.

Sweat streaked slowly down my face, dripping onto his torso. My braid was messy and sticky from exertion. The loosened tresses clung to my arms. I felt suddenly weak like I was the one who had been tortured.

Tarantula gnashed his teeth. "Cease this."

Cease what?

"Ravenal—back . . . away . . . from . . . me." He bit out each word as if suffering the greatest physical agony, which didn't make any sense because the dial was turned off. "'Tis dangerous for thee."

For me?

I scoffed as I held my dagger pointed at his heart. "You're the one in peril."

A breeze dragged down the back of my feverish neck and whispered across my spine. A blissful noise escaped as I shivered with delight.

"Thou art killing *me*. Back away—right now," he said through gritted teeth, fists banging on the mattress, chains rattling.

"Why would I do that?" I asked with genuine confusion. "I hold all the power. *Thou art* at my mercy," I mocked, my voice strangely husky.

Flames of magic smoldered in his eyes as he fixated on my lips. "Back away," he repeated desperately.

I leaned closer and laughed in his face. "I'm not going to give you what you want, ever."

"Ravenal." The scorched ridges of his stomach tensed, the butterfly flapping above his groin. "Thou have *no* idea what I want right now."

I twirled my knife between my fingers, spreading my legs wider as I prepared to fight. "I know exactly what you want—unchecked power."

He exhaled roughly through his nose, moistening his full lower lip. "Over thee."

"Wait . . . what did you say?" I asked, convinced I'd heard him wrong.

"I desire unchecked power. *Over thee*, Ravenal."

"What?" I shivered as the breeze stroked across my collarbone. Long fingers shot out and grabbed my wrist like a vise, squeezing. The dial clattered as it fell from my fingers. He yanked me forward.

I sprawled across his sweaty chest.

I tried to yank my arm away. "What are you—"

"For *many* years, I have desired power over only one thing," he said quietly. "One person." His lashes lowered as he bit down on his lower lip, groaning like my proximity caused him *unimaginable* agony.

"Move a single muscle—" I pressed the tip of my dagger beneath the shock collar at the base of his throat "—and I'll kill you."

"Do *not* say things like that." His eyes were pitch-black.

Both of us were breathing shallowly.

Adrenaline rush.

He arched up, pushing into my dagger; blood welled, tiny droplets streaking down his chest. "*Please* change." He released my wrist and banged his palm loudly against the wall, chains clattering. "I cannot right now. Thou art . . . The outfit . . . Please, don't stand over me . . . Do *not* look at me—not like that."

"Like what?" I asked as he *writhed* beneath my touch.

He stilled. "Change," he ordered, his voice warping with the cold command.

I looked down at my tattered outfit. There wasn't enough fabric present to offend someone's fashion sense. "Why are you so prudish all of a sudden? You were fine earlier when we—"

He breathed roughly, eyes rolling back in his head. "I have never once been fine in your presence, Ravenal."

"It's just clothes—"

"No. 'Tis thou . . . Thou stand over me with a blissful expression, *excited* to torture me. There has never been a woman in all Antichthon as cruel and lovely."

Our chests pressed together, heaving in tandem. I didn't remember moving. My clenched knife dug into the pillow on one side of his head and my fist on the other. I caged him beneath me.

"I ordered thee to cover yourself." His warm lips grazed across mine.

I chuckled into his mouth. "And . . . *why* do you think I would listen to anything you want?"

"Because," he said with a new dangerous softness. "My mind is lost, imagining . . ." He trailed off like he couldn't speak.

"Imagining . . . what?"

"Let it go."

"What are you imagining—"

"I beg thee, sit on my face. Right. Now."

25

Manipul(ate)

I reared back. "What . . . did you just say?" *This can't be the same man who's afraid of my ankles.*

"Art thou happy now, Ravenal?" He slapped the wall loudly. "I am completely undone for thee."

I pointed my dagger down at him. "*Why* would you say that?"

He slapped the wall again and sat up, leaning against the headboard, legs spread wide, chains draped across his bruise-reddened skin. "I told *thee* that my condition was singular and vexing. The desire is real, and 'tis not for anyone else." He scowled and muttered under his breath, "Unlike thee."

"You're just confused." I backed away from his bed. My legs bumped into my mattress. The room narrowed. *Nowhere to go.* No way to escape him. For *months* the hostile proximity had been driving both of us mad, and now it was boiling over.

Complete the quest by any means necessary.

Tarantula bit down on his inner cheek. "I am not confused. Thou have afflicted me with this condition. *Everything* is your fault."

"You're just repressed," I said, half pleading for him not to do this. "In your sorry state, anyone would make you—"

"I desire only thee, Ravenal." He cut me off coldly. "Do thou need to hear how watching thee torture me for hours *turned* me on? How I could see nothing in Babilon but thee—Zora Ravenal—sitting indecently on that couch, your eyes glittering with mischief as thou watched me."

I blinked rapidly. "I think it's probably best if you don't share how you feel—"

"I *yearn* for thee to press that knife against my flesh while thou ride my face for hours." His chest heaved. "No one else will do. I exist in agony . . . My obsession is burning me alive."

I opened and closed my jaw, speech impossible. "Take it back."

"No."

"You do not mean that."

"I yearn to do . . . terrible things to thee."

"What is actually wrong with you?" I aimed my dagger at him accusingly. "You don't just *reveal* your intentions toward a woman. Suffer like a man and suppress your feelings."

"Oh—I'm *suffering*, princess." He bit down on his knuckles, and a gust of wind sent my braid whipping in every direction. "Thou art everything that consumes my existence—"

"You're just turned on." *I can't believe I'm saying this.* "It means nothing—"

"It means *everything*." His eyes shone with sinful malice. "I wake up thinking about thee. I go to bed thinking about thee . . . I spend my days thinking about how I shall ruin your life. And yet thou beat me to it—thou ruined *mine* first."

I had no response.

He brought one knee up to his chest, his elegant pants pulling at the seams, tight around his crotch, as he wiped his thumb across his lower lip. The intensity in his eyes was now easily identifiable: *lust*.

Electricity had made the room unbearably hot. Both of us were near naked and covered in sweat.

His nostrils flared wide. "Thou art afraid . . . I can smell it on thee."

How dare he.

"Cow—ard," he taunted cruelly.

Complete the quest.

We'd spent so many long, tortuous weeks together; he thought he had me all figured out, but he had no idea who he was dealing with.

I will complete the quest.

I will beat him.

"You're just a prude, right?" I asked quietly as I twirled my dagger lazily and stepped closer to his bed.

Complete the quest.

Do not hesitate.

He stopped breathing. "What . . . art thou doing?"

Hunt him down. With both hands balanced on the edge of his mattress, I leaned toward his face, wetting my bottom lip. "What . . . do you want me to do?" *Spring the trap.*

An icy breeze caressed the side of my face.

I closed my eyes, leaning into it, sighing with contentment. It felt divine against my overheated skin.

He panted loudly in the heavy silence.

I opened my eyes. He'd leaned forward, his golden eyelashes fluttering against my cheek as he slowly blinked.

"Sit on my face," he repeated quietly. "*Please.* Let me—" he paused like he was sharing a dangerous secret "—suck thee off."

I shook my head.

He nodded his yes.

"Are you . . . sure?" I asked hesitantly. "That's what you really want to—"

"Yes." He smiled indolently, feigning casualness, but his fingers twitched like he was ready to jump out of his skin.

"Oh." I felt possessed. Unspoken desires burgeoned in the room.

"I yearn," he purred darkly, "to *taste* your cunt on my lips."

I backed away from him, fighting the pull, mouth dry, legs clenched together as I wavered. *He'll ruin me.* His teeth dug deeply into the pillow of his full lower lip as he held my gaze.

"Please," he rasped.

I stepped toward him.

He reached out, fingers sliding down my long braid.

I pulled away, faltering, and his hand hovered.

"Come to me, Ravenal," he ordered, fingers clenching and releasing. "Or art thou scared?"

Complete the quest.

Seduce him.

You know you want to.

I stepped forward and leaned my head against his outstretched hand. "I hate you," I said.

"I know." He stroked across my cheek and tangled his fingers in my braid, eyelids lowering.

I pressed my palm against his chest. We both stared down at where I touched him, silver strands of magic glittering as they rose off him and wrapped around my wrist. Our skin glowed brightly. Gently I pushed against him, but he didn't move.

"I'm in charge here."

His eyebrows rose. "Art thou sure about that?"

"Yes."

He chuckled, a dark light in his eyes. "Whatever the lady desires."

I shoved.

He collapsed back onto the mattress, playing helpless beneath my touch. A heady, tingling rush of power made me woozy.

"Do it," he taunted.

I held my knife up threateningly, and he smirked at it like I amused him.

I'll show him.

Shimmying my hips, I dropped my pants slowly, letting the ruined chiffon puddle at my feet.

He froze; all mirth fled from his expression as his eyes turned coal black. Moon rays disappeared behind cloud cover, his silver haze the only source of light. The hollows of his cheeks sharpened in the shadows.

Leisurely he slid down the headboard until he was lying flat on the bed—waiting. For me.

What we're doing is wrong.

Climbing up, I straddled his hips, my thighs spreading wide. I rubbed myself against his hardness, needing the friction.

He swore with a tormented groan as he grabbed the front collar of my shirt. *RIP.* He tore the buttons off and threw the garment away, then he did the same with the tiny strap of fabric across my chest, like the clothing deeply offended him. His pupils dilated, breath hitching.

He raised his glowing hands up toward my skin but stopped inches away. "May I?" he asked quietly, voice deeper than ever.

"You may."

He still didn't move, his fingers hovering centimeters from my shoulder. "It would be . . . rude of me."

"*Very* rude," I agreed.

"Deeply inappropriate."

"Completely."

"Unethical."

"Of course."

"Art thou . . . sure?" He studied my gaze, expression grave.

"Yes."

His finger pads were warm and roughly calloused; he inhaled swiftly through gritted teeth as if racked by horrible pain.

I disintegrated into pieces.

He groaned deeply, and I nodded in agreement. His touch was fire, and I was incinerating. Nothing had ever felt so *sublime*, and he was just dragging his fingers over my arm.

Slowly I crawled up his body.

The heat in his eyes burned as he tracked my ascent. His hips thrust upward, hands trailing down my spine possessively, leaving a wake of destruction.

He brought his mouth to my ear. "Just so thou know . . . I will let thee do *anything* thou want to me, *body or soul*, for the rest of my life."

I jolted, dragging my nails across the heated muscles of his chest.

"*Anything*." He licked my ear, and I shuddered.

Adrenaline made me weightless with euphoria, and I nodded in agreement, unable to speak.

"Can I taste thee?"

I swallowed hard. "Please do."

Gently he wrapped his long fingers around my waist. He pulled me forward, up, and over his chest until I was positioned on top of his face. My legs spread.

"Noble, perfect Ravenal," he said hoarsely as he stared at my core. His breath fanned hot, and he inhaled deeply. I started to speak. He licked me hungrily like he had a sweet tooth and I was pure maple syrup. *Curse it all.* My thighs spread wider as I sank lower onto the pillow, giving him more access.

Heat coiled deep, pleasure mounting as he sucked, hard, on my clit. I leaned forward helplessly, clutching my knife in one hand and gripping the headboard with the other.

He *devoured* me.

"Zora," he rasped darkly, and my name sounded wickedly corrupt on his lips. "Why do thou taste of the most exquisite nectar?" he asked accusingly, like I'd somehow tricked him.

I whimpered, desperate for more.

"Ride me, Knight," he ordered.

Gripping my thighs in his punishing hold, he pulled me even lower onto his face, his tongue needy as his calloused thumb slipped down, scraping deliciously across my ass. He lapped and sucked on my clit like he was desperate as he pushed his pointer finger slowly into my spasming heat.

Bucking, I obeyed and rode his face.

Heat uncoiled deep in my stomach, a precipice approaching.

"Don't stop—Sazha," I begged.

His tongue stilled.

He mumbled something straight into my core, tongue flicking my clit. A second finger joined the first, slowly exploring, pumping in and out. He paused each time to see how I'd react, learning my body. *Bastard.* Two fingers plunged deeply in unison, and pleasure spiraled. I arched my back as he hit a highly sensitive spot. Slowly he did it again.

I swore, slapping the wall as a flush set my face aflame, muscles tightening as I hurtled toward a cliff.

Unrelenting, *repeatedly*, he hit the spot as he sucked noisily on my clit. Flutters increased, and I tensed down on my inner muscles, trying desperately to hold myself back from coming.

He whispered kisses across my inner thighs. "Say my name again." His teeth scraped as he thrust his fingers. "Please. *Speak* it on your tantalizing tongue."

"Sazha," I gasped.

He bit down, *hard.* Sharp pain streaked up between my legs, morphing into blistering heat.

Gripping my ass tightly, he made a tortured sound and lifted his head, lapping at me like a starving man. I clenched down on my inner muscles harder, desperately trying not to shatter into pieces.

"Thou taste decadent," he said against my sensitive flesh with awe. "Sweet, tantalizing . . . *integrity.*"

Silvery tendrils of wind caressed my face, neck, chest, and stomach, skin humming as his magic stroked me with a reverent touch. His teeth scraped my clit. He sucked, and a sharp pinch seared upward. *What was that?* Every muscle in my body tensed; agonizing, wondrous heat exploded.

I clawed at the headboard. Raw euphoria crested as I hurtled over the edge, spasming, eyes rolling all the way back in my head. Stars sparkled as flutters of white-hot pleasure convulsed through me.

He sucked without mercy.

The pricking sensation sharpened, heightening the ecstasy. Wetness dripped down my inner thighs as I gushed onto his tongue and face. He lapped at me ravenously, eating me out like a man possessed; I jerked helplessly against him.

One hand gripped my hip with almost painful tightness, pushing me down harder like he wanted me to suffocate him. The other pumped ferociously, two fingers still mercilessly hitting the same oversensitive spot, stretching me wide.

Gusts of wind blew gently across my skin, teasing featherlight touches. Nothing had ever held a candle to him.

Apparently Tarantula was a sex god. *And he's never touched anyone but me.* I cried out from the aftershocks of flutters as he continued to wring my orgasm from me. When the trembles finally subsided, I slumped against the wall, arms shaking, barely able to hold myself up.

Zip.

Heaving for air, I looked over my shoulder.

The fly of his golden pants was unzipped and parted wide. The butterfly glittered low between the striated Adonis belt of his hips as he fisted his cock. His shaft was long and *impossibly* thick and had pulsing cobalt veins. It was the largest I'd ever seen.

Oh, come on.

How is it that big?

Small silver butterflies glittered where they were tattooed across the top and sides of his cock.

I stopped breathing. He pressed his hand across my stomach, calloused fingers wide as he gently guided me back until I straddled his waist. I stared down at where his shaft protruded.

"May I . . . fornicate with thee?" he asked with a gravelly timbre, face twisted with agonized longing.

"Who says fornicate?"

"I do." His eyelids lowered with malevolent intention. "Or should I ask . . . may I *fuck you*?"

"You may." I waved my dagger at him tauntingly. "But do try to impress me."

His eyes smoldered. "Can thou handle me, princess?"

"Don't princess me, *princess*," I said.

Laughing, he flung his head back. "Then let me amaze thee, *Knight*."

He grabbed my hips and lifted, sliding off the bed and standing up. He repositioned us both. Laying me boneless on my back, perpendicular across the mattress, he stood between my parted legs, holding me up.

"Thou art divine," he praised. "And thou art *mine*." Biting down on his lip, he stepped closer to me, calluses dragging across my thighs. "Scoot your hips forward, darling."

I obeyed, the flush spreading across my nipples, which his gaze devoured. Head spinning, mind hazy with delight, I *needed* him, desperately.

The large butterfly tattoo shimmered on his lower abdomen, flapping as he flexed. Lean muscles, forearm veins, and taut sinew surrounded me. Silver tendrilled between us.

"Why is your magic . . . doing that?" I asked, staring down at the metallic glow.

"Thou art my syxzal." A flush spread across his chest as his abdominal muscles tensed. "My woman . . . in *every* way." He licked my juices off his shiny lips.

Fisting his thick tattooed cock, he brought it down to my core. He nudged forward little by little with a treacherous amount of control. I wrapped my legs around his hips, clawing at the sheets as he stretched me impossibly wide.

The growing pleasure-pain burn was too much. *There's no way it fits.* I tried to speak. I couldn't. He was too big, and each subtle thrust was overwhelming. I could feel him in my heart, pounding in my throat, and all the way to the tips of my toes.

"Lift your hips a little higher, my valiant Knight."

I did as he requested.

"That's *my* lionheart," he praised.

Holding my ass up with both of his calloused hands, fingers curling, nails digging in, he gripped me harder, *possessively*, as he kept pushing his immense width deeper inside of me with painstaking patience.

I looked between us; the tiny butterflies slowly disappeared.

I was stretched to the point of breaking. It was so intense that I couldn't feel my face. I was obscenely full, skewered on his thick shaft.

He gripped me with desperation, like he was trying to crawl into my skin.

With each thrust forward, the larger butterfly flapped across his stomach muscles, flying.

Dozens of silver tendrils rose off him, wrapping around my wrists like restraints. A hum of energy shivered through my bones where his magic held me.

Slowly, pushing even *deeper*, he leaned forward, blue veins standing out in stark relief across his biceps. He rested his forehead against mine, sweat dripping off his face and streaking onto my own.

"May I . . . kiss my princess?" he whispered, voice gravelly with lust.

I shook my head. "No."

He froze.

"The princess may kiss *me*."

Chuckling, he brought a hand to my forehead. *Why are his fingers trembling?* He raked his nails slowly across my scalp and fisted my braid. Pleasure exploded in his wake.

"Never—" he spoke against my forehead like he was praying

"—in all the realms has a woman been so intoxicatingly *good.* Thou art perfection incarnate, Zora Ravenal."

I gasped, and his tongue slammed into my mouth, sweeping deep like he was trying to consume me. A rough growl rattled from his chest, into his throat, vibrating through my lips as his tongue battled mine, fighting for dominance.

I pressed upward, pushing, tugging roughly at his hair with my dagger still in my fist. He pinned me down against the bed with his cock and mouth, fingers tangling in my messy braid.

He made an unholy sound as he ripped his mouth away, thrusting forward with one powerful lunge, seating his throbbing shaft fully inside of me.

"Thou art taking me so splendidly," he praised softly.

I yanked at his silky curls with growing desperation. He pulled back and drove into me harder.

Tugging at my braid in rhythm to his thrusts, he pushed deeper. Gently he dragged his rough thumbs over my cheekbones, mapping my old wounds.

"Syxzal, thou art . . . *everything.*" Tingles exploded as his magic caressed my silver scar.

With a tormented sound, he cradled my face, kissing me tenderly like I was the most precious thing in the world. Gusts of wind fluttered across my nipples. Pleasure sparked down my chest. He licked into my open mouth, our breaths mingling.

I tipped over the edge again, clenching around his burning size, and he swallowed my orgasmic cries with his mouth.

"Do thou know?" he panted. "Thou art the ideal—the most perfect person to ever exist . . . No one is like thee, and no one could *ever* match your fire." His hips bucked, and he pressed deep, devouring my mouth, warmth pulsing between us as he came. Our chests were pressed together. He lay on top of me, our hearts beating wildly in tandem.

His face blurred as my eyes filled with tears.

He lifted himself up. Again he grabbed my face with both of his hands. He pressed a gentle kiss to my forehead.

"Art thou okay, beautiful?" His eyes were stunning, the color of clouds reflecting a rainbow of sunlight. They brimmed with uncharacteristic benevolence.

I nodded, unable to speak, trying desperately to hold my emotions back.

Again he kissed my forehead softly, the tip of my nose, the very top of my cupid's bow, my fluttering eyelashes. He repeated the path, peppering my face with endless gentle kisses.

Reverently he dragged his hands through my tangled hair. His expression was nothing short of distraught.

"Thou art more precious than any jewel, my sweet Zora," he said, nodding, like he meant it. "Nothing in all Antichthon holds a candle to thee."

I couldn't speak around the lump in my throat.

He brushed his warm lips across the corners of my eyes. "I shall clean thee up."

I didn't know what to do with this dangerous man worshipping me with more tenderness than anyone ever had. No one had ever . . . touched me like him. No one had ever spoken to me so sweetly.

Moisture filled my vision.

He was being *so* . . . earnest.

It wasn't fair.

Hastily I wiped away a tear before it could fall down my cheek and give me away.

Voices shouted from the hangar, and I tried to sit up, but he gently pushed me back down. "Careful. Let me take care of thee . . . Thou deserve to be worshipped."

"We should see what's happening," I said.

He shook his head. "No—we should not." Softly tracing circles over my hips, he gingerly turned me so I lay back with my head on the pillows. I let him position me.

"That's my precious girl," he said quietly. "So fucking *good*."

He stared at my face, eyes shining with delight as he slowly climbed on top of the bed and slid lower. He spoke with intense reverence, like he was referring to something *beyond* sex.

"I thought you were getting a towel to clean up." I tried to hide a sniffle.

Voices echoed louder in the hall.

Tarantula smiled contentedly as he settled between my legs. "My fair, valiant Knight—I do not need one to take care of thee." He lapped, cleaning me with his tongue, bringing my body back up to impossible heights.

He pressed two long fingers into my core, then a third as he sucked harder, applying more pressure. His other hand plucked at my nipples.

I tried to fight it, but somehow *another* orgasm crested, breaking over me in endless waves.

He rested his chin on my pelvis, watching my face with hooded, smoldering eyes as I shivered through the ecstasy, my inner muscles throbbing.

The bottom of his face gleamed, covered in my juices and . . . *blood*?

He smiled; his canines extended, razor-sharp.

Silver steamed off his curls like a debased halo. Gaze molten, he tipped his head down, the whites visible beneath his pale irises. *Evil eyes.*

Someone yelled something outside, and it sounded like "new threat from the Empire." My instincts screamed at me to act. This was the Marshal's plan. She'd said to go to her when events unfolded.

It was time.

Eyes watering from pleasure, I stared at the knife still clutched in my fist, thoughts racing.

I should stab him through the spine.

He'll never see it coming.

I could end this right now.

All of it.

Do it, Zora.

Do it quickly.

He lowered his head and groaned into my core, eating me out with renewed desperation. Tears streaked down my face. Flipping the dagger over, I gripped the blade tightly, muttered a prayer to the old god for strength, and slammed the hilt across his temple with everything I had.

He slumped, unconscious.

For the quest.

26

Escape

Clatter. Stinging lanced across my hand as I dropped my bloody dagger to the floor. Long seconds passed. I stared down at the red line cutting across my palm and fingers.

Tarantula lay limp, his face still between my thighs, a purple lump already forming on the side of his head. I gently pushed him away, but his unconscious body slipped off the sheets, falling to the floor with a loud thud.

I swore, fighting the urge to check to make sure he was okay.

Voices echoed outside.

Compose yourself.

Scorching emotions clawed up my throat. I scratched at my neck like I could physically force them back down. Some women were made for soft romances, but the rest of us were built for war. The world wouldn't save itself.

~~*It was just for the quest.*~~

~~*It was just for the quest.*~~

~~*It was just for the quest.*~~

Throwing myself off the blood-splattered bed, naked, I tried not to look down at Tarantula's spread limbs. Even blacked out, he sprawled elegantly across the floor.

Wrapping a bandage around my stinging palm, I quickly changed into exercise pants and a long-sleeved shirt. Straightening my shoulders, trying to shake off the sluggishness of orgasmic bliss, I positioned a sleepy Squire on my collarbone and put the shock dial into my pocket.

Under the bed, I pulled out the two bone knives I'd hidden for emergencies and tucked them into the holsters in my combat boots.

Before I left the room, I walked back to the chess game and knocked his queen off the board, exposing his king. Neither of us had ever been the pawn in this war. I was closer than I'd ever been to winning, and yet I could still feel his warm lips pressing gentle kisses across my face as he thrust slowly into—*Do not think about it.*

Out in the hall, I pointed at a soldier. "What's that?"

The man flinched as I snatched the *Democratic Papers* out of his hands. The front page said:

Knight Zora's Mother Has Been Taken Hostage by the Empire. Emperor Urges Zora to Meet Him This Week for Hostage Trade at Port Crow.

Port Crow was one of only two operational trading posts run by the Commonwealth and was known for its savage pirate inhabitants. They lived uncivilized without rules and city walls like in the Communes. They were officially "neutral" in the Storm Wars, aka they sided with the Empire.

My hands shook as I read.

A black-and-white sketch was drawn below the title, depicting a Royal Mage with short, cropped hair, a thin mask barely covering his eyes.

The Mage clutched my mother against his chest possessively, and she scowled up at him while he stared down at her with a soft expression. Vale's decapitated head lay at his feet. *He killed her bodyguard.* The worst part—an ouroboros tattoo was stark around the Mage's right eye.

It's the man from Mom's journal.

The caption below it said:

Master painter Marge witnessed the kidnapping and drew the event.

My blood ran cold.

The paper crumpled beneath my hands.

"I'm going to speak with the Marshal," I said to the soldiers, voice calm, face relaxed, as my heart pounded painfully. "Tarantula's incapacitated from torture."

They nodded, and one escorted me through the base to the Marshal's door. She opened on the first knock and pulled me inside the room.

"It's time," she said quietly. She pressed the materials into my hands. I tucked them into the secret waterproof pouch she'd had sewn into my exercise bra for this exact moment. "Good luck, soldier," she said. "You're going to need it."

"Always lucky," I muttered numbly.

She gave me an odd look.

I didn't elaborate.

The Marshal's eyes narrowed. "He *will* come after you. Be ready. Remember your quest—keep him close. Do not give up, soldier. No matter what. We have *one* of these left. Tracker . . . Tsiolkovsky's equation . . ."

Technical math terms garbled together, meaning nothing to me. I zoned out, panicking.

". . . reaching speeds of three hundred thousand miles per hour," the Marshal finished with gravitas. "This is our *only* chance."

"Yes, sir."

I turned and ran, feeling stupid.

In this early morning hour, the hangar sat mostly empty. The base didn't wake up and mobilize until the sun had crested over the horizon. Metal was cold against my chest.

I sprinted to the stables. Shadow Swords had saddled the largest, meanest-looking steed in the hangar. It snapped its fangs at me, swiveling its ears back and forth with distrust. I fought the urge to snap back like a wild thing. *Black Beauty* was engraved across the stable door. She whinnied, eyeing me with blatant suspicion. Ryse handed my reins to me with an awkward bow, and I looked away.

A few minutes later, I was saddled on her broad back. We trotted at a fast clip out into the sand. The cool night air was warming in the morning light. I fought the urge to turn around and ask the twins to come with me. I couldn't keep putting the people I cared about in danger. There weren't that many of them left.

I dug my heels into Black Beauty's side, and she sprinted across the rolling dunes as if charging into war. So swift were her movements that we barely sank into the sand. Thighs straining, I concentrated on matching her pace.

We thundered east.

"The mission?" Squire hooted, dry wind ruffling his feathers as the world blurred around us. He perched precariously on my shoulder, wings flapping as he struggled to stabilize himself.

"We're going to save Mom," I said, watery eyes stinging as I squinted through the grits of sand and tried not to break down. I yanked on the reins as hard as possible, nearly falling forward out of the saddle as I brought us to an abrupt stop.

Damn it all.

My mind finally caught up with my body.

The Marshal had said she had a plan, a player—the man with the ouroboros tattoo. She'd orchestrated Mom's kidnapping. This was her plan. Does that mean Mom's safe? What if the Marshal is being tricked by the Mage?

In the portrait, his eyes were evil. *Mom could be in grave danger.* Bent over, unable to handle the pressure of the moment, I screamed at the top of my lungs.

Black Beauty spooked, dancing sideways, and I bit down hard on my cheek. Blood flooded my mouth, but I barely noticed.

"I'm so stupid," I said.

Squire pecked at the side of my face, giving me kisses. "You brave, Zora."

I stared at him.

You can do this.

I yanked on the reins, turning around. *Go back and confront the Marshal.* No. *There is a bigger enemy.* We spun in a circle. *I must complete the quest.*

Digging my heels in, we once again took off at a fast clip—east, toward Port Crow.

Hair whipped across my face, exhaustion battling with adrenaline. It had been a long twenty-four hours. Sleep-deprived, wrung out from trauma and euphoria that I refused to ponder, I felt my heart cracking under pressure.

Focus on your duty.

No one else was going to save my mom; no one else was going to stop the Emperor from enslaving all of us.

I needed to ruin him.

Chapter one of *A Gentleman's Guide to Slaughtering* stated, "Always attack first." Chapter two explained, "Never let them see it coming." We were now on chapter three: "When committing a deceit, you must see it through to fruition."

Black Beauty leaned her head forward as she realized I wasn't going to hold her back and accelerated. Wind whistled as we picked up to a staggering speed, exactly what I needed. I glanced back nervously over my shoulder, but a mirage of heat lines danced across the dunes. No one followed us.

For some reason, it made me want to cry.

I had hours before Tarantula would come for me. The Marshal was convinced he would follow quickly, but she hadn't seen his face. His look of pure longing as he lay between my legs. He was going to be so livid. *He might not come. Not after the betrayal.*

Feeling sick, I tried not to panic, because it was the only plan we had. The quest depended on him following me.

Bending down to be more aerodynamic, I grabbed the long mane and held on. Squire hooted on my shoulder and leaned his tiny head lower, following suit.

Hours dripped away like sand in an hourglass.

We rode hard.

Exhaustion increased. The concussion Sibrain had given me must have been worse than I first thought, or maybe it was the heartbreak. Head spinning, I could barely focus on the changing landscape.

As we rode eastward into the waving grasslands, rolling dunes were replaced with hills of green. Strange-looking trees dotted the landscape. They had squat trunks with dozens of meandering branches that spread wide instead of high. Their leaves were bright oranges and reds, nothing like the evergreens of the North or the lush foliage of the South. The Mist was a thin, light blue fog across the ground.

The tree-lined dirt road we headed down led to crumbling abandoned towns without walls. Evidence of a time before the Mist and the Storm Wars.

Thunder boomed off in the distance, and bright light flashed. Lightning struck a tree with a blistering crack. Angry clouds churned across the horizon, blocking the last bits of sun.

The sky opened up with a roar. Cold droplets rained down.

Magic throbbed in my skull.

I tipped my head back, face wet as I stared up at the weeping clouds. I'd read about heavy rains that fell in a torrential downpour, but I'd never experienced anything like this all-consuming deluge. The pounding in my head increased, and it felt like I could breathe deeply for the *first* time in my life. Pure, unadulterated exaltation.

Unlike snow, which glanced off blubber-treated clothes, rain soaked me straight to my soul, drenching everything. It drowned the world. Hair plastered my face and skin, so I reached up and rebraided it.

I shifted in the slick saddle, my soggy clothes clinging. My socks squelched uncomfortably in my combat boots. Despite the discomfort, I sat up straighter, jittery from the surge of magic.

This is what it feels like to be alive.

I held my glowing hands up. A silver haze steamed from my fingers, hissing.

Squire huddled under my wet braid, trying, *and failing*, to stay dry. He chirped with annoyance. Hooves smacked into puddles, water and mud flying as Black Beauty kept sprinting over the jagged hills. She leaned her head low, charging through the shower.

Visibility decreased as the rainfall intensified. Mini floods sent water cutting through the rocks, gushing down the hills. The world was a somber shade of gray, and my exposed skin glowed with magic.

Black Beauty reared back abruptly, neighing. I shouted and Squire screamed as we careened, mud flying. Hooves grappled for traction as we slid sideways along the rocks. Finally she came to a stop.

Squinting through the growing darkness, I spit out dirt. Nothing but air to our right and a roaring crash down below. I gasped. A rocky cliffside plummeted into the sea, and we stood on the edge.

We were at the Moor Ocean.

Over ten thousand miles of uncrossable waves.

Shivering, I folded inward to stay warm as the scent of salt filled my lungs.

"We drown?" Squire cawed as he huddled against the back of my neck, hiding from the elements as Black Beauty shook her head, backing away from the free fall she'd narrowly avoided.

"No, dear, we can swim."

"Is this sea?" Squire hooted with excitement.

"Yes," I said with awe. "We've finally made it to the ocean."

Squire ducked as rolling thunder shook the land.

Grief hit me out of nowhere. *Aurora never got to see the ocean.* Mom was also out here somewhere, scared. The feelings were crippling. I pounded my fist against my chest, trying to restart my heart. Numbness had spread.

Squire bobbed his head. "Survive we must—"

"—it's up to us," I finished the poem, rain sputtering off my lips.

I leaned forward, the sharp rocks rising jaggedly below. There was no easy way down off this cliffside. *I'm going to have to jump.*

I screamed into the wind, voice cracking.

Lightning exploded over the churning white-tipped waves that crashed against the sheer face. The flash illuminated a single long, meandering path that led all the way down. It passed under a gate and ended where stone buildings stood by a pier.

A monstrous ship rocked in the waves. Its sails were lowered, and a heavy tarp covered the deck. Its bow bobbed violently, a gigantic figurehead protruding high over the sea—a roaring dire lion with arching dragon wings, the symbol of the Draconis Empire.

They were here to take me to Mom.

"I, Zora Ravenal, am a Mage, a Keeper of the Barren Forest, the Bear of the North, a hunter, and a peasant," I shouted, drawing strength from the storm that had showed me my path. "I *will* complete my quest!"

Just as quickly as the port appeared, it disappeared under the dark deluge of rain. My hands glowed with a guiding silver light. I led Black Beauty tangentially along the edge of the world as we traversed down the exposed, wet path at a slow clip with trepidation. Hooves slipped on rocks, and each step downward was more dangerous than the last.

Finally we made it to the arch with *Port Crow* whittled into the top.

Wanted posters were nailed up and around the structure. A black object hung below the arch on a rope. It blew back and forth in the blustery wind. I squinted through the icy rain and reared back in my saddle, clutching Squire.

The posters depicted a woman covered in blood holding up a masked royal with a knife in his stomach: me and Tarantula.

Further proof that the pirates of the Eastern Coast were loyal to the Empire. *Treacherous cowards.* Cold determination intensified. *I will not lose.*

Head throbbing, I let the rage warm my icy limbs. Black Beauty neighed, flashing sharp canines as she shook her head. She walked around the arch, refusing to go beneath it. Squire cawed out with horror.

I looked back and felt sick. The black object fluttered as it rocked, wings spreading wide in the rain. It was a corpse of the port's namesake: a dead crow. The lack of respect for life was despicable. After I hunted, I always buried the remains of the animal corpses that weren't used by the Commune.

Rule of survival: Respect life or it will not respect you.

Down the path, Black Beauty walked into the town. Misshapen stone buildings towered along both sides of the road, their third floors leaning at sharp angles, lower floors too narrow, like they were built inverted and were seconds from crumbling.

Waves crashed loudly against a low stone wall, the white foam spraying high into the salty air. Soggy wanted posters with my face on them were nailed to the hanging lantern posts that lined the curving empty street.

Rain hissed, falling faster.

The pier came into view, the ship towering above the buildings. Up close, the entire deck was covered with an immense tan tarp. Black Beauty came to a halt. I snapped the reins and dug my heels in, but she refused to move forward.

I dismounted with Squire perched on my shoulder and unsheathed one of my bone knives.

A sound echoed behind me. I whirled, holding my knife at the ready, head on a swivel.

A tall, scraggly man stood a distance away in the rain. His head cocked to the side as he stared at me. His dark beard was long and braided, covered in chains. He coughed loudly, a dry rattle. *The wasting sickness.* I squinted through the gloom. He was missing an eyeball.

"Who are you?" I shouted.

He smiled, and there were no teeth, just black gums. "The bounty's here!" he shouted at the top of his lungs with a coarse accent.

I backed up.

Three more men joined him, each holding machetes and coughing intermittently. They were skin and bones, and their infected tattoos bubbled as gaudy jewelry glinted on their necks.

Pirates.

Two more joined.

I turned, preparing to flee, but Black Beauty had run off—and five more men blocked my path. The wasting sickness had given their complexions a green pallor, and their eyes were a sickly shade of yellow.

They surrounded me. Squire trembled on my shoulder.

Rule of survival: Meet the danger head-on.

Gently I picked Squire up. "Fly to the wall and don't look, dear," I said as I kissed his soggy head. He hooted and flapped over, settling onto the wall. He swiveled his head, obediently looking out to sea.

With a war cry, the pirates charged.

"You must fight for those who cannot help themselves."

The men stalking toward me were riddled with disease and emaciated by starvation. I wasn't sure if my new duty included them. *Will Barren punish me for killing them?* My magical scar itched.

I wasn't willing to take any chances.

Ducking under an arm, I stabbed one of the pirates in the chest from behind, purposefully missing his heart. He cried out in pain as I broke his outstretched arm and ripped his machete from his hold.

He dropped as I spun away. He clutched his chest, but he was *still alive.*

Another approached, and I glanced down at the new machete in my hand. I dropped low and sliced it across the tops of his thighs, not deep enough to bleed out. Incapacitated, he also fell to the ground.

I chucked my bone blade with my left hand, and it buried deep into the fleshy part of a shoulder—another pirate toppled.

A blade glanced off my arm as I failed to duck low enough. The sharp pain awakened my senses. Kicking, I spun and raked the machete down the back of a pirate who got too close. He fell to his knees with his spine shallowly cut open.

Pain sliced my side as I flung myself forward, the very tip of another blade piercing my skin. I ran and slid low across the wet grass, dodging swiping weapons, then dropped to a squat and picked up a second machete. I severed the backs of ankles as gently as I could. *Sorry about that.* Pirates fell to their knees, unable to stand up.

Back on my feet, I spun in a circle.

Four new men converged. Light with adrenaline, I strategized the best way to incapacitate, flipping, jumping, lunging. Blood splattered in arcs—quickly washed away by the rain—as I sliced a path through the men.

The longer we fought, the sloppier the pirates got and the calmer I felt. Each movement was precise, and the number of foes dwindled as I incapacitated them with accuracy. They were panicking, and I was hunting. *We are not the same.*

Blades swung blindly while I sliced with cold, exacting precision. I bounced on my toes in the puddles, pulsing with energy. The Bear of the North had awakened.

"Shiver me feathers!" Squire screeched, getting into the spirit of the melee as a wave slammed against the wall. Chilly salt water sprayed over the road. Pirates moaned in pain. I spun in a slow circle, machetes raised defensively, hands glowing like the moon.

The ocean roared; I shouted with it, expelling the built-up pressure. The waves grew in size, shimmering with my magic.

I turned, but there was no one left to fight. Bodies lay around me in a large circle. Some of them crawled away, but most clutched at their injuries, moaning.

Straightening, I lowered my incandescent arms, cracking my neck. High on a wellspring of my magic, I bounced back and forth, practically vibrating. *Is that it?*

"Ravenal!"

I froze.

It was what the Marshal wanted, but I still couldn't believe my eyes as a majestic brown dire horse sprinted down the cliffside, cutting through the rain.

"Ravenal—how *dare* thou!" The familiar masculine voice was warped by the downpour, hoarse and gritty.

An ominous hush descended as the spectral figure neared. The world fell eerily quiet. I stepped back, and a pirate grunted in pain as I tripped over his injured body. Blood mixed into the puddles that dotted the ground.

Waves exploded higher into the air.

Magic glowed bright silver around Tarantula, surrounding him and his dire horse. Hooves crunched over bodies as they both came to a stop twenty feet away.

Tarantula sat stiffly atop his steed, soaked to the bone. Golden chiffon fabric clung to his leanly muscled torso, creating the illusion of nudity. His curls were wild, disheveled around his ears.

Prisoner chains shackled his limbs, and his platinum mask did nothing to conceal his blistering rage. Metallic flames flickered around him like a bonfire, and for the pièce de résistance, he held *my* bone knife outstretched in his hand.

The one I'd slammed against his skull.

After we had sex.

"Tarantula," I said casually, schooling my face to hide my shock.

I tried not to contemplate how I'd left him in an unconscious heap, or how his face had twisted with rapture as he held my hips tight and licked his lips while he thrust deeply into— *Don't you dare think about it.*

He shouldn't have recovered so quickly.

He'd been out cold . . . *right*?

I coughed, eyes watering and sinuses burning from the sheer magnitude of magic pouring off him. He was more of a force of nature than he was a man.

"Thou art a treacherous, deceptive, sadistic *brat*." His accent thickened with each word.

"I won the chess match," I blurted, unable to stop myself from gloating. I waved my new machetes. "Did you notice?"

"Oh, I noticed, *princess*." He smiled, and it was all teeth. "I was never unconscious. Do thou think a little tap to the head is all it takes to best me? 'Tis beyond insulting."

SNAP.

With one violent motion, he yanked his hands wide, and the titanium chain that bound his wrists snapped in two as if it was nothing but string. Solid metal clanked as the chains hung broken.

He'd freed himself for the second time.

This is not good.

His mouth flattened into a straight line. *It was just between my thighs.*

I forced my shoulders to relax and made a show of rolling my eyes at him like he hadn't just played me for a fool. *This is a calamity of diabolical proportions.* With him, every step forward felt like three steps back.

He spun my bone knife expertly between his elegant fingers, *the same ones that were inside of me earlier— STOP thinking about it, Zora.*

Tarantula didn't break eye contact, still not blinking. With precise control, he raised his arm and leveled *my* blade forward. Icy winds howled from every direction, thrashing my braid into a frenzy.

The cataclysm happened slowly, then all at once.

Sinful lips curled up with insolent aggression as he flung my dagger straight at me.

27

CAPTIVATING (HOST)AGE

Thunder cracked.

Icy rain slammed down in gray sheets as Tarantula flung my bone dagger through the storm. It barreled toward my face, traveling too fast to duck but just slow enough to inspire abject fear. *This is going to hurt.*

I flinched.

Thud.

A body dropped dead. Lightning flashed, illuminating the pirate who'd been sneaking up behind me, now sprawled on the ground with my knife protruding from his skull. I hadn't heard him coming.

Whipping my head around, I raised my weapons. More bodies stepped out of the shadows.

We were surrounded, again.

The pirates had seemingly multiplied and were trailing out of buildings, coming from everywhere. There was no end in sight to their numbers. They brandished machetes and long swords in their tattooed hands.

ROAR.

Golden scales shimmered as the tarp covering the colossal

ship's deck was flung away, revealing Plague. She was covered in thick leather straps that were attached to the ship. She shook her head, sitting as if waiting for instructions. *That's how their ships traverse the Moor Ocean. The fairy tales must be right; dragons really can fly over three hundred miles per hour.*

Up on the deck, men shouted to each other, and the oversized sails slowly rose up the towering masts.

The Emperor has Mom.

Is she on that vessel?

Plague tipped her head back, her fire billowing into the rainy sky.

I will complete my quest.

I must complete my quest.

Failure is not an option.

Steel slammed against steel as I spun, ducking and shoving with all my might, dislodging the machete locked with mine.

Tarantula dismounted and threw gusts of wind at the pirates, fighting to get to me. I swung my blade, focusing on only injuring as I battled my way toward the ship, rain flying off my braid.

The pirates seemed to be endless, dozens of bodies swarming around us, blocking me from getting to the dock.

"*Zora*," Tarantula bellowed, fear in his voice.

"Mom!" I screamed.

Silver exploded from his hands, and he flung a dozen pirates high into the air. They slammed down against the stone wall. Bones cracked. Silver-streaked waves lashed over the barrier, pulling the screaming men out to sea.

I took the opening, incapacitating man after man as I inched closer to the ship. A pirate rose from the ground. In stretched-out seconds, I turned, but I was too slow.

A heavy object cracked against my temple.

Nausea hit instantly. Swearing, head screaming with pain, I staggered back from my attacker, blinded.

When the dark spots faded, I was on my knees, and men were closing in all around with weapons raised.

"ZORA!"

Ten feet away, Tarantula lifted his hand, and a metallic wave exploded from it, filling the world with violent magic.

Crack. Crack. Crack.

The men around me snapped backward. Blood sprayed as their spines burst out of their abdomens. They collapsed with horrified screams.

Squire shrieked, wings flapping as he hovered in front of my face with his talons raised defensively.

Another wave of magic shot from Tarantula.

More pirates screamed as they dropped. Eerie silence descended. There was no one to fight because every single person had been massacred. *Instantly.*

Clutching the lump on my head, trying not to throw up, I fell to my side. The dial tumbled out of my pocket in slow motion, and the edge caught on a cobblestone. *No.* It turned all the way up.

Electricity sizzled hotter than ever, amplified by the rain and salt water. Tarantula dropped to his knees.

I passed out.

The world rocked as salt, brine, and copper filled my nostrils.

FLAP—whoosh—FLAP—whoosh.

A strange cadence filled the air. Sluggish awareness pounded through my aching head as pain mixed with debilitating grogginess.

Tacky eyelids pulled open as I forced them apart. I was soaked to the bone, and shivers racked me. The wooden floors, walls, and ceiling were moving. Fishing nets rocked above as everything pitched back and forth. Something heavy and warm covered my back.

Waves roared outside, and my glowing fingers hummed with awareness.

I'm on a ship.

"Mom . . . Squire . . . Ella . . . Axel?" I said hoarsely, my tongue sandpaper, throat rough as I shuddered miserably. Shallow wounds covered my body, but the physical pain was nothing compared to the dawning realization of silence. No one had responded.

The emptiness of the world stretched, anxiety a dense weight in my stomach. Unfathomable panic mounted.

You're by yourself, Zora.

Desolation hollowed out my chest.

There's no one left.

I trembled harder, my skin clammy.

"Squire," I cried out in misery. "My sweet darling."

My heart grew heavier.

A tiny head filled my vision, and disheveled feathers stuck out in every direction. "Zora love me?" Squire hooted sleepily, silver wafting from his beak. Wide yellow eyes peered into mine as he cocked his little head to the side and studied me with his perpetually nervous expression.

I tried to lift my hands, but crushing lethargy made it impossible to move. Wetness dripped down my face. "Of course, dear. You're still with me," I half sobbed as he rubbed his cheek against mine.

"Zora is me family," he sang solemnly.

"And Squire is mine." I rubbed against his face, savoring the familiar scent of magic and feathers as he pressed himself to me. We were still together.

On closer inspection, I lay sprawled on my back surrounded by something warm as Squire perched on my collarbone. Panic receded in a dizzying rush. It was astounding the difference a friend could make. Relaxing back into the splendid heat, I tipped my head with a tired sigh and looked up.

Pearlescent eyes met mine. I screamed; Squire shrieked in solidarity (helpful).

Tarantula stared down at me with his lips pressed into a frown. His cold gaze studied my face behind his blood-splattered mask.

Oh.

No.

I was draped across his chest as he cradled me with his hands spread possessively over my lower stomach. Long legs surrounded me, his thighs dwarfing my own, providing endless heat. He gently stroked wet hair off my temple and repositioned my braid. Then he pressed his wrist against my forehead.

"Ravenal, thou have a fever," he said sharply. His tone dropped an octave in anger, but he held me gently.

"Zora, a *sickly* woman," Squire sang mournfully.

"Yes." Tarantula stiffened beneath me. "She is ill because she foolishly rode through a storm for *hours*. Then she fought pirates instead of retreating to safety. Her core body temperature is struggling to regulate itself. She has needlessly put herself in danger . . . again."

Squire cawed defensively, "Zora me friend."

"*Zora* is a danger to herself," Tarantula argued. "Never has a woman been more threatened by the pernicious effects of her own hazardous decisions."

"Me like seeds," Squire hooted, clearly overwhelmed by the intensity of the conversation (understandable). He hopped down, curling up on my lap.

"She," I said weakly, "is *fine* and doesn't appreciate being discussed without—" A coughing fit interrupted my speech.

"Oh yes, thou art *obviously* fine. Thou have *clearly* proven me wrong once again," Tarantula said meanly, but his right hand stroked my head tenderly and his left hand rubbed at my hip. "Insolent, disturbed woman."

Sarcastic bastard thinks he's so witty.

I made a face.

"Insufferable, rude harlot," he grumbled.

"Happy to serve the cause—" More coughs racked me miserably.

Tarantula swore louder.

I delighted in my small victory of angering him.

He reached for an earthen pitcher that sat to the side. Long-broken chains rattled as they dragged across wood, cuffs glinting on his wrists like decorations.

He snapped them like they were nothing.

"Swallow," he demanded as he gently brought a cup to my lips and tipped the water into my mouth. "Careful—tiny sips," he warned as I gulped rapidly and choked.

When my lungs finished spasming, I leaned back against him limply, a warmth spreading through me that I refused to identify.

"Another sip—please." He poured more water into my mouth.

I drank it down.

"Yes, just like that," he said quietly, his voice taut with unidentifiable emotions. "Thou art doing great."

Am I really?

"Thou art going to be the death of me," he said almost wistfully as he put the cup to the side.

I nodded. "Correct."

"Thou wish," he muttered under his breath as he resumed rubbing my forehead and holding me tenderly. "Such lofty goals for a peasant."

"There he is—the royal bastard."

He smirked lazily and winked down at me like we were having fun. *Are we?* I couldn't tell anymore.

ROAR. A dragon's call echoed, and the flapping intensified. The ship pitched violently beneath us, rocking forward and back with intensity.

Plague is pulling the ship.

The memory of her golden scales and ferocious fangs sent chills down my spine. Tarantula squeezed me tighter, rubbing my arms for warmth. He seemed strangely content to just hold me, exuding the heat of a furnace.

Squire crooned quietly on my lap, swaying with the rocking ship, enjoying the seafaring adventure.

Tarantula shifted, dangerously alive, as he cradled me. I tried to sink deeper into my hunter's mind, to remain cool and detached, but it was impossible in his embrace. Whenever Mom touched me, my mental defenses crumbled, and no one else's presence had ever disarmed me. *Until him.*

Waves crashed against the side of the ship. People shouted above, something about a mast and starboard. *Pirates?*

Harsh reality broke through the warm, feverish haze. "Where is my mom?"

"They are bringing us to her," Tarantula said.

"The pirates are taking us to Aleksander?" I repeated. "To make the trade?"

His hand stilled on my forehead, his thumb stroking back and forth in a way that was delightfully maddening as he breathed out roughly.

"Yes," he said.

I waited.

He didn't elaborate.

I huffed with annoyance.

"I mean—I assume so," he said quietly, the subtle movement of his thumb still scrambling my senses. "I was too busy being electrocuted."

"Ah," I said. "Sounds like divine intervention."

"Yes . . . 'Tis fate, syxzal."

His other arm wrapped around my chest, holding me closer, pressed back against his beating heart. In the quiet, we breathed in sync, unspoken words screaming between us. The scent of his burned skin still lingered in the air, and thorny vines wrapped around my heart.

"Sorry about the shock collar," I said quietly, trying a new angle to get him to open up. "If I hadn't dropped it, I know they wouldn't have been able to take you—"

"Silence, Ravenal." He cut me off. "Thou do not know everything."

I stiffened and tried to sit up and pull away, but it was a weak attempt. His intense dark cherry scent spiked with notes of . . . *homicidal tendencies*? I inhaled deeper. *When did he start to smell less like danger and more like safety?* Peril mounted by the second, my defenses flagging.

"Do not hurt yourself," he ordered.

"I have to save my mom," I said, reminding myself of my goal, desperately searching for a barrier to put between us. I didn't know where my body ended and his began. He'd shifted, and his long legs were intertwined with mine.

"Thou . . . were never going to make this journey alone."

What an odd thing to say.

"Don't pretend you're on my side." I shook my head, trying to dispel the intimacy. "You serve the Empire."

"I serve myself."

"Exactly. We both know they're the same, so don't pretend to care about me."

Fingers tucked a wet lock of hair behind my ear. "Who says . . . I am pretending, Ravenal?"

"Then what are you doing right now?" I asked.

He cocooned me protectively with his body like I was precious. His warm lips glanced across my forehead in the most innocent and tender of kisses. I struggled to breathe. *Why does he keep kissing my forehead?*

"I think," he said quietly against my temple, "we both know what is happening here. Do not play obtuse. Thou art far too intelligent." The sharp scents of magic and man intensified, burning my lungs, everywhere he shouldn't be.

"You can't do this." I struggled to organize my incoherent thoughts. "We're *not* on the same side."

He notched his chin over the top of my head. We fit perfectly together. Chills multiplied. *It's all just from the fever.*

"But . . . what if we were?" he asked solemnly.

I swallowed around the lump in my throat. "Dreaming about the impossible . . . doesn't make it so."

"Says who?" He nuzzled the side of my face, pressing delicate kisses against my icy skin.

"Hoo?" Squire chirped.

Tarantula nodded. "The ugly, minuscule bird gets it."

I bristled. "Don't call him ugly. It's offensive."

"Perhaps that is our problem. I find great pleasure . . . *offending* thee."

"You serve the Empire," I repeated, needing to find strength in hatred that was suspiciously absent. "You serve *tyranny*."

"I think I may have found something else that I want to serve."

"You don't mean that."

He chuckled darkly. "Thou keep telling me how I feel, Ravenal . . . 'Tis very unbecoming of a woman."

"So, loathe me."

He pressed another kiss to the side of my face as we rocked together with the ship. "I don't think I will anymore."

"You must."

"I shan't."

"Be quiet and hate me," I snapped, losing all pretense of control.

"No."

"Screw yourself."

"I'd prefer to fornicate with thee . . . Thou taste *exquisite*, Ravenal." He inhaled with masculine satisfaction. "Nothing in all Antichthon is sweeter."

He really has to stop saying stuff like this.

"Aren't you supposed to be a prude?"

"People can change."

"Stop playing games. Did you forget the part where I knocked you unconscious?"

"No. I pretended to be asleep . . . 'Twas just a lovers' quarrel." He shrugged. "I have read about them. These things happen when emotions are running high."

"I *bludgeoned* you."

He stroked his thumb slowly down the front of my neck. "Thou see me for what I am. 'Tis endearing."

"You're mad."

"Exactly. It runs in the blood. Thou *comprehend* me. Let me take care of thee . . . Let me be yours, Ravenal," he whispered against the shell of my ear. "I beg thee, take mercy on a yearning man, princess."

"You're the princess," I grumbled, flushing as I remembered arguing with him while he thrust into me. He chuckled huskily like he'd had the same thought.

I shook my head, eyes closing. How wondrous it would be to let someone else handle everything. For some odd reason, he seemed to mean what he was saying. Protection had never been so tempting. Soul aching, I reveled in the tender heat of the moment because I'd never tasted safety before, not like this.

He was like the Barren Forest. Beautifully dangerous. *Soul-corrupting.*

Turning my head so our faces were inches apart, I lost myself in the steely depths of his emotion-filled eyes. Lashes fluttered as he smiled insolently.

He thinks he's winning.

He always did.

"You don't make peace with evil," I said as I leaned so our noses were pressed together, needing him to understand. "You *destroy* it."

He flinched, and the ship pitched violently forward, but he held me tighter. "Just because a dead poet wrote it down and thou recite it—" his voice sharpened, his accent disappearing "—does not make it true."

I bared my teeth. "That's something that only evil would say."

He stiffened and pulled away from me. "It does not have to be like this. Thou could be accommodating." He turned his head, glaring up at the rocking fishing nets. "Thou could have been *mine*."

My lips pulled up, cheeks aching. I tried to fight it, but a laugh burst from me. He had the audacity to look insulted as he glared down at me with confusion.

I patted his thigh.

"It was *always* going to be like this," I said. "You ensured it the moment we met."

His eyes narrowed suspiciously. "What do thou mean?" he asked slowly.

"You attacked me in the woods."

He went rigid.

"You killed Aurora and kidnapped my mom."

He relaxed beneath me, breath whooshing from his lips. "People can change," he repeated.

"No—they can't."

His expression transformed in the blink of an eye; it was downright hostile. "Thou art right." His arms tightened around mine.

"I know. And this lust you feel, it will pass."

"Shall it?" His expression turned cruel.

I nodded with conviction. "Yes."

"So 'tis just infatuation," he purred darkly as he reached for my face. "And thou feel *nothing*."

"Nothing." My voice hitched as he stroked down the front of my throat.

"Thou art a disastrous liar, Ravenal."

"So are you."

His smile turned cold. "No—I am not."

"Hmm." It took every inch of training I possessed to keep my face blank because he thought he had me deceived. *You poor fool.* As if he couldn't help himself, he resumed rubbing my forehead tenderly like the motion soothed him.

Eyes closing, I turned my head and cuddled against his wide chest, leaning into him as the ship careened. We were sailing toward certain doom, but unlike him, I wasn't lying to myself. The chessboard was spread between us, and I saw his strategy. It was only a matter of moves before everything crumbled. For now, we would both pretend.

Until it was time.

To fight to the death.

28

L(OVER)

"*Tie the sails—anchor drop. Release Plague!*"

I opened my groggy eyes. A loud clanging echoed and then a dull thud like something made of heavy metal had dropped. Pirates shouted above, and feet pounded across the deck. Squire hooted, jumping off my lap as he looked up with wide, anxious eyes.

Waves crashed, and the ship rocked as if something had been detached—*Plague*. Then we steadied like we were being held in place at a pier.

"Ready the prisoner!"

Curious, and expected, use of the singular.

Bright light cut through the gloom as the hatch door opened above with a loud crack. Noise intensified. A pleasant breeze gusted inside.

Calloused hands rubbed my arms comfortingly. Tarantula stared at me pensively.

A pirate climbed down the rickety steps. "The Emperor is ready for ya, lass." He bared two rotting teeth and stomped toward me. Reaching, he grabbed my arm and—

Crack.

The weight of his hand disappeared as wind flung him backward. Squire flapped his wings with distress, hovering in the air. The pirate's arm had snapped at the elbow. His hand faced the wrong direction. He collapsed against fishing nets and slid to the floor.

"Do *not* touch her," Tarantula said dismissively as he got to his feet and gently pulled me up. He scowled as he studied the cuts on my skin, lifting my hair off my nape to inspect the damage.

The pirate whimpered in the corner, curling into a ball.

Tarantula didn't seem to notice, too busy tucking a loose tendril behind my ear. He pressed a soft kiss to my forehead and placed a hand to my lower back, then guided me up the steps that led out of the hull.

"Careful," he said, grabbing my arm as he steadied me. "Watch the steps—one at a time."

Squire settled onto my shoulder as I glanced back at the mutilated man. Tarantula shifted so he stood in front of me protectively, exiting first up onto the deck.

I followed.

"*Never make peace with evil,*" I muttered under my breath.

"Did thou say something?" Tarantula asked as he held his hand out, waiting for me.

"No."

Stomach balled with nerves, I steeled myself as I let him pull me out into the light. An ocean stretched as far as the eye could see, and our ship was tied off to a jutting pier.

I inhaled the sun-warmed mild air, savoring the soft floral scents. Colors were richly saturated: the periwinkle sky shimmered with magic, and the frothing ocean was a vibrant, bright blue.

Azote had a dreamy, ethereal quality.

The dock led to a dense forest that was straight from a storybook. The immense white trees were leafless but covered in a lilac moss, and a fog of teal Mist rolled around their trunks.

On the glittering horizon, where the naked trees ended, mountains jutted breathtakingly into the sky. They were *far* taller and sharper than the peaks in the Barren Forest and had a smooth, rocky white surface with a spattering of greenery.

Straight ahead, a mind-numbingly high mountain towered above the others. Clouds parted at its peak, revealing a grand white structure with platinum spires. I'd only ever read about such a structure in the ancient fairy tales.

It was a magnificent castle.

Are the fables real?

The scale of the structure was truly shocking, but it was the romantic architecture that stole my breath away. No tale had ever accurately described such *sparkling* opulence.

A bone-chilling roar reverberated as Plague flew above the forest, heading for the top spire of the castle. Fire exploded into the air, golden scales flashing as she landed atop it. I felt light-headed. A cloud of blue ice joined the heat as Pestilence flew up from somewhere off in the distance. Clouds dissipated as their long tails swung through them.

Plague and Pestilence both wrapped themselves protectively around the largest platinum spire on the castle. Mammoth wings fluttered, magic gathering around their snouts with such magnitude that it formed a silver haze above their heads. They roared at each other.

"Do not be afraid," Tarantula said quietly beside me, but it was far too late for reassurances.

Down below, a man stalked out of the forest, heading straight toward our ship. He wore a familiar white fur cloak, and a golden mask concealed his entire face. His short black hair was slicked back atop his head.

Ice spread at his feet with each step, thickening as it coated the pier in a light blue sheen. Dagger-sharp icicles formed beneath him, jutting below the boards, breaking off as waves crashed against them.

In my peripheral vision, Tarantula stared down at me. His lips pressed into a tight line as if he was cataloging my reaction. I kept my gaze on the approaching man.

"Welcome, Emperor Aleksander," a pirate announced, and the dozens of men on board fell to their knees.

They bowed low and kissed the ship deck in deference as he climbed up the gangplank and walked past them.

The Emperor ignored them all. He stared at me.

I straightened taller, clasping my shaking hands together, fingers still glowing silver from proximity to the ocean. His golden-scaled boots clicked against his magical ice as it slowly spread across the deck around him.

Finally the Emperor stopped directly in front of us.

Up close, his eyes were a familiar colorless shade; the opalescence, like cruelty, ran in the family. *So does the madness.*

Squire trembled on my shoulder, hiding his beak behind my ear.

The Emperor's cloak hung still behind him, unmoved by the ocean breeze.

No one spoke.

Tension mounted.

A muffled, anguished moan came from below the deck. Off in the distance, two dragons roared as they grappled for dominance, flames and ice exploding high into the shimmering sky.

"Welcome, Zora—to *my* Empire," the Emperor said as he opened his muscular arms wide, gesturing to the vibrant landscape. "How was your journey from—"

"Where is my mom?" I cut him off, done playing their games.

Tarantula stiffened beside me, and the Emperor dropped his arms. He glanced over at Tarantula and then back at me. "I shall bring thee to her," he said slowly. "First come with me back to—"

"No, we make the trade now," I said. "Me for her. Those were the terms."

"Ah." The Emperor rocked on his heels. "But this is Draconis land . . . Thou art no longer in the Commonwealth. We do things differently here. There is decorum, and there are other . . . *formalities* to honor. We shall bring thee to your mother and—"

"I'm not stepping a foot off this ship until I see her." I took a pointed step back.

The Emperor glanced again at Tarantula as if looking for assistance. "Then thou will be escorted."

"No. I won't be."

"Ravenal," Tarantula said quietly, grabbing my elbow as he leaned close. "What is the meaning of this? Obey his order."

Yanking away from him, I threw my head back and laughed, a broken, harsh sound. "And *why* would I listen to him?"

A muscle ticked in Tarantula's clenched jaw as his nostrils flared. "He's the Emperor." Silver-streaked wind howled loudly as ocean waves crashed violently against the ship.

I held his gaze.

"Is he?"

"What—" Tarantula trailed off, narrowing his eyes "—is the meaning of this? Why art thou acting belligerent? I thought we knew the—"

"I think you know *exactly* what I'm doing."

He smiled thinly. "I have *no* idea what thou art alluding to right now."

"Now who's playing obtuse?" I pursed my lips mockingly. "It's not very becoming of a man . . . *Especially* one of your stature."

He stilled. His head cocked slowly to the side as he studied me like he'd never seen me before.

"No," he said with disbelief.

"Yes."

"Thou art bluffing." He exhaled slowly like he was calming himself. "Thou art just posturing because thou have no leverage for your mother."

"Ah, there's that infamous arrogance," I said as I backed across the deck, the pressure in my skull increasing to a fever pitch as my fingers burned with magic. "But you don't know me—not really. You never did. That was your mistake. You assumed."

He tipped his chin down, the bottoms of his eyes yet again in stark relief. "What is your angle, Zora?" he demanded as wind battered the tied sails and the scent of *death* intensified.

Eyes watering, I bared my teeth. "How about you tell me yours first—Aleksander. I believe they started calling you *the Sadistic* . . . after we met."

The ship pitched violently.

Waves crashed against the side, water spraying high and dousing the deck. Pirates near that side screamed as they scrambled on their hands and knees, falling overboard as they tried, and failed, to hold on to the slick railing.

I balanced and kept my feet. *Like riding a snowboard.*

Next to me, the man who called himself Tarantula withstood the rocking as he shook his head slowly. His mask reflected my determined expression. Looking furious, he whirled on his heel, stalked over to the other Mage wearing the golden mask, and whispered something to him.

The second Mage bowed low, his golden mask dipping beneath his knees with reverence, then he stood up, turned, and walked straight off the edge of the bow, ignoring the gangplank.

Waves froze as they crashed up along the ship's edge, forming a perfect set of glistening silver-blue stairs. With his shoulders pulled back and posture perfect, the man in the golden mask stepped down his icy magical steps.

When he finally made it to the pier, the crystalline stairwell cracked into pieces behind him, chunks of ice falling into the ocean. As he stalked away, he glanced back over his shoulder, leveling me with a look of abject loathing. He turned and disappeared into the lilac-covered forest.

I exhaled with a strange relief.

It was *finally* time.

From across the deck, the Mage in the silver mask sauntered toward me. It was the same posh gait he'd had when he was fifteen years old.

I took a step back, struggling to catch my bearings.

"I know your game," I said, pointing at his face, and he froze mid-step. "I've known all along who you were. Calling me brat was a nice touch, but your deception was doomed from the start . . . No one else in Antichthon has ever called me a *filthy serf*." I mimicked his voice.

His face hardened, hands clenching into fists. "Thou don't know *anything*, Ravenal," he said slowly. The diamonds on his shock collar caught the light. "Thou *never* did."

"Sazha is a nickname for Aleksander," I said. "Isn't it?"

He smiled and resumed walking toward me.

I shook my head, covering my mouth as I tried not to be sick. "I would recognize your sadistic eyes anywhere, Aleksander . . . You bit my throat as a child, and it was always *your* wind choking me."

Maroon lips pulled up. He shivered as if experiencing a sudden bout of excitement.

"I could smell it on you," I whispered, articulating the secret I'd only ever shared with one person—the Marshal. "I could always sense your nefarious desires . . . I can smell your wicked intentions."

The man who'd been calling himself Tarantula for years came to a stop in front of me. Wrath and magic seeped from his pores. His expression turned wicked, his tattered chiffon shirt hanging open, nearly ripped away from the earlier fight. The ridges of his skin gleamed.

"My eyes are up here, Ravenal," he purred. "And what thou smell is attraction for me."

I scoffed. "No, I smell *death* . . . There's nothing impressive about—"

"Thou sense my strength." He dragged his graceful fingers down his stomach until his thumb rested suggestively on the waistband of his blood-streaked pants. "And thou thought differently when thou were *screaming* my name . . . and gushing onto my tongue."

I struggled to swallow around the dry lump in my throat. "It meant nothing to me," I said, voice cracking.

His thumb traced the ridges of his lower abdomen, drifting over the glittering butterfly. His lips twitched, expression cruel as he oozed malevolence. *Seductive evil.*

"So thou art saying thou *let* your tyrannical *archnemesis* eat your cunt . . . That is what thou art admitting right now, Ravenal?" He dropped the subterfuge. "Thou filthy little—"

"Aleksander," I cut him off. "You forget that, unlike you, I'm not repressed." I blew a mocking kiss, heart pounding, lungs seizing. "Many men have feasted happily on my—"

"*Silence yourself!*" Cobalt veins stood out across his neck and jaw in stark relief.

"It wasn't even good," I taunted. "Not memorable at all. I've already forgotten about it."

Silver steamed around him. He slowly smiled, an awful, wicked expression. He inhaled deeply. "Liar . . . Thou forget, I can smell it too. Thou yearn for me."

"What you smell is that I yearn for your violent demise." I inched away, hating how my hands were shaking, knees weak.

"Thou yearn for me to make thee mine. I will cherish thee forever . . . Rule by my side." He held out his hand for me to take, his smile charming.

Memories flashed rapid-fire.

He stood between my legs. The image changed. *He lay beneath me, groaning as he ate me out.* I shook my head. *He rested his chin on my hip bone, licking his lips.* No. *He peppered gentle kisses across my forehead, whispering hoarsely.*

"No," I said, taking another step back.

He sauntered closer, hand still reaching for me.

"Thou will come with me. Stop pretending."

"I'm not." I shook my head, desperation growing as I pointed at his masked face. "I always saw through your royal scheme. You've never had the upper hand—and I will *never* go willingly with evil."

He slowly dropped his hand, eyes darkening as he saw something on my face that made him stiffen. He rolled his neck, veins protruding from his jaw and forehead like he was struggling for control.

"It all meant *nothing* to me," I said louder.

"Thou art a terrible liar." He stopped a hand's length away, close enough to kiss. His bottom lip gleamed as he wet it. "Such stubborn insolence . . . refusing to admit that thou art just as desperately obsessed as I am. We are ruined for each other."

"You mean nothing to me!" I screamed with all my might, like it would make it true, as I backed away.

He shouted back, "Thou mean everything to me!"

"Leave me alone."

He shook his head, eyes glittering with emotion. "Never."

"Then take off the mask. What do you have left to hide?"

He scoffed. "Why would I listen to thee—"

I pointed my glowing hand at him in fury. The silver-streaked sea roared high as it crashed against the side of the ship, rocking it. Foam sprayed across the deck. More waves rose, each one higher than the last.

He froze, staring out at the ocean and then back at my glowing hand with confusion.

"Do it!" I waved my fingers, and the sea spray exploded high in the air around him. "Stop hiding, you lying coward!"

The ship rocked, dragons roared on the horizon, and Squire screeched into my braid.

In slow motion, Aleksander lifted his slender fingers up to

his face and pulled off his mask. Magic sizzled as it detached, and he pocketed the platinum.

I'd *known* the truth, but it still shocked me. The same realization, the one I'd had when I'd removed his mask after he'd kidnapped Mom, settled into my bones. *I was never paranoid.* He was just a megalomaniac royal who played a twisted game, and he thought I was too dumb and poor to know the rules.

He studied me with his hauntingly familiar features. Since I was fifteen years old, I'd seen him in every one of my dreams *and nightmares.*

The jagged face of a cruel boy had filled into the sharp angles of a ferociously attractive man. Puberty had been *far* too kind to Aleksander. He was stunning. Tall and lean with whipcord strength, he was vastly different from the scrawny boy I'd first met.

Disturbingly gorgeous.

Aleksander the Sadistic smiled at me across the deck, wind tousling his curls, and the effect was devastating.

"Lying spider!" Squire squawked with outrage (helpful).

The golden shade of Aleksander's eyebrows matched the undertones in his curls, complementing his features. The *real* Tarantula had no dimension in his white-blond hair. *Small details matter.*

There was no question—no one in all Antichthon had eyes like the man before me. It wasn't the unique color—the cloudlike white, shimmering with a rainbow, surrounded by the faintest ring of icy blue. It was the *cunning* in their depths.

Chills trailed down my spine as I held his burning gaze. He'd been sculpted by the enemy of the old god to seduce and destroy unsuspecting mortals.

He waited.

"You dyed your hair and eyebrows as a child," I said, remembering I'd thought it strange how light his lashes were all those years ago. *A common practice among elites to remain undetected.* "You *mutilated* your neck to hide my dagger mark . . . You had your Mage brand himself with a recognizable tattoo long before you even met me—the perfect neat little plot. An easy way for an Emperor to conceal his identity and fool the world. And now the *real* Tarantula's hair is dyed black and he's masquerading as you. Your subterfuge *never* ends."

Aleksander's smile widened. His expression was different than it had been on that snow-covered bridge. Now his mania had a heated, raw edge. *Blatant desire.*

"Ah, my sweet Ravenal," he said softly, pride in his voice. "Too brilliant for your own good. If only thou had played dumb like the rest of them." He flashed perfect white teeth. "It might have been easier for thee."

He hooked both of his thumbs in the waistband of his pants, drawing attention to his Adonis belt. He knew exactly what he was doing because *every* single one of his actions had a purpose. Every move a constant game. *Never has a man been so cruelly calculating.*

"It was never going to be easy for me," I said, trying not to look at his exposed chest. "I met you."

"I think," he said, "it was *I* who met thee . . . not the other way around."

I widened my defensive stance. "Now that we're done with the games . . . *where* is my mom? Bring her to me. Now."

His eyes glittered. "Thou shall come with me back to Palladium, my glorious castle. I shall give thee a tour of the finery, and then we shall discuss the details of the trade."

"No, we won't be doing that."

He arched a perfect golden eyebrow. "Thou have *no* power here over me . . . 'Tis not the bedroom, Ravenal." He bit down on his lip like he was remembering.

Heat flushed across my cheeks as I struggled to stay focused. I raised my hands high, the glow intensifying. "Are you sure about that?"

My head throbbed, fingers burning, because the magic was *everywhere*. I sank deeper into the pressure that had been steadily building inside of my skull since the rainstorm back in Westmere.

Ocean water rose up behind Aleksander in a towering tsunami, a churning endless mass of silvery blue. I brought my hands down roughly, just like I'd practiced thousands of times with the Marshal. It slammed across the ship.

Pirates screamed, crunching as they were thrown against the mast. Dead on impact.

"That was for my mom!"

As water exploded across the deck, Aleksander raised his hands. Wind spun around his body protectively, forming a shield. I sent another wave crashing across the ship, and it dragged the bodies out to sea. Aleksander stood stoic and remained perfectly dry.

The metal on his wrists glowed with bright white light, and there was no mistaking his expression. He stared at me with *blatant* hunger.

"Thou," he said with awe, "should NOT be able to wield storm magic, let alone the *rarest* and *strongest* power. Thou art my made vassal . . ."

In Mom's old book, the five ancient symbols must have been listed in ascending order of strength: *snowflake, fire, lightning, wind, water*. His power was also near the bottom.

Aleksander gasped loudly like he'd realized something. His eyelids lowered. "Unless . . . No . . . Art thou sure Ravenal is your mother's name and not your sire's?"

Razor blades twisted deep in my gut, because Mom had never been able to hold my gaze when she talked about my missing father.

He laughed, head thrown back, ocean water spraying around him. "Ravenal, my darling, brilliant huntress—tell me who your sire is, and I'll tell thee everything thou want to know." He visibly shuddered. "This is a delightful turn of events. I had my suspicions, but this, *this* is a triumph."

He gestured to the ocean and clapped mockingly, the shredded pieces of his shirt falling off as wind whipped around him. Half naked, he was a carved statue of a perfect man.

He bared his canines like a sly dire fox.

I bared mine back.

"My triumphs are not yours to celebrate, *Aleksander*." I raised my hands higher, pressure mounting behind my eyes, vision blurring as I sent the full force of the ocean barreling toward him.

He cocked his head to the side, unbothered by the deadly wall of water pummeling against his shield. "Have thou heard of the dangerous criminal Marx Ravenal?"

"No," I said. "You don't know anything about my father—"

"He's a wicked Royal Mage—"

"—because he was a Commonwealth man of great esteem—"

"—with an ouroboros tattoo here?" He held his fingers up to his right eye. "If memory serves correctly, he wore a platinum mask tinted bronze."

I stumbled backward, unable to disguise my horror. Breathing became impossible. *His name is Ravenal?* That cold-looking man with the snake tattoo couldn't be my father. Mom would never fall in love with the enemy . . . *She's too kind and romantic for her own good.*

I bent over, hands on my knees, gasping.

Mom would.

The missing pieces behind recent events clicked into place.

Marx was looking for her, and he saw Mom's portrait in the newspaper. I bet she never told him she was pregnant. She was in hiding, and the papers blew her cover. It was why she always refused to leave the walls of the North. Marx struck a deal with the Marshal. He was her "interested player," and she sacrificed Mom for the cause.

A horrible sound wrenched from my throat.

Mom was probably so afraid, and I wasn't there to protect her.

I screamed.

"Ah—I see," Aleksandar said. "That is why the Iron Ritual

did not make thee into a Knight. What a violent, *royal* lineage. Now everything makes sense. Thou were never my vassal, but it has been centuries since a halfling was born . . . They must have loved each other very much."

Halfling? He was speaking nonsense.

Standing up with an angry shriek, I waved my arms and threw more ocean his way. Silvery wind directed it straight back to the sea.

Straining, head aching, I sent more.

He flicked it away.

I did it again.

He deflected it.

I pummeled him with everything I had. Wood splintered, the ship cracking between us, breaking apart into two separate pieces.

We each balanced on our halves of the deck.

I panted. Sweat poured down my face as fiery coals filled my chest.

"What did you give to the Marshal?" I asked. "What did you trade that convinced her of your allegiance?"

He arched a single eyebrow, casually leaning against the mast as the ship disintegrated around him. "'Tis too bad," he shouted over the destruction, "that thou do not know everything!"

A metallic haze blurred his features as magic gushed off him.

The shock collar around his neck cracked. It fell off, revealing his gruesome scars, the ones he'd given himself to hide my dagger mark.

Diamonds tumbled across the deck.

Aleksander rolled his head and shoulders, sighing with relief.

It can't be.

The collar had never actually contained him.

The entire time, he'd been pretending to be constrained.

The breadth of his deceit—*unfathomable.*

29

Tropical Cyc(lone)

"No," I said.

He shrugged casually and winked. "It made thee feel safer, so I let thee electrocute me. Day and night. Every—single—time. Diamonds dampen our power, but I am not an average Royal Mage . . . Breaking this toy takes an *infinitesimal* amount of my will."

Cloying emotions clawed at my throat.

"I do not have *some* storm magic," he said with pride. "I am the reigning Emperor of the Draconis Empire. I *am* the storm."

"Stop talking!"

"Thou *never* had the upper hand, Ravenal," he said. "The power was always mine. I told thee to leave the North because I knew thou would join the Crimson Army—and we could finally be together!"

"No."

"I *let* thee stab me in the forest," he said with terrifying calm. "I *pretended* to be incapacitated . . . I let thee pose for that portrait. *Everything* I have done was on purpose to be with thee."

It was as I'd suspected, and yet so much worse. His machinations were beyond comprehension.

"You're vile."

"Close—but not exact." He shrugged. "Same letters but a different word. Thou know exactly what I am, dearest."

"EVIL," I screamed with all my might.

"Only thou know me *so* well, Ravenal. Thou see me for who I am." He clutched his heart like it was romantic.

I quickly sent a deluge of ocean at his half of the ship, trying to catch him unawares.

He flung his hands up. *Boom.* A huge bomb-like gust of wind exploded from him. Thrown with the water, I went flying off the ship, up into the storm. *Oldgodsaveme, he's now at full power.*

Flailing, I raised my arms as I was flung through the air. Squire screeched, holding on to my braid. I gestured frantically down at the choppy sea.

Water rose up in a frothing mass, surrounding me in a metallic blue vortex. It held me upright, hovering in the sky.

Aleksander shouted my name. Jumping up, he deftly climbed the mast of the sinking ship, up the pole to the crow's nest, far faster than any man should have been able to move. His every action defied gravity.

With magic thundering through my veins, I pointed my hands at him.

A jet of ocean torpedoed toward him. He batted it aside playfully. I leaned forward, and water propelled me straight toward him.

Crash.

We collided, my fists pummeling him. He held on to me with his hand cradling the back of my head, fingers tangled gently in my hair.

We spun through the air and skidded across the pier. He clutched me protectively, his back taking the brunt of the impact. *A dragon hoarding his prey.*

We came to a stop, half the wooden pier shattered, water

lapping below us. He rolled so he was on top, his heated skin burning where he pressed flush against me.

"*My* Ravenal." He held my head like I would break, pressing a gentle kiss to my forehead as his heart pounded in sync with mine. His magic wrapped around us in a tender embrace.

I punched him in the jaw.

He brought his thumb to his mouth and slowly wiped away a droplet of blood. "Divine," he said quietly. "That felt exquisite . . . Do it again, *please*, my valiant Knight. Hit me!"

Emotions welled up that I should *not* have been feeling. I scrambled out of his tempting, depraved arms.

I waved my hands. Ocean water rose up and crashed down where he lay on the half-broken pier. He sputtered, drenched to the bone.

I staggered to my feet, backing away. A migraine split my skull. Warmth dripped down my face, and I brought my hands up to my nose. My fingers came back covered in blood.

I stumbled with dizziness, barely catching myself.

Aleksander focused on my bleeding nose. The scent of his magic sharpened, shadows darkening around him.

"Thou art overexerting yourself. Cease fighting me. Thou need platinum to strengthen your magic—"

"Where is she?" I cut him off. "Where is my mother?" The tide receded as the ocean rose in a tsunami, and copper flooded my mouth as I lifted the water up higher, then slammed it down atop him.

He lazily flicked his finger, and his wind redirected the entire mass down onto the pier between us. Posts exploded, splintering away.

He stood on the intact section close to the land; I was on a detached plank, drifting out to sea. Balancing on the churning waves, I struggled to stay upright with my glowing hands in a defensive position.

Wetness poured from my ears, down onto my arms—*more blood.* It sputtered off my lips, dripping from my nose as I gasped for air.

Aleksander watched me with wide, panicked eyes.

I hurled more ocean, but it never touched him. It just mixed with his wind, becoming a silver blur that rose up in the air. Dark clouds spun above our heads.

Gale-force winds twisted with ocean water and spiraled above us in a growing hurricane. Chunks of detritus fell from the sky. The flying projectiles were everywhere.

The force of our magic was unfathomable. It felt cataclysmic.

"Zora, is we in a hurricane?" Squire asked as he clung desperately to my shoulder, wings flapping for purchase. My blood had splattered across his tawny face.

"No, darling. I think . . . we *are* the hurricane."

"ZORA!" Aleksander bellowed over the churning tempest. He stalked down the broken pier toward me. I was floating away. "I order thee to stop hurting yourself and come back with—"

I sent more ocean at him. With a dismissive wave, he flicked it away like it was a nuisance. The water slammed into the forest, felling full-sized trees with a loud, cracking boom.

"Stop telling me what to do," I said, spitting out blood. *Oh nice, I'm also internally bleeding.*

His expression darkened, and silver flames shot angrily off his shoulders.

I wobbled on my plank of wood and fell to my knees, coughing violently; scarlet splattered my splayed hands. Squire hooted with distress as I choked.

Wiping at my blurry eyes, I registered with horror that blood was also dripping from my lashes. *Magical exhaustion.* My chest spasmed. The plank rocked. I grabbed the edges and barely remained on top as I was nearly swept into the roaring ocean.

CREAK.

A familiar silver shield shimmered around me.

"My Zora," Aleksander shouted with concern. We shouldn't have been able to hear each other with the tempest raging all around, but each word was crystal clear like he was standing directly beside me.

Encased in his shield, the plank beneath me groaned unnaturally as it defied gravity, slowly rising *out* of and above the churning seawater. Aleksander pointed his finger.

The wood beneath me creaked loudly as I ascended, propelled by his magic. Higher he sent me, up into the roiling clouds. Wind and water bounced off his metallic barrier.

Quiet descended. Soaked to the bone, teeth chattering, shivering, bleeding out of my orifices, I curled into the fetal position. *This is too much.* Vision narrowing, I gagged with nausea. *I can't do it.* Sounds diminished further. Everything hurt. I was nothing but a sack of brittle bones and throbbing flesh.

"Let spider help?" Squire hooted as he tugged desperately on my braid. "Me get him?"

Yes.

He'll take care of me.

"No," I croaked out, shaking the treacherous thoughts away.

"Why not?" Squire asked with confusion. "Zora sick."

Because I'm not a coward.

Groaning, I coughed up seawater, choking on snot that tasted like iron. As I shifted to sit up, my arms gave out beneath me.

I will not betray myself.

A dozen agonizing tries later, I finally staggered up to my feet.

"We need spider!" Squire flapped in front of my face, his eyes wide and nervous.

I shook my aching head at him sadly. "No, darling, I can help myself."

Knees aching, I balanced precariously on the floating platform, swallowing down bile. It felt like my organs were unraveling as I barely held my ground.

Rule of survival: Make your own luck, lucky woman.

Aleksander stood on the edge of the pier, frowning up at me. Lines of silver glowed across his skin. "It does not have to be this way between us." His voice strummed with gentle sincerity, sharp canines flashing as he spoke. "Please, let me help thee . . . Thou art mine to care for—"

"I belong to no man."

And I will complete my quest.

Roughly I dragged trembling hands down my face, wiping away blood, sweat, mucus, and the lingering cowardice.

"Princess," he said tenderly, pity in his eyes. "I am not a man."

Silver lines glowed brighter on his skin.

The intricate circular tattoo on his back spun and rolled around to his front. The cobalt spider crawled across his jaw, up his face, around his eyes, *alive.* It disappeared down onto his back. His bare face was devastatingly handsome.

The silver butterfly flapped delicately on his lower stomach, and tiny butterflies flew up and around it.

Something was happening to the platinum on his body. His cuffs, his earrings—it all *melted.* Turning to a metallic liquid, it fanned out behind him, forming a nearly translucent shape.

Gossamer platinum wings flapped as he lifted off the ground, flying up into the air until he hovered a short distance in front of me. A hurricane swirled above our heads, and the ocean raged beneath us, but the world was eerily quiet. Apocalyptic.

"Your ancestors worshipped my ancestor as a god while we mined the platinum together, but he—*we*—never died. We simply retreated back to Azote after their betrayal. They ruined Antichthon with their misguided technologies."

Air whistled from my open mouth as the old tales mixed together. There was a lost, ancient god with platinum wings and stories of immortal species who wielded magic.

"Zora, the man scary," Squire hooted as he held on to my wet braid, trying to hide. "He *large* spider-bird."

I nodded absently in agreement as Aleksander raised his hand toward me, his magical wings flapping elegantly behind him.

"I am the Sovereign Divine Emperor of the Storm Fae," he said with royal gravitas. "There is no *rightful* Commonwealth in the Antichthon realm. There are only the Storm Fae and the lesser species. Please, stop hurting yourself and let me explain everything to thee over a warm meal."

Storm Fae?

Lesser species?

"My full High Fae name is unspeakable to humans—so Aleksander is what thou call me."

He said *humans* like he was referring to something disgusting.

It hit me like a punch to the face. *Mom called them fairy's tales . . . It never made sense, because she must have meant* Faerie's Tales. *She knew and was trying to tell me. Mom's journal. The strange language was High Fae. The symbols were their magic.*

In a trance, I extended my hand out toward his.

Aleksander's lethal expression softened further. "Thou art not my enemy, syxzal. Thou art mine to worship." He pulled his arm back, and I started to float toward him as if his magic was connected to mine by an invisible string.

This wasn't about politics like I'd always been taught. *The mortifying ordeal of knowing the truth.* The war wasn't Draconis Empire versus Democratic Commonwealth. It was Storm Fae versus humans, and it was clear from the way he spoke that he viewed humans as lesser. It didn't matter if I shared fae blood. I was raised by a kind human woman who would never hurt a fly.

The exact kind of person he didn't respect.

"Hold on tight, darling," I whispered to Squire. "Look away."

My scalp stung as he swiveled his beak, scratching my neck.

Gathering the last of my courage, I nodded. Aleksander's

otherworldly expression twisted with shadows, glittering platinum wings beating faster as he read the intention on my face.

"You're wrong. Your ancestor is not *my* god." I brought my hand up above my head. "Never surrender to tyrants." I raised a single finger, then brought my hands together, clasped atop my wildly beating heart, and bowed my head. Mom had taught me hope was proof of the divine. "Never make a second of peace with evil," I said the most sacred prayer, feeling naked in my previous foolishness as blood gushed down my chin. *The war was always in the spirit.*

"Don't thou dare hurt your—"

I jumped back off the floating plank, out of his shield, flipping through the air. "I will defeat you, Aleksander," I whispered, held together by a solid anchor, my soul, the indomitable human spirit, the only real thing in this illusory world full of monsters.

"ZORA," he screamed as he tried to fly forward, but water threw him backward. "MY SYXZAL!"

I plummeted face-first, hurtling downward through the hurricane. Willing the ocean to meet me, I reached for it with both hands.

Magic pulled me with impossible speed straight into the churning darkness of sudden cognitive awareness. Everything I'd ever imagined was real, in the worst way possible.

Splash.

Bubbles exploded as I sank into the inky depths, one thought repeating on a tormented, grateful, cursed loop:

I want to complete my quest.

30

DEVASTATION

ILLUSTRIOUS STORM FAE HIGH EMPEROR
ALEKSANDER THE SADISTIC

Knee-deep in mud, I searched desperately for Zora, climbing along the sea-soaked shore.

Unholy terror pounded through my corrupt soul. I gasped, heart in my throat. Storm magic swirled bright silver around me, drowning the world in a haze. Hours ago, I'd thrown myself into the roiling ocean after Zora jumped. Swimming with everything I had through the hurricane, I'd searched for her in the cold water to no avail.

Now I climbed through the mud, covered head to toe in filth. Fear bubbled hotly, every second without her more devastating than the last. "ZORA, WHERE ART THOU?" I bellowed as I trudged forward, throwing muck.

Dozens of tornadoes spun all along the coast. Ancient trees cracked as they uprooted, and thunderous explosions boomed. Unrestrained storm magic *screamed* within my blood.

Plague roared from the sky, acute devastation pounding through our bond as she flew above, breathing fire into the tornadoes.

Zora Ravenal might be the most consternating woman in all Antichthon, but she was *my* consternation. Mine. When I was fifteen years old, my magic had come alive, sparking on a swaying bridge with my teeth buried deep in her throat.

I had meant it when I told her, *"There is no corner of Antichthon where thou could hide from me. I shall find thee* every *single time. Your fate is already decided."* I'd tasted her fate—our fate—that day when I licked her blood off my lips.

It was why, at twenty-one years old, I'd shaved off my dyed black hair and eyebrows and taken on the alias of my most dangerous Mage, Tarantula. *Anything* to get close to her.

A dozen new tornadoes touched down as Plague landed beside me with a fiery roar. Her spewing flames joined my churning wind, setting the forest on fire. I climbed up her golden scales, seating myself in the gilded saddle—my throne. Her wings beat fiercely as we rose up through the air. I half hung from her saddle, using my thighs to keep myself aloft as I scanned the ground.

Where would she go?

I yanked the reins, steering Plague toward the mountains and thicker forest. *Burn it all,* I said down our bond. Plague opened her maw, fire rushing out in a steady stream of orange. Wind exploded from my fingertips, and the flames turned silver, shooting across the forest with destructive fervor meant to flush her out.

Failure was not an option.

Minutes bled into hours, the sun setting red across the violet horizon as I leaned as far as possible off Plague's saddle and laid siege to the lowlands. Covered in sweat, straining from magical overuse, I'd need to feed soon. We searched slowly in circles, no wood untouched.

"*There!*" I pointed down at where a figure moved fast through the flaming forest, a sprinting blur. Only someone with insane courage would sprint through wildfire. *Why wouldn't she stick to the shore? There is nowhere here for her to run to.*

Plague roared as she banked viciously, flying low above the lilac moss-covered treetops. I removed the cuffs attached to the saddle and didn't even think about it. I jumped from above the trees, plummeting eagerly downward.

Crack—crack—crack—crack.

Fallen branches snapped as I rose to my feet, standing among the flames, directly in her path.

"You," Zora whispered accusingly. Squire squawked with distress on her shoulder. I shot him a glare. *Even after I've given thee all those seeds?* He cowered. Zora pointed her dirt-covered arms at me, but silver glowed faintly on her fingers and then disappeared.

I inhaled deeply. She smelled of magical exhaustion.

Unacceptable.

Trails of dried crimson dripped from her nose and ears; her eyes were bloodshot and rimmed with dark circles. *She needs platinum.*

Zora turned and ran, sprinting away from me into the smoldering forest. Unfortunately for her, I was much faster. As gently as possible, I tackled her to the ground.

I've got thee now.

There was a time I would have fainted at the mere thought of touching Zora's tender person with such liberties, but that was before I'd been locked in a room for *months* with her. I'd been gripped with delusions, thinking I would educate her in decorum. In the end, she had taught me.

Her lesson: romance was war.

It was a different battleground, but the fight was just as physical as hand-to-hand combat. Deception offered a different flavor of passion, and I was always an exceptional pupil. She'd rejected me outright, so I'd seduced her cloaked in deceit. It was the only way to get close to her, and I'd do it again a *billion* times over.

The past few months with Zora were the best of my entire life.

Nothing could compare to the sweetness of watching her

scowl above me, turning her little shock device, feeling powerful. She'd slapped me like she *wanted* me. It had been glorious.

Now she kicked out as we tussled, throwing mud, punching desperately—*she's still touching me*—as Squire squawked traitorously in my face. "Stop it, little bird," I ordered the admittedly adorable creature.

"Die, spider-bird slut!" he screeched.

"How dare thou."

Zora rolled her eyes as I easily grabbed her wrists and brought them in front of her. *Click.* The platinum cuffs secured her arms, a long chain hanging from them, but most importantly, the metal would help her recover from her magical exhaustion.

Squire chirped with distress, hiding behind her muddy braid as I yanked her closer so we were heart to heart.

I'd donned the platinum-reinforced belt that was always attached to Plague's saddle—the one I used when I captured enemies of the crown—and now I secured her chain to my belt hook, satisfaction rushing through me. *I've got thee now, darling.*

Zora bared her teeth, my fearsome warrior. "You're still just the pompous boy I met on the bridge, a terrorist to peace who—"

"Do not taunt me with that day when thou ran away from me . . . thou ran from *us*." I pulled her face closer, lost in the light brown of her honey eyes. "We both know we have progressed *far* past the initial courtship stages."

Magic crackled as it swirled between us. We were lying together in the mud and Mist. I clutched her to me as the trees burned above, ash falling on us like rain.

"What are you talking about?" she said softly, sooty lashes fluttering as exhaustion leaked from her pores. She'd put on a display of power so mighty the ground had trembled. "We're nothing."

"Stop lying to yourself." My stomach swooped with the falling sensation that was specific to her presence. I'd gotten a butterfly tattooed on my lower stomach the day after I met her. In her proximity, I came *alive.* When we were apart, I was nothing.

I reached for her, fingers shaking with desperation.

"Don't touch me." She dodged my caress, rejecting my gentle affection. *Again.*

A ripping sensation tore through my heart. Agony mounted, her dismissal unbearable. I yearned to be with her, and she felt absolutely nothing. *How is it possible, after we've made such sweet love?* It was like being ripped to shreds and burned in dragon fire for days with no respite.

My affections were unrequited.

Please, blessed storm spirit, help her see the light.

"We belong together," I said hoarsely, hating how ruined I sounded. I was a pathetic mess for her.

Making love to her had been transcendent, life-changing, irrevocably tender, and afterward she could have stabbed me with her dagger. I'd seen the moment she'd considered it. Instead, she'd merely hit me with the hilt. It showed her intentions were pure. She *cared* about me. *I knew it.*

"Please," I bit out.

"No." She shook her head, jaw set stubbornly, a sadness in her eyes.

Why is she still lying to herself?

It wasn't supposed to be like this. She was supposed to fall head over heels and bow at my feet. This chemical compatibility, this overwhelming attraction, she shouldn't have been able to fight it. She shouldn't *care* if I murdered a couple useless humans to get my way. It didn't make any sense. In all of history, a rejection of this magnitude had never come to pass.

Maybe it's her heritage? Marx Ravenal was known as a Dark Storm Fae, which meant he was one of the cruelest Royal Mages who had ever lived, and among an immortal population, that was saying something. He's been a wanted criminal for centuries. No one could stop Marx once his intentions were set. He was an obsessive, dangerous man with no ethical code. He refused to recognize my ancestral right to rule over the Draconis Empire.

Centuries ago, he'd openly declared himself an enemy of the crown.

He still waged a one-man war against us.

Now he'd defied my direct orders by kidnapping Zora's mother. I'd have to deal with him later. Just like I'd have to deal with the real Tarantula for putting a bounty on Zora's head, dead or alive, when I'd *specifically* told him only the latter. There would be lots of consequences dealt out once I retook my throne.

The portrait circulating of Marx holding Zora's mother confused me. There was a strange story there, how such a violent man had reproduced with a human. He was, by all accounts, a morally black hedonist of the highest degree, and his daughter appeared to have inherited his stubborn temperament—just like she'd inherited his rare ability to wield water magic.

No woman has ever been so lovely.

"Let me go," she breathed out quietly, as if hearing my thoughts, still not meeting my gaze. "You've gotten it wrong." Her chest rose and fell faster, pulse racing at the tender point beneath her jaw, practically leaping out from under her perfect bronze skin. I could smell the raw attraction simmering in her veins.

"Then why," I whispered, mouth lowering to hover over hers, "art thou panicking, syxzal?"

She stopped breathing. "I'm not. You misunderstand."

"Thou art the one who does not understand," I said roughly, pressing my nose to hers, needing her to *see* me. "There has never been a more perfect match. It is *thou* who is wrong."

"No," she repeated with growing desperation. My knees sank deeper into the warm mud, embers glowing orange as they landed on her hair and shoulders like snow.

I was supposed to remain suave and coldly removed around her as I led her through a courtship with the subtlety of an Autumnal Fae's waltz. In theory, she was the one thing in my life that was supposed to be easy. She was the only person who made sense and the only person who was supposed to *understand* me.

But she had taken one look at me and seen every inch of my rotten soul. I could not hide my true self around her. My passions were too . . . volatile. She disarmed me to a dangerous degree.

Zora scoffed, but her lashes fluttered, her back bowing as she pressed against me. "You're delusional."

"Incorrect." My mouth brushed over hers, inhaling her with every desperate breath as I couldn't help but gloat, her proximity the most dangerous aphrodisiac. "I am Aleksander the Sadistic, illustrious High Emperor of the Immortal Storm Fae, and now it is my turn—to hold all the power."

I stood up and tossed her over my shoulder in one swift motion. *CRUNCH.* Trees were crushed to pieces as Plague dropped from above. She landed in a blur of golden scales, bowing low for me to mount her.

Zora beat her fists against my back, but I reveled in her touch, shivering with ecstasy as I climbed up into my saddle with her hanging across my back. The chain connecting us rattled loudly as she fought.

Plague roared beneath us as she took to the sky, flying us to Palladium.

Zora grappled desperately, grabbing at Plague's scales behind me, trying to get purchase.

I laughed at her futility, looking off into the sparkling violet horizon.

She screamed at the top of her lungs, the sound grating.

Wait, what was that?

I listened, but it was just her voice ringing in the air. I could have sworn a woman's voice had spoken when she screamed. *Madness runs in the family.*

Zora resumed beating her fists on my back, and I relaxed, enjoying her touch. I urged Plague to fly slower, spiraling lazily through the sky as I savored the sunset with my woman.

Zora had never stood a chance that day on the bridge. I'd already decided she would be mine. But when I tasted her blood, *everything* changed. Rare and precious beyond belief, she was a jewel that came along only once in many immortal lifetimes.

An Emperor with a rare syxzal by his side was unstoppable. More myth than real, she was the type of providence that inspired the bestselling Storm Fae romance of all time, *Faerie's Tales*.

"You never understood," she said cryptically as she stopped struggling.

We banked in a wide circle.

I rubbed the backs of her legs soothingly. "Do not fret, my princess . . . thou art my syxzal. Everything will make sense soon."

"You're a fool," she said.

"Yes—I am a fool for thee. If thou need warmth, I shall set myself aflame . . . If thou art injured, I shall open up my vein . . . If thou need to feel powerful, I shall let myself be electrocuted and stabbed for months on end. Anything and everything, all of it, I do for your satisfaction."

Her breath hitched, heart racing where it pressed against my back.

Plague banked lazily, and we tilted to the side, riding an air current high above the romantic cloudscape.

Blue streaks tendrilled up from the ground.

Why is the Mist chasing us?

"But what if . . . I'm dissatisfied by *you*?" she asked loudly. "Aleksander."

Tremors of delight jolted through me. "Then there will be chains," I said, distracted by her. "Until thou feel differently, syxzal."

I wanted her love more than I wanted power. Zora Ravenal would never be free of me.

She trailed her nails up my back.

A loving caress.

"My Zora," I gasped out, shuddering with pleasure as she did it again.

"My Aleksander," she repeated.

I relaxed back in the saddle and loosened my hold on the reins. Laughter burst from my lips. Joy rushed through my veins because this was it. *My pinnacle.*

The success . . . the world . . . all of it was mine for the taking. I tipped my head back, clutching at my chest, laughing with an endless glee that I'd never felt before.

In my highest moment, she struck.

Quicker than I could process, Zora rolled off the back of my shoulders, flipping over. I grabbed for her legs, but it was too late. I turned my head, and we made eye contact. She balanced on the back of Plague, wind blowing through her long hair, scars stark, covered in bruises and dried blood. High above the clouds, rays of darkening scarlet light drenched both of us.

"Goodness will prevail over Antichthon," she said, eyes haunted like she was reciting someone else's words.

"Zora," I said calmly, reaching for her like I would a skittish animal. "Do *not* do anything rash—"

"You said you would do anything I want." A halo of sunlight shone behind her head as she pressed a cuffed hand over her heart, fingers flexing. "I want to win the Storm Wars."

A red light flashed at her feet.

Something was protruding from Plague's back. *An arrowhead?* It was the reason the Mist was following us.

"Checkmate," Zora whispered. "For those who cannot fight for themselves."

She jumped.

The chain pulled around my waist, and there was a split second of abject horror as I was yanked forcefully from my saddle.

Down we plummeted, chained together.

A loud whistling echoed *high* above in the atmosphere. There was a sonic boom. A missile hurtled down toward Plague with impossible speed. Mist streaked closely behind it.

Zora hadn't been grabbing at Plague's back trying to get away. She'd implanted the device, and she'd screamed to cover up the woman's mechanical voice. The memory whispered dangerously in my ear. *"Target designator activated."*

It had been tracking us the entire time.

"NO!" I roared, platinum wings exploding from my spine. I started to shoot back up, counteracting gravity, returning to Plague. I faltered, wings pulling tight to my back. Zora was attached to me. *I can't put her in harm's way.*

We plummeted down through the sky, away from Plague, who roared with confusion at the top of her lungs. Fire exploded in every direction. Fear whistled down our bond. Her confusion—*why is my bonded leaving me?*—echoed through my skull.

I reached a hand up, platinum cuffs burning my flesh as they channeled eons' worth of power. My storm magic exploded up at the monstrous technology, battering against it. The ginormous missile wavered but didn't stop its descent. The speed was too great to counteract. It was like nothing I'd ever seen before.

A moment of awful silence stretched.

Missile slammed into fire-breathing dragon.

"PLAGUE!" My voice sounded far, far away, moisture streaking down my face.

Bloody golden scales, and flames, exploded in every direction. A secondary dull thud echoed. *BOOM.* A mushroom cloud ballooned, sickly white in the violet sky, and our bond flatlined. *We were supposed to have centuries together.*

Plague was gone.

Vibrations punched through my stomach, shock waves flinging us away, hurtling us toward the mountain valley.

Screaming, spinning, heart breaking in my chest, I wrapped my fist around the chain and yanked it, link by link, pulling Zora through the air toward me.

I grabbed her cheeks, holding her head close, wanting to *tear* her smile off her betraying face.

"How could thou?" I breathed out. "How could thou . . . do . . . *this*?"

"Why did you kidnap my mom and take Aurora from me?" Zora's voice was terribly quiet.

Her smile is full of pain.

Colors lost saturation as my world crumbled.

As I stared into her bleak desolation, a horrible understanding dawned. I had to make this right. Gripped, *possessed*, by the overwhelming urge to earn her absolution, I said in a rush, "I wanted thee for myself. Tarantula disobeyed my orders. Aurora was not supposed to die . . . Forgive me. I only wanted to win thee over. *Please.*"

Her eyes were a searing, burning amber—the gaze of a hunter. "You did nothing but take them from me, and now I've taken from you."

It was too late.

Zora was in my arms but out of my reach.

Worlds separated us.

All this time, I thought we were the sun and moon, chasing after each other, but really we were two asteroids on a collision course.

Everything was suddenly so obvious. How did I not see it? She had her father's ruthless eyes.

I've misjudged . . . everything. The depths of her loyalties. The lengths she'll go for revenge. The consequences of what I've done to her. We were far more alike in temperament than I'd ever comprehended, in the most awful of ways.

She's never going to forgive me.

Zora tipped her head back, arms up, not even bracing for impact. I wrapped mine around her head protectively, pulled my wings wide, and flipped, taking the brunt of the fall.

Cratered deep in the smoking dirt, broken and bruised, I held her to my aching chest as droplets splattered down on us both, soaking the ground crimson.

Dragon blood fell like rain.

31

DUPLICITY

ZORA RAVENAL
MONTHS AGO . . . THE DAY OF THE
IRON RITUAL AND MAGIC TEST

"Tell me everything," the Marshal whispered so quietly I could barely hear her.

The scar on my throat tingled with phantom pain as I brought my lips to her ear, and obeyed.

The Marshal's eyes widened, pupils consuming her irises as her face turned a sickly shade of green. I told her the tale of a boy with dyed hair becoming a man, who stole the alias of his right-hand assassin and then *let* me stab him in the woods, pretending to be captured. The same boy had *begged* me to go with him back to Azote.

I whispered so softly I could barely hear myself. "The man calling himself Tarantula, held captive on the base, is the Emperor in disguise. We do know his storm magic. It's wind. I recognize his speech, his eyes . . . his *scent*. I'd bet my mom's life on it. It's him."

The Marshal covered her mouth like she was holding back vomit, breathing loudly through her nose. Abruptly she straightened, completely composed, brushing her fear away like it had never existed. Duty had forged her into a woman of steel and fire.

She spoke in a rush, quick-witted and cunning. Faster than imaginable, she outlined an awful, brilliant plan. She opened a box on the side of the board and pulled out a golden figure—Plague. She sat the Emperor astride it and tossed them both down to my feet.

"The dragon is the asset," the Marshal whispered. "We use what *he* wants—you—to get close to what *we* want—Plague." Her voice shook with excitement. "We break the stalemate of mutually assured destruction, and then . . . we're closer than we've ever been to winning this damned war."

She smiled. It was laced with menace, shadows stretching long across her features. For a second, I saw *him* in her.

"Code name: *Quest.* Your mission objective is to seduce Aleksander so he ultimately brings you to Plague. When the time comes, I will give you a tracker and detonator to keep hidden on your person. You will place it on Plague, and you will activate one of our last intercontinental high-speed ballistic fusion-propelled missiles."

"No." I shook my head, stomach revolting. "It's a suicide mission. It's impossible—"

She slapped me, hard.

I choked on panic, but when she offered me her hand a few seconds later, I took it because I'd joined the Crimson Army to defeat the Empire and this was my chance—an awful, terrible, impossible chance, but a chance all the same.

Rule of survival: Take the opportunities given to you, especially if they scare you.

The Marshal didn't release me as she hauled me upright off the floor. She pulled me close and whispered, "There is no one else in all Antichthon who can pull this off . . . no one else he cares about. All the ships in our harbor are ablaze with dragon fire. There is *no* safety to retreat to. The Democratic Commonwealth is counting on you to save all humanity. They're coming for us all."

I yanked from her hold.

The pressure was unfathomable; I backed away, straining under the weight of impossible circumstances.

My task: deceive the devil and destroy his most cherished monster.

As I panicked, a memory sparkled, starlight in the pitch darkness. Mom used to sing the same eleven words to me before bed, even when I grew up and came home later each night covered in dried animal blood.

"Lucky girl, you can do anything you want in the world."

She must have foreseen.

What the world would ask of me.

Epilogue

Storm Fae Crown Prince Aleksander,
Fifteen Years Old
Eight Years ago, on the Bridge

The brick walls of the Northern Commune towered pitifully behind me. Why the Marshal was hosting peace talks in Westmere's poorest, most barely civilized city was beyond my understanding. *They are all fools.*

The Draconis Empire was never going to negotiate for peace, especially not once I took the helm, but thus we pandered to their human politicians, pretending to play along.

We needed the location of the last mine, and my illustrious ancestor, the first emperor—*Chriztoph the Raving*—had the information, which was why the humans had been holding him hostage for centuries.

Not for long.

Military strategizing was my passion.

Everyone said youth was supposed to be glorious and free, but I was shackled by duty. Royal festivities, dragon riding, and the endless Storm Fae court politics were all of no interest to me. There was only one singular thing that mattered in my life—solving the Iron Trap Dilemma.

We were vastly outnumbered by humans, outdistanced and outclassed by technologies. There were only a few of us, but power was our birthright.

Storm Fae *were* magic, and all the humans had was thievery, but to beat them at their ways, I had to play their cunning little games. I'd read through every book the palace had on Westmere, but they were all poetry written in medieval dialect. It was how I'd learned their language.

If manuscripts from humanity's modern era had ever existed, Ryzar the Flaming, who could manipulate fire, had burned them to ash in one of his infamous rages.

Typical.

Centuries of my ancestors had failed to break the Iron Trap and spring Chriztoph free. One thing they had done right: they'd carefully selected their partners with the sole purpose of bearing a child who had enough ruthlessness to solve the dilemma.

Darkness fell with the crackle of snow across ice.

My bloodline had finally succeeded. Storm Fae were immortal, and birth among my kind was a rare miracle. We did not *perish* pathetically like the humans. Instead, we followed extensive rules of power and succession. I'd already proven smarter than Father, besting him at games of strategy and intellect. Thus it would soon be my turn to rule.

I'm going to spring the Iron Trap.

It wasn't hubris, because I knew it in the same way that I knew the sky was violet and composed of eighty percent nitrogen. Father and Uncle were far too weak, but I was vastly different from them. I was cruel and manipulative enough to *actually* get the job done.

I perceived the patterns.

Everyone else thought small—a battle here, a threat there. Their ideas were as pitiful as they were futile. When they got angry, they lashed out. Ranting as they raged, murdering indiscriminately, and enslaving pockets of humans because it made them feel better about their failure to find the location of the last platinum mine. Our people needed it desperately.

I rubbed the royal platinum cuffs on my wrists, and a whisper of fear prickled, because without them, my magic would destroy me from the inside out. The doubt disappeared as quickly as it surfaced, and there was nothing inside me but cold determination.

My rage was silent. Calculated.

Instrumental aggression.

Useful.

To spring the Iron Trap without setting off the humans' monstrous atomic bombs, I needed years of planning and the strategic manipulation of unwitting pawns. Humans had to work *beside* me. They had to help, whether they knew it or not. I'd need to curry their favor and get close to the source.

I'd need a disguise.

At the incipient age of ten years old, I'd begun laying the foundation. At eleven, before I'd yet to make a public appearance, I dyed my naturally blond hair and eyebrows pitch-black. When it was finally time to take on an alias, no one would suspect anything, because they'd never seen the real me.

At twelve, with hair as dark as my soul, I'd met and signed treaties with the fearsome dire bear shifters of the rural North. They were helping me hunt the humans in exchange for future protection, an extremely *satisfying* alliance.

Now, at the mature age of fifteen, it was time to make more . . . *prolific* moves. I needed to manipulate the humans into helping me spring the Iron Trap. Countless Emperors had failed because they all approached from the outskirts.

It needed to be an inside job.

Everything was up to me.

The pressure was as crushing as it was exhilarating. I assumed it was, at least. I didn't feel much of anything. Never had. That was the problem when thou were so much better than those around thee, more intelligent, and built to dominate. The other Royal Fae were so easily distracted, pursuing romance and carnal pleasures. Both repulsed me.

I had no urge to *touch* another being.

Until I dismantled the Iron Trap, secured the location of the last platinum mine, and freed my ancestors from this farce of a war, there was *nothing* to feel. Without the Iron Trap left to protect them, nothing would save the humans.

The sweet cherry taste of blood flooded my mouth as my fangs accidentally lengthened, stabbing deep and automatically releasing my dark venom into my bloodstream.

Pain lanced down my spine and across my hips as I shifted my aching limbs. Puberty was my current damnation. It was no small feat for a child to become an Emperor.

If I were of any other Storm Fae lineage, I would have already been crushed by the force of what was growing inside of me. Alas, I was better than everyone else.

Howls filled the night as dire beasts prowled. Northern Westmere was reminiscent of home with its snowy mountains, but the lack of castles and dragons made it unsettling. It was foreign, just like the desert lands on this cursed continent.

These woods, Barren's forest, had an aura of malingering menace that I'd never felt before. These were no normal pines. They were *his*. Branches rustled, and I listened intently, waiting to see if I could hear the famous elven whispers that drove shifters, witches, vampires, and Storm Fae to madness, or in rare instances—greatness.

Barren was one of the most powerful elves, an ancient people of peace, but most importantly—*power*. Barren had also famously chosen one of the most powerful Storm Fae ever to be a Keeper—Chriztoph the Raving, my most esteemed ancestor. He was the only fae ever chosen for the role.

A Keeper was without a doubt the *greatest*, most honorable

title any warrior could receive. Elven power did not come easily. Constrained to their magical land, and a naturally reclusive people, they rarely walked among men or fae.

After digging a hole in the snow, I sliced my pocketknife across my palm and bled onto the frozen grass. *Choose me.* With my cunning and Barren's power on my side, domination of Antichthon would be assured. I'd be the greatest, most impressive Emperor who'd ever lived.

Branches clattered loudly, the sound coldly ominous.

My blood disappeared as it was sucked into the frozen dirt. The ground shook violently—judging.

Silence.

A strange heaviness settled in my bones.

The dirt turned black, and so did the snow around where my blood had dripped. Nothing grew. No figure appeared.

Barren had rejected me.

Whatever. I don't care what a half-witted elven thinks of me. It's probably more of a responsibility than a help anyway.

His cursed land meant nothing to me.

Absolutely *nothing.*

I didn't want his help because I could do it myself.

If it wasn't for the old platinum mines, my ancestors never would have bothered with this land and been trapped into the Storm Wars. I spit with disgust as the unnatural Mist twined around my ankles. The humans had ruined *my* world with their awful technologies.

Ennui grew, cerebrum liquefying with boredom. I daydreamed of flying away on Plague with Chriztoph the Raving seated safely behind me. I fantasized about dragon fire, finding the hidden mine, and a quiet world full of peace where the Storm Fae reigned over all Antichthon.

Wind churned, a mini-tornado swirling snow at my feet.

I rested against the towering brick wall, ancient parchment

fluttering in the magical wind as I read the pages for the thousandth time. It was a first edition of *A Gentleman's Guide to Slaughtering.* The tome was priceless, less than three had been made in the entire world, hand-bound and hand-inked two centuries ago, worth more than everything within this cursed Northern Commune, including all the inhabitants.

Long-term plans required immense amounts of patience, which I had in spades, but there were still . . . consequences. Restlessness was the cause—annihilation the result.

It didn't help that these nights I lay awake, trembling in agony as puberty kept stretching my aching bones while storm magic found a home in me. I turned the page, slowly reading text that I could recite with my eyes closed.

Crunch.

I stilled, blending in with the darkness as I tucked my treasure into my waistband.

Footsteps?

None of the bumbling human peasants in this provincial Commune ventured outside their walls. *Ever.* All week, I'd watched them scurry around like rats, hiding from the wilderness, struggling to walk without breathing heavily as they pretended they didn't exist within its maw.

Crunch.

There was a figure in the dark.

It was the same one I'd glimpsed earlier hurtling down the mountain, flipping through the air on a strange wooden board.

Torches flickered against the city wall, casting light across the narrow path leading to the entrance gate.

A spotted carcass with long, curved fangs and a mutated, distended chest—a lethal dire coyote—was stretched across the person's narrow shoulder. Its blood splattered across the snow. The board was slung across their other shoulder, almost as big as the person carrying it.

"You lost the race," a high-pitched voice crooned. "Me win!" The smallest owl I'd ever seen swooped down on tawny wings and landed on top of the person's head.

The figure laughed and shook their head no, jostling the owl back and forth as they approached a trunk with purpose. They ripped down a tree branch, cracked it over their knee, then poked and prodded at the snow. Falling to their knees, they cleaned away the white, revealing jagged metal teeth glinting in the night.

A jackalope struggled in the trap, still alive.

"The horror," the owl squawked, swiveling its head around to look away. *What a strange creature.*

Unlike the owl, the person didn't hesitate.

Crack.

They snapped the jackalope's neck—a swift, unflinching action—then bowed their head, praying over the carcass.

I jolted. A strange warmth spread deep in my stomach, because unbridled strength shone in the movement. Duty and domination, I recognized. They didn't want to act, but they did it anyway, because they *had* to.

The person stood up with a grunt, struggling to keep the coyote carcass across their shoulders, hold their board, and keep the owl balanced on their head as they gently handled the dead jackalope.

Arms full, they moved with shocking strength and agility toward the Commune walls. There was something mesmerizing in the swaggering canter of their steps. Self-assurance and strength practically oozed off them. The same energy had them throwing death-defying flips on the mountainside.

The tip of my tongue tingled. Awareness hummed across my skin.

I inched forward.

Lift your head. Let me see. Yes, just like that. Turn toward me so I can see thee—

I stifled my gasp.

A teenage girl scowled. Firelight caressed bronze skin; her almond eyes were a startling shade of light brown. *Golden amber.* Her face was round, cheeks full of adolescence. A long brown braid hung down her back, silky pieces wisping around her head.

The most captivating part: three scars covered the right side of her face in streaks of raised white from eyebrow to jaw. The longest of them *glowed* silver with storm magic. *She has been marked by a powerful magical being.*

I inhaled deeply, and she smelled of weakness—human.

Who would mark such a magicless creature? Strangely it also shimmered in a bright white light around her, a shade only fae could see, as she casually readjusted the predator draped across her shoulders like it was a silk shawl. She was being tested by someone, monitored with magic.

Who is she?

The storm magic inside my chest ached as it churned hotter like it was attempting to tell me something. The air was rich with pine and the lingering scent of something *intoxicating*—her. A profile of notes that bewitched the senses and befuddled the mind. I licked my lips, mouth uncomfortably dry. She smelled like my . . . destiny. *No, it can't be.* Syxzals were so rare they were practically a myth.

The only way to know for sure was to have her blood. The old stories said thou could *hear* destiny singing in your ear with the taste of a single droplet from your syxzal.

A beast howled out in the night, and the owl cried out with terror, but the girl didn't so much as flinch. Slamming her boot down on the mechanism beside the gate, she turned and backed into the city, eyes scanning the forest with cold cunning as she reengaged the door.

I shivered with awareness.

The way she existed with her surroundings was nothing short of . . . *exhilarating.* I waited a beat and then slipped through the shadows, following the magnetic pull. I couldn't have fought it even if I wanted to.

One street over, on the outskirts where the poorer citizens lived, she hung both carcasses on a front porch and put her board away inside.

Returning, she pulled a wickedly sharp blade from her waist holster and carefully cleaned it off with a rag. Untying her blood-covered boots with the owl balanced on her head, she paused in the entrance, checking the street like she could sense my gaze. She disappeared, locking the door multiple times behind her.

I crouched in the dark and waited, barely noticing the passage of time. Her scent still lingered in the air. I inhaled greedily, half mad with delirium.

Before dawn cracked over the horizon, she stalked back outside and carried her prey down the street. I followed in the shadows.

The owl sat silently on her shoulder.

After dropping off the carcasses at the mess hall in the center of the city, she stopped back at her house. Minutes later she emerged in full hunting gear. Citizens milled around her, walking much slower as they went about their provincial morning. She sped past them as she headed back out into the wild.

She slunk through the forest, setting dozens of traps at the bases of trees, and then she crouched behind a snowbank and waited, *for hours*. She watched the trees with wide, alert eyes, like a dire wolf hunting in the brush, blending fully into her surroundings.

I didn't just watch her. I *consumed* her with my eyes.

Never had a human appeared so at home among nature's talons. Unlike the rest of her species, she did not shy away from the danger. She melted into it and adopted its ferociousness.

Hours later, she stood up and stretched with three small carcasses slung over both her shoulders. Her owl flew above her head, spiraling in the sky as she ran inside the walls and back to her house. Disappointment stabbed through my heart because her day was surely over and I wouldn't see her again for— Her front door opened.

I stopped.

Why is she dressed like that? Her neck and wrists were exposed under her skimpy shawl. *Extremely* inappropriate. A strange flush filled my cheeks as a bead of sweat streaked down my spine.

The bronze arch of her graceful neck was beyond indecent. The delicate bones of her wrists were just *there* for everyone to see. I stumbled, nearly faint with the urge to carry her to safety. *No, my syxzal would never show herself in such a state.*

Anyone in the Commune could feast upon her bare flesh. The impropriety was nauseating, and icy winds gusted down the street in cyclones of snow as hot coals burned inside my gut.

Whistling happily in her state of abject ill repute, she practically *skipped* down the snowy street, the owl once again on her shoulder as she slipped outside the walls. Ire fought with confusion as she took a different path than earlier.

It can't be.

"There you are—what took you so long?" A gangly, pathetic human boy bounced on his feet. He nervously looked around, jumping as tree branches swayed. Unlike her, he *reeked* of fear.

She tipped her head back, the delicate arch of her naked throat catching the sunlight. Wind howled louder as a flush warmed my cheeks. The boy feasted on her exposed skin like a starving louse, his lack of etiquette repulsive.

Somehow unaware that she was being completely disrespected, she laughed, offering him her hand. Wrists and all.

They touched *bare* fingers, and a sickness like nothing I'd ever felt stabbed through my empty rib cage. Sweat beaded across my forehead because his dirty oils were rubbing against her precious skin. My etiquette teacher would have passed out by now, and I had half a mind to do so myself.

The display was beyond vulgar. *They might as well just be screwing in front of me.* She could not be mine.

Her reputation had been compromised, and he'd proven himself to be a tactless, uncouth swine of the lowest breeding. To add to the indecency of the moment, the girl led him below the swaying bridge, under the overhang.

I stepped onto the bridge, wind gusting through my dyed hair as an odd pressure swelled beneath my ribs.

He wouldn't dare sully her— Kissing noises carried on the wind.

I staggered, clutching the railing to keep myself upright. Wind exploded, the bridge creaking as it swayed beneath me. This continent was a den of heathen iniquity, and it ought to be burned to the ground.

The situation was *far* more dire than I'd ever contemplated. Even if she wasn't my syxzal, someone had to step in and defend her honor.

Someone needed to do something to protect her from this tactless rube. Her tantalizing scent drifted on the wind, and I inhaled raggedly, half high on it. She was clearly superior, like myself, but was a provincial peasant who had not had the opportunity to learn proper etiquette.

I would save her.

From herself.

It was irrational, inexplicable, and borderline suicidal. I was supposed to stay focused. Solving the Iron Trap was my only purpose in life.

Until yesterday, it had been.

Now I had a second purpose. Rescuing this misguided girl from her stupidity. *She will thank me for educating her on decency.* I smiled, despite the burgeoning rage, and nodded. She would bow low, exposing the pretty curve of her neck, in a show of submission. She would offer me a gentle taste from her tender flesh, and I would know the truth about us.

Even if I was wrong about her being my syxzal, this would be the start of a *beautiful* acquaintanceship. Perhaps when we were of a proper age, I'd take her back to Palladium and start a courtship, delicately wooing her with my riches, dragons, and castles. We would hunt together, discussing politics and current events.

She would thank me for civilizing her, and I would be nothing but gracious to her, taking care of her for the rest of her pathetically short mortal life. She'd ride Plague, cheering from the safety of the sky as I sprang the Iron Trap.

A flush spread hot across my cheeks, and warmth smoldered deep in my heart. Pressing my fingers to my lips, I held back laughter. Down below, the object of my affections made a throaty sound, and then a loud kissing noise carried on the wind.

Heat blinked out inside my chest, leaving a frigid sickly rage. *How dare she.* "Only harlot girls kiss boys before marriage!" I called out with a sneer, unable to stop myself.

All noises stopped.

"Excuse me? What did you just call me?" Her voice reverberated, raspy and lower than I expected. Edged with danger, it did *things* to me.

"Call me," the owl squawked ridiculously.

The bridge swayed beneath my feet, and a distant part of me, an amalgamation of thoughts that resembled a conscience, wondered if she could feel it approaching, the tangled web of my intentions. Spiders were my favorite animals because thou could learn everything thou needed to know about a person by how they reacted to venom.

Wind howled louder.

"Thou heard me," I snapped back, grimacing because I was supposed to be *wooing* and educating her, not fighting. Despite my best intentions, I prickled at her responding scoff. She was more . . . *hostile* than I'd anticipated, and I never stepped down from a fight. It lived in the Emperor's lineage, simmering within our blood, the urge to dominate—*everything*. It was why we made the most exceptional leaders—we were born warriors. Admittedly romance was not in our purview of talents.

'Tis her lead I shall follow.

Attempting to stay calm, I tried to appeal to her softer womanly sensibilities.

I quickly discovered she had none.

Apparently the object of my affections preferred violent fisticuffs and cutting verbal swordplay. Another thing we had in common. Our courtship would be more volatile, more *perfect*, than I'd originally anticipated.

My infatuation: immediate.

Obsession at first sight.

Finally I took Zora Ravenal by surprise and sank my teeth into her tender neck.

Oh.

Oh my blessed Mages.

The storm magic in her blood didn't sing. It *screamed* that she was my syxzal.

My soulmate.

My soulmate.

My soulmate.

These sudden and new possessive inclinations were cripplingly intense. Nose pressed against her flesh, I was sure I *had* to be misreading her, because her scent was unmistakably . . . *virtuous*?

Notes of valor mixed with courageousness, dark heroism, extreme loyalty, and— *No. It cannot be.*

It was.

My soulmate reeked of saving the world.

She smelled like Knight armor, freshly spilled blood, storming a battlefield on behalf of those too weak to defend themselves, and screams of righteous anger.

I licked across her warm skin, eyes rolling back as I savored her probity, and a delirium-inducing hunger thundered as my ribs barely caged my racing heart. She didn't taste like anything I'd ever had before.

She was pure, unadulterated *goodness*.

A new objective took shape. The nascent flutters of a scheme involving deception, aliases, and torture—*mine*—emerged in the blackest depths of my corrupt soul. I needed her, spiritually, and no action would be too extreme. *She* was my cult because I was born to worship Zora Ravenal, the girl with the silver scar.

I was going to ruin the world so I could watch her try to save it.

Acknowledgments

Thank you so much to my mom for spending weeks editing every single sentence of this book by reading it aloud with me. It was truly special how you argued with me over . . . *everything*. My favorite was when you told me that the "italics are annoying me, make them a different slant," which is a physical impossibility, and then you refused to let it go. There is truly no one else on earth I'd want to talk to (scream at through the phone) for basically months on end.

With each book we do together, we've somehow found a way to make the process more fun (hostile), but I'm not joking when I say I'm the luckiest author in the world to have you as a mom.

Special thank you to my beta readers Marissa, Patricia, Cha, Jamie, and many more who read different drafts of this book *multiple* times, sometimes within the same week. Without all your feedback, this book wouldn't be anywhere near what it ended up as. You guys are amazing!

This book also wouldn't have been possible without my wonderful editor, Cat, and the rest of the great team at HarperCollins: Alex, Lindsey, and Kamille. Also, shout-out to Elizabeth from Harper Voyager UK for her insightful edits, and thanks to Lyss Em for proofreading.

Huge thank you to Siana Park for all of the jaw-dropping character art! Also, thank you so much to Maria at Steamy Designs for helping me with the graphics on the cover and with the chapter heading designs.

Big thank you so much to my amazing agent, Kimberly Whalen, and her assistant, Nina, for getting my books into more than twenty countries around the world. Thank you to Benoit and Glenn in France for believing so much in my stories, and to all my international publishers for your continued support.

Tiny shout-out to my brother and my husband, who, for the first time, *actually* read small sections of this draft. You both pointed out weaponry/action scene edits I never would have thought of. Way to do the bare minimum, guys. I'm so grateful for all my family and friends who continue to be shocked I'm in bookstores (real) and send me a picture *every* single time they come across one of my novels (also real).

Also, thank you to my emotional support cat, Boo-Boo, who is so cute and sassy. Finally, thank you to my girlfriends, who make my heart so full and keep me sane. Taco Tuesday is a lifestyle.

We *are* the people in our lives, and I'm so grateful for everyone.

Subscribe to Jasmine's newsletter at blog.jasminemasbooks.com for a free exclusive bonus chapter of *The Emperor's Enemy.*